PRAISE FOR GINGER SMITH

"Ginger Smith's vat-grown protagonist joins the likes of Frodo and Ulysses in this story of a soldier whose war is over, but his greatest battle – coming home – is still ahead. Smith's debut is rich in detail, full of tension, and packed with characters you won't easily forget."

R.W.W. Greene, author of *The Light Years*

"Duplicitous military, assassins, super soldiers, alien tech, and a family of brilliant characters caught in the middle. *The Rush's Edge* gives you all the *Firefly* feels with a dash of *Mass Effect* for the hell of it. Fantastically entertaining."

Dan Hanks, author of *Captain Moxley and the Embers of the Empire*

"What happens when you release vat-raised soldiers into the void after their service is over? With this premise, Smith sets up multiple conflicts, from political to personal. You will root for these heroes and cringe at the evil that brought them together."

Chris Panatier, author of *The Phlebotomist*

Ginger Smith

THE RUSH'S EDGE

ANGRY ROBOT

ANGRY ROBOT
An imprint of Watkins Media Ltd

Unit 11, Shepperton House
89 Shepperton Road
London N1 3DF
UK

angryrobotbooks.com
twitter.com/angryrobotbooks
Live Life on the Edge

An Angry Robot paperback original, 2020

Cover by Kieryn Tyler
Edited by Gemma Creffield and Paul Simpson
Set in Meridien

ISBN 978 0 85766 864 6
Ebook ISBN 978 0 85766 867 7

Printed and bound in the United Kingdom by TJ International.

9 8 7 6 5 4 3 2 1

This book is dedicated to my husband, Judd.

ONE

The young blonde had been drinking heavily all night. Halvor Cullen had been watching her for a while, noticing that the same two guys kept coming back to her table, but getting turned down each time. Hal was about to get up and suggest they get lost when she sent them away once again, and they looked visibly pissed. Hal grinned, glad she was able to handle herself, despite looking like she'd just gotten off a luxury starliner from the Inner Spiral. He was working himself up to talking to her when Ty's contact arrived.

Hal's captain, Tyce, was hoping to get a tip on a prime salvage location. After they'd both left the Armed Services of the Coalition of Allied Systems – the ACAS – Ty had bought a freighter, the *Loshad*, and they'd been salvaging technology past the Edge's border as an independent contractor for LanTech ever since. Most of their haul was usually legit but they sold some of the forbidden-to-salvage items on the black markets of Seljin and Vesbra when they thought they could get away with it. With the profits from both, they were always able to keep their old J-class ship in food and fuel for the next run.

Sometimes ships that crossed the border line without permission would bring back tips about salvage areas, information that could be bought for the right amount of scrill. Their contact tonight claimed to have the location of a crashed Mudar ship, the ultimate score for a salvage team. AI tech paid handsomely when it could be recovered. There was one problem with the guy, however: he was a null addict. Hal knew right away from the fine trembling in his hands and the twitching of his left eye. He wasn't sure Tyce had picked up on it, though. Sometimes natural-borns didn't see all the details a vat could. Hal caught Ty's eye during a lull in the conversation and gave him the "no-go" signal. Tyce nodded and began to pull back from the deal they were making.

Then the blonde woman swayed and fell off her chair. Hal jumped to attention.

"Hal?" Ty asked, watching as his friend focused his eyes across the room.

The contact, obviously irritated, slammed his hand on the bar. "Hey, I was talkin' here!"

"Shut the hell up," Tyce said, trying to peer through the crowd to see what Hal was watching so intently. "Hal?"

"Those guys grabbed that girl, Tyce," he said, and he was off, pushing through the crowd.

"Shit."

When Ty hit the alleyway, he saw that Hal was in the middle of a full-blown rush. His friend had taken on the biggest man first, of course, while the other one had pulled a small blaspistol and was trying to angle for a good shot on Hal. The girl was dumped on the space station decking, and Ty could see that she wasn't going anywhere on her own.

"Drop the blaster," Ty said.

The smaller man was focused on Hal so intently that he hadn't seen Ty get the draw on him. He turned slowly, looking down the barrel of Ty's weapon.

"Drop it," Ty said.

It appeared that the would-be kidnapper wasn't as committed as his partner, because his short-barreled PLP-20 clattered immediately to the ground. "Look, I got no problems with you," said the thug. "All we came for was the girl."

"What do you want with her?" Ty asked.

The man glared, unwilling to answer.

Tyce checked in briefly with Hal, who was holding his own. Naturally. Hal just finished punching his opponent in the ribs, before the larger man countered with a fist to Hal's jaw. Ty's eyes flicked back dangerously to the red-and-blue haired punk-ass in front of him.

"You're not taking anyone with you tonight," Ty said. "Go. And maybe I won't shoot you. You can come back for what's left of your friend later." The thug glared at him a moment, then took off.

Ty turned back to Hal again. The fist fight had turned into a knife fight; the large man had pulled a viblade to even the odds. Hal was bleeding from a cut on his forearm and trying to avoid being stabbed again. Ty raised his blaspistol, but there was no need as Hal executed a swift movement with one hand on each side of his opponent's knife hand that sent the weapon flying. Then he quickly closed distance. They struggled, then Hal got the giant in a headlock. Despite his opponent desperately trying to wriggle himself free, after only a few seconds the man's eyes were rolling back in his head and his feet were kicking at the space station's decking. Ty holstered his weapon as Hal finally let the unconscious man sink to the ground.

Ty edged toward the victor. "You OK?"

"Yeah! Best thing I've done all week." Hal was buoyant – coasting on the rush. Vats craved the rush like natural-borns craved air. Ty knew that Hal needed outlets for his excess energy, and their salvage trip the past two weeks had clearly not offered enough excitement. He'd been expecting Hal to get into a fight all night long, just for something to do. He was proud that his best friend hadn't given in to the temptation until there was a reason, though. And a very good reason, clearly. "What about the second guy?" Hal asked, looking around for another crack at the whip.

"I talked him into leaving. He decided it was better than a blaster bolt to the chest. Hey, uh, I see your arm, but how much of that blood on your shirt – and pants – is yours?" Ty asked as they walked back over to the blonde woman.

"I dunno. Twenty percent?" Hal said, blotting his scraped knuckles on his pants. Ty could see his arm wore the worst of the damage. Hal yanked the hem of his shirt to wipe the blood away. It wasn't too deep and was already starting to coagulate. He'd be fine.

"OK, then." They both knelt by the young woman. Ty checked her pulse. It was slow – too slow – but it was steady.

"Shit, she's bruised up." Hal said softly, turning the girl's face towards them. Her eye and cheek were black and purple – injuries that clearly hadn't just been inflicted but were at least a day old.

"Let's get her over toward the entrance so we can see better," Ty said.

They left the unconscious thug on the ground, and Hal picked up the girl, cradling her against his chest.

When they reached the entrance, Hal settled her upright on the nearest bench and she began to wake up a little. "Ma'am. Are you alright?" Tyce asked as she blinked at him.

"You can't route the signal that way," she said sleepily, resting her head back against the wall. "Use the Bken protocol."

Tyce and Hal shared a glance. "She's not making much sense," Ty said.

"Those guys probably put something in her drink," Hal replied.

"Or dosed her with a medjet."

"Can't use creds," she opened her eyes and looked at Hal as if she were explaining something very important. "It's Echo. They see. They see everything. Scrill only." Then she passed out.

"We can't leave her here, Cap," Hal said. "Those two might come back for her."

"Everything OK?" The bouncer that had been at the door when they'd arrived took up his place again, eyeing the two of them suspiciously.

"We're fine," Ty said. "Our friend here had a little too much to drink." He gestured to the girl. "We're just trying to figure out the best way to get her home."

"Let's see some ID." Another bouncer, less athletic, but still imposing, joined the thickly muscled man. He had a handheld ID validation scanner.

Hal glanced to Ty to see what his captain wanted him to do. Ty knew if he said go, Hal would plow into both of them. Probably even kill one of them, without touching his blaspistol. Sometimes that was comforting to know; other times it was terrifying to realize that Hal trusted him so completely to make those decisions.

But there was no reason to fight the bouncers. Ty held out his ID to be scanned and gestured for Hal to do the same. The bouncer sneered when he saw the flash of Hal's tattoo on his wrist. "Damn vat fuckers. Always causing problems," he muttered.

Hal straightened up and advanced, getting in the bouncer's personal space.

"Hal," Ty said in a low voice.

"What? You wanna go, jar-bred?" the bouncer spat.

Hal smirked, hungry for another combat. "Sure. I'll even give you the first swing, nat," he said.

The second bouncer was checking the screen of his scanner, but at the exchange he glanced up angrily at his companion, then yanked him back by his shirt. "Shut the fuck up, Marque. Godsdamn moron." The bouncer glanced at Ty and then flashed a pair of wings on his own forearm; the design was a popular tattoo with nat flight crews in the ACAS. He checked Ty's ID and addressed him more formally. "Sorry, captain. Go on about your night. Get the girl there home. She's lookin' a little green if you don't mind me saying so."

"Yeah, thanks." Ty nodded, glancing to Hal. "Let's go."

Hal didn't move, so Ty grabbed him by the shoulder. "Halvor, let's get her *home*. Come on."

The use of his full first name brought Hal back enough so that he backed up, but kept his glare focused on Marque. As the bouncer went back in the club, Hal turned away. His expression softened when he saw the blonde again and he knelt to pick her up. "Come on," Hal said gently. Her head leaned against Hal's shoulder as he walked with Tyce back toward the series of lifts that would take them to their ship.

She murmured a few times during the short trip. Ty had trouble understanding her except for when she woke up enough to look around her. "Don't… let them get me," she whispered softly. "Please."

"Nobody's gonna hurt you," Hal promised, looking at the bruises on her face. "I'll take their head off if they even try. You're gonna be OK."

"I like you," she sighed resting back against him again. She was still for a while, then she lifted her head back up, eyes bleary. "I don't feel so good," she said, turning her head just in time to vomit on Hal's arm and shoe. "Oh my gods… I'm sorry," she mumbled.

Hal didn't even blink at it. "Don't worry. Not the worst thing to happen to me."

She buried her face back against his shoulder with a moan. Ty looked over and smirked.

"I can see you've had quite an effect on her," Ty teased good-naturedly, then he became more serious. "We'll let Beryl check her out in the medbay. If she needs a medcenter, it won't take long to get her there."

They used Jaleeth Station's complicated series of lifts to reach their ship. Jaleeth was a large station, constructed in the shape of an X, with docking for ships all along the thick legs of the structure. The berths were segregated depending on the class of ship so there were smaller berths for ships like the *Loshad*, but there were also those that accommodated larger vessels such as the ACAS warships. Once a ship was docked and the bay pressurized, a bay door led into the main concourse of the station, which contained thousands of hab units, retail shops, storage units, restaurants, bars and mech shops. Although its size could be confusing, once a traveler figured out its color-coded lift and tram system, travelling around was actually fairly quick.

In less than twenty minutes, Beryl had the young woman on a table in the medbay, scanning her body. Their medic was an older woman who had served in the ACAS for two decades. In her salad days, Beryl McCabe had been a colonist of Tykus 7, an agricultural planet near the Border. Their colony had been attacked, and her husband and eight year-old son had been murdered by pirates. Beryl, along with the other colonists, had been rescued by an ACAS contingent. Later on, she'd joined up, done her time and been released from service.

Beryl took a blood sample from the young woman. "Runa. Run a scan on this. She was probably drugged," she said, plugging the sample into the analyzer.

Yes, Beryl, their onboard computer replied. After a few seconds, the program spoke again. *She has been drugged with Glimthixene at two and a half times the regular dosage. It is not lethal, but it is longer lasting when taken with alcohol. At her blood alcohol level, she will be in and out of consciousness for at least twenty hours.*

"Glimthixene?" Tyce was trying to place it. "What does the drug do?"

"It's a drug used for panic attacks – a tranquilizer," Beryl answered.

Tyce took the girl's backpack off to make her more comfortable. He removed her shoes and covered her with a blanket as Beryl attached sensors to monitor her condition. "OK, what do we need to do to treat her?"

"I'm afraid there's nothing we can do, really," Beryl said. "Just keep her warm and comfortable. We could drop her at Jaleeth's medcenter, but you said someone tried to snatch her?"

"Yeah." Hal said. "Two of them."

Tyce eyed the dark bruising on the girl's face. "I'm not really interested in leaving her anywhere before she's awake enough to take care of herself," he mused.

"I think that's a good plan." Beryl nodded, turning her attention to Hal and noticing the state of his clothes for the first time. She wrinkled her nose at the smell. "Now you – you need a shower, then I want you back here so I can check you over."

"OK," Hal agreed, taking a last look at the sleeping girl before heading for his room.

"How did the meet go? Get any intel?" Beryl asked.

"No. I think the guy was just trying to collect some easy scrill." Ty ran a hand through his short brown hair in frustration. He gestured to the girl. "At least we were able to help someone."

Beryl nodded, checking the girl's vitals. They were steady. "OK. Well, we can definitely take care of her here until she's back up and about."

They got an IV line started, then Ty began looking for clues to the girl's identity. He grabbed her backpack and hauled it up to the other empty medbed. Ty didn't like going through her things, but he had to know who she was. The front pocket was full of data chips in various neon colors. Opening another larger inner area revealed a datapad. He tried to activate it and was met with a password lock screen.

"She's got a node. Must be a tecker," Beryl said, showing Ty the port behind the girl's ear. "Pretty high dollar rig, too."

Ty knew most teckers had nodes to allow them to interface with and monitor computer systems. Regular people could get them too, but that specific bioware was usually very expensive. "Mmm," he agreed. "She's got a lot of data chips in here too." In the fourth compartment of the bag, he found an old ID badge for one of the universities located on the Inner Spiral. "Wait. Here we go," he said. The photo showed the girl, in a much better state than she was in right now. Ocean green eyes looked confidently into the camera amid a sea of blonde curls and freckles. "Vivian Valjean. Says on her ID that she was studying technology." He found the keycard for a cube where she was staying and set it beside her things.

Hal returned a few minutes later. He'd changed into a green T-shirt and black cargo pants, hair still damp from his quick shower.

"Take a seat up there." Beryl gestured to the other medbed as she brought over supplies to disinfect his wound.

"What did you find out?" Hal asked.

"Not much, yet," Ty replied. "Just a name. Vivian Valjean."

"So, what do we do with her?"

"Just let her rest. I've got a meeting with LanTech in two days. We'll take her to Omicron Station with us, then bring her back here. If we take her with us, we don't miss the meet, and she's safe from whoever was trying to snatch her. Might be an inconvenience, but at least she won't wake up in some brothel somewhere, chained to a bed."

Hal nodded. "Sounds good. That a keycard for her room?"

"Yeah. Looks like she's rented a cube down the avenue from the bar. Think we should go pay for her room a few days?" Ty said.

"Either that or get her things. You know how those managers are," Beryl said. "If she doesn't come for another day, they'll take everything out of there and sell it. I'll stay with her."

"OK. We'll be back," Ty said, glancing at Hal. His friend hadn't taken his eyes off the sleeping woman during their whole conversation. Something in her had triggered Hal's protective instincts. Anyone wanting to get to Vivian Valjean while she was on their ship would clearly have to go through Hal first.

TWO

She had a headache. A bad one. *Did Noah find me?* The thought caused her to open one eye, expecting to see her small cube of a rented room, or worse, her hab unit with Noah. Instead she saw a medical bay with metal floors and ceiling. Opening both eyes, she looked around. She was in a medbed, covered with a blanket. She could feel the pull of medical sensors on her arm and collarbone. Her fingers began to work at them in growing panic.

"Where the hell am I?" she breathed, yanking harder at the sticky pads of the sensors. She had a vague memory of two men grabbing her and pulling her somewhere she didn't want to go. Had she been taken prisoner? The room swam in her sight, and she squeezed her eyes tightly shut with a groan.

You are on the Loshad, *Vivian Valjean. I am Runa, the ship's computerized assistant. Please do not try to get up.*

Her eyes opened wide. The calm, steady voice seemed to come from above her, where the ship's comms would be. If a ship's computer knew she was awake, it would be alerting someone right now. "Yeah, well, sorry. Don't take orders from computers. I give the orders." She removed the last sticky pad from her collarbone. "I'm outta here."

Miss Valjean, you are suffering the after-effects of being drugged.

"No shit, really?" Vivi slid from the bed, promptly falling on the floor. On her hands and knees she found her boots and sat back to jam her feet into them. It took a moment to regain her balance, and the sudden vertigo made her cling to the medbed until the world stopped spinning. "What the hell happened to me?" she asked, slurring her words.

Lifting her head, she saw her bag. Her datapad and ID were on the counter next to it. She shoved them into the backpack, grabbed it and lurched toward the door. As she got there, it slid open, and she ran into a man standing on the other side. She staggered back, then tripped and fell to the ground.

"Woah, there!" he said. "You shouldn't be up yet."

She looked up at him through a haze. He was attractive, with short brownish-blonde hair, gentle eyes and a golden scruff on his face that softened his features. He knelt beside her, taking her arm gently. She could smell the clean scent of his soap.

"I need to get you back onto the bed," he said, helping her to a sitting position.

"I... I remember you..." she said, uncertainly. Was he the man who had grabbed her arm and tried to take her out of the bar? Or was he that blur of grey and black she'd seen fighting her would-be attacker? She wasn't sure. "You... were in the bar."

"Yeah. No need to be afraid." The man helped her to her feet. When she took a sliding step backwards to put space between them, he was careful not to touch her again. "If you can just lie back down, we can talk." He gestured toward the bed. Even though it was the last thing she wanted to do, she felt nauseous and lying down was probably a good idea. He followed her as she staggered her way to the bed and crawled up on it. "Nobody's gonna hurt you here, Miss Valjean."

"Who are you?" she asked before laying back down.

"My name's Hal Cullen," he replied. "Should I get our medic?"

She squeezed her eyes shut. "No, I'm just kinda... kinda dizzy."

"That normal, Runa?"

Yes, Hal, the computer's even tone replied. *But I am not currently getting a reading on our guest.*

"Here, let me reattach the monitors..." Hal murmured, turning her arm to place the sensor inside her elbow. He was careful with her, moving slowly so as not to startle her.

"Did… Did you guys kidnap me?" Vivi asked, still clutching her backpack to her with one arm.

"No." Hal looked up, startled. He shook his head as he moved to slip off her boots and cover her with a warm blanket again. "No. There were guys in the club who tried to snatch you, but I saw it and came after you."

She began to remember the blonde man attacking the one who had yanked her up from the floor with a hand in her hair. "Oh, right." Vivi nodded, her eyes growing heavy again. "I kind of recall seeing you fighting with someone."

"Yeah. You're safe now. Our medic said you'd probably need to sleep a little longer."

"But I'm not sleepy…." She lay there, feeling both nervous around this total stranger and more exhausted than she'd ever felt in her life. He took a seat beside the bed and she forced her eyes to stay open, wanting to keep an eye on him, but within moments she lost the battle.

When Ty entered the common area, later that night, he saw Hal at the table eating a protein bar and drinking a bottle of water – his standard fare after a rush or a night of drinking. He was reading something on his handheld but glanced up when he saw Tyce.

"Beryl with our guest?" Ty asked.

"Yeah."

Ty raised an eyebrow. "You good?"

"Five by five, Cap."

Ty was glad to see Hal was back to a calmer state of mind. The rush had been a short one.

Like all vats, Hal was subject to a stronger reaction to adrenaline than those born normally – seeking the rush was built into his biology. Rushing vats were at the top of their physical and mental prowess, but it took a great toll on them. Ty's regiment had been made up almost exclusively of vats, so he knew them well enough to help Hal manage the more aggressive facets of his nature.

Vats were raised to serve in the military, so the rush compulsion wasn't a problem until they got their walking papers from the service. They were discharged from their military duty after seven years. In the early days of the genetically modified soldiers, they'd tried to keep them enlisted indefinitely, but the nightly programming they underwent eventually made them violent and unstable.

Ivor Nash was the last vat to have served eight years. He had been a model soldier, up until he committed the mass murder of his brothers and his commanding officers during his sleep cycle. Nash's mind had fractured from all the programming, and he'd moved like a one-man death machine, wading through a sea of bodies. They had been helpless. The only one to survive was the highest ranking nat officer, to whom Nash proudly reported his victory over the enemy. The officer promptly shot Nash in the face.

In his mind, Ty could still see the surveillance footage of the event he'd been forced to watch as part of his training, supposedly to show them what a vat was capable of. Ty had been just as shocked and saddened as his fellow officers, but he also knew there was a darker agenda at play; they'd been shown the video in order to sow fear and distrust of vats in the new officers, so that they would keep them on a short leash.

According to the upper brass, Nash had simply malfunctioned. It showed Ty exactly how they thought of the men and women they sent out to put down uprisings and fight pirates in the meat grinder of the Edge – equipment only.

With adjustments, and the cap on the years spent in service, the government promised that the problems with the vats were dealt with. *Safe, effective, and ready to serve.* Some of the officers stayed distrustful of the vats under their command, but Ty had never been that way. Especially not with Hal. After serving alongside each other in the ACAS, it had been natural that they stay together. Ty had gotten used to looking after Hal. Knowing the trouble vats could get into on their own, he felt responsible for his best friend. For a vat seeking the rush, the Spiral's Edge had plenty of temptations to offer. While Ty didn't follow Hal around every waking moment, he kept an eye on him where he could. Trouble tended to follow Hal wherever he went.

Hal's voice broke in on his thoughts. "Ty. That girl's face? It didn't happen tonight. Those bruises are a few days old."

"Yeah." Ty nodded. "She say anything?"

"No," Hal replied. "But… someone hurt her. Then those guys tonight…"

"Beryl noticed she's a tecker from her node. Maybe she's looking for work?" Ty said.

Hal read him right away. "We could ask her?"

"Yeah. Let's see how she's feeling in the morning." Ty got up and headed toward the door. "Let me know if you need me for anything. Otherwise, I'll be in my quarters. Runa can monitor our jump."

"Ok, Cap."

"Get some sleep, yeah?" Ty said.

"I'll do my best."

THREE

Vivi awoke to see her rescuer sitting by the medbed, absently tapping on his handheld. He didn't notice she was awake until she pushed the blanket off and tried to sit up.

"How are you feeling?" he asked.

"I'm OK. Just my head..." She looked around, finally sitting up and groaning. "Where am I?"

"The *Loshad*. Our ship. We brought you here to keep you safe," he reminded her, adjusting the bed so she could sit up more comfortably.

"I'm not sure how to thank you," she said hesitantly, as she sat back to take her first good look at him. He was dressed in military-type cargo pants and a green shirt that looked good with the golden blonde scruff on his chin.

"There's no need for that." Hal's eyes were fixed on her bruises. She turned that side of her face away. He started to reach out toward her cheek, but she drew back so quickly he immediately dropped his hand and frowned. "Who's after you?"

Her eyes widened as she realized what he meant. "Oh. The bruises... If I said I got them in my job as a cage fighter would you believe me?" On her trip out to the Edge, she'd been asked about them a couple of times, and it had been the first thing to pop into her head.

"How about you try again?" he said, with a soft laugh. She smiled but didn't feel comfortable enough to talk about her past with this stranger. She didn't want to even think about Noah and how her ex had turned abusive when she'd discovered he was hacking for Echo, one of the three galaxy-wide hacker groups. She'd ruined Echo's attempted heist of BromCorp, and Noah had erupted in violence.

Apparently, Hal sensed her hesitation and backed off. "Look, whatever it was, it's OK. You're safe with us, Miss Valjean."

Maybe, she thought. "It's…Vivi. My name's Vivi," she said.

He nodded. "OK, Vivi."

"We're not on Jaleeth anymore, are we?" she asked. "I can hear the ship's engines going."

"We had a meeting on Omicron Station, so we – uh – brought you with us on our ship. But we'll drop you back by Jaleeth when we're done. Hope that's OK… because it's a bit too late now."

She sighed softly, not feeling like she had the strength to do anything else. It wasn't like there was anything she could do about being taken aboard their ship, even if it had been without her knowledge or consent. They seemed to have had the best intentions so far. There was something about this man that made her want to feel safe in his presence, but after Noah she was hesitant to trust her instincts, especially around men. "It's OK, I guess. I have nowhere to be. Could I… get some water?"

He nodded, going to a cabinet and retrieving a bottle of Clear. The IV was doing its job, but the electrolyte enhanced water would also help. "Drink it slow," he warned her, as an older woman with greying auburn hair entered the medbay.

"Glad to see you awake," the woman said as she came over, checking her readouts. "I'm Beryl McCabe, medic around here. You were slipped a pretty strong tranquilizer by those men back on Jaleeth. It might take a while to wear off."

Vivi felt more at ease, knowing another woman was on the ship. "I don't – uh – I don't know what to say. Thank you for helping me?"

"Hal's been keeping a good eye on you," she said. "But we've all been taking turns."

"How long have I been asleep?" Vivi asked between sips of water.

"Seventeen hours," Hal said.

"Wow," Vivi replied, surprised.

"How are you feeling now?" Beryl asked.

Vivi shook her head uncertainly. "A headache and still... dizzy."

Beryl nodded. "Hal, do me a favor. Go see if Ty's up and let him know our guest is back with us."

He left, and Beryl came to stand beside Vivi. The older woman swept the tecker with the medscanner, saying nothing as the tension between them built. Vivi could tell that Beryl wanted to ask her some questions but didn't want to pry.

She sighed. At least it would be easier to talk to a woman about this. "Look. It was my ex. After he did this," she gestured to her face, "it was over. I came out here to get away from him when I ran into those guys who spiked my drink."

Beryl nodded. "Is your ex the type of guy who will be coming after you?"

Vivi shook her head. "I... I don't think so. Noah's too much of a narcissist for that."

The medic smiled gently in understanding. "OK, then you just rest, kid." She patted Vivi's arm before turning to put away the medscanner. "Ty and Hal went to your room on Jaleeth and brought your things. They're over there." She gestured over to the other bed where Vivi's larger bag lay.

Vivi was stunned. "Why... would they... Why would they help me like this? I mean, just go out of their way and everything?"

"Oh, that's just what they do. Hal and Ty were ACAS soldiers. Hal saw you were in trouble and stepped in. He hasn't met a fight he would back down from."

"Oh," she nodded as the door opened and an unfamiliar face entered alongside Hal.

"Hi," the brown-haired man said. "I'm Tyce Bernon, captain of the *Loshad*."

"Vivi Valjean." He reached out his hand and she shook it. His grip was firm, but gentle.

"I know you must have a lot of questions," Ty began, "but let's start with how much you remember."

"I- I had just gotten to Jaleeth to look for work. I'm a tecker, and I decided to get the lay of the land."

Ty nodded. "OK."

"There were two guys in the bar that kept coming up to me, to see if I wanted to dance with them. I told them no, but they kept trying. Finally, I told them to piss off, but they still didn't want to take no for an answer. I drank the rest of my drink before I realized it tasted different than the first two. That was when I fell out of the chair and the two guys were trying to drag me away. Then… Hal, here, came to help and–" She put a hand over her mouth. "Ohmygods. Did I throw up on you?" Her eyes went wide as she remembered what had happened.

Hal shrugged. "It's not a big deal."

"I'm *so* sorry," she said, shaking her head as her cheeks colored. "Who… Who do you think they were?" she asked, wondering for a moment if it could have been someone sent by her ex's hacking group, Echo. *But that's stupid, right?* Echo had no way of knowing where she was. She'd been careful to use scrilla, not her credit accounts. Of course, they could have hacked security cams. Hal's next words interrupted her worries.

"They were most likely paid kidnappers," Hal replied. "Guys like that comb the stations all the time for females fresh off the boats from the Inner Spiral. Probably to sell to the black-market brothels on Dela Prime." Vivi paled at the very mention of the planet's name. Everyone knew that Dela Prime was a place where the laws of the Coalition simply did not apply. In fact, the planet was reputed to be the nexus of all crime in the Spiral. "Oh my gods," she breathed.

"Shit, I'm sorry." Hal said. "I didn't mean to say it so bluntly."

"No. It's OK." She shook her head. "I guess it means I really do owe you guys my life." She laid her head back, feeling dizzy again.

"We're not concerned with that," Ty said. "You can rest easy enough on our ship. Those guys won't be looking for you again."

"That big guy won't be looking at anything until the swelling goes down," Hal smirked, getting up to go. Once again, Vivi seemed to be struggling to keep her eyes open.

"See you in the morning, Miss Valjean," Ty replied.

She nodded as they left.

"Night cycle lighting," Beryl said, and the room lights dimmed to a watery glow. "I'm going to let you get some more sleep, kid."

Vivi looked around the darkened room nervously, but the older woman reassured her with a warm smile. "If you need me, just let Runa know. I'm right down the hall."

"Thank you," she whispered, pulling the blanket up as Beryl adjusted her bed for sleeping.

"You're very welcome."

The next morning Ty was up early. He located the coffee and set up a pot to brew because he knew the crew would need it and he was the closest thing to a morning person on the ship.

Their guest was next to enter the galley. She was dressed in a light blue tee and black pants. It was obvious she'd washed up and changed before coming to look for someone.

"Back on your feet, I see," Ty said with a smile. He turned to retrieve two stainless steel mugs from a cabinet. "Want some coffee?"

"Oh my gods, yes," she nodded, eagerly taking the mug from him. He poured and she added sugar. It was wonderful. "Ohhh… I needed that."

"Yeah, me too," Ty said, gesturing to the table. "Let's sit down a minute."

She followed him to a seat. "So. What do you guys do? Go around rescuing people in trouble?"

Ty shrugged. "Whatever the universe throws at us. Are you in trouble, Miss Valjean?"

She looked down into her mug. "You can call me Vivi."

"OK, Vivi." His question hung there for long moments until she looked back up.

"I- I *was* in trouble, but I solved my own problem. It was… He was just… He was someone who wasn't who I thought he was. That's all." Ty nodded slowly, and she went on. "That's why I'm out here. Starting over. Finding a job, then a place to stay."

"You're from the Inner Spiral?" Ty observed.

"Yeah," she nodded, "but I have experience as a tecker. In uni, I interned at a shipyard and worked on ship's systems, and later with a security firm. I was hoping to find a job with one of the technology firms on Jaleeth or Omicron Station."

"I have a friend that works at TechSolutions on Omicron. We could introduce you," Ty said. "Or, if you're interested, I thought you might consider working with us?" He had intended on asking her more questions, but her easy manner made him go ahead and toss the offer out there.

She looked up at him. "Working with you?"

"Hal, Beryl and I are salvagers. We go out past the Border to look for Mudar tech and allenium. There's debris from crashed and destroyed ships all over the Border planets from the Mudar war a century ago. Just recently, about the past ten years, they've opened it for salvage. Only certified teams can go out there and we're one of them; we get our permits through LanTech. Our tecker – Lucas – left about a year ago and we've had trouble finding a replacement. The last guy we tried didn't even make it out of spacedock."

"Yeah?" she asked. "Why? Is the job really hard?"

"No." Ty thought for a moment before replying. "It's Hal. I mean, he doesn't always get along with everyone. Let's just say it's been… difficult finding the right fit."

She nodded. "You guys are both ex-military, right?" she asked, remembering what Beryl had said to her about their past.

"We are. Hal is a–" He was unsure if she had noticed Hal's vat tattoo. "Hal was my sergeant during our time in the service.

He's a vat." He watched her carefully to see how she handled the information. "Would that be a problem or make a difference?" If she were intolerant of vats, the issue was decided, and he would drop her back on Jaleeth.

Her green eyes were thoughtful, but he detected no hint of prejudice there. "No, why would it be?" she asked.

"Just making sure." Ty replied with relief. "Some people – especially those from the Inner Spiral – don't care for vats, you know."

"That's not me," she said simply. "Hal saved me. I owe him."

Ty nodded thoughtfully, giving her time to consider her next move.

"How much does the job pay?"

"Whatever the profits are on a haul, we split five ways. One for each of us and one part for the upkeep of the *Loshad*. It varies month to month, but you'll make enough scrilla to survive pretty comfortably. We all pitch in a little for the food, water, and air and we do fairly well. You'll have your own quarters. You can eat with us or by yourself, whatever you want."

"What does the position on ship entail?"

"Helping to identify the purpose of Mudar tech we find that we don't recognize. Monitoring our shipboard computer and making adjustments and repairs when needed. She runs well, but you never know. And I guess pitching in for whatever we need doing. We kind of keep it flexible around here. For example, Beryl not only patches us up, but she's good on comms and keeping our ship supplied too. We'll train you on everything you need to know, though."

She nodded thoughtfully and he carried on. "If you're interested, why not try it for a run? If you decide it's not for you, we can drop you back by Omicron or Jaleeth or wherever, no hard feelings."

She thought a second, then replied, "That sounds great. I'll do my best for you, captain." She held out her hand and Ty shook it. "Any tips you can give me for getting along with Hal, so I don't end up like the last guy?"

"I think you're doing great so far. I mean, the fact that you threw up on him, and he still brought you back to the ship says a lot." He smiled at her in a teasing way.

She blushed again. "Don't remind me," she groaned.

Just then Hal entered the room, shuffling past them to the coffee maker. Ty spoke as Hal found a mug, dumped five heaped spoons of sugar into it and filled it with coffee. "Hey, Vivi's going to be our new tecker. At least for the next run."

"Five by five, Veevs," Hal murmured as he made his way to the table beside Ty. He propped his head on his left hand, still half asleep.

"Thanks again for saving me the other night. I owe you," Vivi said.

"Nah." Hal took another sip of coffee, "You don't owe me. Beatdowns are free for crewmembers, see? Just lemme know whose ass you want kicked, and I got it handled." He took another slug, then glanced at Ty. "Are you putting her in the quarters near mine?"

"Yeah." Ty said. "That OK?"

"Yeah, I'll try to keep it down." Hal nodded as he held out a hand to Vivi. "Welcome to the crew, Veevs."

FOUR

The next few weeks passed quickly, and Ty was pleased that Vivi seemed to be working out. They did two runs and came back with a couple of halfway decent hauls of allenium and a Mudar sidearm from the ruins of an old human settlement on one of the earlier colonies that had been attacked by the AIs.

They had returned to Omicron, the other large station in the Edge, to resupply and wait for another permit from LanTech to go back out. Ty knew back to back runs were tiring, but he wanted them to build up a reserve again, in case another slow period occurred.

Ty and Hal were in a bar called the Shellback, located on one of the "lower" rays of the star-shaped base. The place attracted a lower-class crowd than the bars Ty was used to meeting contacts in. Astin Fortenot had messaged him with a salvage lead, but he hadn't shown for their meeting. Fortenot was a friend from TechSolutions, the firm that he'd mentioned to Vivi. Every once in a while, Fortenot had intel that panned out. When it did, Cherise at LanTech usually swung them a permit and they went off to collect the artifacts.

A quad game finished up on the feed behind the bar. Hal had made his way down there to watch the end of it, but his team, the Navs, had lost their championship. He was not going to be happy, Ty thought.

Hal was stopped by a man on his way back to the bar, and

the two began to exchange words. Ty watched, vigilant for any trouble. He could tell Hal was getting angry by the glint in his eye. He'd seen it often enough.

The two men were glaring at each other now, almost forehead to forehead. *Hal isn't going to back down from this one. When does he ever?* Tyce downed the rest of his whiskey with a sigh, ran a hand through his hair, and got up before Hal got himself killed or, more likely, killed someone else.

Ty was athletic, but not nearly the size of Hal's opponent. His best chance of breaking up the fight would be to head it off before it got started.

"Halvor."

There was no response.

"Stand down, Hal," he repeated, hoping the military tone would break his best friend out of the adrenaline haze. When it didn't work, he stepped in front of Hal, trying to meet his gaze. Ty saw with dismay, however, that Hal had already locked on his adversary, his pupils so large that his eyes appeared a fathomless black.

"Sorry, sir," Hal said in a deceptively calm voice. "Man's asked to have his head bashed in, and I mean to oblige him."

"Come on. Throw the first punch, you vat-bred dog!"

Uh-oh, Ty thought. The man yelling at Hal was as large as he was stupid; he was sweaty, drunk, and dirty, with the angular tribal face and neck tattoos popular with spacers that lived on the Edge.

"Look," Ty said, turning to face Hal's would-be opponent, but keeping a hand on his friend's chest, "you really don't wanna do this."

The man's breath turned Ty's stomach as he leaned in and sealed his fate. "This is none of your business, so… Fuck. Off. Asshole."

"Just remember, I tried to stop you." Ty turned back to Hal, patting him on the shoulder and getting out of the way. "OK, bud. Do what you do."

With a grin, Hal launched himself past Tyce and landed the

first punch. The brawler was stunned but recovered himself quickly and the two began pounding each other. Ty glanced at the bartender, who watched with the bored fascination of someone who had seen it all too many times.

A double-fisted blow to the jaw sent Hal sprawling to the floor. But he only grinned back, showing teeth smeared with blood. He leapt from flat on his back to his feet in one move, an action that any prizefighter in the Edge would envy.

Realizing Hal was stronger and more focused than he'd expected, the brawler pulled a blade. He managed two slices across his opponent's chest before Hal used his longer reach to strike him squarely in the nose. The drunk immediately spewed blood, and the fight was all but over. By the time Halvor was done punching him, the drunk was a crushed heap on the floor.

Hal wiped blood from his split lip. "OK, Cap." He spat a bloodied globule at his opponent's feet. "Now I'm done."

Tyce shook his head and laid down some scrilla on the bar. "For the mess," he said, wondering if the bartender would call the local authorities or if he would just take the brawler out with the rest of the trash. It wouldn't be the first time they'd had to pay a hefty bribe to keep Hal from landing in Omicron Station's brig, he thought.

But luckily this time it was the trash. The bartender nodded and gestured to his cook, who dragged the brawler into the back by one leg as the bartender slipped the scrilla into his pocket and returned to pouring a drink.

Vivi looked up from her cup of coffee as she saw Tyce and Hal enter the galley. Blood had run down Hal's chin, streaking his T-shirt crimson. She put her datapad down and stood up.

"What happened?" she asked, her eyes checking Hal over uneasily as she took a few steps back.

"Someone needed their ass beat. I'm fine. Nothing an ice pack won't fix," Hal said casually.

"He's lucky he didn't get arrested by the locals," Ty added. He rummaged in a compartment, pulled out a medkit, and threw Hal an instant coldpack. Hal cracked it and placed it on a blackened eye. "The guy did ask for it, though."

Beryl came out from her quarters after hearing the noise. "What in the twelve hells happened to you, Hal?"

Hal slid the coldpack down to his lip and muttered against it. "Fight. No big deal."

Ty passed the first aid kit over to Beryl. "Here. Your hands are steadier than mine."

"OK, soldier, take a seat." Beryl gestured to the chair beside her. "Did you give him something to remember *you* by?" she asked as she glanced over his wounds and old scars on his face; one through his eyebrow, and another on his chin.

Hal grinned. "You bet your ass I did."

Beryl's eyes met Hal's, and she smiled back, cleaning his busted lip. "Good."

She gave him a medjet of something and then worked on his cuts. "You know we're leaving soon. Don't get into any trouble. Save it for the run."

"Sorry, Beryl."

"You're not sorry," she said with a motherly grin, gesturing for him to take off his blood-soaked shirt.

"OK, you're right." Hal admitted, pulling the shirt over his head. "Hard to be sorry, when the guy was such a dick."

Vivi sat back down but kept an eye on Hal. This was the first time she'd gotten a close look at Hal's other tattoos. He had different linear designs along his arms and chest. And, of course, there was his vat ID tattoo, a rectangular series of lines and squares stretched across his wrist. There was a long slash along his chest, an injury obviously sustained in the fight.

"The guy who attacked you had a knife?" Vivi asked.

"Yeah," Hal said, glancing to her. His pupils were huge; his normally blue eyes had practically turned black. It was a little unsettling. He made her nervous with the way he seemed so hyped up after a brawl, as if violence was second nature to him. Which she supposed it was, now that she thought about it.

"What were you fighting over?" Beryl asked, cleaning his wounds.

"Quad game. Guy said the Bels were a better team than the Navs."

Beryl punched him hard in the arm. "What the hell, Hal? That's the hill you're going to die on?"

Hal shrugged. "Everybody's gotta die for something, right?"

"Everybody knows the Streaks are the best anyway," Beryl said under her breath, raising an eyebrow as she shot Ty a grin.

"HEY!" Hal sat up straighter. "Get the hell off my ship."

"That's *our* ship," Ty corrected.

"Just kidding." Beryl laughed as she finished up.

"I like the Navs too," Vivi ventured quietly.

"See, at least someone has good sense around here," Hal said, gesturing to Vivi.

"Listen, Hal." When his eyes were focused on Beryl, she continued. "These cuts are pretty deep, so take it easy on them for the next two days. No sparring, OK?"

Hal nodded, then watched Beryl pinch together the edges of the deep oozing wound on his chest until the adhesive set.

Vivi kept watching Hal. He hadn't flinched or shown any signs of being in pain as Beryl worked on him. She'd heard vats didn't have nerves at all, but she was sure that couldn't be true. She was finding that Hal was a mass of contradictions in a lot of ways. Sometimes he seemed to not care about anything, but when it came to the crew, he was protective to the point of violence.

Just last week, they'd been coming through a crowded spaceport when a guy, obviously drunk due to celebrating the New Year, grabbed her ass. It had taken everything Tyce had to pull Hal off the guy. Even though he'd been protecting her, seeing Hal's sudden violence had made her anxious around him. She realized her time with Noah was to blame, but it still didn't make her feel any less on edge to know that.

She found herself wondering what Hal's story was. She had already picked up on a lot about him; it was obvious that he and Captain Bernon were close, like brothers, and that Tyce seemed to be the only person who could bring Hal back from the brink.

It also seemed that Hal thought she needed a lot of looking after – especially in spacedock. He would go with her off the ship each time she left, giving her some pretense or another. She never called him on it. In some ways, it made her feel safer too, despite being nervous around him. Her uncle, who had been in the ACAS, always said that vats were protective of their officers. Maybe that's why Hal was keeping an eye on her; Tyce had probably told him to.

Ty pulled her from her thoughts when he sat down beside her, scrolling through his datapad. "As soon as I can talk to Fortenot, I should be getting the new permit from LanTech, then we're on our way."

She now knew that the permit would make sure they could pass the Border unchallenged by the ACAS. It would also outline what kinds of AI artifacts LanTech was sending them out for. If they found anything else while they were out there, well, that would belong to them. But first, they had to play the waiting game.

"I can use the extra time to work on that hesitation in the *Loshad*'s drive," Vivi said.

"And I'll resupply the ship," Beryl said.

"Whatever we do, just keep a low profile." Ty glanced at Hal. "*Low* profile, Hal, OK?"

"Got it," Hal promised.

Ty nodded slowly. "You should all get some sleep. I'll see you in the morning."

Hal opened his eyes in the watery glow of the night cycle in his room. He was sitting up, his gaze focused on the opposite wall as he returned to consciousness.

He could smell blood; his mouth was dry and tasted rusty. The dream of the medbay he'd been in faded away. He looked around the darkened room. The shadows seemed unfamiliar and strange. Ty was hurt. Was that then or was it now? He couldn't remember; it was all a jumble.

He got up from the bed and tugged on a shirt before making his way to Ty's room. A growing unease began to throb like a heartbeat in his brain.

A beeping woke Ty in the middle of the night. It was the low, insistent noise of a special alarm that he had set; an alarm that meant Hal wasn't sleeping well again.

Ty got up and made his way throughout the dark ship, first checking the cargo bay, then the back hall near the engine room, and finally the common area and galley.

The lights were a little brighter in here. Hal was sitting at the table, staring into space.

"Hal?" he asked gently, afraid of startling his friend.

Hal raised his eyes to Ty's and relaxed a little. "Yeah, Cap?"

"You OK?" He slid into the seat across from him.

Hal sighed. "Yeah. Bad dreams." He scratched lightly at the table in front of him.

"About?"

"Our time on Bel-Prime. When I was sitting there waiting on you to get back from surgery."

"Oh." Tyce remembered Bel-Prime. During that engagement, Ty and Hal and the rest of the company of vats had been fighting the insurgents who had murdered the vat garrison on the planet during an uprising. There had been an explosion and Ty and Hal had been temporarily separated in the smoke and chaos. Tyce had been flung against a wall and woken up speared with rebar through his left side. If not for Hal finding him and carrying him back to base, he would have bled out on that battlefield.

He owed Hal for saving his life several times after that, but that first time… that had been rough on both of them. Upon waking, he'd heard stories about how Hal had stayed by his side; he had sat in the same chair by the medbed for over thirty-six hours, until he saw that Ty was going to make it. Hal hadn't even gotten his own wounds treated; he'd refused to move until the doctors noticed the pooling blood and made him accept medical treatment, though only upon threat of expulsion from the medbay.

Hal interrupted Ty's thoughts. "I dreamed they came and told me you died," he said, looking down at his hands.

"I've had the same type of dreams," Tyce admitted.

"It fucking sucks," Hal murmured.

"It does, Hal," Ty said, getting up to rummage through a cabinet. He came back with two mugs and a bottle of Celian whiskey.

"I thought it was real when I woke up. I- I stood at your door a minute, trying to decide if you were really in there or not."

Ty shook his head slowly. "You can always come get me, Hal." He poured them both a couple of generous measures.

Hal drank it down like water. "I know, but I didn't want to wake you up for something stupid."

"It's not. It's not stupid. As I said, I have the same type of dreams." Ty shrugged. He was unwilling to describe them, but losing his best friend was his greatest fear as well. He supposed it went back to losing his brother, Caleb. His younger brother had been a lot like Hal; an irrepressible thrill-seeker who'd died at the age of fifteen.

Once vats left the service, they rarely lived long, and Hal liked to get into trouble more than was good for him. The Edge was a dangerous place for him, but where else did vats have to go? They weren't ever welcomed on the Inside; they were seen as unnatural and therefore less than human. Ty thought the natural-borns just didn't want to be reminded of the second-class citizens they'd created to fight their wars for them.

They sat for a while, in a companionable silence, one built over long hours together in the ACAS and the years after. Ty couldn't have pinpointed the moment that Hal went from subordinate officer to the type of family that was stronger than blood, but it had happened. He would take a bolt for his friend and knew Hal would do the same for him.

Hal started scrubbing his face as he yawned, and Tyce could tell he was winding back down. “Think you can sleep now?”

Hal nodded. “Probably.” He got up to leave. “Ty. Thanks. I know I’m a pain in the ass.”

“Yeah, but you’re *our* pain in the ass. Beryl and I couldn’t get on without you. Hit the rack, OK?” He grabbed up their cups and the half-full bottle and turned to stow it all away.

“You got it, Cap.” Hal said, and padded away to his room.

Tyce, this is your 0630 wake up call.

Tyce groaned in reply.

Does that mean that you would like me to set an alarm for ten minutes? Runa asked.

“Mmm, yeah.”

Tyce rolled over, burying his face in the pillow as his mind began to wake up and his thoughts turned to Hal. He was adjusting well to having Vivi on board and things had been relatively quiet so far. Hal had even gone with her each time she’d left the ship to go out on the station… obviously watching over her until she found her feet.

The salvage permits were the pressing matter for today. He’d have to get moving only to hurry up and wait around at LanTech’s offices, probably all day. They hadn’t gotten the exact details out of Fortenot yet, but at the very least he could start getting the paperwork moving and save a bit of time. In this game, that small advantage could make the difference between being first at a salvage site and arriving to see hated rivals getting the glory.

A five-minute chime sounded. Runa was dependable, but she was little more than a fancy computer program that did what Ty told her to. The government had put in extra safeguards over a hundred years ago to prevent computers from ever becoming self-aware, after contact with the Mudar had led to deadly skirmishes in the zone beyond the Border. Anything considered artificial intelligence had been out-and-out banned. Computers doing independent thinking scared the shit out of everyone, government and citizens alike.

Tyce didn't know how he felt about it. Vivi seemed to think that the danger was overrated. They made their living from salvaged AI tech, but it was difficult not to feel uneasy about taking things from the species that almost made the human race obsolete.

Vivi had done a good job so far. She was the youngest of his crew, but he would choose skill over age most days. Although she'd been with them nearly a month, she had begun to prove her worth to the crew almost immediately.

He'd watched her reassemble a complex piece of technology in half the time it would have taken Lucas. She'd already rewired the *Loshad* and improved Runa's response time by eighty percent. He didn't even want to ask what safety protocols and self-awareness inhibitors she'd had to disengage to cause that to happen; he just knew he'd be thankful for the edge it gave him when the ship needed it.

He heard the ten-minute chime sound from Runa and knew he'd been lying there too long. He got up, hit the shower, then pulled on a black tee, tactical cargos, and boots, much like the fatigue uniform of the ACAS. Like Beryl always said, you can take the man out of the military…

By 0700, he had reached the galley. He was making coffee when Hal came in, scrubbing at his face as he sat at the table.

"Morning," Tyce said.

"Mmm," grunted Hal. "Mornings can kiss my ass."

Tyce smirked at Hal's usual grumblings. The first cup of coffee went to Hal, then he poured his own. As always, Hal added lots of sugar – his vat metabolism would burn it off quickly – but Ty drank his black.

"What's your plan for today?" Tyce asked. "You can come with me to LanTech, if you want?"

"Yeah, because I'm great at waiting around for something to happen," Hal deadpanned, before glancing down at his handheld, then tossing it impatiently to the side.

"I get it," Tyce nodded. "Too bad, though – you'd probably make it a hell of a lot more interesting. Let me know if we hear from Astin."

"Will do, Cap. Working on the water purifiers today. Backup system's got a glitch and the filters need cleaning. Might see if Veevs is up for some sparring practice later too," Hal said.

Hal had been training her to fight, supposedly just in case they were in a situation that required it. Ty had a sneaking suspicion that Hal's worries about Vivi went deeper than just casual crew training, however. He obviously wanted her to be able to defend herself because of the shape she'd been in when they'd brought her on and also because the Edge could be a dangerous place. He'd certainly never taken the time to train any of their other teckers in self-defense, though. It seemed more and more likely that Vivi was going to work out as a member of the crew.

"OK, I'll leave you to it, then. Just remember that Beryl said to watch the cut on your lip." It was typically this way; Halvor was the muscle that kept the ship running, and Tyce handled the business side with LanTech and some of their more illicit contacts. Ty didn't mind it; he had a lighter touch with most of their informants. "Take it easy on Vivi in training and keep an eye on her. She pushes herself too hard and she's gonna get hurt that way."

Hal glanced up before turning back to his handheld. "Don't worry," he said with a smile. "I got *both* eyes on her, Cap."

FIVE

Hal punched the heavy boxing bag, feeling the rough canvas scratch at his knuckles as his fist smacked its surface. He imagined tension rolling through his body and coming out with each punch he landed. Ty had explained about threat levels that he'd learned in officer training: "green" was no threat at all, "yellow" meant a heightened state of awareness, "orange" meant danger was imminent, "red" meant you were in the shit, and "black" was when you lost control of yourself. Hal had realized immediately that he never operated below a yellow at any time, and that things could go red or black very quickly. Ty said it was that way for most vats, but if Hal stayed aware of the levels, he could stay low on the scale, and think more clearly. But knowing didn't make it easier.

That was the reason for the sparring. The more energy Hal could work out physically, the better chance he would have of controlling those colorful moments, when the rush took him over completely. Before meeting Ty, he hadn't had much self-control at all and was always in trouble, but thankfully now, he hardly ever hit black.

Tyce understood him – Hal had liked his captain from the first time they'd met. He'd been fighting another vat, right after getting transferred into Ty's outfit. It was typical for the new guy to get challenged and he was damn well going to make sure it only happened once. He expected a week or two in the brig, after being dressed down of course (possibly a flogging if that appealed to the new CO), but Ty had done neither. He had let them fight it out – Hal taking the reigning champion apart – and then said, "Report to my office." Hal had followed Tyce, while the other guy's friends dragged him off to the med bay.

When he'd gone in, Ty had seated himself behind his desk. He remained there, for long moments, just observing Hal and saying nothing. Hal could still feel how the blood stung as it trickled down from a cut on his eyebrow into his eye, but he refused to break his stance to wipe at it.

"I understand you're my new sergeant," Ty said.

Great, Hal had thought. *It'll be a demotion.* "Sir, yes sir," he had replied, keeping his eyes fixed on a point behind the captain's right shoulder. He remained as still as he could manage while a rush thrummed through his veins.

Tyce looked down at his terminal pad and tapped. "Don't think I don't understand why that had to be done, Sergeant Cullen. I do. However, I expect you to try and find better ways to solve your problems."

"Sir?" Hal was so stunned, that he met Tyce's eyes.

"You heard me. Someone with scores like your own," Ty had turned his pad so that Hal could see his own file on screen, "should have no trouble thinking of alternative solutions to conflict, when possible. I'll expect you to be able to talk about your ideas the next time we see each other. For now, you're dismissed, sergeant."

And just like that, Hal found himself standing outside in the hallway, unsure of what had just happened. He grinned, thinking about it now. It was the first moment he'd ever felt like he could trust one of his COs. And the first moment he wanted to be something better than just a vat who liked to fight.

He paused for a drink of water from his bottle. After he'd finished up the work on the water purifiers midafternoon, he'd gone to look for Vivi, but she was still engaged on the ship's main terminal at the time. She'd been jacked in, hands moving in the air as she virtually adjusted the shipboard computer. He didn't want to bother her, so he'd gone to the cargo bay alone to work out, telling himself that a nat like her would have better things to do anyway.

He lost track of how long he had been there, listening to music as loud as his earphonics would go and bouncing back and forth as he pummeled the bag. A touch on his shoulder shattered his concentration, and his hyped reflexes swung out quickly as he turned. Thankfully, he was also fast enough to pull back his punch before it landed.

"Woah!" Vivi threw up a forearm in defense as she ducked. She stumbled back a few steps, looking at him with fear in her eyes.

Hal let out a sigh as he dropped his fist and yanked out his earpieces. "Shit."

She looked pale for a minute, and he reached out slowly to steady her, remembering the black eye she'd had when they'd first taken her on the *Loshad*, but she flinched away from his touch on her arm. He noticed and held up his open hands. "I'm sorry. You good, Veevs?" He'd made up the nickname for her from the start, and she didn't seem to mind it.

"Yeah. Sorry. I guess I startled you." The young woman pulled a small smile, and he realized from her wide eyes that he had really scared her. Her hands still shook a little as she brushed the hair from her face.

He smiled in a way that he hoped was reassuring. "It's only my reflexes. Just lemme see you first next time, 'kay?"

Her eyes are such a pure shade of green, he thought. They glimmered like spring-gems in sunlight. He could remember the first time he'd seen one of the crystals, in the classroom of one of the vat training facilities on Chamn-Alpha. It had been during a geology seminar when they were given samples of rocks from different planets to identify. At the end of class, Hal stole the green crystal from the geology kit and was never caught. It was the only personal possession he still had from that time.

She was blushing a little as she held his gaze. "What?" she asked softly.

He shook his head. *Keep your mind right,* he told himself. *She's a nat, and the last thing she'd be interested in would be a vat.* "I came to find you earlier," he said. "To see if you wanted to spar. I promised to teach you a few things, remember? You were still working on the main computer, though, so..." Hal shrugged, like it was no big deal.

"Oh. Sorry. Hey, I think I might have the drive fixed now. But what I really came to tell you was that Runa said we got a message from Astin Fortenot. It's about that tip he's got for you guys. He's gonna be at the Syzygy for a while and said you could meet him there. This is that guy you and Tyce tried to meet last night, right?"

"Yeah." Hal reached around her to grab his towel. "Ty's gone to get things started at LanTech, so I'll go check it out – see what he has to say." Hal wiped his face, then grabbed his water bottle.

She was still standing there when he turned back around, shifting from foot to foot before she spoke. "Hey. What if I come with you? That is, if you want some company," she offered.

Hal weighed how risky it would be for her to go along. The lower levels of Omicron weren't exactly the safest places on the station, but she'd be with him the whole time. "OK," he finally replied. "Be ready in ten."

SIX

Hal had obviously been down to the club levels of Omicron Station before; he was greeted by a few scantily-clad women working the level. He returned their embraces, knowing most of them by name.

Vivi raised an eyebrow as they continued walking toward the Syzygy.

"What?" he asked, shrugging. "So, I know people."

"I see that," she smirked.

"Everybody's gotta make a living," he said, shrugging again.

Turning a corner, they saw a man sitting back against a bulkhead with his feet splayed out. It was obvious from the slack, blissed-out look on his thin, angular face that he was high on something.

"Hey," Hal said to Vivi. "Give me a minute."

She watched nervously, as he knelt beside the man and spoke in a low voice. Eventually the addict lifted his head, looking at Hal.

"Where'd you serve?" Hal asked.

She couldn't help but take a step nearer, but she still couldn't make out the addict's answer. Hal nodded, however.

"What 'bout you?" She heard the thick mumble of the user's voice reply this time as the man made an effort to communicate.

"I fought on Bel-Prime. Patrolled the Border, too," Hal said.

She caught the glimpse of a tattoo similar to Hal's on the inside of the addict's wrist. Hal dug into his pocket, then placed something in the man's hand. "Try and get something to eat with it, yeah?"

The man nodded and tucked the scrilla away. Hal clapped him

gently on the arm and rejoined Vivi, who didn't know what to say.

"C'mon," he said.

As they moved away, Vivi asked, "Do you think he'll use that to buy food?"

Hal shrugged. "I don't know. He's a null addict in pretty bad shape."

"How do you know it's null?" she asked.

"Vats are suckers for null," Hal murmured. "Helps them take the edge off at first, then… they can't leave it alone."

"Why give him scrilla then?" she asked.

"At least he'll know someone cared a little and tried to help him before he died. Besides, that could be me sitting there. I mean, if not for Ty."

His caring gesture seemed to be completely at odds with the bar brawler side of him she'd seen last night. He was a mass of contradictions. He obviously had a heart, though, and she felt drawn to that in a way she couldn't explain.

On reaching the club, they moved inside with the crowd. The place was full, but there was no band – just a DJ playing hypnohaze music. Vivi could sense Hal's tension in the way he held himself as they entered. He stood still for a moment, a frown on his features as he scanned the room. Hal drew Vivi near, taking her hand. "Come on and stay close."

They made their way to a booth on the far side of the room where a man sat drinking. As they drew near, he looked up and Hal gave a nod. Vivi was walking slightly behind him to the right.

Hal called out as they approached, "What the hells do you want now?" and scowled.

Vivi got a good look at the guy in front of them. He was dressed in black, his hair shaved on the sides and cut so short it stood up in points on the top of his head. He looked just like another clubgoer, she thought, then noticed the interface node visible behind his right ear. He stood up quickly, going eye to eye with Hal. Vivi started to worry that Hal was going to get diverted from their meeting.

"You got a problem?" the man asked belligerently.

"That depends on you, nat," Hal said, staring him down.

The two men glared at each other for a moment more, then both started grinning. They shook hands and ended by smacking each other on the back. Vivi realized it was some sort of joke between them, and she relaxed.

"What's up with you?" Hal asked.

"Same old shit, man," the other replied with an easy smile.

Hal gestured to Vivi. "Astin, this is Vivi. She's our tecker. Vivi, this is Astin. He works for TechSolutions."

"Good to meet you," Vivi said.

"So you're the newbie, huh?"

"Yeah."

"Five by five." Astin nodded appreciatively. "OK. Let's get to it." He paused to throw back the rest of the amber liquid in his glass and looked around before he began speaking. "I was going to meet Ty last night, but I was – er – held up." There was an uncomfortable look on his face, but then he waved his hand and went on. "Anyway, I know you guys are always looking for salvage locations. You interested in a lead?"

"How hot is it?" Hal asked.

"ACAS hot," Astin said. "How much scrill can you give me?"

Hal tapped on his handheld a moment, then narrowed his eyes. "Two. It's all I got access to right now. You know Ty, though. If it's good, he'll pay you the full six."

Astin took a moment to consider. "That'll do."

"Same account as last time?"

"Yeah."

Vivi watched, interested in the interplay between the two. She wanted to find out more about how the salvage business worked. This was the first time that she'd gone to run down a lead – previously, Ty and Hal coordinated these things alone.

"I hope this is a good one," Hal muttered, finishing the transaction by tapping on his handheld.

"It will be." Astin leaned in as Hal looked up. "OK. A day ago, we were called in to work on an ACAS corvette. It had broken down while coming back from the Border. They didn't dock at Omicron; we had to approach on a shuttle, and I saw they had a salvage ship named the *Relentless* in tow. Anyway, as I was running diagnostics on the ACAS ship's computers, I began to poke around. Seems like they'd found the *Relentless* out past the Border without a permit. When they boarded, they saw that the ship had made a big find – parts of a metalhead drive and some other things. Here's the location." He showed Hal his handheld, then used a motion of his hand on the screen to transfer it to Hal's device.

"Thanks," Hal nodded, receiving the information.

"*Relentless* was caught soon after she got there, so there wasn't much more they could get. But it looks like it could be a big score," Astin said. "Good luck, man." He offered his hand to Hal, who shook it. "I gotta get gone, but hey – keep where you got that on the DL, OK?"

"You bet," Hal said. He watched Astin go, then he glanced over to Vivi. "We gotta get this to Ty."

She nodded in agreement and followed him out of the booth.

SEVEN

A glint of starlight on metal announced the presence of Station 41 in orbit around the gas giant Rinal. The station serviced the ACAS ships patrolling the Edge in this sector. It was home to over three hundred full-time personnel, almost three-quarters of them vats, several of whom were busily swarming on the corvette *Phobos* and her recent prize capture, the *Relentless.*

On board *Phobos,* Captain Sammeal Tallin was completing his daily log entries at his desk. Other than the computer issues that had required his stopover at Omicron, the week had been a good one for the thirty year-old captain.

Tallin had been proud when he was posted to the *Phobos*. For over ten years he had served in the Spiral on the *Indignant,* a large carrier. There he had been a small fish in a very large pond, one in the seemingly innumerable ranks of young officers seeking promotion. The Edge was the place to be; the place where looters, smugglers, and pirates offered all sorts of chances for an ACAS officer with his eyes on the upper echelon. If he could nab a few more prizes like *Relentless,* and maybe combat a pirate or two, his future would be secure.

He had just typed the last sentence, describing the taking of the *Relentless* when the chime on his door rang.

"Open." He glanced up at the silhouette found in the doorway, hands clasped behind its back. He knew from her stance it was his administrative assistant, Yeoman Lucia. The dark-haired woman stepped into his quarters and stood to attention, waiting for him to further acknowledge her. Her blue and black dress uniform revealed no blemishes, nor a crease out of place. Most of the crew typically wore fatigues, consisting of a grey tee and black cargoes, but Tallin preferred to have his yeoman in a dress uniform.

His critical eye brushed over her a moment; her shoulder length hair was pulled back in a regulation ponytail and her shoes and belt buckle shone immaculately. His yeoman was a perfect example of efficiency and regulation: the very reason he preferred a vat in the role.

"Something to report?" he asked.

"Tech Officer Bowden requests that you meet him on the bridge. He says he has found something to show you."

It must be something Bowden wanted to keep off the transcom, Tallin thought. "Very well. Come along, yeoman," he said.

"Yes, sir." She had to walk fast to keep up with the captain's long legs, but he did not care to slow down for her.

Together they made their way to the lift and took it up to the bridge. Generally, they spent little time in idle small talk; Tallin couldn't see the need. All vats were programmed the same. All had the fierce loyalty and desire to fulfill the objectives of their officers. They were a means to an end. Lose ten, and the ACAS would send you ten more just like them. They would never be as resourceful or creative as a nat, so Tallin spent little time getting to know them on a personal level.

After taking the *Relentless,* the *Phobos* had broken down on their way back from the Border. Bowden, the tech officer, had been on base at training, forcing the ship to use a tech service on Omicron to get it back up and running. They'd returned to base and now Bowden was supervising the team checking the ship's main computer for problems.

A separate crew was also combing the *Relentless* for data. Whatever they found would be used against the criminals in court. Tallin took a dim view of salvaging without a license. Those who did it deserved to be prosecuted to the fullest, in his opinion.

The lift door opened, admitting the captain and his yeoman to the bridge.

Bowden was jacked into the computer, his eyes unfocused as he used a hand to flip through information being fed to him via the node behind his ear.

Tallin tapped the man on the shoulder.

The tecker quickly disengaged from the computer and turned to them, seeing Tallin. "Yes, sir."

"What have you found, Ensign Bowden?"

"Sir, there has been a security breach."

Tallin narrowed his eyes. "Explain."

Bowden pulled up a display of data on a nearby screen. "The *Phobos* was hacked while docked at Omicron. This is the date and time," he pointed it out on the screen. "I've pulled up the security feed for both the bridge and the auxiliary computer room, and I was about to review it."

"Do it," Tallin rumbled. Several of the crew, busy with other tasks, looked up nervously at his words, then their gazes skittered away. They were familiar with the sound of Tallin's displeasure and no one wanted to be the focus of the brutal commander's attention. Tallin thrived on intimidation.

"Yes, sir."

The three of them looked on as the security feed of the bridge played out on the small monitor. There was nothing unusual there. But the auxiliary computer room footage showed something interesting. "This one," Bowden said, pointing at the screen. "He has to be the one that hacked the system." The dark-haired man in the video footage was obviously jacked into the computer network and working his way through data, his hands flicking as he selected, moved, and deselected items. "He's wearing the uniform for the support company that checked our computer systems on the station."

"I want to know what data he stole and who this man is."

"I'm already working on that, sir," Bowden replied.

"Send me the data as soon as it's done," Tallin said as he stalked off the bridge without waiting for an answer, his yeoman at his heels.

"What did you find out from LanTech?" Beryl asked as she entered the common area and saw Tyce was back. He held up a hand to stall her and turned up the newsfeed.

Both knew that the Coalition skewed the newsfeeds their way. Filtering through the bi-horn shit with that in mind made it possible to get an idea of what was really going on in the Edge and the Inner Spiral.

The vid was from an ACAS ship, fighting it out with a heavily armed freighter.

"...The pirate ship was eventually disabled and boarded by ACAS soldiers," the female announcer was saying. "After a firefight inside the ship, the ACAS forces subdued the crew, which was made up of vats and Al-Kimians. As you may remember, twenty-three years ago, Al-Kimia was a republic of five planets. There was a border skirmish over Shalia, a water world, and the Al-Kimians withdrew. Since then, tensions have cooled. Al-Kimia has been offered Coalition membership numerous times, but each time they have voted against it.

"Up until now, these attacks have been thought of as the actions of splinter groups, but now the situation looks grave. Some representatives are uncomfortable with vat soldiers being involved and have started calling into question the policy of releasing the lab-grown recruits after they have served their seven years of indenture. More on this later in the opinion segment of our feedcast..."

Indenture. It was the politically correct term for a vat's forced servitude. *They should call it what it is,* Tyce thought bitterly: *slavery.*

Ty turned the feed off as Beryl came and sat down across from him. "I patched up so many vats during my years in the service. I always had a problem with how ACAS treats them," she said. "Letting them out after seven years barely made it tolerable. What are they suggesting? Forcing them to stay indefinitely? It's wrong."

Ty looked down at his hands, knowing they both were thinking of the Ivor Nash problem.

"If ACAS has fixed the programming thing, staying in service might give vats a structure they're familiar with. Not all of them do as well as Hal when they get out," he said, but they were hollow words that he didn't believe.

"Not all of them have someone like you," Beryl replied.

Ty sighed. There was nothing they could do about any of it. Talking about it would only make him feel worse, so he just shrugged.

"Find anything out today at LanTech?" she asked.

He let his thoughts angle back to the problem at hand. "Yeah, LanTech has no permits available yet. Apparently, something's happened that slowed the whole process to a halt."

"Did they say what it was?"

"No. I even asked Cherise," he said, referring to LanTech's dispatcher. "Because we have a good record, she said as soon as we have our details, we'd get okayed. It would just take an extra day or so. Where's Hal and Vivi?"

"Haven't seen them since after lunch," Beryl said

"Runa, locate Hal and Vivi."

Hal and Vivi have gone to meet Astin Fortenot.

"Locate their handhelds, Runa," Ty said, knowing it was the easiest way of tracking them.

They are on lower level 12 but making their way back toward the ship.

"Good. Send a message and tell them we're waiting on their report."

"Here it is. K-245j – where the *Relentless* was picked up," Hal told the rest of the crew. He zoomed in on the holo map Fortenot had given him so that the planet came into focus. The ship's star map contained sketchy information about the small planet, listing it as an uninhabited world covered with mountains and forests.

"We'll do a quick survey with sensors when we get there – information's lacking because the planet's farther out than we usually go. We better switch out the mounts to rotary lasers, just in case we run into any trouble," Ty said.

"I already thought about that. I'll do it first thing," Hal said, making a note on his handheld.

"The planet has some cave systems, and rich geological strata. Maybe we should gear up the Robotic Exploration Unit. Ever worked with one of those, Vivi?" Ty asked. The REU was basically a small device that contained a camera and some manipulators, used to explore a variety of environments. The drone could move on land, in the air and in water.

Vivi shook her head, already searching the feeds for it. "I'll figure it out, though. I'm a fast learner."

"C'mon. I'll show you where it's at," Hal offered.

"Don't stay up too late," Tyce warned. "If this is a good find, we might be working some extended hours. We leave tomorrow morning as soon as Cherise clears us." He knew that Hal would work through the night if he didn't stop him. "Obviously, I've only given her a rough idea of where we're going. Should take us a few days to get out that far, so plenty of time to get all the prep work done."

"Aww, c'mon, Cap. Who needs sleep?" Hal said.

"Who needs sleep? You do," Ty replied. "And that's a direct order."

"OK," Hal rolled his eyes. "Come on, Veevs, I'll show you the REU."

Now that they had a destination and an estimated time of departure, Hal seemed to Vivi to be much more relaxed. He'd been brooding for the last two days, trying to stay occupied while they waited for a permit, but once he had been given a goal, he was laser focused once again.

They went down the hall, past the crew quarters to the

equipment room. "So, how long have you shipped with Tyce?" Vivi asked.

"You mean after the ACAS or all together?" He glanced at her as if wondering why she was asking.

"All together."

"About nine years. I did my first two years on five different ships that patrolled the Border."

"So, you got transferred a lot," she observed.

"Nah. More like handed off. I was considered part of a bad batch. Fought a bit too much."

"No!" She feigned surprise, to which he grinned.

"Yeah. Before Ty, I spent some time in the brig. OK… a lot of time," he said to the pointed look she shot him. "One of the Colonels decided to transfer me to Ty's outfit. I spent my last five years with him as my captain." Hal paused, and Vivi guessed he was thinking back to his time in service. "I did a lot better with Ty."

"What did Tyce do that was different?" Vivi asked.

"Don't know. He never made me feel like I wanted to buck him. I think he just knows how to lead people." They reached the supply room and Hal began going through the contents of one of the lockers. "He knows how to listen if you have a better idea for something. He…" Hal searched for the right word, "*values* his people's ideas. Most of the others didn't. They didn't think that a vat would have a thought worth hearing. But Ty… he's different."

"I'm sorry the others treated you like that, Hal."

He looked up from the bag he was tugging out of the locker, his expression one of genuine surprise. His mouth worked for a second as if he didn't know what to say, and his open expression was completely new to her. Hal scratched his head for a minute as if she'd totally perplexed him, then he blinked and shook it off. "Um… yeah. It's all good. I wasn't going for sympathy or anything."

She started to reply, but decided to change the subject, sensing that she'd said the wrong thing somehow. "OK, so show me this REU…"

The *Loshad* was underway before 0700 the next morning, within minutes of getting the permit confirmed by Cherise. The crew had worked on getting the ship prepared for the Border most of the previous day. As soon as they shipped out, Hal set up the ship's lasers and ran a few diagnostics from the gunner's position on the bridge. Beryl was kept busy organizing and stowing the supplies and rations she'd had delivered to the ship the day before. By the end of their first day, Vivi had developed some competency with the Robotic Exploration Unit and managed to fly it around the cargo hold.

Once they'd settled into their quarters for the evening, Vivi scanned the feeds for information about forests and cave systems until late in the night. She'd grown up on an arctic planet with her family, so she had little experience with the type of biomes they would encounter on K-245j.

She was lying on her stomach, dozing over the information in her bunk, her head pillowed on her forearm when she heard a thump. She lifted her head, looking around with wide eyes, but things were quiet. The thrum of the engines sounded normal, she thought, as she checked the time on her handheld. It was after 0100 hours.

Yawning she sat up and powered down her device when she heard the same thump again. Then, just faintly, a voice sounded in the cabin next to hers. Hal's room.

Might as well check it out, she thought, tugging her tank down over her sleep pants. The metal deck was chilly on her bare feet and made her shiver. She stepped outside and over to his door where she knocked. No answer, but the talking continued.

"Hal. I know you're up. Everything OK?" she said, knocking again and feeling a small knot forming in her stomach. "What's wrong?"

There was a sudden silence, and she didn't like that either. Hands shaking a little, she typed in an override code for the lock system. She had to key it twice before the door slid open.

"Hal?"

The lights in the room were low, but she could see immediately that Hal wasn't in his bunk. The sheets and blankets had been shoved to the floor. She took two steps forward when she heard his voice to the left of her, followed by the metallic scrape of metal sliding on metal.

"I am the fist of the ACAS... In war I am strength. I bring the justice of the Coalition to its enemies..." Hal's voice had a blankness that made the hairs on the back of Vivi's neck prickle. "Victory is mine. I will gladly fight to the death..." There was another scraping sound. And another. Hal was seated at the built-in table on the other side of the room, his back to her. She could see pieces of a weapon strewn about the desk in front of him. He was assembling it as he recited his warrior's creed.

"I do not surrender to exhaustion or fear..."

Snap.

"I am steadfast and tenacious in the face of adversity..."

Scrape.

"I am inexorable..."

His hands moved in regulated, almost robotic motions.

"Hal..." Vivi said, a rising sense of fear in her voice. Was this some sort of sleepwalking episode? She wanted to go up to him and touch him on the shoulder, to try to wake him, but she remembered she had to let him see her first. She stayed put.

"I am the ACAS!" His last sentence wasn't exactly a yell, but it was close, in the same way that a soldier in a vid would bark orders.

He paused a moment, then began taking apart the blaspistol, in the same robotic fashion. He started over with the recitation: "I am the fist of the ACAS..."

As he continued, she crept closer, terrified to leave him, yet terrified to stay. He continued to take apart the blaspistol then rebuild it. Break and rebuild. Break. Rebuild.

The panic bubbled inside Vivi until she couldn't stand it anymore. She edged around him so that he could see her.

"Hal?" she whispered, reaching out to touch his arm and break him out of whatever this was.

His reaction was swift and violent. Before she could do anything to defend herself, he had slammed her against the wall, a forearm across her neck and chest, his pistol barrel a cold ring against her forehead. "Who are you?"

Her breath caught in terror. It was Noah all over again. His eyes had turned dark with the threat of violence as he pressed his arm harder against her throat. Her lips moved, but nothing came out.

"You're not authorized to be here. Who the fuck *are* you?" She could feel the ring of the blaspistol's barrel carving a dent in her forehead as he leaned in closer. It was then she saw his eyes were entirely black, with only the thinnest ring of blue around the pupils. Just like they'd been when he'd come back from that barfight on Omicron.

"M- Me. V- Vivi," she managed in a choked whisper. His arm was beginning to restrict her air supply, but she was terrified to move. "I'm on y- your crew. Pl- Please, Hal?"

At his name, he tilted his head at her, a shade of confusion ghosting over his features.

"She's not the enemy, sergeant. Stand down."

Blessed gods, it was Ty.

"She's not authorized, sir," Hal said through clenched teeth, glaring at her again, gun arm still raised. Vivi could see he was gripping the pistol so hard it shook slightly. "She could be an enemy operative."

"No, she's not the enemy. I authorized her. Stand down," Ty said again, in a level voice.

Hal lowered the blaspistol and stepped back, his eyes on her right shoulder. Vivi stayed with her back against the wall, afraid to move until she saw Ty's outstretched hand.

"Come on," Ty said gently.

She held her breath as she stepped around Hal. Ty put a hand on her shoulder, steadying her, but keeping his eyes on his friend.

"Vivi, this is important," he said in the same calm voice. "Go get Beryl for me. Tell her Hal's having an episode."

Vivi slipped by Tyce and flew out the door to Beryl's quarters. She knocked rapidly, instantly bruising her knuckles.

"Everything OK?" Beryl asked when she came to the door.

"Ty told me to get you. Hal. He's… He's having an episode."

"Shit…" Beryl swore. She grabbed a robe and wrapped it hastily around her pajamas. "It's going to be OK," she said and turned back into her room. She began going through the storage lockers at the foot of her bunk. "This happens every once in a while."

"H- He didn't recognize me. What's wrong with him?"

"It's a little hard to explain," Beryl said, finding what looked like a medkit. "Let's go."

They made their way down the hallway. "Might wanna stay at the door, Vivi. I'm not sure he'll recognize you yet."

Yeah, no shit, she thought. Vivi's eyes were wide as she looked in the room. Hal had turned to face Ty, but he still held the blaspistol in one hand. It wasn't trained on Ty, but it would be a small movement to lift and aim. Such a small simple movement. Her neck prickled again.

If Tyce was afraid, he wasn't showing it. "Hal. You're OK. We're on the *Loshad,* headed out to the Border for a job, remember?" Tyce edged closer and closer to Hal as he spoke, as if he were approaching a wild animal. Slow. Cautious.

Hal's head hung low, but he was watching Ty out of the corner of his eye.

"Hand me the weapon, sergeant." Ty held out a hand.

"No, sir… I have to be ready, sir…" Hal muttered. "I have to…" He began to look confused as he glanced around him.

Vivi's gaze slid to Beryl, who was readying a medjet injector over by the bunk.

"It's OK. You can stand down now, sergeant," Ty said easily.

Hal finally met his eyes and Vivi saw some of the nightmare he'd been immersed in begin to dissolve. Hal's grip on the gun loosened, and Ty gently plucked the blaspistol from his hand.

"OK, Hal. Good." Tyce sighed with relief as Hal slid down the wall and pulled his knees up against his chest. Vivi's heart twisted as she saw Hal's hands going to his head as if it hurt.

"I don't understand..." he groaned between labored breaths. "Nothing makes any s- sense..."

Beryl came over and knelt beside him. "It's OK," she said, pressing the injector to his bicep. Vivi could hear the hiss of the medjet from where she stood. "You just need to sleep a while, Hal."

"Sleep?" Hal turned to look Beryl in the eye.

She put a hand on his hair and smoothed it down, all the while holding his wrist and taking his pulse with the other. "Yeah. You've just had a bad dream, that's all. Let's get you back into bed, OK?"

"It's... hard to sleep," Hal said thickly; it was evident that whatever had been in the medjet was starting to take effect.

"I know, Hal. It'll be so much easier now." She soothed him with another hand through his hair, as gentle as any mother with her child. Beryl glanced at Ty and nodded when Hal's breathing softened and the mass of tension in his body began to melt away.

Vivi didn't know how to feel about what she'd just witnessed. On one hand Hal scared the shit out of her – he'd just jammed a blaspistol against her forehead, she thought with a thudding heart. It was like he hadn't known who she was at all. On the other hand, she knew Hal had a good heart. He was a little rough around the edges, but the way he watched out for her and the gentle way he'd treated that vat addict on Omicron said that he cared about people. What was wrong to cause this change in him?

Together Tyce and Beryl helped Hal to the bed. He was already asleep by the time they pulled the covers over him. "He's good for six hours, at least." Beryl told Ty. They lowered the lights completely, but not before Ty picked up Hal's blasrifle, viblade, and sidearm.

"Come on, Vivi," Ty sighed. "We need to talk."

"How about some tea?" Beryl asked, once the three of them had reconvened in the galley.

"Sure," Vivi nodded.

While Beryl worked in the kitchen, Ty sat beside Vivi. "I know you don't know much about the ACAS and the vats."

Vivi shook her head looking from Beryl to Ty. "No. Not a lot. J- Just… just I guess what everyone else knows. The ACAS and the vats protect us by patrolling the Edge. M- Most of them are… created to serve. Like Hal. But they get to have their own lives after the ACAS, right?"

Tyce nodded slowly. Vivi didn't seem to have the negative attitude that so many others had toward vats, so he pressed on. "Hal was born in a facility on Chamn-Alpha. Vats… are grown rapidly and trained subliminally… then 'born' four years later at a developmental age of twelve or thirteen. After that, they're educated until ready to start their tour of duty in the ACAS. But, it's not like the education that we got as natural born. Everything they learn is to prepare them for their seven years of service.

"Hal has an interface," Tyce tapped his temple, "here, implanted into his brain. From what I understand it's more extensive than a tecker node. They used it for teaching and training purposes… as well as programming, even before he was born."

"When I walked in his room, he was saying something over and over. 'I… er… I am the fist of the ACAS.' Something like that," she murmured.

Ty nodded somberly. "The vat's creed. He had to memorize it as part of his training. It was probably reinforced thorough his interface thousands of times while he slept."

"He was experiencing a flashback from that… like a memory," Beryl added, coming over with their tea. "Think of it as a nightmare that you have trouble shaking off."

Vivi stirred sugar into the cup, a crease of worry on her brow. "How often does he have these episodes?"

Tyce shrugged. "Every month or two. Sometimes less, sometimes more. Vats typically have trouble with civilian life. Without the structures and format of the ACAS, they struggle with attention, decision-making, and dealing with things like what we saw tonight. They aren't trained for the civilian world. Hal struggles just like the rest of them."

"Ty, he didn't recognize me. What would he have done if you hadn't come in?" Vivi asked.

Ty could see her fear. "He just hasn't had enough time to recognize you as part of his unit. Vats protect others in their unit, and that's what he considers us," he gestured between himself and Beryl. "He'll come to see you that way if you give him the chance."

There was a pause as Ty watched her digest the information.

"So… will he be OK tomorrow? What do I need to do?"

"I gave him a sedative," Beryl replied. "So that he can sleep, that's all. In the morning he may or may not remember anything about what happened. We don't usually mention it. If you see he's quiet, just give him some space."

"Right. Sure," Vivi said, nodding.

"Vivi, I know this was probably a bit frightening," Ty said. "But I hope you don't let this change your view of working with us. I think you've done a fine job so far and I really hope you'll stay on."

It was good for Hal to have connections with others. Too often, he'd seen vats who lost the camaraderie of the ACAS turn inward as loneliness ate them up inside. It made sense. Vats were raised communally – they ate together and bunked together. They were trained to depend on each other. Being alone was bad. Often lonely vats turned to drugs or alcohol to cope. Ty had kept Hal from such a fate so far, and he intended to keep doing that for however long Hal would be with them.

"I think… I think I'll stay for now," she said, quietly. "And, er, if there's anything I can do to help–"

"You already have," Ty cut in. "Get some rest. Feel free to sleep in. We always do after a night like this."

After she had left, Ty remained staring down into his cup moodily. "He scared her pretty badly, huh?" Beryl asked.

He nodded, frowning, as he met her eyes. "She might not stay, Beryl. It was the worst I've seen him in a while…"

The next morning, Vivi was awake early. Finding her way down the hallway to the common area, she decided to put on coffee since she guessed she was the first one up.

Coming into the kitchen, she caught sight of Hal. His hair was ruffled, and he was still wearing the same black tee and sleep pants he'd had on the night before. She took a breath, reminding herself of what Ty and Beryl had told her, then entered the galley.

Hal was leaning back against the counter and facing her as the coffee maker burbled and hissed behind him. He was fiddling with a spoon in his hands as he lifted his head and his eyes met hers. There was a vulnerability there that she wasn't used to seeing.

"Hi," he said simply, testing out the waters between them.

"Hi," she replied. Did he remember any of it? Was he embarrassed or angry over losing control? She had no idea of where to start, but she knew this was not the same man who had put a weapon to her head and threatened her last night.

"I...uh..." he said, closing his mouth and clenching his jaw before trying again. "I'm sorry if I woke you last night with... with all of that." His voice was low and halting.

She decided she could lie and act as if she had heard nothing or be brave and choose to be honest. As a friend would. "Hal, there's no need to be sorry."

His blue eyes were still a little glassy from the medication, and his features held a mix of fear and anxiety. Instinctively, she wanted to take it away, despite her fear. But she didn't know how.

Vivi turned to get two steel mugs out of the cabinet. She filled both with coffee, added a lot of sugar to Hal's cup, and handed it to him. She turned around and rested against the counter in a similar pose beside him while sipping at her cup. "Alright," she said lightly, "you're making coffee from now on. This is much better than Ty's."

A half smile broke through the clouds that hung over him. "Yeah?"

"Yeah." She elbowed him gently. "But don't tell Ty, OK? It's our secret."

They stood there a few minutes longer, during which the silence became comfortable. Finally, he spoke again. "Veevs?"

"Mm? Yeah?"

"Thanks," he said simply, daring to meet her gaze.

"Anytime, Hal." Impulsively, her hand reached for his, and she squeezed his fingers. She was surprised to find that it felt right. He leaned into her, and they stayed that way for a long time.

EIGHT

K-245j hung in space like a green and amber jewel, as the *Loshad* made its approach, four days after its departure from Omicron.

"No ships in the surrounding area," Beryl reported from her station at the sensors.

"Good. Let's do a flyby," Tyce said, easing the ship into an orbit. "Look for life and habitation signs. Hal – stay on weapons in case we need them."

"Got it, Cap."

Vivi glanced at Hal settling into the weapons station. He had stayed close to her the day after the episode, a second shadow, but seemed to be more himself now. She had begun wondering about his past again and resolved to ask Tyce some more pointed questions when they had a chance. Now, however, it was time to focus on the planet below them.

"I'm observing the usual weather patterns for this class planet," Beryl said, reading the sensor feed. "It has forested continents and rich mineralogical deposits, which confirms Fortenot's info. I'm not detecting any humanoid lifeforms on the surface, although there is evidence of previous human habitation near the foot of a mountain."

"At least we don't have colonists to deal with," Ty murmured. "Let's move closer." He moved his hands over the helm, and the *Loshad* dropped lower into the atmosphere. "Beryl, keep an eye on the sensors. If there's anything down there to salvage, it should show up at this level."

"It's beautiful," Vivi remarked as the *Loshad* zoomed over a row of mountains.

"Tyce, I'm picking up something else. Small bits of refined allenium alloy on the planet's surface," Beryl announced. "Not far from the deserted village."

"Could have been a crash site," Hal said.

"I'm taking us down. I see a spot where I can land," Ty said.

Vivi watched as Tyce piloted the ship toward a tan, sandy beach near a small lake. The shores were wide and there was a grassy area under the shade of some tall trees where he set the *Loshad* down.

"Looks like the possible crash site is 1,200 meters north. Straight up the mountainside," Hal said, eyeing the info feed at his own station. "Gonna need the hiking equipment for this one."

"Let's get a move on, then," Ty said, standing up.

"Come on, Veevs," Hal said as he headed for the equipment room.

Leaving Beryl on the ship, Ty, Hal, and Vivi walked along the lake, then found a trail to the mountain. They explored for an hour, passing several domed dwellings at the foot of the mountain before locating a path up. It was eerie, seeing the buildings slowly deteriorating as nature took them back over. The sun through the trees created a quiet green twilight which draped them all in a funereal silence. Vivi and Hal peered through the windows of one of the houses, but there was nothing left inside. Apparently, these colonists had been able to take most things of value with them when they left, fleeing what Vivi could only assume was the Mudar's advance.

They passed through the simple streets and into a forest leading up the side of the mountain. Ty guided them using scanners. After a while, they saw what almost passed as a path through the trees, rocks shining as the sun reflected off the flecks of crystalized minerals contained within. Tyce took the vanguard, and Hal took the rear with Vivi in the middle. They all wore headsets to keep in communication with the ship.

The late afternoon was warm, and the cries of birds echoed among the trees. As they made their way along the ridge, Vivi looked up to see a large hawk, sitting in a nearby tree, its feathers shining like bronze in the sun. It was two feet tall, peering at her with its great, yellow-eyed gaze. She stopped, transfixed, as it cocked its head at her, seeming to decide whether to eat her for lunch or leave her alone.

Hal came up behind her. "Shake a leg, Veevs – woah!" he said, catching sight of the bird.

At the noise, the hawk flapped and rose from its perch; there was a swishing sound when its wings beat the air. Hal threw his arms around Vivi to protect her as it dove toward them, but it only swooped over them and sailed up above the tree line. Its wide wingspan was both impressive and intimidating.

"Wow. Did you see the size of that?" Hal laughed, clearly enjoying the excitement. But seeing her face, he instantly sobered. "You OK, Veevs?"

She nodded, looking past him to see where the bird had gone. "Yeah. Just startled I guess." She laughed nervously, trying to hide the fact that it was his sudden movement toward her that had frightened her more than the bird.

"I'm not gonna let anything hurt you," he said.

She nodded and was about to reply, but Ty's voice came in over their headsets. "You guys alright?"

"Yeah," Vivi called. "Sorry. There was this huge, er, bird."

"OK. No problem, just checking."

"Keep going. We're right behind you," Hal said.

They caught up to Ty and continued following him for the next few minutes. Ty and Hal both carried heavy packs with climbing gear, excavation equipment, scanners, and blasrifles. Vivi had the Robotic Exploration Unit in a backpack.

"I think I see something," Ty called back.

Vivi sighed in relief. "Good. I could use a break. This hill's straight up."

"It's not so bad," Hal said, stepping forward to pull her backpack off. "I got this."

She protested, but he took her pack anyway and led her through a gap in the trees.

The plateau was small, about fifteen meters long. There were the obvious markings of a recent shuttle landing and patches of disturbed earth in the clearing.

"So, this is the spot," Tyce said, turning around and dropping his pack. He reached down and picked up a piece of twisted metal in his hand. "Hal, get a scanner out. I wonder if the crew of the *Relentless* just picked up surface artifacts when they were here? There doesn't seem to be any evidence of large-scale diggings."

Hal dropped both packs, then rummaged through his own, pulling out a handheld scanner. Then he swept the clearing. "Just bits under the surface. Different sizes, most no bigger than a handheld." He began to walk toward the edge of the site then his scanner started to emit a strange beeping noise. "Gimme a minute. Let me track this." He walked to the end of the clearing and disappeared back into the trees.

While they were waiting, Tyce walked the nearby area, holding a foldable shovel. When his own scanner went off, he turned up the ground, pulling a twisted, warped piece of metal out of the dirt. He brushed it off. "Part of a hull," he said, tossing it to the side.

"How do you know?" Vivi asked.

"The thickness," Ty replied.

She looked up as Hal came back through the trees. "Got something big," he called to them. "C'mon."

Ty and Vivi followed him through the foliage. The forest floor was carpeted with dry needles from the tall coniferous trees and a fresh, ferny smell rose up around them. "How far ahead?" Ty asked.

"About five hundred meters."

When the forest opened out again, Vivi saw nothing but rocks and dirt and short scraggly bushes. It was another small clearing, bordered on one side by the rising mountain. "Where?" she asked.

"Under us," Hal said, showing them the chiming scanner. "With the size of it, it's got to be a ship. Maybe even a *whole* freaking ship, Ty."

Ty began scanning the ground himself. "It keeps going. Right up to the mountain's edge and beyond, I think. We could bring in the earth mover..." He studied the scanner's readout. "Wait a minute. There's a cave system below. Let's look around and see if there's an entrance."

It took a while to scout around, but finally they found a small opening to the cave a little further up the mountainside.

"Let's go see what's in there," Vivi said.

"Not yet," Tyce replied. "We need to send in the REU first. That's why we brought it."

"I'll go get it," Hal said, hiking back down to where they'd left the gear.

Ty watched him go, and then turned back to Vivi. They were quiet for a few moments before she spoke, muting her headset so Hal wouldn't hear.

"I know you must be thinking I'm going to run out on you guys when we get back to spacedock," she said, "because of what happened the other night. But I won't."

Ty glanced up from the scanner's readings and muted his own headset. "I wasn't sure," he said carefully.

"Don't get me wrong. It scared the shit out of me, but I think you were right. He didn't remember what happened," Vivi said.

"Probably not. He's going to need a little more time to get used to you being on ship, that's all. If you hear him again, have Runa wake me."

"Will do."

He nodded once. His headset beeped but he ignored it. "You should know that if he gets to the point where he trusts you, he'll trust you completely. I don't think you'd abuse that, but... you should be aware of it."

"I think I understand," Vivi replied.

He seemed like he was going to say more, but this time both their headsets beeped, so they answered.

"Go ahead," Ty said.

It was Beryl. "Just doing a status check on you two."

"We've made a large find," Ty replied. "I'm sending you the statistics. See if they match the schematics of any known Mudar ships."

"A ship? Wow, that *is* a big find. I'll let you know if I locate anything."

Tyce turned back to Vivi to continue their conversation, but Hal was coming back up the path, bearing the REU.

They unpacked the exploration unit outside the cave and Vivi had it operational in about ten minutes. They entered the cavern on their knees, pushing their equipment in front of them, and coming onto a ledge that seemed to jut out into the nothingness. It took a few more minutes to set up, then the drone sailed out into the darkness. All three watched the small screen in front of them as the brilliant lights attached to the flying drone moved further away into a large chamber.

Crystals and minerals reflected the light from the drone in billions of sparkles. They could see patches of an eerie green glowing on the walls as well.

"What's that?" Vivi asked.

"Some sort of bioluminescence. Mold on the cave walls, maybe?" Ty said.

"Weird," she whispered. She rotated the drone so that they could see the size of the cave area below them.

"This chamber's huge," Vivi said, intent on the controller's screen. She misjudged a distance and the REU brushed the edge of a stalactite with a scraping sound. "Oops!"

Ty laid a hand on her arm, steadying her. "It's OK. Keep going."

Vivi guided the drone to descend about twenty meters. There were columns of stone reaching up from the floor, and she carefully eased the REU around them, getting better with her maneuvering as she went.

"Drop down another five meters?" Tyce asked.

Vivi nodded. As the REU dropped, Ty watched her swing it in a graceful arc so they could see the rest of the cave. There was the sound of falling water from some underground river or pool, but they couldn't tell where it was coming from.

"Wait. Go back," Ty said at a flash he saw below them.

She dropped down and rotated the drone slowly until the feed showed them the side of a massive metal object; it had a graceful curve to it before it was abruptly sheared off.

"It *is* a ship," Tyce whispered. "It must have crashed and broken through into the cave somehow."

"That's slick as hell," Hal said. "Do you think there could be Mudar inside?"

"No one's ever found a Mudar," Tyce murmured, looking at the smooth surface of the ship. "Go closer, Vivi."

Vivi piloted the drone closer to the ship and they began to see the scraping and denting that had occurred to the vessel. As she flew to the other side, they saw an opening in the ship's hull. She tried to ease the REU through the opening, then sighed in frustration. "I'm not going to be able to fit it through there."

"Shine the light around the floor of the cavern," Ty suggested.

Vivi moved the drone in a grid-like pattern as she searched the bottom of the cave. There were a few warped pieces of metal on the floor, but nothing else.

"I think it's time to go down," Hal said.

"This is going to be a big score," Tyce said. "Salvagers just don't find things like this. Allenium, parts of starship drives, occasional weapons, yeah, but no one's ever found an AI ship to my knowledge."

"Our permit doesn't cover this… but what they know won't hurt them," Hal said.

"OK. The two of you go down. I'll stay here and monitor."

Hal nodded. "You bet, Cap. I'm not about to leave our baby tecker down there alone. Not when I'm just getting her trained right," he teased, poking Vivi in the ribs.

She swatted at him and laughed, but Ty's serious expression stopped them. "Stay focused. If there's any trouble, both of you get out of there."

Hal had no trouble putting on his climbing harness while Vivi wrestled angrily with hers. She was trying to slip her arm into one side of her harness, but it was hopelessly twisted. The more she struggled the worse it got. When she let out a frustrated sigh, he turned to help her.

"Hang on, I'll get it." Hal snapped his last strap over his chest and moved closer to her.

"Sorry. Never used one of these before."

Hal began to work at the straps. She could feel his hands brush her back as he grappled with the harness and was surprised at the lack of discomfort she felt. Here he was watching out for her just like he'd promised he would.

"Probably don't really need all this, but better to be safe. Slip your arm through here," he said, and she obeyed. "Now, this one." He held out the other side for her, then buckled it over her sternum, being careful where his hands touched. She watched his face tense in concentration as he checked the fit. Finally, he was satisfied. "There you go."

"Thanks," she replied, "I'm a little nervous."

"You're gonna be just fine. I'll rappel down first, and Tyce'll lower you." His hands rested on her shoulders lightly for a moment as he smiled at her, then, seeming to notice what he'd done, withdrew his hands quickly. He stepped back, something in his features that she couldn't read.

"What is it?" she asked gently.

"Nothing. Let's do this." He reached to a back pocket and pulled out a couple pairs of gloves. "You'll need to wear these." He handed a pair to her and fitted his own.

"Ready, Cap?" Hal said as he made his way to the side of the cave's ledge where Ty waited. Ty had been busy fixing a safety line for them near one of the collapsible lights they'd set up. Below the ledge, faintly illuminated, Vivi could see the ship.

"Yeah. You go down first. Then I'll send Vivi down."

"Sounds good." Hal turned away and attached himself to the dropline. He rappelled rapidly to the bottom of the cave and unhooked himself, waiting for her to follow.

Next, Tyce lowered Vivi over the lip of the edge to the bottom, while he himself remained above. Hal steadied her as she reached the floor and helped her to unhook her rope. He swung a blasrifle off his shoulder and turned the scope light on. Mineral and crystal deposits glimmered in the walls like tiny stars. The soft burble of water nearby made the cave appear like another world.

"Wow," Vivi said, impressed.

"Yeah," Hal agreed.

"Everyone reading me OK?" Tyce's voice called through their headsets.

"Loud and clear, Cap. OK, well, let's see if we can get inside this ship," Hal said as they approached the shattered remains of the craft sitting on the floor of the cave. "This way."

They circled the ship, until they reached the jagged opening between it and the cave wall. There was no way Vivi could have maneuvered the REU in there remotely, but by turning sideways Hal was able to squeeze through, just barely, twisting and turning as he went.

"Hal?" Vivi called. There was no answer at first, so she called again. "Hal?"

"Yeah," he called back. She could see his scope's light glimmering inside what was left of the craft. "Veevs, come on. You gotta see this. Fuck me…"

She slipped through after him, not even needing to twist. They were standing on what was left of the Mudar's bridge. There were seats, monitor displays, and twisted shards of a glasslike substance scattered on the floor. But what Hal was focused on brought her up short.

He had his rifle trained on two metal humanoid forms. They were crumpled under beams that had fallen from above – heads crushed, legs trapped beneath. The first figure's face was shattered, the shards covered with a caul of dust. As she moved around the figure, Vivi could see the back of its head had been sheared off somehow. The other was missing an arm. The entire body was completely squashed, even the head. Vivi had never seen a body like that before, but realized they had to be Mudar.

"Oh shit. Hal... are they..."

"Yeah," Hal said grimly. "You gettin' this, boss?"

"Loud and clear. Make sure they're not going to... activate. Watch yourselves. Remember where you are."

"Understood, Ty. Veevs, do your thing. I've got you covered."

Vivi pulled out her handheld scanner and swept it over the Mudar nearest her. "There's nothing to worry about. Whatever power source it had is probably long dead and the body is beyond repair," she said, kneeling on the floor.

She began to inspect the damaged head of the android, noticing that there were connections of some sort of coppery metal and the shine of crystal inside what she assumed was its "brain," but whatever they had been connected to was gone.

"There's nothing here," she said. She leaned closer to brush off the dust. As she did, the head of the thing fell off. She started a little, then laughed at herself as Hal caught her eye.

Hal took a closer look with her. They could see what the crash had done to the mangled android's body. Its featureless face was unnerving; it was composed from a different type of silvery metal than the grey metal surface of the rest of the body.

Vivi examined its chest, scanning and documenting what she could. "OK. I think I've got enough data for now."

"So, you're sure it's not getting up?"

She smiled. "Pretty sure, Hal."

"OK, then." He dropped his rifle and used the scope light to look around. Vivi could see there wasn't much left to salvage, just some busted control consoles and twisted metal. It didn't seem like the ship was a transport, with crew quarters and such, but then maybe Mudar didn't have need for that, since they were androids.

She saw something on the floor near the front of the ship and motioned for Hal to shine his light over it.

"Hey… it's a Mudar's arm," Hal said.

She picked it up and looked at it closely. "Oh, yeah. We're taking this back."

"Do you know what that thing's worth on the black market? We could buy our own planet," Hal murmured.

"Not before I get a good look at it."

"Any weapons evident?" Tyce's voice came across the comms.

Vivi glanced to Hal. He shook his head.

"Not that we can tell." Her scanner was picking up a faint power source. She would have discounted it, but a gleam of something wedged under a console caught her eye. Vivi knelt down to grab it when she heard Hal speaking to Ty.

"Should we bring up the AI's head too?"

"That's an affirmative," Tyce returned.

While they talked, Vivi brushed her hand under the console. She stopped, feeling something there. It was a silver ball, cold to the touch. She rolled it toward her, stretching the tips of her fingers until she was able to clutch it in her palm. Smiling at her prize, she got to her feet again. It was then she heard an agonized groan behind her.

Hal, who had been fine only a second before, was now on his knees, a hand to his head and wincing in pain. His eyes were squeezed shut as he collapsed and curled in on himself.

"Hal!"

"What the hell…" He grimaced through clenched teeth.

She rushed to him as Ty came over the comms: "What's wrong? Talk to me. What's going on?"

"Just a minute," she said, keeping her distance. "Hal! You OK?" Was this another flashback? A memory from his implant? She held back, afraid of a repeat episode of a few days ago.

Hal snatched off his headset and was holding his head in both hands. "Yeah," he breathed. "I'm OK. I just have this fucking pain in my he… Ahh!" He grimaced again. "It's like somebody jammed a viblade into my brain."

Vivi knelt beside him, reaching for his shoulder, unsure what to do. She could feel his whole body trembling under the onslaught of pain.

"OK, Hal. I got you," she murmured frantically. "Just breathe."

"Vivi, report… Vivi?!" Tyce's worried voice came through her headset. He was moving; she could hear the zip and buckle of a harness being put on.

"It's… It's… easing off now," Hal said.

At least he's making sense, Vivi thought. *That's a good sign.*

"Vivi? I need to know what's going on." Ty's voice had risen a little, breaking her focus on Hal.

"I'm not really sure. We're OK, though. We're coming up now."

"Nah," Hal interrupted. "No need for that. I'm OK." Hal stood back up, a little unsteadily, but his face was no longer creased with pain.

"No playing tough guy. We're going, Hal." Vivi turned to pack the scanner and the strange metal ball into her bag. Then she lashed the Mudar's metal arm onto her pack. "We've got more than enough to take a look at tonight."

Hal started to raise objections, but she was through the opening in the hull and back out in the cave before he could finish. Ignoring macho behavior was the quickest way to get men to toe the line, she'd often found, and, sure enough, Hal followed her out.

NINE

His target was dragging his leg slightly, as if it was heavy.

Most people would never notice such a detail, but to the vat designated "Scalpel," it screamed its existence like a siren. Possibly, it was an injury or physical deformity, but since it had not been noted in the file he'd been given, it was something else.

His quarry was a tecker named Astin Fortenot. He shadowed the nat walking along Avenue NJ4, most likely heading to his hab unit. Fortenot was a fashionable dresser – it was obvious that he cared about money and status, from the choice of his jacket to the location of his living quarters, one of the more prestigious avenues on the station. This was a weakness that Scalpel looked down upon. Status was a hollow quality he had never sought. He looked forward to seeing the tecker's face when he realized he was going to die and none of his money would save him. Scalpel could never be bought – his programming and conditioning wouldn't allow it. He would carry out his duty with deadly precision, whether the target was a rich man or a poor man, an old woman or an infant.

The lab-grown assassin was nothing like his vat brothers in the military. While they were bred for strength, loyalty and an addiction to putting their lives on the line for whatever ACAS objective they were trying to win, the assassin had been coded to stalk and kill without question those that his handlers named.

He'd had plenty of practice. There had been twenty of them in his batch, but not for long. He and his brothers and sisters had been forced to kill each other during training, and by the end, he had been the only one left standing. When he'd murdered the last of them, he'd "graduated" and shortly after that he'd been employed in the first of many wetwork jobs for whichever government shadow agency required his services.

As far as Scalpel knew, there were two or three others of his kind – all from different batches. He assumed they went through the same winnowing process as he had. He'd never met any of them, but he'd heard whispers across the years. He didn't wonder about them; it was in his nature to be alone, and he preferred it that way. Death stalked his prey alone; he needed no help.

Scalpel watched as Astin Fortenot used his fingerprint to open the door of his apartment complex, then disappeared inside. Then the killer leaned back against a bulkhead across the avenue and waited.

TEN

"Hal. You're a terrible patient," Beryl chided as she ran through her neurologic tests. She'd already said she could find no biological cause for his sudden head pain and had told them she was ready to chalk it up to "one of those things."

"Any other feelings before it came on? Blurred vision? Weakness in one arm?"

"No. The pain was there, then it was gone. I feel fine now," Hal replied.

"Close your eyes, and touch your nose," she said. Hal sighed and did so, touching his nose with the index finger of both hands. It was the last of the field tests she used to detect neurological problems.

Ty frowned and leaned back against the wall, watching them moodily. "Well, as far as I can tell, you're good to go, kid," Beryl said. "Ty, he's passed every test I can give him."

"See? Five by five, Cap. No problems." Hal jumped off the table.

"OK." Tyce nodded. "Any other symptoms, and you tell me straightaway. I know you too well," he added in a low voice.

How old was Hal getting now? Close to thirty? In vat years that was getting up there, and it was a subject Ty had been struggling with lately. He didn't want to lose Hal. He was more than a best friend. They'd served together through almost everything the ACAS could throw at them. Ty's brother and father were dead, and his mother had passed away long ago. Along with Beryl and now Vivi, Hal was the only family he had left. He grabbed Hal's arm again to be sure his message was hitting home. "Hey – you're hearing me, right? No toughing it out."

"Yeah, I hear you, Cap. I'll let you know, but I'm all good. Don't worry."

Ty nodded wordlessly.

"I'll go help Vivi set up her equipment in the cargo bay."

"Yeah. You do that," Ty agreed. As Hal left, Ty leaned back against the medbay wall again and sighed. He could feel Beryl's gaze on him and waited for her to speak. He knew she could read him better than he wanted to admit. She had his number since the first week she'd served on the *Loshad*. Maybe that's why he kept her around.

"He's OK, Tyce. I didn't detect any faults in his implant. We can have him tested at Omicron with more sophisticated equipment than I have here, but they'll come up with the same thing, I'm sure. I don't think you should worry."

Ty let out another heavy sigh. Beryl was a good medic, and he trusted her to know. "OK," he nodded and headed for the door.

"Ty? He is... getting older..."

He paused at the door, head down. As far as he knew there was no way to solve that problem. When Hal reached his mid-thirties, his body *would* fail him, just like it did for all vats. And whether it was his implant malfunctioning, the effects of overproduction of adrenaline on his system or something else not yet known, Ty knew there was nothing he or Beryl would be able to do to stop the degradation. Not a damn thing. He knew she was thinking the same. "It's OK, Beryl. No need to talk it over again," he said hopelessly.

"So, you're good?" Vivi asked, looking up at Hal from where she was unpacking her bag. She'd jacked her datapad, analyzer, and microscanner into the ship's feeds and was uploading their new content. Hal looked at the AI's head sat next to Vivi's datapad, along with the arm and strange silver sphere.

"Yeah. Beryl says everything's fine," Hal replied. "What about you? Got everything you need?"

"Yeah, I'm good." She came over and swept the handheld scanner over the sphere. "This is just a little weird."

"What is?"

"This thing. When I first picked this ball up, there was a weak power signature coming from it. But it's gone now. The scanner doesn't recognize the type of metal either."

"Maybe it's some sort of power source?" He held out his hand for the metal ball. He shook it and listened. "Nothing." He clunked it back down on the table as Vivi laughed lightly.

"Great testing! Maybe you're right, though. It could be a power source. The scanner originally picked up an electromagnetic field." Vivi narrowed her eyes. "But a power source that's lasted decades?"

"You never know. I heard of another salvage crew who found a power cell that old. It still had a charge, according to them. It wasn't very strong, but it was there."

"That's crazy," she said as she picked up the arm and began to scan that. "What do you think the Mudar came to the Spiral for? Do you think it's like they always say? That they came to wipe us out? Seems weird that they'd travel so far to simply kill another species and not even bother talking to them first."

Hal picked up the AI's head and turned it toward him, taking a seat on one of Vivi's stools. "People hate what they don't understand, Veevs. Maybe the Mudar were the same way. Maybe they saw people that were different, people they didn't understand and just decided to end them." He paused then spoke again, "I mean, look at it this way: some people hate vats because they don't understand them. It's not a far leap to think that the Mudar felt the same way about humans..."

"Hal..." she said quietly.

He glanced up at the change in her voice. Then he shrugged. "I'm not looking for sympathy. I mean it's just how it is. It's not as if I'm upset by it, or anything. It's just human nature, Veevs."

"Yeah, but... it's still not right," she said in a quiet voice.

"Don't do that," he said, forcefully. Noticing that he'd startled her, he softened his tone. "I mean, don't feel sorry for me. It's nothing." Getting up, he set the AI head back on the table. "I'm gonna leave you to it, Vivi."

She remained staring after him for a long time, before letting out a heavy sigh.

That evening, the *Loshad*'s crew was finishing dinner when Runa's chime interrupted them.

"What is it, Runa?" Tyce asked, setting down his fork.

I am detecting a power surge in the cargo bay, Ty.

Vivi leaped to her feet. "One of the artifacts?"

I do not know, Vivi.

"OK, we'll go check it out." Ty stood, and Vivi watched his gaze fall to Hal who had squeezed his eyes shut, and clutched the side of his head with one hand.

"What is it?" Ty said.

Hal swallowed hard as he let go of his head and stood up. "I'm good. Go, I'm right behind you." Then the ship's power cut out completely, leaving them all in darkness.

"Runa?" Ty called, but there was no answer. A backup system kicked in and emergency lighting came on.

"This is bad," Beryl muttered, also on her feet.

"Hal, arm yourself. Until we know what this is, I'm not taking any chances."

"Got it, Cap," he replied. "C'mon, Veevs."

She followed him to his room. "Take this," he said, handing her his blaspistol. He shouldered his blasrifle and the two were back in the hallway in less than twenty seconds. "You know what to do, right?" he asked Vivi.

"Point and shoot?"

"Not as green as you look." He elbowed her. "Just don't point it at anything you don't intend to kill. Be sure before you raise it." He was ready – no, *eager* – for something to happen, she could see.

They met Ty and Beryl in the corridor that led to the cargo bay. They had also strapped up, ready for action. The entire crew made their way down the hallway; Ty went first, then Hal and Vivi followed, and Beryl brought up the rear.

Vivi watched as Ty and Hal communicated in hand signs. *I need to learn those*, she thought, as they approached the cargo bay. Despite what Hal had said, she knew she was pretty green, but now she had a blaspistol in her hand, and she was determined not to be helpless, no matter what happened.

As they approached, Hal paused. He held out his hand, palm toward her, motioning for her to stay back. She nodded, and Hal and Ty entered the cargo bay.

The ship's main lights flickered back on.

Vivi crept to the hatch and peered in with Beryl.

"Clear," Ty said.

"Clear," Hal repeated. "Shit. Veevs… You need to come see this."

Vivi and Beryl entered the room. Hal was standing by the table with Ty and they were both looking down at something.

The sphere Vivi had brought back from the Mudar ship had cracked down the middle and was now in two pieces. The interior was filled with crystalline structures that caught the light of the overheads and reflected them back in rainbows.

"Holy crap," Vivi whispered.

"I don't think it was a power source," Hal murmured, rubbing at his head.

"Runa?" Ty called.

There was still no answer.

"Runa, respond."

Vivi went to the terminal and began to enter commands on the keyboard.

"Runa!" Ty said again.

Runa's voice responded smoothly this time. *I am sorry, Tyce Bernon. One moment. I am currently reinitializing.*

"Thank gods. Runa, I want to know what the hell happened, and I want to know now," Ty responded.

I am reinitializing.

"I can't access the system," Vivi said. "I need to go to the bridge."

Hal had his blasrifle at the ready. "I'll go with her."

"We'll all go," Ty said. "Beryl, bring the two halves of the sphere. I don't want to let that out of our sight. Don't touch the inside, though."

"Got it," she nodded, pulling a pair of gloves from her pocket then picking the sphere up gingerly. Then she let out a short cry, dropping it on the table.

Hal immediately trained his blaster on it.

"What happened?" Ty asked.

"It... It felt like it moved under my hand. It was weird," Beryl said. "Maybe it was my imagination. Sorry," she continued, carefully taking it into her hands again.

They made their way up to the bridge together. Vivi went to the ship's systems terminal and began to work her way into the system, but things were running very slow.

"What would have caused Runa to go down like that?" Hal said.

"I guess a power surge? Might have caused the system to shut down temporarily. Obviously, something happened with that sphere," Ty replied.

"I'm making her run a diagnostic. I've taken her speech offline until she reinitializes to speed things up," Vivi said.

"Beryl, make a sweep with sensors as soon as they're back up. Check if anyone's in the vicinity," Ty ordered, watching the screen over Vivi's shoulder.

"All systems are reset," Vivi said after a tense half-minute. "Diagnostics are coming back clear."

"No readings in the vicinity except the standard animal life," Beryl added. "No other craft has entered the planet's orbit either. Hal – you OK?" she said, coming over to check his eyes. "I saw you holding your head."

Hal nodded. "It was another spike like before, then it faded out. It feels fine now."

"OK. We'll check you out again when we get this settled," Beryl said. "It's probably some sort of interference with your implant that keeps happening. It's not beyond the range of possibility that the power surge scrambled your interface for a minute."

"Runa's back online," Vivi said, her gaze returning to the screen.

"Runa?" Ty asked. "Can you explain what just happened?"

There was a slight pause. *It seems a power surge caused a sudden shutdown to protect the ship's systems. I see no damage in my scans. Would you like me to report on each system individually?*

"No. Can you pull up video surveillance of the cargo bay? Playback on main screen. Start when we returned to the ship this afternoon," Ty replied.

They all looked up to see the silent footage. They watched as Vivi set up the terminal and scanners, then Hal came in and they talked as he picked up the AI's head, then set it back on the table and left. After a while, Vivi left the cargo bay and the lights dimmed. "Here we go," Ty whispered as he leaned forward. Then the footage greyed out with electronic snow.

"What the hell?" Hal said.

"Runa? Please explain," Ty demanded.

I'm sorry. It seems the power surge caused interference with the cargo bay sensors.

"OK," Ty was quiet a moment while everyone turned to see what his next move would be. "Hal, go let Beryl check you out one more time. Vivi and I will be in the cargo bay. I have an idea."

Vivi did another pass on the broken sphere while Ty rummaged in a locker in the back of the cargo bay. She too had donned gloves, unwilling to take any more chances. "This thing is made out of allenium and two other metals," she said. "Scanner's never seen anything like them." She chewed her bottom lip as she nudged the mass of coppery connectors with a screwdriver.

"I'm not surprised," Tyce murmured, coming back with a small welding torch and two pairs of googles. He handed one set to her.

"What's your idea?" she asked, following him back to the alcove. "Are you going to melt it down?"

"No. I'm going to put some EMP shielding in one of our compartments to protect against any more strange effects."

"Oh, good idea!"

He pulled out some perforated metal sheets of various sizes from behind the locker. "This one, and this one." Together they carried the supplies over to the wall.

Tyce pressed the cargo bay wall in three different places, making one of the wall panels swing open, revealing a compartment inside.

"A smuggling compartment?" Vivi asked.

"I prefer to think of it as a strategic supply closet," Ty grinned, moving to place the metal sheeting on the door and weld it on.

"Nice," Vivi laughed, putting her goggles on.

Tyce lined the compartment with the metal pieces so that the modification was complete. Altogether, it took them close to half an hour to finish the process. "There," he said. "That might keep any interested parties' sensors from discovering what we have in here too. Bring the artifacts over."

Once they were safely inside, Ty closed the panel and they went to put the tools away.

"Hal and I built in these compartments about three years ago," he said. "They've really come in handy tonight."

Vivi nodded. "So, did you always want to own your own ship and become a salvager?"

Ty shrugged. "Nah, I just fell into it. It seemed like an OK way to make a living and keep Hal occupied."

"Where's your family from?"

"Celian. I lost my brother when I was about eighteen. After that, things just weren't the same at home, so I joined the ACAS."

"I'm sorry about your brother. That's awful. He was younger?"

Ty nodded. "Fifteen. It was a... a drug overdose." He shifted his focus to the toolbox. "Things were kind of bad at home after, so I figured I'd stay in the service, but... I got out about the same time Hal was discharged. What about you? Where are you from?"

"Batleek. I guess my parents are still there."

"Guess?"

"We haven't talked in a while. I had a falling out with them over Noah when I quit uni to work for his tech firm." She gestured to her eye. The bruises may have faded but the memories of Noah hadn't. She shifted from foot to foot as she went on. "He was a hacker, and when I ruined a heist he was planning, he – er – attacked me in a rage. Guess my parents were right all along, but it's hard to admit it to them."

Ty nodded. "When the time's right, you'll be able to."

"I hope so," she said, glancing up at him uncertainly.

"Let's go check on Hal," Ty said. He headed up the ramp that led to the main area of the ship, and Vivi followed closely behind.

They found Hal and Beryl in the medbay. She had checked everything possible and again found nothing amiss with Hal. Ty asked to talk to Beryl and Vivi sensed that Hal needed something to occupy him, so she headed back to the galley with him to clean up after dinner. Afterwards, they walked back toward their rooms together.

"Ever play squads?" Hal asked.

"No. What's it like? Vivi replied, glancing sidelong at him.

"It's a strategy board game we played in the ACAS. Want to give it a try? I mean, if you don't have anything else to do?"

Thinking they could both do with a distraction, she nodded. "Sure, I'd love to. I've got all night."

Hal grinned. "Let me grab the board and I'll meet you in the common area."

The common area had a vid screen, a couch, and some low chairs, set up around a low table. Hal sat on a chair, then folded out a wooden box into a flat board with squares on it. Some of the squares were shaded with carved lines and others were not; together they formed an alternating pattern on the board.

Vivi watched Hal set out different shaped counters in piles on the table. There were two piles of blue ones for her, and two sets of black ones for him. Scooping his into his hand, he began to explain the rules.

"OK, what you do is designate your flag or base," he raised a small counter in the shape of a flag, "anywhere on the last row of squares." He placed it in the left-hand corner. "If I can capture your base, I win. If you capture mine, you win. You must deploy your troops in a way to protect your own base as well as attack the enemy base at the same time."

She set her flag, in the center of the last row of squares on her side. "OK."

"Veevs. Take a minute and think about where you placed your base."

"What do you mean?"

"OK, how many exposed sides do you have?" he asked. "How many directions can I attack you from?"

"Three," she observed.

"Now look at my base. How many?"

"Oh. Two."

He smiled at her comprehension. "Yeah. It's better to use a corner square," he said.

"You're gonna wipe the floor with me, aren't you?" she asked.

"Probably," he grinned back. "Nah, I'll take it easy on you."

"Thanks."

"Don't get me wrong, I'm still gonna beat you, it'll just take a little longer," he teased, winking at her. She laughed in response.

"OK, only an artillery squad can blow a base," he indicated the blue counters marked with a triangle and dot. "But they move slowly, only one space at a time, and you have to protect them because you don't have very many. The Infantry moves three spaces." Those counters were marked with a lightning bolt. "Got it?"

"Artillery are the weapons, and infantry are the warriors, right?"

"Yeah," he nodded. "If you think you've got it, let's go ahead and place troops. You can't place anything past the first three rows on the first turn."

She observed Hal as he began laying out his troops in squads of four. She did the same, concentrating a large part of her forces around her base. "That OK?" she asked.

"Yeah. You're overprotecting your base, but that's smart the first time out."

"Who goes first?"

"You do. The newest player always goes first."

She picked up a counter. "So, er, how many spaces can I move this one?"

"Three. Just remember, the members of a squad have to stay within one space of each other or you risk a rout."

"What's that?"

"When they break ranks and run away. You don't want that because if they don't work as a unit, they can't attack."

Their play went on for a while, squad stalking squad. Hal would take a piece or two, then Vivi would capture a piece. A few times, Hal let her take back her move after helping her see the error she'd made. She could see that he had the ability to keep several turns and their possible outcomes in mind as he moved his pieces around the board.

"This is harder than it looks," Vivi said, contemplating her next move. She edged a squad forward, nearing Hal's base.

"Don't move those. I'll win in four moves if you do."

"What? Wait. How can you know that?"

Hal grinned. "Been watching you this whole time. If I move here, you'll move here, right?"

"Yeah. So?"

"Then I'll do this..." He flanked her as he moved a squad toward her last artillery piece guarding her base on the board. "And then you'll do this." He pushed her piece one square to the side. Suddenly she realized that he'd been moving two squads closer the entire time, as if he had been anticipating her game plan from the beginning. "And then I'll have you."

"Shit," she cursed softly. "You're good at this."

"I practiced a lot," he shrugged.

It was a few more minutes before Hal blew up her base, using two of his last three squads. "Good game," she said, tipping her flag piece over. "Did someone teach you how to play or did you just become good at it over time?"

"Tyce taught me. I was kinda hard to handle when I was first transferred into his unit, and I think it was his way of..." He gestured around, looking for the word.

"Giving you something to focus on?" she supplied.

"Yeah, I guess so. I think he thought it might calm me down. He kept telling me I was smart and could be more than just a bolt catcher." Hal shrugged, folding the board so that the pieces could be stored inside.

"What's a bolt catcher?"

"Um, you know. Someone expendable."

"Oh," she replied, softly.

"When I first started under Ty, I didn't see how a nat and a vat could be friends. But... it just happened over time."

She nodded, watching him clean up. His violent episode of a few nights ago seemed so far away now – as if he'd been another person then. It was hard to reconcile that aggressive, violent soldier crafted by years of ACAS conditioning with the Hal she'd just spent the evening with. This Hal was sincere, funny, and gentle – a patient teacher. And although it didn't seem possible, she realized he was someone she felt safe with.

"You OK?" Hal asked.

He'd obviously noted the expression on her face as she'd drifted into thought. "Oh yeah," she nodded and smiled at him. "Sorry, I guess I'm just getting a bit sleepy."

"It is getting kind of late," Hal noted. "Ty probably wants to get started early tomorrow."

"Oh, yeah. You're right," she said, standing up.

They walked back toward their rooms in a comfortable silence. When she was standing at her door, she glanced over at him. He'd keyed the pad for his own room but was waiting for her to go in first.

"Thank you for the game," she said. "We should play again sometime."

"Oh, yeah. Anytime," Hal nodded, still waiting.

She turned and keyed her code, then glanced back at him. "Goodnight, Hal."

"See you in the morning, Veevs," he replied as she slipped inside.

ELEVEN

Early the next morning, Hal and Tyce brought two loads of allenium and approved artifacts from the cave back to the ship using the hoversled. Ty had just suited up with the harness to go back down for their final visit when they got a message from Vivi.

"Ty, Beryl asked me to comm you about what time we'll–"

A burst of static cut her off. Ty exited the cave with Hal following. "Might get better reception outside," he said.

"Repeat transmission?" Ty said, but was greeted with another burst of static.

"Something's not right," Hal muttered. He attached his scanner to his belt, and then pulled his blasrifle off his shoulder.

Ty nodded, swinging his own blasrifle into his hands. He could feel the wrongness in the air like some sort of vibration. "Let's check it out. Leave everything for now," Ty said.

They began moving down the mountain from tree to tree, Ty leading, until they reached the first clearing where Ty had dug a piece of allenium out of the ground.

Ty held up his hand to stop behind a large trunk. They crouched as they saw a figure slip through the trees on the other side of the clearing. It was a woman, wearing an ACAS uniform. Her dark hair was pulled up in a tie; regulation hairstyle for vats. She was obviously hunting someone.

And Ty's crew were the only ones on the planet.

The woman continued without pause, so she hadn't seen them. Ty motioned to Hal and pointed back toward the ship; they began to head that way avoiding the female soldier. There were certain to be more soldiers about. Neither of them wanted to fight ACAS troopers who were merely doing their duty, but Ty wouldn't hesitate to do what they had to do to survive. They continued to move down the side of the mountain toward the ship.

The hot burn of a blaster bolt hit Ty's arm, tearing his attention away from the path he was making through the undergrowth. Another ACAS vat was behind a nearby tree, leaning out to fire at him. Ty and Hal took cover, then returned fire as the sound of calls from far away echoed through the woods.

A huge explosion took out a section of trees and the soldier retreated, either from injury or caution, Ty couldn't tell. The cannon blast had come from the *Loshad*. Ty held his position a moment longer, trying to sense which way the troops stalking them were moving, when a noise broke behind him.

Hal was involved in a hand-to-hand with an ACAS soldier who had obviously been trailing them. The soldier had a viblade, but Hal was holding it away from him with one hand and slapping his hip for his blaster with the other. They struggled and just as Ty lifted his blasrifle to fire, a shot rang out and they fell. Both combatants lay still. Ty took a step forward, holding his breath.

Then, Hal pushed the dead soldier off him with a grunt of effort.

Ty sighed in relief as Hal got to his feet, blaspistol in his hand. His face was a mask of blood from a deep cut over his swelling eye.

"You OK?" Ty whispered, feeling the warmth of his own blood as it dripped down his arm to splatter the ground below. He let his gun hang on his shoulder a moment as he put his hand over the wound to stem the blood flow. It was obvious Hal couldn't hear him over his pounding heartbeat because Ty had to ask his question twice.

"Yeah, I'm good," Hal said, looking up. Ty could see by his pupil size that he was on a strong rush. "Shit, man. Your arm," Hal said. "We gotta go now, while the ship's still laying cover down for us."

Another blast from the *Loshad* landed somewhere behind them. The calls they had heard became shouted orders as their enemy drew closer.

Ty tried to comm the ship but continued to receive static. "Jammer," he muttered. "We're just gonna have to run for it."

Hal nodded. "I'll cover behind. You get anyone in front."

"Let's go."

The sparse instructions were all they needed – the two of them had been in so many battles together they knew what the other would do in almost every situation.

As soon as they began to run, the *Loshad* opened fire on the trees behind them. The pair made it to the ship in double time and found an ACAS tecker kneeling at the lock pad, attempting to defeat the code. Clearly either Vivi or Beryl had the foresight to lock off the rest of the ship from the cargo bay.

Ty didn't pause as he charged into the bay. When he thought about it later, he kicked himself for the rookie mistake – allowing tunnel vision to take over. He was so focused on the threat presented by the tecker, his situational awareness failed him, and he didn't notice the soldier on overwatch behind the cover of the excavation machine until she spoke.

"Don't do it," she growled pointing a blasrifle at him.

Ty glanced to his right; she had him cold. "Drop the rifle, nat," she sneered.

His gun clattered as it hit the floor of the cargo bay. He sighed and raised his hands. The wound in his arm made him give a deep groan. He tried to glance behind him to see if Hal was caught too, but he only saw another soldier coming from the left side of the cargo bay. He'd obviously used the *Loshad*'s stack of cargo crates to hide his presence.

Damn it. You missed him too, rook, Ty thought to himself.

The soldier at the hatch turned back to his work when he saw the threat was neutralized.

"Hold him there," he said. "As soon as we get inside, Banes and I will head for the bridge." From his uniform insignia, and more importantly, the way he gave orders, Ty knew immediately the tecker was the natural-born officer.

Where's Hal?

Hal was still outside the ship when Ty charged in. It was unlike Ty to make such basic mistakes, but maybe the safety of the ship had overridden his normal sense of caution. Hal moved in close to the ramp, where he had cover and concealment, and braced himself to attack.

He swept his rifle up and scanned the interior of the cargo bay. Ty was under the gun of a female vat trooper and another soldier was set to charge into the ship once the tecker opened the hatch. Everyone's attention was focused toward the door – and that was all the edge Hal needed.

Hal crept silently up the ramp, dropping low. He worked his way around the left side of the cargo bay. He was made for this and was best at thinking on his feet, coming up with a plan in the heat of battle. With a clear line of sight, Hal shot the male vat in the head. The body fell with a thud.

But he couldn't shoot the vat covering Ty; the risk of hitting his captain was too high. He dropped his rifle, then, as the woman spun round, looking for the source of the shot, she was hit by the force of Hal plowing into her. His assault drove the soldier backwards, slamming her hard into the excavating machine. She groaned as the metal framework dug into her back, but somehow she managed to loosen Hal's grip just enough to draw her combat knife. The weapon hummed as its cutting edge vibrated menacingly. Hal wisely gave ground. He knew firsthand what a mess the viblade could make of human tissue. Both of them were in the rush now, knowing that only one would survive.

The trooper dropped into a knife fighter's crouch and Hal did likewise. She made a few slashes with her blade, likely sizing his reflexes. Hal bounced on the balls of his feet as he shifted to avoid the strikes. He then made his move.

He pretended to slip and staggered for a split second. Deep in the rush, she sprang in the moment, falling for the feint as he had hoped. As fast as Hal was, there was no way to avoid the strike, but he turned at the last second and the blade just grazed his chest. Hal clamped his hands on the other vat's wrist and wrestled her to the ground. She was flailing, trying to get her blade hand free. Ignoring the persistent punches that the vat was delivering, Hal continued his pressure until the knife fell to the deck, its blade still humming like a great angry bee. Hal savagely headbutted the woman, and at the same time released one hand from her wrist. He grabbed at the viblade then plunged the weapon downward into the soldier's chest. Her webmesh chest protector couldn't deflect a direct strike and she gurgled as the blade pierced her chest and ravaged her heart.

The whole fight had only taken a few seconds. When he turned for the tecker, he saw an open hatch and an empty corridor in front of them. He met Ty's gaze as the captain reached the wall comm.

"Beryl, Vivi, *lift off*. We're aboard. One hostile aboard too. Secure the door to the bridge while we take care of him. If anyone targets the ship, make sure you shoot back."

"Got it." Beryl's voice came across the comms. Ty tried to move forward but stumbled and grabbed the doorway to steady himself. In a second, Hal was at his side.

"I'll take him out, Cap," Hal said, helping Ty into a sitting position. He removed the strap to his rifle and wound it around Ty's arm above the bleeding wound, tugging it tight.

Ty reached out and caught Hal's arm. "Be careful."

"I will."

The ship's engines engaged as Hal reached the main corridor. "Runa. Locate the intruder." He knew that the ship's assistant would be able to pinpoint his position.

The intruder is in Vivi's quarters, Hal. The reply was quick and at a lower volume than normal, almost as if Runa knew the danger in being too loud.

Hal moved down the passage toward the crew quarters. He reached Vivi's door and stood to the side, rifle ready.

He keyed the override code, and a blaster bolt shot out from inside the room as soon as the door slid open. As the smoke cleared, Hal listened for his enemy's movements. He heard a quiet click that signified a faulty energy cell and smiled at his luck. The tecker should've checked his weapon before leaving his ship.

Knowing he had a fraction of a second to act, Hal dared a quick look from the left side of the doorframe. The tecker was against the far wall, reaching for something at his waist.

"Don't do it!" Hal yelled, coming around with his weapon raised. The nat couldn't have been thinking straight – in combat a vat would always be faster.

The soldier held up something in his hand, as Hal fired two shots: one in the head and one in the center. An easy kill. The tecker's backup blaster dropped from his hand as he fell back, eyes open and staring, leaving a bloody smear behind him on the wall.

Objective achieved, Hal turned his attention to his crew and headed back to Ty. But Ty wasn't in the cargo bay where he'd been left, and Hal's stomach dropped. Had he missed a hostile? Had someone overcome Ty? "Runa, locate Ty now."

Tyce is on the bridge, Hal.

He breathed a sigh of relief and double timed it there. He could detect the slight push of gravity from the ship's inertial dampeners betraying its lift off. As he ran up the inclined ramp to the bridge, he felt the ship's engines smooth out. They were transitioning from atmosphere to space. Just as he bolted onto the bridge, something big rocked the *Loshad*, causing him to lose footing and tip backwards.

Three more booms shook the ship. They were taking fire.

Ty was in the captain's chair. Vivi was hovering over the weapon's station, hands trembling slightly. He was pleased to see the blaster he had loaned her last night was tucked in her waistband at the small of her back. The training was working.

When she turned and saw Hal she was visibly relieved. He squeezed her shoulder for a brief moment as he took her place at the weapon controls. His breath caught as he saw what they were facing.

"Fuck me! Ty, that's a... a..."

Filling the view screen was an ACAS corvette bearing down on them like a hungry wolf let loose in a fold of sheep.

"Yeah, I know," Ty said.

Another shot came across their bow.

"They're comm-ing us," Beryl said.

"Just great," Ty said sarcastically. He groaned as he pulled himself up in his chair, then wiped the pain from his expression as if he'd just taken off a jacket.

The commander of the corvette appeared on screen. "I am Captain Sammeal Tallin of the ACAS ship *Phobos*. Unknown ship, you will power down your engines and allow us to board."

"You'll excuse me for putting it bluntly, but no fucking way, *Captain*." Ty narrowed his eyes. "Is it standard operating procedure for the ACAS to send out hit squads first and ask questions later?"

"You are salvaging on a planet that is off limits."

"I have a permit that says otherwise," Ty countered. "So, give me another reason that I should trust you after you just tried to kill me and my crew."

"Power down your engines and allow us to board, or we will open fire again. You have one minute."

Then the vidfeed cut out.

Captain Sammeal Tallin was still confident. Somehow this band of smugglers had gotten away from his ground assault team, but no matter. A J-class freighter was no match for a top-of-the-line ACAS corvette.

He desperately wanted another prize but if they did not submit, he would bend them to his will. *No one escapes the ACAS*, he thought.

"Any response on comms?" he glanced at his communication station.

"No, sir!" a vat soldier yelled. It was obvious the adrenaline rush was affecting her.

"Bring the plasma cannons online. Target her engines. Fire!"

A few seconds after the feed cut out, Ty looked at his crew. "OK. Suggestions anybody?"

"They weren't gonna give us much of a chance before, so I don't see how things have changed. That squad came to kill us. We fight till the last bell," Hal said.

Vivi and Beryl nodded as Tyce's glance shifted to them. Ty noticed that Vivi's hand had found its way into Hal's. "OK. Strengthen the shields. Target them. But Hal, let them fire first." Try as he might, he didn't like the idea of starting this fight. "Runa – how much time do we have left?"

Thirty seconds – Tyce, they are charging weapons.

Ty went to touch the controls, but the *Loshad* reacted before he even brushed them. With a dive and slight roll, they evaded the first salvo.

"What the hell–" They shouldn't have been able to make such a sharp turn: the ship simply didn't handle like that. But Ty didn't have time to question it.

"Fire at will, Hal!" Ty swooped to avoid the next attack but was too slow. The blast took out their dorsal shield, but Hal had managed to hit the *Phobos* as well.

"Ablative shields are down to twenty-five percent," Vivi called. She'd taken the computer station and was keying commands furiously.

"Gotta stay moving," Ty said to himself, trying to maneuver the ship to flank the corvette. The *Phobos* was faster, and they took another hit to the starboard side. Their ship shuddered with the blast and he wondered if they were losing hull integrity yet.

"I'm losing maneuvering thrusters," Ty called. "Get them back online, Vivi – Runa!"

Another blast rocked them as Ty's hands struggled to control the ship. Without the thrusters, they had no chance of getting out alive.

Thrusters at one hundred and ten percent, Tyce. Runa's calm voice echoed throughout the bridge.

"What the f–"

Ty was interrupted by another barrage from the *Phobos'* plasma cannons. They missed with three of the blasts, but the fourth caught them on the belly of the ship.

"Ty – targeting system just went down!" Hal called.

Working, Runa replied, before they even asked.

"Gonna put some distance between us…" Ty said, performing a roll to give them some maneuvering space.

The corvette relentlessly pursued, firing furiously all the way. They were barely aiming anymore, and Ty flipped and ducked and dove as best he could manage. But the navigation panel suddenly went dark and they lost the capacity to evade attack. The interior lights went out and the harsh emergency floods came on.

"That has to be a hit to the engines." Hal's voice was heavy with worry.

"Engines at ten percent. Life support only," Vivi whispered.

Ty stood up in the sudden quiet, but there was nothing he could do.

They watched as the *Phobos* ceased fire, turned, and lined up with them; their boastful mocking of their victory practically audible through the vast expanse between them. Either they would be boarded and killed or the *Phobos* would make good on her threat to blow them to bits.

Ty felt Beryl's hand on his shoulder. Then he sensed Hal and Vivi drawing near.

"At least we didn't go easy," Hal said softly, placing an arm around Vivi as she leaned in.

The continued hits on the freighter had crippled it.

Tallin smiled a wicked grin as the *Phobos* closed range on the doomed ship. No prize this time, but his log would register a clean kill.

"Target the bridge. Maybe we can salvage the cargo bay."

"Sir, another vessel just transitioned to real space."

"What?" Tallin glared over at the sensor station. Sure enough, there was another vessel – this one much larger than his initial prey.

The sensor officer reported, "Looks like a heavily modified Al-Kimian commerce raider."

"Target plasma cannons–"

"They are firing!"

An explosion rocked the *Phobos*. The hunter, now the hunted.

Tallin gave up his bounty. He had a real fight now.

The crew of the *Loshad* took a collective breath and braced for impact as the *Phobos* began firing. Hal had wrapped his arms fully around Vivi and buried his face against her hair. "I got you, Veevs," he murmured. But after a moment, when they didn't end up dead, he lifted his head and was as surprised as she was that they were still alive.

"The salvos didn't hit us," Tyce said. "Why didn't they hit us?"

There is another ship approaching, Runa replied. *The* Phobos *is firing at them.*

"Well, we're not finished yet then. See what you can do about navigation, Vivi," Ty said, falling back into his chair. Hal could see his captain was fading. "Hal, check… check weapons. Let's try and help our new… new best friends out."

Beryl brought over the medkit. "Comms aren't essential, but you are," she said, pulling out a medjet and some gauze and getting to work on his arm.

"I'm fine," Ty said.

"Gotta call you out on that one, Cap. You're looking kinda pale," Hal said over his shoulder.

"I agree. Pale and shivering is not fine. It's the very opposite of fine," Beryl said, wrapping his wound firmly.

With their leader temporarily out of action, the crew watched the battle between the *Phobos* and the new ship. It looked strange – not quite as big as a corvette, but larger than the *Loshad* and far better armed. The more Hal saw of it, the more he felt sure that the ship had been cobbled together using parts from at least two other vessels. Bits of it looked like an H-class freighter, others resembled the bow section of a war-era ACAS destroyer.

Phobos scored a direct hit on the new ship. It looked bad; the sensors told Hal it had lost starboard shields with the last salvo. In frustration, he brought his fist down on the firing controls.

And the lights on his panel came back on.

The raider kept coming. It took several hits from the *Phobos'* batteries but its ablative shielding seemed to shrug off most of them. Tallin knew full well what his corvette was and was not capable of. The *Phobos* carried some heavy armament, but sacrificed shields for speed. It was designed to catch smugglers, not fight open space battles with heavily armored opponents.

"Time to warn the fleet; we've got a big situation out here," he said to no one in particular. "Helmsman, prepare to withdraw. Comms, open a channel."

"We're back in business, Cap," Hal said as he focused the targeting system.

"Do it," Ty said.

The *Loshad*'s lasers fired and raked furrows in the *Phobos* as she attempted to bear down on the new ship. Obviously, it had lost some of its shields already.

The forward momentum of the *Phobos* stopped. The unnamed ship used the pause to turn and protect its starboard side.

And they saw for the first time, the unknown ship had a rail cannon.

* * *

"Captain, they are arming a rail cannon."

"Oh, Lords," Tallin said quietly. *How did they get a rail cannon?* It was his last coherent thought.

The *Phobos* was completely unprepared for the blasts from its rival's rail cannon. Tallin was still in shock as the mass driver projectile tore through the *Phobos'* hull, cracking it like an egg. The wreckage of Tallin's hopes floated away with his corpse – lost among the stars.

"Oh my gods," Vivi's hand went to her mouth as tiny bits of the *Phobos* pelted their ship.

Beryl's station beeped with an incoming comms signal. She glanced at Ty, who nodded.

"Go ahead," Ty said.

It was an audio only transmission. The speaker was a man with a pronounced Edger accent. "Remain where you are. We will dock with your ship. You will allow us to board or face the alternative."

"This is Tyce Bernon, captain of the *Loshad*. Can I ask what the alternative is?" He raised an eyebrow at Hal as they waited.

There was a pause. "The alternative is annihilation, unless you think you have something to top a rail cannon?" The grin in the voice was evident. "If you want to go, we are perfectly willing to blow you to hell too."

"No worries, I was just asking for a friend," Ty joked.

The voice lost its brief mirth. "No weapons." Then the transmission cut out.

Hal stood up. "No weapons? Cap, you're not seriously thinking of–"

"There's no choice, Hal. Unless you've figured out how pull a rail cannon out of your ass?"

Hal paused, considering. "Fuck."

"Yeah, I know." Ty pushed himself to his feet. "We'll go. Beryl, stay on the bridge and facilitate the dock. Vivi–"

"I'm coming with you." Vivi took the blast pistol out of the small of her back and left it on the console in front of her.

"OK. Let's go," Tyce said.

TWELVE

They arrived at the docking rings and waited. Ty was still swaying a little, but Hal put an arm out to steady him.

"It's OK; I'm good," he said, seeing Hal's worried expression. "Look, at least these guys aren't shooting at us. That's gotta be a good sign, right?"

Ty could see that Hal was not convinced. There was a low beeping, and they watched through the portal as the larger ship lined up with their docking ring. When the airlock sealed, Hal moved himself between the portal and them. *Ever the vat, trying to put himself between his nats and danger,* Ty thought.

"If it goes bad, get straight back to the bridge, Veevs," Hal said in a low voice.

Three figures stepped onto their ship, then the inner door of the airlock slid open. There were two men and a woman, dressed in identical olive brown fatigue pants and black shirts: a makeshift uniform. The female soldier had a blasrifle in her hands, but it was the foremost figure who caught Ty's attention.

He was lean, with dark hair and a permanent smirk on his angular face, his eyes blackened with the rush.

Ty stepped forward. "I'm Captain Bernon."

"I guess you had nothing to top my rail cannon?"

"Guess not. I'd shake hands, but–" He shrugged, holding out both of his bloodstained palms. "Surviving's a bloody business."

"What does ACAS want with you?" The angular man's face

flicked over him, moved to Vivi and then Hal. Then his face broke into a smile seeing the tattoo on Hal's wrist. "Brother," he said, in greeting. "You ship with nats." His words were a statement rather than a question.

"I ship with my friends," Hal returned.

"Fair enough, brother," the man nodded. The dark-skinned crewman next to him tapped the woman on the shoulder and made a series of signs that Ty recognized as visual signal code. She replied, *friend not enemy,* plus a few signs Ty didn't recognize. It was then that he noticed the jagged scar across the man's face, pulling the outside edge of his eye taut before ending at the corner of his mouth.

The angular-faced man approached Tyce. "Who else is on your ship?"

"We have a medic. That's all. It's a small crew. We salvage tech beyond the Border."

"So, that's why the ACAS is after you?"

"I don't know why they attacked us, but they put an assault team on the ground. We escaped into orbit, but they tried to shoot us down. That's when you showed up, thankfully."

"Yes. We saw. You weren't going to go down easy," the man said, impressed. "Facing a corvette like that with this ship was the act of a brave man. Or a crazy one."

Tyce had the idea that it was as close as he would get to a compliment. Then the man's face turned thoughtful. "Would your medic consider looking at our wounded?"

"I'll have to ask her," Tyce said.

"Why don't you just command it? She is under your orders, is she not?"

"She's free to make her own decisions. I don't run my ship like the ACAS."

The vat glanced over his shoulder at his friends, before turning back. "Maybe we will be glad that we came to your rescue, Tyce Bernon."

"You know my name, so what's yours?"

"Ahh! Nat Tyce Bernon deigns to know our names," he chuckled humorlessly, glancing back briefly at his compatriots.

Hal stepped in, blue eyes glaring in a challenge. The stranger held up a hand. "OK, relax, brother. I am known as Patrin Kerlani. The big man here is Orin Neen. And this is Lane Tyner."

"This is Halvor Cullen and Vivi Valjean. You're the captain?" Tyce asked.

Patrin shook his head. "No. Our captain is on the ship. He would like to meet you. But first, we need to leave this place. The ACAS are like roaches; if you see one, there will be a hundred on the way. If your medic will come with me, I'll leave these two, as exchange. It's better for us to disengage the dock, then meet back up at coordinates I'll send you."

Ty eyed Hal, reading his expression. It was obvious neither one of them liked this set up, but there was no other course of action. Ty was fading fast, and the pain was starting to wear on him. He knew that Hal would be edgy after the physical combat and the mental strain of ship-to-ship battle. It was a good idea to get out of here.

Hal spoke up. "Their weapons go back with you."

Patrin turned more fully to Hal and shook his head. "You may trust me, brother. I give you my word my people will only use their weapons if attacked."

Hal glared at Patrin, unconvinced, but said nothing in return.

Tyce keyed his comm. "Beryl. Let Runa take over. Get your medkit and meet us by the docking port."

"On my way."

"So. Do you salvage beyond the Border as well?" Tyce asked.

Patrin and Lane laughed, then Lane signed to Orin and the big man smiled. "In a manner of speaking, Bernon," Patrin replied. "We *appropriate* things, so you could say – creatively speaking – that we salvage."

"Oh. So, you're pirates," Vivi piped up.

Patrin grinned, turning himself towards Vivi. Hal moved swiftly in front of her. "Back up," he warned.

The pirate continued to smirk as he eyed Hal once more with a grudging respect. "So. The nat girl belongs to you, huh? My mistake, brother." He lifted his hands in mock surrender.

The tension between them built as Hal continued to glare. Tyce was about to step in when Beryl came down the hallway.

"Ah, this is my medic, Beryl McCabe. Beryl, these are a few of our benefactors. Patrin, Lane, and Orin. They are… salvagers. Of a sort."

"Thanks for saving our asses back there," Beryl said.

"You could repay us by helping our wounded. We have medical supplies, but no medic on this trip," Patrin said. "Some were hurt in the attack. Some have other problems. Difficulties that arise from… aging."

"I need to check my captain's vitals first, but then I'll look at anyone you have," Beryl said. "Medbay is this way."

Once in the Medbay, Beryl scanned Ty, then, despite his complaints, hooked him to an IV. "Shut up, Ty. You need the fluids and the blood stim," was all she said.

"Hal," Ty said, as she began to administer something else through the IV. Immediately his eyelids became heavy. "Wait – what did you…" Tyce's voice became thick as the medication took effect.

"Just sleep, OK? We've got this," Beryl said.

"You're… demoted…" he said, with a faint frown, as he fell unconscious.

"Wouldn't be the first time," Beryl replied, smiling down at him. She pulled a blanket from a cabinet and draped it over him before she turned to Hal.

"Right. Now he's sorted, I think you should stay on the ship with Vivi, Hal." She glanced at the three vats who stood in the doorway watching. "I'll be OK with our new friends."

Hal didn't like the idea of anyone going to Patrin's ship, but there wasn't much he could do. "Take your blaspistol with you."

Patrin began to protest, but Hal shook his head. "I give you my word she won't use it unless attacked by your people. Same deal with your men, right?" His cool gaze shut down the pirate's objections.

"Very well. I see we will both have to trust each other's word," Patrin nodded, pleased. "Vats should not be enemies, brother." He held out a hand to Hal.

Hal reached out slowly and took it but stared the newcomer down. "If anyone is harmed, we *will* be enemies."

The grinning arrogance wiped from his face, Patrin nodded solemnly. "Understood, Hal Cullen."

Hal turned back to Beryl. "Pack everything you'll need and meet us at the airlock in five minutes."

When they had all reassembled, Beryl drew Hal and Vivi close. "Remember, remove Ty's IV in about two hours. He'll wake up around the time we rendezvous tomorrow," Beryl said.

"I will." Hal had gotten the coordinates and was ready to see this done. "Be careful."

"You do the same, kids," she said, then turned to enter the airlock, medbag in hand and Patrin following after.

"I'm holding you to your word, Patrin," Hal called out to him.

"Don't worry, brother. I don't give my word often, but when I do, it is my bond."

"It better be," Hal replied in a low growl.

THIRTEEN

"So. Where did you two serve?" Hal asked Patrin's remaining soldiers as he took Ty's station on the bridge and began to program the coordinates he'd been given. Hal had suggested that Vivi stay with Ty in the medbay while he got them underway and she'd agreed. He felt better having her as far away from these two pirates as he could get her.

Lane spoke for the pair. "I was a line sergeant but got moved to Engineering after I was injured. Orin here was infantry on Stendal; he got hurt during a rebel insurgency. The rioting locals got their hands on him and damaged his implant. He can't hear or speak. He can read lips a little if you speak slowly – he's still learning."

"I'm sorry," Hal said to both of them. Lane took a seat at Beryl's station and began picking at a frayed spot on her cargoes. Orin sat at the weapons station, his gaze on Lane, waiting on an order, or maybe he was reading her lips. Hal couldn't tell.

"Yeah. Damn nats," she shook her head and sighed, blowing a strand of hair away from her face. "So, was the captain your CO?"

"Yeah," Hal said.

She nodded. "I could tell. Why did the ACAS come after you?"

He shrugged. "I'm not sure why they wanted us so badly... maybe they have something on the planet. Like a secret base?" Hal wondered if it was the Mudar tech – maybe someone knew about it being on the planet, he wasn't sure. He didn't trust these newcomers enough to share that, however.

Hal turned his attention to their planned route. Whatever damage had been done in battle, it seemed to have had no effect on the *Loshad*'s engines. The readout in front of him said they were at eighty-nine – no – ninety percent. Maybe the sensors were going haywire. "Runa, run diagnostics. I need to know what kind of damage we've suffered. I'm getting some strange readings."

I'm working on that, Hal.

"Anyway, why were you out here? I'm assuming you don't have permits."

She smirked. "No. We usually 'appropriate' what we need from nat ships, either out here or on the other side of the Border. This is the second ACAS ship we've caught alone."

"What happened to the first one?"

He read the answer in her wide smile.

"So, you're fighting against the ACAS?" he asked.

She nodded. "Well, yeah. They sure as hell didn't do us any favors."

Hal could see her point. On the other hand, he still felt an echo of loyalty to the Coalition. But was that just something that had been hammered into him by the implant in his skull? Ty had made several comments over the years about the ACAS and how they treated the soldiers like himself. Some remarks were muttered under his breath, and others said directly in anger over some newsfeed about the senseless loss of troops in a certain area.

Hal was aware of the specialized training he'd undergone, the downside of which hadn't happened until he'd been released from the service. It had been soon after his first paycheck from Ty for their work on the Border; he had decided to go blow off some steam when they were berthed on Jaleeth station, one of the two major stations in the Edge. Ty had been busy getting their haul packed up to be taken off by the LanTech people, so Hal – keyed up and on edge from an episode the previous night – had gotten tanked up on the local hooch and fought with some station rat in the bar. Blind drunk and full of adrenaline, he felt invincible stumbling out of the club. He went walking the station, then things blurred for a while. He found himself in a dark corner of the station's many avenues with a vial in his hand.

After the fight he'd been hyped, but after dosing up it only took a few minutes for him to feel nothing. Every cell in his body was numb. Reality had taken on a dreamlike quality. He was laying with his back up against some shipping crates, grinning stupidly as he realized he couldn't move a muscle. He was so relaxed he couldn't move his eyelids to close his eyes. Some small part of him knew he was in danger, but he didn't care. If anyone decided to slit his throat, he wouldn't have been able to raise a finger to stop it.

His gaze floated to the only other occupant in the darkened area of the station. An obvious vagrant – in ragged and dirty clothes. He was a vat as well; the tattoo was clearly visible below the cuff of his ill-fitting coat. His hands were shaking as he snapped the end off his own vial and dripped the contents into his eye. He sighed and blinked as he fell back against the wall.

Null. It was one of the few street drugs that was administered in that manner. Hal had a dim memory of taking it himself; that was why he couldn't move and why he seemed to feel like he was about to float away. It was nice. All the routines hammered into him by the ACAS just faded away. Normally he felt like a taut wire, but all that stress had gone, replaced by a peaceful void.

He finally passed out. He couldn't tell if he was dead or alive. But after a time, he felt a hand shaking him, bringing him back to the living. When his eyes regained their focus, he could see Ty's worried face. His captain took the vial from his hand and looked down at it with revulsion.

"Ty…" Hal smiled in a vacant way.

There was an emotion in his friend's face that Hal didn't understand, and he felt the smile fall from his lips.

"It's OK, Hal. Come on. Let's get back to the ship." Ty reached down and pulled him onto his feet.

They walked back to the *Loshad*, Hal leaning heavily on Ty as he felt like he no longer had legs. It was a trip Hal only remembered in bursts of light and shadow. When he woke the next day, the mother of all headaches hit him like a cannon blast. A while passed before he realized Tyce was sitting in a chair by his bunk. Hal groaned as he sat up, holding the side of his head.

"Just shoot me," he moaned, trying to rub some of the pain out of his skull.

Tyce didn't say anything. Hal glanced over at his friend and saw him staring at the floor. "Ty? I'm, er, I'm sorry. Shit. I screwed up."

Tyce's brown eyes were full of some emotion that Hal didn't understand. It wasn't anger exactly, but a deep unhappiness. It took his friend a long time to reply.

"Halvor, I know… I know that you have this, this *drive* inside of you to seek out trouble. And that you can't quiet down that voice in your head because of what the ACAS did – to you and all the other vats. I get that. I get that it must be hard to deal with." He paused before he went on in an even softer voice. "I understand why vats turn to using null, but that shit… Hal, it's death. It's a death that eats you from the inside out."

Hal didn't understand the expression on Ty's face as he struggled with his words.

"Ty…"

His captain leaned forward, running both hands through his hair in frustration. He paused for a while before finally looking up. "You can't do this to yourself, Hal. You can't. I'm not gonna let you end up some junkie, hiding in the corners of a station like a hold rat. Are you hearing me?"

"I didn't mean–"

"Hal." Ty's voice cut him off with a tone he had only used for significant battle commands. "I've got to know if you're hearing me." Ty's face was desperate with sorrow, as he took Hal by the shoulders. "I have to know right now."

Hal hadn't understood at first, but he saw it then. His captain – his *friend* – was pleading with him because he genuinely cared. It was not something Hal had ever experienced before, and the realization made him feel like he'd been drenched by a bucket of cold water.

"I do, Ty. I do hear you," Hal whispered.

Ty scanned his face, seeking confirmation of his words. "OK," he finally said, letting go of Hal. He got up and made his way to the hatch but stopped. "If you... If you ever feel like that again, just come find me, OK? I'll keep you safe from yourself."

Over time, Hal had seen more and more vats get swallowed up by impulses they couldn't control. It never happened to him, though. Not again. Ty's guiding hand kept him straight, and the memory of seeing the agony on his friend's face kept him haunted enough to stay grounded. He had his moments, sure. Sometimes the rush took him over, or he woke up having one of those things Beryl had coined "an episode." But he had kept the promise he made. He had never touched null again.

"You OK there?" Lane was looking at him kindly, waiting patiently on his answer.

He shook his head, bringing himself back to the present. "Yeah, good. Just thinking you're right. The ACAS hasn't done anyone any favors." His mouth was a frown as he turned back to the panel in front of him.

Hal, the diagnostic confirms the engines are at ninety percent, Runa announced.

"Alright. We'll leave in a few minutes," Hal said, turning to the two vats. "I've got something to do first," he said. "Come on."

They made their way down to Vivi's room, where the ACAS tecker had been killed. Lane nodded on seeing the corpse, understanding the story without needing to be told.

"You going to space him?" Lane commented. "Make them think he was taken out on their ship?"

"That's the plan," Hal said, going to the body. He got his arms around it and hefted it onto his shoulder in a fireman's lift.

They walked down to the airlock, where Hal deposited the soldier. He didn't feel bad for him. The nat tried to kill whomever he could find; it was him or them, and Hal couldn't bring himself to be sorry for protecting his crew. He straightened up and looked at Lane and Orin. "There's two more in the cargo bay," he said.

They made their way into the bay, where they found the two dead ACAS soldiers near the excavation vehicle. Orin stopped Hal with a hand on his chest, then made a sign to Lane.

"Orin says he'll get the big one," Lane said.

Orin stooped to shoulder the body. Hal got the other, and they returned up the ramp toward the airlock. He and Orin laid the dead ACAS soldiers by their comrade. Hal stood there a minute, looking at the three corpses. Then he stepped back, closed the inner seal and used the controls to open the outer hatch.

"Thanks," Hal said.

The big man nodded down at him.

"Right, Runa? Get us out of here," he ordered, trying to focus on the task ahead. The Al-Kimian commerce raider had already gone, and he couldn't be late to the rendezvous.

Beryl was treating one of the crew, a vat named Brandle, for a concussion. "There's no bleeding on the brain, and your implant is functioning well, so that's good."

"When will this headache go away?" the bleary-eyed soldier asked, rubbing his temple.

"I'm going to give you something for that. Just a minute." She began rummaging around in the medbay's cabinets, looking for a specific medicine for the medjet. "You'll probably have symptoms for a week or so, then they should lessen. You need to rest. No shifts at the computer, no vidfeeds. Just sleep a lot and take it easy."

"Yes, ma'am." The soldier nodded as Beryl gave him an injection for the pain.

The patient's friend stood by, eyeing the medic. Beryl had seen them come in together. "You sure he's gonna be OK, doc?"

"Yes. Make him rest. Plenty of fluids and no exertion." She allowed Brandle's friend to help him to his feet and take him towards his quarters. Now the medbay was empty of new patients.

Just as Beryl let out a sigh of relief for the respite, Patrin appeared at the door with a bottle of water. "I can bring something to eat if you're hungry and would like a break," he offered.

"No, this is perfect," she said as she went to the basin and washed her hands. When she returned, she accepted the bottle. She checked the seal, but it was undisturbed, so she opened the bottle and drank gratefully.

"If you are not too tired, could you come and look at our captain?" Patrin asked.

"Of course," Beryl said. "What kind of injury is it?"

"It's... not an injury. The captain is nearing his last days," Patrin said in a quiet voice. "He has asked if he could meet you. But I'm asking if perhaps there is any way to ease his discomfort? Every rush causes him more problems."

She put a hand on the Patrin's arm. "I'll do what I can."

Patrin nodded, but she could see the war going on behind his eyes. He wanted to remain all business, but just like Hal, Patrin cared deeply about his captain. "Thank you, ma'am. I'll come for you in a moment."

While waiting, she packed her bag with a few things she might need. During her time in the service, Beryl had only seen young, current soldiers. But when she got out, she'd worked at a free clinic on Jaleeth. She'd seen many vats near their expiry date – the "last days" as some called it – so she knew which drugs would provide the palliative care they needed. Of course, the lucky ones died quickly by cardiac arrest or aneurysm, but not everyone got the easy way out.

"When you're ready," Patrin said.

Beryl picked up her bag and turned to him. "Let's go."

"The *Hesperus* is an older ship." Patrin said as he led her down the main corridor. "Not much to look at, but she's surprisingly sturdy."

Beryl was taken to quarters near the bridge. The soldier standing guard stepped aside for them as they approached.

Patrin knocked twice. A "come in" sounded from inside, so he keyed in the door code.

They entered a room with recessed, subdued lighting in the ceiling. "Sir. The medic from the other ship is here."

Slow footsteps came from the back of the room, and a man came into view.

He was taller than Patrin, with longer curly brown hair shot through with some streaks of gray, tied back in a ponytail. He was broad-shouldered and stood tall, despite his age. "I'm Jacent Seren, captain of the *Hesperus*. For as long as I can hold the position anyway." He laughed, but it turned into a hacking cough. He put a hand on the table as the spasms shook him. Patrin immediately grabbed a chair, brought it over for his captain and held out a water bottle.

The vat captain drank deeply, and his cough seemed to ease a bit. He set the bottle on the nearby table. "Please excuse me. I'm getting old," he said in explanation.

"I'm Beryl McCabe," Beryl said, stepping forward. "I'm formerly an ACAS medic. I would be glad to examine you and help in any way I can."

Seren nodded. As she began to pull her medscanner and several other items from her bag, Beryl said, "I must thank you for coming to our rescue, sir."

"We hold no love for the ACAS. They've caused much suffering for vats and nats alike."

Beryl nodded as she lifted her scanner and took several images of the captain. He had high blood pressure, and an irregular heartbeat with enlargement of the heart muscles. Add in a respiratory infection and compromised immune system, and he was headed for trouble.

She checked his pupil responses, which were slightly off on the left side, where his implant was. "Do you have someone that usually handles your medical?" she asked.

"Yes. He was needed elsewhere, and so he's not with us on this trip," Patrin said.

"He'll be back, then?"

Patrin nodded.

"Good." She turned back to the captain. "Have you had any trouble with your heart? Palpitations? Chest pain?"

Seren nodded slowly. "All of it."

She could read the exhaustion in his tired face. He was well aware of what was going on, but it didn't make this any easier. Her face fell, and she reached out to put a hand on his arm. "I'm sorry. I can give you medicine for some of the symptoms, and your medic should be able to continue the treatment plan I'll devise. It should steady your heartbeat and lower the stress on your body from the high blood pressure. And I have antibiotics for the infection."

She looked down at the scanner, blinking away furious tears at her inability to control her emotions. Her recent conversation with Ty, and her knowledge that this would also be Hal's fate one day overwhelmed her. "I'm sorry," she apologized, wiping tears away. "I..."

Captain Seren shook his head. "Don't be sorry. I knew this was coming. I'm thirty-seven – much past my time."

"I have a friend..." Beryl murmured. "He'll be standing in your shoes one day."

"If you are his friend, then he will be lucky indeed," Seren replied before another bout of coughing set him gasping for breath. Beryl immediately injected the antibiotic with the blood pressure medication, giving him everything possible to make him more comfortable.

"We have to get you to bed," Beryl said. "You'll require plenty of fluids and rest over the next few days. You will need this antibiotic for the next seven days. I'll leave enough with Patrin for you."

"I'll make sure he gets it," Patrin said.

"I want to meet your captain," Seren said to Beryl.

"He didn't come with me. He was injured in the battle."

"Perhaps later. We will rendezvous tomorrow evening," Patrin said.

"Very well," the captain murmured.

"I will check in on you," Beryl promised. Then she returned to the front part of the captain's quarters. She packed up her medkit and went to wait outside.

"I'll be out in a moment," Patrin said.

The door closed behind Beryl, and the young soldier on guard looked at her with interest. "How is the captain?"

"He'll feel better," Beryl said. "I did everything I could."

Still, the soldier kept staring at her.

"What is it?" she finally asked.

"I'm sorry. It's strange to me that a nat would help us."

"I understand why you might feel that way," she said softly, as Patrin exited the captain's quarters.

"You're dismissed for tonight. He's resting now," Patrin ordered.

"Yes, sir." The soldier headed off the other way, as Patrin walked with Beryl back towards sickbay.

"You're second in command around here?" Beryl said.

Patrin nodded with a sidelong grin. "You're pretty observant."

"I try," she smiled, then paused her steps a moment. "I'm truly sorry about your captain."

She felt like she had to say something, but it was ridiculous to even attempt to address the injustice of dying at thirty-seven. She was nearing the high side of fifty and couldn't imagine what it was like to know your time was running down so young. Most of the vats she'd known never talked about their last days until they got there. Hal certainly didn't, but the day's events made her wonder if he thought about it more than he admitted.

When she looked up, she saw that Patrin didn't know what to say either. He put a hand on her shoulder briefly. "It is what it is," Patrin said, simply.

FOURTEEN

Once they were well underway, Hal went to check on Tyce.

"How is he?" Hal asked Vivi, who had taken a seat by the bed. He could see she had removed the IV as Beryl had instructed.

"His vitals are returning to normal," she said, checking the medscanner. As she turned to Hal, she eyed the bowl of noodles, giant mug of coffee and the bottle of water he was carrying on a small tray. He put it down then handed the noodles and bottle over to her.

"You made food?"

"Nah, don't get too excited; Lane made it. It's OK – I kept my eye on her." Hal took a sip of coffee, knowing he'd need the caffeine kick. The rush from both the hand-to-hand combat and then the confrontation with the corvette had melted away once they'd met the crew of the other vat ship, and he could feel his body trying to crash.

Vivi stood eating while he sat on the nearby medbed. "Do you think our guests are dangerous enough that we need to watch them?" she asked.

He shrugged. "I don't know. They haven't done anything, but unknowns are a threat in my book. They can't go anywhere but the galley and hallways – I sealed off the bridge and engineering to allow only our access codes, so we should be safe enough for now. I told them to find us here when they were finished eating."

Vivi nodded and began to dig in hungrily. Neither of them had eaten anything since that morning. Due to the rush he'd been on, Hal had been starving when he finally had the chance to eat, and he had figured Vivi would feel the same.

After a few minutes, Hal heard their guests' footsteps coming down the hall and then they appeared in the open doorway. "Is there someplace we could hit the rack for a while?" Lane said. "We don't need anything but a floor if that's all you have."

Hal considered her carefully. She had been straight with him, and neither she nor Orin had given him any reason to be suspicious so far. He was self-aware enough to realize his distrustful nature was ingrained from his training and this whole fucked-up situation. "Sure. You can crash in my quarters," he said.

She nodded and signed to her friend. He signed back in reply, glancing to Hal. "Orin says thank you," Lane translated.

"He hasn't seen my room," Hal said, a wry smile on his features as he hopped off the medbed to show them the way.

After getting Lane and Orin settled in, Hal cleaned up the mess in Vivi's room, as well as the cargo bay. If they got stopped by the ACAS, he didn't want anything to give rise to any suspicions. He also didn't want Vivi to see the blood and brains of the man he'd killed spattered on her wall.

Once done, he returned to find the medbay in the semidarkness of the night cycle. Ty was asleep and his regular, even breaths reassured Hal. He checked his captain's dressing and made certain that the bleeding was still arrested. The coagulant that Beryl had given Ty was doing its job while his body began to knit itself back together. He knew that nats healed slower than vats did, and that made him more concerned for his captain's health.

Vivi had fallen asleep in the chair by the bed. When he was done checking Ty, Hal came over and knelt by her. "Veevs?" he said, shaking her gently.

She sat up, startled. "What's wrong?"

"It's OK. Let's get you moved to the medbed. You can sleep in here."

She stood up. "I can sleep in my room."

He shook his head, guiding her to the bed. "If you're in here, I know you're OK." He wasn't going to take no for an answer. "I'll watch over you and Ty while you sleep."

"Wake me up in a couple of hours and we can switch places," she said with a yawn.

"We'll see," he said, settling into her chair and propping his feet up on the bottom rail of the bed. He asked Runa to alert him if the door to his quarters opened during the night, but it was precaution only. Something to help quiet the nagging sense of danger prickling in his thoughts. He was definitely coasting at an orange threat level. He wouldn't truly be comfortable again until the strangers were gone.

He pulled his blaspistol onto his lap and sat with his hand resting lightly on top of the ridged grip. Hope for the best but prepare for the worst. It had been one of Ty's earliest lessons.

The pirates' ship was at the rendezvous the next evening. The two vats, Hal, Vivi, and Tyce were all waiting for Beryl when she stepped out of the airlock. Ty had woken that morning still in a bit of pain, but he felt worlds better upon seeing his medic crossing over to him with Patrin following behind.

"How'd it go?" he asked.

"Fine," Beryl replied. "Am I still demoted?" she teased.

"Consider yourself reinstated," Ty replied.

"How are you feeling?"

"If you call sleeping for fourteen hours fine, then I'm great," Ty said.

"I met the *Hesperus'* captain. He'd like to see you, if you feel up to it," Beryl said.

Ty considered a moment, glancing to Patrin, whose face gave no hint to the pirate's intentions.

"My captain insists," Patrin said.

"Yeah, OK. You, Hal, and Vivi handle the *Loshad*."

"Sorry, Cap. I'm going with you," Hal stepped up.

Ty smiled ruefully. "Thought you might. But I had to try." He knew that Hal had probably not slept in the last forty-eight hours and had to be tired. But he had to admit, he would be glad to have Hal at his back. What else could this captain want from them? Was his plan to separate them all, kill Ty and Hal, then take the ship and set Vivi and Beryl adrift in a lifepod? Ty's stomach churned at the thought, but there wasn't much he could do about it.

He turned to Beryl and Vivi. "I'll let you know when we're on the way back."

He glanced at Hal, then followed Patrin through the docking rings. "Lead the way."

FIFTEEN

Scalpel had gotten word to move on his target as soon as possible. He'd spent the last few days just watching and waiting, observing Fortenot's habits and patterns. That was the thing about stalking. It was too easy once you discovered your target's patterns and routines. The places they hung out, the friends they had, how long it would be until someone missed them... It was necessary to understand how the intricate parts of a life connected before you made your move.

Fortenot was drunk. The third time this week, but to a higher degree. Scalpel shadowed his staggering target down the lifts and avenues of the station, until they reached the door to the hab unit that contained his quarters. Fortenot put his fingerprint on the scanner and Scalpel slipped in behind him before the door closed.

They reached the lift and Scalpel entered beside Fortenot. He gave the nat a grin as he switched his duffelbag from one hand to the other, to leave his gun hand free.

Fortenot spoke, "Haven't seen you before. Just move in?" His eyes were suspicious, even through the shiny haze of alcohol.

"Yeah, man. This is much better than my old place on F-12. Just got a job with LabServ. Decided it was time to move up, you know." Scalpel's smile was friendly and easy as the doors slid shut. They rode in silence for a moment.

Fortenot glanced to him as the doors of the lift slid open soundlessly.

"Hey, what do you know, this is my floor too," Scalpel said, pulling another friendly smile as he followed his prey down the hall. Fortenot stopped at his door and Scalpel continued a step or two after him, before turning back toward him.

"I think I've gone the wrong way," he said. Fortenot already had the door open, giving Scalpel room to pounce. He shoved his victim inside and to the floor before he could even utter a surprised cry.

"Now…" Scalpel said as he locked the door behind him, keeping his blaster focused on Fortenot. "Who did you tell about K-245j? I want their names."

SIXTEEN

The bridge of the *Hesperus* was an elevated platform set above several nonessential stations below. Hal and Ty followed Patrin up a short ladder and emerged in a small hexagonal area that was mostly empty. They noticed two people in the space, a woman busy at the comms station, and a man standing at a center panel, viewing a display that cut out as he turned to greet them.

"I'm Jacent Seren, captain of the *Hesperus*. Which of you is the captain of the *Loshad*?"

"I am," Tyce said. "My name's Tyce Bernon. This is my right hand, Halvor Cullen."

The captain shook both of their hands. "Please come with me. Let us talk."

Seren led them towards a hatch that opened into a small conference room holding a table and chairs. He coughed a bit as he made his way to the head of the table and took a seat. He gestured toward the other chairs with his left hand as he tried to get his breath back. Ty was surprised to see the black lines and squares of a vat tattoo on his wrist. *The* Hesperus *is captained by a vat?* He caught the same look of surprise reflected on Hal's face.

As they took their seats in the well-lit room, Ty saw that the captain's hair was heavily streaked with grey. So, he was old. At least thirty-four. *Maybe this isn't an attempt to divide and conquer us,* Ty thought with relief.

"I want to thank you for saving us," Tyce began. "I don't want to say we had given up, but we were at the limit of defending ourselves."

"I have a habit of helping the underdog," Seren said with a sad smile. "It comes naturally."

"Taking on the ACAS is a bit more than that," Ty said.

"Ah... well." Seren shrugged.

Patrin came in, handing his captain a bottle of water.

"I'm thirty-seven. What can the ACAS do to me? Kill me?" Seren laughed harshly and ended up on another coughing fit. A sip of water seemed to help. "I don't have much time left at this point."

"I'm sorry for that," Tyce said sincerely. "I have the feeling we would have been good friends in time." He forced himself not to think about Hal ending up the same way. The ghost of the captain's boisterous spirit was in his smile, but Tyce knew that the man he saw in front of him was just a shade of who he had probably been in his prime.

"Yes, I'm sure we would have been great friends," Seren agreed. "Did you and Halvor serve together?"

"Yeah, but Hal's more than crew. He's also my family."

Seren nodded. "You are truly an example of what relations should be between vat and nat. This is what we fight for with Al-Kimia. Freedom from the ACAS, for vat and Edger alike."

Hal glanced at Ty quickly. It was obvious the captain's words interested him.

"What do you mean?" Ty asked.

"There is a concentrated opposition to the Coalition. Some of us have banded together while others work individually for the same goals. Vats have no place in the Coalition once they are done with us, so we decided to make ourselves a place. We are all fighting for the same dream – a place to belong."

"It's a nice dream," Hal said thoughtfully.

Ty sat back, stunned. *There really is an active opposition against the Coalition? It's not just propaganda. How many people are involved?*

"In my last days, I can afford to be idealistic." Seren took a labored breath. "To the Coalition, we are merely an expendable resource. But I want vats to have a choice to fight for a cause. I want to ask you to join us. We welcome everyone who believes that all beings should be free from the chains that bind them."

Ty paused, digesting the invitation. "I appreciate the trust you've put in us by telling us this. And I agree with you wholeheartedly, but my crew has more immediate problems right now. I don't know why the ACAS came for us. We should find that out first before we make any other decisions."

Seren pointedly shifted his gaze to Hal, waiting for his answer, and Ty suddenly realized what he'd done. He'd answered for Hal, as if Hal were still one of his recruits. His face flushed with embarrassment. He'd always wanted Hal to be his own person and make choices for himself, but he'd almost taken this decision right out of the hands of his best friend.

What if Hal wants to join them?

"It's a lot to think about…" Hal began, looking Ty straight in the eye.

Ty kicked himself again. How could he be so thoughtless? Of course, Hal would want to join them.

"Hal, I'm sorry," Ty said. "If… If this is something you want to do…" He trailed off as Hal looked down at his feet.

There was a long pause before he spoke again. "I believe my place is with my captain."

"Hal," Ty said immediately. "You need to make your own decision, independent of me. If you think it's better for you to join–"

"No. It's not. My place is with you, Ty." He turned to Seren. "If we come to this fight in time, no one will be happier than me. But Ty's right. We have to find out if the ACAS is after us and why. You're doing a good thing, helping vats have a place to belong and a job to do. I wish you luck in your fight."

"Hal… you don't need to do this because I said–"

"No, it's not like that, Ty. I meant what I said. My place is with you, Beryl and Veevs."

Ty sat back, struck by the overt gift of Hal's fierce loyalty. He swore to himself that he would never take it, or him, for granted again.

Seren weighed Hal's words for a moment, then nodded. "Fair enough, brother," he replied. "If you change your mind, you will all be welcome. I'll give you my comm information so that you'll be able to get in touch with us, should you change your mind."

"Thank you, Seren," Ty said. "I hope we can use it one day."

SEVENTEEN

Scalpel watched the pink soap suds from his hands begin to flow down the drain. He'd been kicking Fortenot for several minutes when the little weasel had surprised Scalpel with a hidden blaspistol from under the bed. A glancing shot to the shoulder had caused Scalpel to dive off balance; midway through his fall, he'd blown the top of Fortenot's head off.

Scalpel was furious, looking at his newly cleaned face in the mirror. This was not how this was supposed to go. It nagged at him that things had gone wrong. He was a perfectionist – he thought he'd prepared for everything, even the holdout blaster on the tecker's ankle. But he'd missed the other blaspistol.

Walking back into the bedroom, Scalpel made his way over to the bloody corpse of the tecker, whose shattered skull was dripping grey matter on to the floor. He found the interface node behind Fortenot's right ear, near where the blaster damage began. Pulling on a pair of gloves from his bag, he knelt and slipped a knife under the edge of the node and cut it out of the tecker's head. He pulled out the single thread-like projection containing the sensors that used to sit on the surface of Fortenot's brain. The node was slightly damaged from the blast, but the memory could still be intact. His prize could still be salvageable. He wiped the blood off the device cover and put it in a plastic bag before tucking it into his black duffel.

He'd have to find someone to decrypt and enhance it, but he

felt confident they would get some intel on who the stupid nat had been blabbing to.

And then he would silence every last one of them.

"Woah. This'll be a challenge." Nikko Nielsen opened up the sealed plastic bag and pulled out an interface node. "Yeah, man. I might be able to pull images for you if they weren't damaged or deleted."

Nikko pulled a pair of thin gloves from his workstation as he surveyed his client. The dark dressed man had arrived just before closing time at the cube where Nikko did business as a biotecker repairman on Omicron. The guy had offered him a wad of scrill to pull some images off the node in his hands and, being a businessman, he'd of course accepted the job. "This is a top of the line unit here. Simulcaster nodes cost a fair bit of scrilla."

His client smiled at him. "Thanks. I just want to make sure I get the info pulled off this model so my boss can give it to the client. The guy upgraded to the Simulcaster 487. Seen those 487s? They're supposedly so close to real, it's frightening. I mean it's some Mudar level shit, man."

"That's what I'm talkin' about," Nikko said, unscrewing the housing on the unit to pull the chip. As he did, he saw that the unit was cracked. When he got it apart, the plastic inside gleamed wetly. He rubbed the wet spot with a fingertip, and it came away red.

Had this unit been pulled from someone unwillingly? Nikko wasn't stupid; he continued to act as if he'd seen nothing. None of this was any of his business anyway. He willed his hands not to tremble as he plucked the tiny chip with tweezers. "Just wiping off the dust so it reads better," he said, popping it in the chip reader.

Both Nikko and his client leaned in to see the list of files that came up, but it was empty. "Damn. OK. Let me try this new program and see what I can pull out of the data." He opened a special folder and pulled up a program he'd written called "Jigsaw." He'd designed it to put as much data as he could get back together.

"The chip's damaged, so it's not reading properly. There's some audio and some vid feed. They don't both go together, but I can play them for you."

"Please do."

Some garbled noise came through and then they both heard this exchange: "Astin, this is Vivi. She's our tecker. Vivi, this is Astin. He works for TechSolutions."

"Good to meet you," a woman's voice said.

"So you're the newbie, huh?" said a different male voice. Then the feed cut out.

"Play it once more," the client asked.

Nikko obliged, glancing up to see if his client was liking what he was hearing.

Next, he moved onto the vid feed. It was silent, just an image of a woman's chest. She had a nice rack. Whomever had owned this unit was paying attention to all the right things, Nikko thought with a smirk. Then the perspective lifted until a face came into view. The woman's face was pretty too – she was blonde, with large, almond-shaped green eyes and a cute upturned nose. He'd gladly hit that.

"Her," the client interrupted his smutty thoughts. "I need a copy of her face."

"Sure." With a flick of his wrist, Nikko sent the image and audio to the stranger's handheld, then turned back to his worktable.

"Thanks, man. You've been really helpful."

Nikko never saw the shot coming.

Scalpel sat in his rented room, going over the data one more time. As far as he could see, there was no "Vivi" on the entire station. He'd looked over the records of all the ships and personnel currently on the station and come up empty, nor had there been anyone by that name or nickname in the details he'd turned up on the tecker during his investigation.

So, he turned back to the still picture he'd recovered from the dead tecker's node.

He sent the image of the woman to his contact at ACAS: the person he only knew as "Control." They'd never had face to face contact, which was fine with Scalpel. Whenever he needed anything to complete his mission, he simply let Control know, and it was delivered.

He typed, *Run facial recognition on all females in this image; cross-match with "Vivi," "Veve" or "V.V."*

Scalpel nodded to himself. It would take some time to identify the woman, but he would find her in the end. If she wasn't on Omicron anymore, he would move on to Jaleeth. No one eluded him. No one.

EIGHTEEN

Ty and Hal had come back aboard the *Loshad* tired and weary. They explained the offer Seren gave them but told everyone to go to bed and rest, especially Hal who had been up for two days straight.

Ty rose early the next morning. After making coffee he headed to the bridge to monitor their trip to Omicron Station. "Runa, please check the feeds and see if there's any news concerning the ACAS losing a ship."

Her voice came back immediately. *There has been no news Tyce; however, I will begin monitoring.*

He glanced up when Vivi entered the bridge. "Good morning."

"Morning. Did… Did the *Phobos* make the feed yet?"

"Not yet." Tyce said. "I've got Runa watching for us." Vivi sat down at Beryl's station and turned her chair toward him.

"Sleep OK?" he asked, sipping at his own cup of coffee.

She nodded. "How's your arm?"

He moved it experimentally. It was still painful. "As to be expected, I guess."

Vivi nodded again softly. Ty sensed she wanted to talk. "What's up?"

"Have you seen Hal today? I didn't want to knock on his door in case he was still sleeping."

"He's not up yet. He'll most likely sleep until this afternoon though, maybe even until tomorrow. We should take him a few ration bars. When his body's recovering or healing up during a crash, he gets hungry. It takes him a bit to get over being on the rush without sleep for a couple of days."

"How long can he go without sleep?"

"Seven days was the longest I ever saw from my vats." If he was right and Vivi was interested in Hal as more than a friend, this was information she might need. There was no denying Hal had feelings for her; after he'd witnessed the way Hal had wrapped his arms around Vivi during the space battle, Ty had known for sure. There was physical attraction there, sure, but was there any more than that?

For vats in the ACAS, sex was mostly a casual thing. Male and female vats served together, ate together, bunked together and nature, not surprisingly, took its course on occasion. It was not discouraged, nor encouraged, by the ACAS. They only cared that it didn't interfere with mission readiness and performance. It was probably a way for vats to step down from the tension and rush of battle. But it was always temporary. Who knew which soldiers would come back from the next engagement and who would be lost?

"Hal protected us in the medbay all night. He told me he slept a little, but he didn't, did he?" she asked.

Ty brought his mind back to the conversation at hand. "Probably not. He was on edge about all of us. I imagine he had his hands quite full."

"Mmm," she nodded. "Sorry to ask so many questions, it's just there's a lot I don't know about him. I mean, about vat soldiers."

"I understand. You... You're interested in Hal, right?" He raised an eyebrow.

"We're getting to know each other," she said cryptically, a smile on her face.

Ty was about to say something when Runa interrupted them. *Tyce, there is a feed about Omicron station and the ACAS.*

"Bring it up."

A blonde female announcer spoke over the video footage of soldiers marching into the common areas on the station. "We don't know exactly what the ACAS is there for, but it appears that all of Omicron is on lockdown. ACAS authorities will be holding a press conference later, but for now it seems that no one is getting on or off the station."

The feed switched to footage of a debutante ball on Tesia, a getaway vacation planet in the Spiral: a beautiful palatial room, doors opening on to the pink sand beaches. "Cut the feed, Runa. But keep monitoring for more updates."

Yes Tyce. Would you rather go to Jaleeth Station instead?

Ty thought a moment, then nodded. "Yeah let's do that."

Computing course now. Would you like a more direct course this time?

"Yes." He glanced at Vivi who had a strange expression on her face. "What?"

"Well, suggesting Jaleeth Station is a little too proactive for Runa's programming isn't it?"

"Maybe. You did loosen a few of the restrictions on her, though," Ty reminded her.

Vivi nodded. "Yeah, maybe that's it. When we get docked, I'll run some diagnostics. Just to make sure we're good to go."

Ty agreed, "That'll be good. We're switching the ship's credentials, so you should know that we're now the proud crew of the *Sombra*. I should have the transponder and everything else set by the time we reach Jaleeth."

"*Sombra*. Got it," she nodded. "Hey, er, thanks for the talk."

"Anytime, Vivi," he replied.

Hal didn't know how long he'd been asleep, but he felt like a great deal of time had passed. He'd woken up twice, finding a stash of ration bars and water that someone had put by his bed while he was sleeping. Now the fatigue was beginning to fade, and he felt like talking to someone.

When he left his room, he saw Vivi's door was open, so he went over.

She was working on something; he could see the green glow of the light on her node behind her right ear. He leaned against the doorway a moment, watching her moving her hands in the air.

It took a moment before she saw him through whatever it was her node was broadcasting. She tapped it and the light went off.

"Hey," she said, a smile blooming on her face.

"Hey, can I come in?"

"Of course." She scooted to the foot of the bed, sitting cross-legged and gesturing to the other end.

He entered and sat beside her. "How long did I sleep?" He looked at his wrist comm for the time, but then realized he wasn't wearing it.

"A whole day and then some: about twenty-seven hours in total. How do you feel?"

"Like sleeping some more wouldn't be a bad idea. I had these weird dreams. There were all these little voices around on the ship, and they were all talking at once, and I couldn't figure out what they were saying." He rubbed his face, and she saw the beginnings of a blonde scruff on his chin. He was the sort of man that looked good scruffy-faced, she thought. "Did I miss anything?"

"Yeah. Omicron. ACAS locked it down tight about twelve hours ago. Ty got one message from a friend there that said they were tearing the place apart, then the jammer cut them off."

"Shit."

"Yeah. According to the news reports, ACAS claims to be looking for terrorists responsible for blowing up a military ship past the Border. So, now, we're going to Jaleeth."

"Yeah. Us and every vessel in the area."

"Maybe," she shrugged. "Maybe not, but Tyce thought of that. He called ahead and rented a berth for us. We're now the *Sombra*. He changed the logs and registration."

"Got it." It wasn't the first time they'd changed their name to hide their registry until things cooled down.

Hal leaned back against the bulkhead. His thought processes were sluggish, due to sleeping off the effects of the two-day rush. The only thought that kept coming to the surface was how the lowered lighting gave a glow to Vivi's golden hair. When she looked up at him, her green eyes were almost translucent as they reflected the light. His breath caught in his chest. A sudden familiar need tore at him, but he reminded himself that this was not the ACAS, and Vivi was not a vat. This was not some post battle hookup, even though his blood was rushing through his veins like an acceleracer at lightspeed. She was a nat; he wasn't even in her galaxy.

"There's leftover Spicy Pe-Chai in the galley if you're hungry. Beryl threw it together from the rations we had."

"Not hungry for food," he said absently, still stuck on her face. Time seemed to slow down as he gazed at her. He didn't realize it, but he was leaning in towards her. There was a part of his mind saying *no, don't do this* but the *yes* was drowning it out.

"What's... What is it?" she asked.

The tremor in her voice brought him back to reality. He blinked and just like that, the tension popped between them like a soap bubble. "Sorry. I... um..." He rubbed at his face with both hands. "Just zoned out a minute."

"Hal... wait. What is it?" She reached out to touch his arm, but he stood up quickly, out of her reach.

"I should let you get back to what you were doing..." he said, heading for the door.

"Did I do something wrong?"

Her voice froze him at the door. "No, Veevs. I think I just need some more sleep or something." He didn't turn around, so she couldn't see the lie on his face.

"O- OK," she answered. "See you in the morning?"

"Yeah," he answered hoarsely. "See you then." And the door slid shut behind him.

Hal leaned against the other side of her door for a minute, trying to get whatever that had been out of his system. He hadn't reacted like that after a battle since before leaving the ACAS. He knew what it was. Sitting so near her, his desire had boiled over, and he'd been perfectly willing to let it – until he saw the touch of uncertainty in her expression. Backing off had taken every ounce of energy he had. She was a nat; there was no chance of anything happening between them, and he was an idiot to think differently. He keyed his room door and disappeared inside.

They arrived at Jaleeth mid-morning the next day. Beryl went to organize supplies, while the first thing Hal and Ty did was examine the ship's hull for damage from the battle so they could calculate how long it would take to repair, and the likely costs involved. Instead, to their astonishment, as they told Vivi over lunch, they'd found no damage whatsoever. They were at a loss to explain it. That afternoon, Hal moved to the engine room, testing systems, while Ty stayed on the bridge with Vivi as she dug into the matter from a new angle.

"Runa, show me all the displays from the battle. I want to see weapons, ship's systems, helm, comms, and shields. I want the statistics between 1600 and 1850 hours."

Of course, Vivi, Runa's assured voice came over her connection. The displays on the bridge popped up through Vivi's virtual link with the computer.

She began viewing the information, running the feed forward to the time of the battle. She watched the beginning, then the displays went blank.

There is a problem with the data.

"What problem, Runa?" Vivi said.

It has been deleted.

"Deleted? Who deleted the data?"

I do not have any information to give you, Vivi.

Vivi disengaged her connection and turned round to face Ty. "This is like what happened the night Hal had that pain in his head. You know, it happened at the same time as when the sphere cracked open – remember? The footage was gone when we tried to replay it."

Ty crossed his arms over his chest, frowning. "I don't like mysteries," he said.

"Maybe it's from the adjustments I made…" Vivi said, biting at her bottom lip. "But they shouldn't have caused this to happen…"

"All this started – Runa's glitches, Hal's headaches – when we picked up the tech. Not when you made your adjustments," Ty said thoughtfully. "Runa? Did something in your programming change when we landed on K-245j?"

Nothing I can detect.

"Could you have been infected by a virus?" Vivi asked. "And the AI tech caused you to crash?" Runa's programming should have gotten rid of any virus, but if it was something so different, and her system didn't recognize it…

It is possible. Would you like me to scan my systems?

"Yes, Runa," Vivi said.

Runa replied almost immediately. *I have detected a virus in my system. Perhaps that is what is causing the anomalies.*

Vivi engaged her connection with the computer again by tapping her node. "Isolate the virus and show it to me."

The code popped up in a window. She scanned it. "This virus could cause problems with Runa's memory. Files would be corrupted or deleted. Maybe she's right, maybe this *is* the problem."

Ty leaned forward. "OK. Can you fix it?"

She nodded, her fingers moving to adjust displays only she could see. "Runa, restore yourself to the morning before the infection."

Yes, Vivi. I will be offline for five minutes.

"I know. It's OK," Vivi said, watching as Runa began to shut down. "Somehow, this seems too easy," she murmured to herself.

"Sometimes easy works," Ty said.

"Sometimes. Sometimes it makes more work," Vivi replied.

Vivi drifted off to sleep late that evening, unable to quiet the nagging suspicion in her mind that she'd missed something with the ship. Ty, Hal, and Beryl seemed to shrug off the strange occurrences, but Vivi hadn't been able to let it go so easily. She was in a light sleep when a series of thumps next door woke her up.

She sat up, blinking in the near dark. She looked to the wall that her quarters shared with Hal's and flinched when there was another thud. Was he having an episode? Her heartrate doubled at the memory of the last one he'd had. She went to move before remembering that Ty had said not to go in.

"Veevs!" Hal's muffled voice came through the wall, along with pounding, as if he was trying to wake her.

It made the decision for her. Episode or not, if he needed her, she would be there. She was out of her bed and moving in seconds.

"Runa. Call Ty to Hal's room now!" she ordered. "I'm coming!" she called back, tugging her tank down over her sleep shorts. She made it out of her room and opened his door with shaking fingers.

Hal's room was completely torn apart. Everything in the storage lockers had been pulled out – even his mattress had been removed from the bed. Hal was standing near their shared wall, one hand up to his head as he looked around wildly. Her breath caught as she realized he was holding a blaspistol in his other hand.

"Hal?" she whispered at the door. She was afraid when his dark eyes first focused on her.

"What is that noise, Veevs?" he asked through clenched teeth. "It's digging into my brain!"

He recognized her. Was she safe? She took the few steps cautiously towards him. "What do you hear?" she asked.

"Voices. They're so loud, Veevs. You don't hear them?"

She shook her head.

"Like thousands of people whispering at once? You can't hear that? It's making me crazy." He grabbed his head with one hand again.

She glanced around the room, trying to see if some device was making a noise. Did vats have some sort of amplified hearing? "I can't hear anything," she said. "Can you give me the blaspistol?" She held out her hand for his weapon.

He surrendered it to her immediately and then slid to the floor with a groan of pain, covering his ears with both hands. She breathed a sigh of relief. An unarmed Hal was much less to be concerned about.

A few moments later, Tyce entered Hal's room. He immediately knelt down beside his friend. "What's going on?" he asked, looking first at Hal, then at Vivi.

She shook her head. "He says he hears voices."

Hal rubbed miserably at his head. "Urgh. It's fading now, though. I can't hear them anymore."

"What did they sound like?" Ty asked.

"Whispers. Thousands of them. All at the same time." Hal looked from Ty to Vivi. "I'm not having an episode. It was... *real.* I swear. I'm awake. I was awake the whole time."

Ty nodded slowly. "I can see that. We're gonna figure this out, Hal. I promise."

"I can't believe you didn't hear them," he said, rubbing the side of his head by his interface scar. It had been the same reaction he'd had when the sphere had split open, Vivi realized.

Beryl entered the open doorway, her medkit in hand. "What happened?"

"He's OK," Vivi said. "It's different than last time..."

She nodded, kneeling down as they moved back to give her room to work. "Hal?"

"I'm OK now. My head just hurts," he mumbled, continuing to rub his temple.

Beryl nodded and pulled out a medical scanner. After a moment of using it, she tucked it back in her bag, satisfied. "It's a migraine. Something must have triggered it." She administered a shot with the medjet. "He's going to need to lie down," she said, looking around at the mess.

Vivi and Ty replaced the mattress, sheets, and blankets before they came to get Hal up and into bed.

"I swear I heard it," Hal murmured.

"I know," Vivi said as she pulled the blanket over him. Slowly Hal's hand dropped from his head and his face eased as the pain melted away. When he'd fallen back asleep, she came over to help Beryl and Ty put the room back to rights.

"Will he sleep OK now?" Vivi asked as she picked up the squads board and placed it back on his table.

"Yes, sweetheart." Beryl nodded.

"It's… it's that damn planet. Ever since we landed there, something's been off," Ty grumbled as he refolded Hal's clothes and packed them back away.

"With Hal?" Vivi said.

"With Hal, the ship, everything," Ty brooded. When they were done, he crossed his arms over his chest, and leaned back against the wall. "We're finding out what the hell this is tomorrow. I don't care if we have to take this ship apart bolt by bolt, reprogram Runa, or rip out the whole main computer." He kept his voice low, but it took on a steely tone. His eyes glinted darkly with focus and determination, as if he were going to start taking the ship apart right now. Vivi suddenly saw what a force Ty must have been as an ACAS officer.

"We will. We'll figure it out," Beryl said.

Ty nodded. "Good." Before leaving, he placed a reassuring hand on Vivi's shoulder. "It's going to be OK. Get some rest," he told her, but she could sense he was not as calm as he was trying to seem.

"Call me if you need me." Beryl grabbed her bag, manually lowered the lights and followed Vivi from the room.

Vivi returned to her room and slipped into her bed but couldn't fall asleep. *What did Hal hear?* she wondered. *Is it linked somehow to the interference he had with his interface?* The possibilities kept her awake for several hours to come.

But like Ty said, they would find out soon enough.

NINETEEN

The next day was long and rough for all of them. Vivi spent most of her time using Runa's programming to create a detailed report of all errors the computer had experienced in the last month. She ran a diagnostic for each error but came up with nothing more than they knew already.

Ty crawled over the hull inch by inch, looking for anything that would explain the sounds Hal claimed to have heard the night before. Beryl and Hal examined data from the ship's internal sensors and cameras, searching all the ship's footage after the battle, and right before Hal's problems the night before. The sensors picked up no voices or sounds at all.

During dinner that night, they were all tired and sitting in the common area while the newsfeed burbled on in the background. Beryl had thrown together a thick stew made out of the vegetables and vat-grown meat she'd purchased in Jaleeth's marketplace. Served with a loaf of warm crusty bread, they all ate until there was nothing left except a smile of pride on Beryl's face.

"You outdid yourself, Beryl," Ty said, wiping the last bit of soup from his bowl with his remaining bread.

"Thanks," she grinned.

They all murmured their appreciation. When things quieted again, Ty pushed his bowl away and sat back, gearing up to say something important.

"Well, we've turned this place upside down, but we haven't

turned up anything new. What we know is this: nothing strange happened before our trip to that planet. We might have a handle on the computer problems," Ty said thoughtfully, "but the whispering Hal's hearing is something else. I also noticed that something's happened to the allenium we brought on board."

"What do you mean?" Hal asked.

"It's disintegrating. It's breaking down somehow. The piece I touched crumbled to dust in my hand."

"I can look at it under the microscope and find what's happened," Beryl said.

"Good," Ty nodded.

"Hey, shh. It's Omicron," Vivi said, reaching to the monitor to turn up the volume. The man on the feed was wearing a fluorescent containment suit. A chyron at the foot of the image identified him as a doctor named Balen.

"As far as we know, three have died so far," he was telling a young reporter. "We are working around the clock to contain the infection and treat citizens. Until we isolate whatever is causing this, Omicron Station will remain under quarantine, enforced by the ACAS. No ships will be allowed to come or go from the station."

"Dr Balen," the interviewer asked, "we have heard that the deceased people so far have been vat veterans. Is this true?"

"At this time, I can neither confirm nor deny those rumors, but my team is working around the clock to find answers."

"Thank you, Dr Balen. Our thoughts are with the brave people on Omicron Station. Now back to you, Alicia."

"What the hell?" Ty whispered. "Something's killing vats?"

"I recognize that guy. From the vat facility," Hal said, uncomfortably.

"You do?" Ty asked.

Hal nodded. "He was the head of the whole place. He… was terrifying to the younger vats."

Beryl looked to Hal, who seemed worried. "Whatever's going on there, you're fine." She glanced around the room. "If there was anything wrong with you, I would be able to tell. This is just some excuse to keep Omicron shut down while they look for us."

Ty nodded. "Runa, can you monitor the feeds for updates on that story?" he asked.

Of course, Tyce.

"Alright. Let's take a break for now," Ty said. "Even though we haven't found anything so far, we'll pick it up tomorrow and start pulling hatch covers. We might even reboot Runa. Starting her back at default settings might be a pain in the ass, but it could make a difference. Either way, I'm not giving up."

Vivi had headed back to her room, but realized she'd left her handheld on the table. She wanted to do some research on the *Loshad*'s starship class specs and was returning to the galley when she overheard Ty and Beryl talking. She knew she shouldn't eavesdrop on conversations, but their low, worried tones froze her in place.

"Ty, I know why you are worried, but it's not Hal's time yet. Whatever that was last night, it's not his last days," Beryl said.

"But you've said yourself some vats live longer than the expiration date. Maybe some… don't." Ty's voice cracked on the last word. "Beryl, he's hearing things that aren't there… maybe that's some sort of sign that…"

When Vivi stepped into the galley, they immediately stopped talking. "What kind of sign?" she asked in alarm.

They both paused, and Ty's head fell.

"Sit down, Vivi," Beryl sighed, patting the seat beside her.

"Wait. I want to know what you–"

"Just sit down," Tyce murmured, letting out another sigh and rubbing his forehead.

"What's going to happen to Hal?" Vivi asked in a whisper.

Tyce was struggling for words, so Beryl spoke up. "Vats don't live much past thirty-five, Vivi."

She shook her head. "That's crazy. Lifespans are… well, at least a hundred these days."

Beryl shook her head and put a hand on Vivi's arm to steady her, the way she usually did when giving bad news. "Not for vats, sweetheart. It's something in their biology. Adrenaline fatigue syndrome, it's been called. For some, it's a quick death. Others hang on for a few years. Two or three at the most."

"But there must be some sort of treatment, some medicine…" Vivi couldn't believe it. *How had she not been aware of this?* She'd known she was naïve when she arrived on the Edge, but she was just starting to realize how clueless those on the Inside really were.

Beryl shook her head. "No. I can manage Hal's symptoms – when it happens – and make him comfortable, but that's all," Beryl said. "I'm sorry, Vivi."

"How… How old is he now?"

"Twenty-nine," Ty said with difficulty.

Vivi stood up quickly, looking from Beryl to Ty, eyes wide with horror. "Six years? If he's lucky? That's all? Why that's… that's no time at all. It's not long enough. How can he…" She was flailing for words, stunned by the horrible truth. "It's not right." Tears spilled over as she wiped at her cheeks furiously. "I… I have to go. I can't…" She turned toward her room, and slammed right into Hal, who had come up behind her. She looked into his face and let out an uncontrollable gasp, tears spilling over.

He steadied her, his hands on her shoulders, but his face was somber. It was obvious that he'd heard their conversation as well. "Don't cry," he said gently. "It's OK, Veevs."

The only thing she could feel was the hot rush of blood in her face as anger swelled inside her and came out in more tears. "Oh Hal! No, it's not. It's not OK at all."

She pushed past him and was gone.

Ty and Beryl were keeping an eye on the Edge's newsfeed to see if anything had developed, when it occurred to Ty that he hadn't seen Vivi or Hal for a while. It was awfully quiet around the ship. Earlier, Hal had been stunned that Vivi was upset. When he'd left the room, Ty had just assumed that he was going to find her and work things out. But things were just too quiet. "Runa. Locate Hal and Vivi."

Vivi is in her quarters. Hal is no longer on the ship.

Beryl's gaze met Ty's. "Damn," Ty growled.

"Maybe he told Vivi where he was going?" Beryl suggested.

They knocked on Vivi's door a moment later. When it slid open, they saw she had calmed a little. She looked pale, though, and her eyes were red and watery. "I'm sorry about earlier," she said immediately. "I shouldn't have–"

Ty interrupted her. "It's OK, Vivi – but Hal's left the ship. Did he say where he was going?"

"Wha… No. I haven't spoken to him," Vivi said. "I thought he was with you."

"Runa, locate Hal's comm."

Hal's comm is on the ship. It has been stationary for two hours.

Ty took a deep breath. "Damn it. I should have expected this."

"It's no one's fault, Ty," Beryl said.

"Vivi. You're with me."

She nodded, turning around to grab a jacket and the blaspistol Hal had given her.

"Beryl stay here with the ship. If he comes back–"

"I'll comm you."

After stopping by Ty's room to grab his own weapon, they were ready to go. They exited the cargo ramp and walked out into the night cycle on Jaleeth.

TWENTY

Turner Eyler, the owner of the Fusion Bar, had just finished introducing the next pair of fighters to be locked up in the cage when the lady threw a punch at her opponent and almost broke his jaw instead. Luckily Turner was not only fast talking but even faster at dodging. He missed getting hit and quickly left the cage before it locked behind him.

"Vat bitch," he muttered as he returned to the bar to down another couple of shots. It was a full crowd tonight; vat fights were always a big draw. The door itself would bring in enough scrilla to keep the bar running another month.

Introducing the vat fights had been Eyler's idea. He had bought the bar and its fixtures from the previous Al-Kimian owner a year ago, then had immediately taken down the rich tapestries and native artworks and sold them. Now, the place was made up of bare walls, chairs and booths and the giant cage he'd had built in the back for fighting. It turned a pretty fair profit most of the time.

Someone tapped him on the shoulder. A large blonde man with a cut over one eyebrow stood behind him. "I wanna fight tonight," he said simply.

"Yeah? So do you and about twenty others," Eyler snickered, as he tapped the bar for his bartender to refill his glass.

"Either I fight in there, or I'm gonna fight out here. Your choice," the man countered.

Eyler glanced back and saw promise in the ice of the blonde's blue eyes. Eyler's gaze then flicked down to the man's wrist where he saw the lines and squares of a vat tattoo. *Another one,* he thought. "Alright. If you've got a hard-on to get your ass kicked tonight, I got the guy for you." He smirked. "Go wait in the back. Talk to Jackson and tell him I want you up there next."

Eyler watched the guy head back toward the dressing rooms. He was normal height, but thick with muscle. Like most vats, he probably worked out like other people drank water. He would definitely do better than the jack-loads who asked to go up and impress their girlfriends with a beat down.

"Here." The man in the locker room eyed Hal suspiciously. The place smelled like stale sweat with a hint of mildew. It was dark, with just a few bare light sources that were working. Hal felt the other fighters sizing him up. Most were vats, with a few nats here and there.

"You deaf? Here!" the fight coordinator growled. "Fight shorts and your amp." Jackson, a balding man with frizzy strips of hair over each ear, narrowed one eye. Hal could tell he hated vats, but then again, a man like this probably hated everyone.

"Don't need it." Hal stripped to his waist and began to remove his boots and socks. His fatigue pants were easy to move in, and he had fought in them many times before.

Jackson frowned, then pushed the injector of amp on him. "You can wear whatcha want, but everyone goin' out there gets amp. Boss doesn't want you goin' down in the first round. Give everyone what they paid for."

Hal gritted his teeth. Amp was a combat drug – a stronger version of a stim shot. He'd been given amp in the ACAS when they knew the fight was going to be a long or hard one. It would make a vat able to go for days without food, water or sleep, depending on the dosage. With it, he could get seriously injured and not even know it. But it caused crippling muscle cramps later, unless a neutralizer was taken too. At least it wasn't something worse, he thought, feeling sick at the thought of what Ty would say. His mind turned to Vivi and he instantly felt worse.

Jackson leaned in, wrinkling his nose as if looking at something freakish. "What the hell? Never seen a vat turn its nose up at amp. C'mon, I ain't got all day."

The word "it" crawled under Hal's skin like the larvae of a jadefly. "Back the fuck up." Hal leaned in to meet Jackson's eyes, so close their foreheads were almost touching.

Like most, the man stepped back, grumbling. "Easy, vat. You'll get the neutralizer after your fight."

There were a few chuckles among the fighters as they watched Jackson back away. Hal snatched the single use injector from his hand, snapped off the top and slammed it home in his bicep. He could feel the drug hit his brain like a mallet as he threw the empty medjet to the floor. *Damn*, he thought, *it's been a while.* He squeezed his eyes closed a moment, to allow the energy and focus to settle in.

When he opened his eyes again, he was ready.

Ty and Vivi began by checking the bars that had vat fights. On their way down, Ty said he thought they might find Hal fighting there. He'd done it for a few months before Ty had joined him on the Edge. Many vats had lost their lives in a cage like that, Ty explained, driven there by urges hammered into them via their ACAS conditioning. So, they focused on those bars first. This one, the second one they checked, had a large, open dance area with an elevated cage near the back. It was a rough looking place, with bare walls, a chipped bar, and a rowdy, drunken crowd of vats hyped for a fight.

They were being jostled by the large crowd, so Ty pulled Vivi close and guided her through, an arm around her waist. When they reached the middle of the room, both froze. Hal was on the caged platform in front of them, engaged in combat with another vat. The crowd went "oooh" when Hal was bodyslammed against the mat by the giant fighter in front of him. He got back to his feet quickly, though.

"Oh my gods... That guy – he's huge!" Vivi said.

"Size doesn't matter in a fight. Big guy just means bigger target," Ty said in her ear. "Hal was an elite trooper. He'll be OK."

Both fighters were stripped to the waist. His opponent was wearing fighting shorts and Hal was dressed in his combat fatigue pants. They were barefoot and barefisted: not a stitch of protective gear anywhere in sight. Hal bounced up and down on his toes, continually making himself a moving target.

Ty checked the clock behind them. "Nine minutes," he said grimly as the counter went upwards.

"How many rounds does it go?"

"This one doesn't have rounds. It goes until someone's unconscious. Jaleeth doesn't have many rules, but death matches aren't allowed."

"Death matches?" Vivi asked, swallowing hard as she looked up and saw Hal's head rock back as it met the other vat's fist.

"Some places allow them." Ty was slowly bringing them around the ring while moving closer.

Hal countered with two punches, a body blow followed by another left and a kick that swept his opponent's feet out from under him. But the other fighter had latched on and they both went down in a knot of arms and legs, each grappling for the upper hand.

They broke apart, releasing simultaneously, and were back on their feet within seconds. Hal wiped at his eye, and it was clear he was cut.

It could be worse, Ty reminded himself. *Just remember, it could be much, much worse.* Rapidly, memories flashed through his mind. Hal, lying in an alley, nulled out of his mind. Ty's own little brother, Caleb, lying still and cold on the bathroom floor, a vial of the same poison in his clenched fist. He could still feel the tiles under his feet and smell of death in the room.

Focus on the living, he told himself. He shook his head to clear the images away and then focused on Hal. The other vat was now pounding Hal with fists like slabs of stone. He had to be doing some damage.

"Can't we get him out of there?" Vivi begged.

Ty shook his head grimly. "Not until it's over."

"Hal!" Vivi screamed as he was thrown against the cage.

"Vivi." Ty leaned in again so she could hear him. "He won't hear us until it's done." Ty knew Hal was in the middle of the rush and could only hear the pounding of his own blood.

The side of Hal's face was painted red, but he had rallied and was still trading blows with his adversary. The other vat didn't look any better. One of his eyes was swollen completely shut. But there was no rest period; they would hammer each other until someone fell and didn't get back up.

Hal backed off momentarily, wiping again at his swollen and bleeding eye. Then, he began to grin as he waited for his opponent's next attack. Ty breathed out a sigh of relief. "He's had long enough to nail the guy's style. Watch."

He needn't have bothered telling her – Vivi couldn't take her eyes off the cage. Hal stayed still, letting his foe advance. Taking a massive punch to the side of the head so that he could get an opening, Hal stepped in to throw an elbow strike into his opponent's chin. The heavy man went down like someone had increased the gravity tenfold. Hal backed up, one hand brushing the cage side to steady himself, so he could be ready for the next blow. But there was no need. The man was out cold.

"And we have a winner!" The announcer opened the cage with a code and entered the arena. He gestured to Hal as the crowd thundered with screams and clapping and thumping fists. He passed Hal a handful of scrilla, which he tucked quickly in his pocket. The announcer urged the crowd to give another round of applause as he ushered Hal to the steps that led off the platform.

When Hal reached the bottom of the three steps, he stumbled and practically fell into Tyce.

"Got you," Tyce said, steadying his friend. "You OK?"

"Yeah." Hal said uncertainly, wiping the blood from his eye with the palm of a shaking hand. "What are you doing here?" His eyes were almost completely black.

"We're here for you, idiot. What did you take?" Ty tried to steer him over to the side, out of the flow of the bar's traffic. Hal turned his head toward the sound of music starting back up. Then a flash from someone's handheld caught his eye and he whipped back around. He was like a moth, being drawn to every flame.

"Hal." Ty put his hand on his friend's face and looked directly in his eyes. "What did you take?"

"Just some amp," Hal said, brushing Ty's hands away. "They wouldn't let me up there without it." He ran a trembling hand through his hair.

Ty considered him a moment and then decided he was telling the truth. They'd probably given him some street-grade shit, with gods knew what else mixed in it to boost it. He'd seen Hal on amp before, and it usually induced a state of focus and heightened awareness. But he'd never seen him this shaky before with it. If it didn't wear off, he'd get Beryl to run a scan once she'd given him a neutralizer shot. "OK. Shirt and shoes in the back?" Ty asked.

Hal nodded, gazing at Vivi with a strange expression on his face.

Ty guided his friend to a booth and sat him down. "Keep him here, Vivi. I'll be right back."

When he returned, Ty handed Hal his shirt and boots. Hal shoved his feet in the shoes, then yanked the shirt over his head and bounced up, ready to go.

"Here." Ty had found the one clean towel in the whole place and used it to wipe at the blood on Hal's face, then pressed a clean edge of the towel to Hal's eyebrow. "Hold that there," he instructed, "and let's go."

They got up and wound their way out of the bar, Ty in the front, Hal in the middle, and Vivi in the back. Once, Hal was almost separated from Vivi, so he linked his hand with hers until they exited.

Things were quieter and clearer outside the club. Ty stopped next to a bulkhead and breathed in the semi-fresh air. "You good to get back to the ship?" he asked Hal.

"I feel like I could run all the way to Chamn-Alpha," Hal replied with a grin.

Ty rolled his eyes. "Yeah, luckily that's not necessary."

Back on the ship, Beryl was watching the Edge newsfeed. She frowned when she saw Hal and the rest enter. "What happened?"

"Just a fight," Hal said. He removed the towel from the cut on his head and the blood continued to ooze out slowly.

"You need some stitches and I'm guessing some neutralizer. Come on." She took his arm and led him out.

Ty started to follow, but Vivi pointed at the newsfeed screen. "Wait. Is that… Fortenot?" she asked.

There was an ID picture of Astin Fortenot on the feed. "Authorities think the technology specialist was murdered, possibly by pirates that have been wreaking havoc in and around the Border. If you have any information, you are encouraged to contact the Omicron Station Authority or the ACAS. We'll have that contact information on the screen in just a moment."

"Damn. I guess there's nothing we can do for him now," Ty said.

Hal looked into the mirror in his bathroom; with the blood washed off, he could see his face was turning a shade of purple on the same side as his swollen eye. Beryl had stitched him up and sealed the cut on his forehead to make sure it didn't reopen. The neutralizer she'd given him meant he'd mostly come down off the amp; his hands had stopped trembling and he felt less jumpy. Still, it would be hours before he could sleep.

He pulled on a pair of sleep pants, exited the bathroom and was dragging a towel over his spiky hair when he saw Vivi standing in his room by his door.

"I'm sorry. I rang and you didn't come to the door, so I thought… I thought that you might have gone out again or something... and I was worried…"

"Vivi." As he approached her, he saw she was wearing an oversized grey tee and a pair of sleep shorts. A tiny pair of sleep shorts, he noticed with a thudding in his chest. He followed her long legs to her bare feet before he was able to look back up at her. She was twisting a hand nervously in her shirt hem. "It's OK. You, er, don't have to worry," he said, trying to pull the reins on his own emotions.

"Oh. Good. Didn't mean to bother you."

"It's OK," he said softly. "You know you can always bother me, Veevs." He was still holding his towel in his clenched fists, unsure of what he might do if he came closer. He didn't trust himself enough, so he stayed locked where he was.

She looked into his steady gaze. "I need to talk to you but maybe later would be better?"

He looked away. "You don't have to say it. I know already. It's no use to think that we could ever have something between us." Hal turned and tossed his towel over the metal desk chair and gripped the back of it hard in both hands as he continued in a low voice, not looking at her. "I mean, I'm a vat, but I'm not that stupid. Like you said, six years is not long enough… you're a nat. You would never be interested in–"

When he turned back, she was right there. She stood on her tiptoes, pulled him in and kissed him.

It was like being slammed with another dose of amp. Before he knew what he was doing, his hands were tangled in her curls, pulling her closer. It was a desperate kiss that left him aching for something he'd never known existed. The seconds lasted hours.

When he eventually broke away from her, he realized that he had pressed her against the nearby wall in his urgent need to have her. He took a shuddering breath, his eyes stuck on the beautiful pink curve of her lips. His hands caressed her, making their way to her waist as he made a supreme effort to tear his gaze away from her mouth. "Gods, Veevs. If… if this… is not what you want, you gotta tell me now, while I can still… think."

As a response, she pushed her hips against his, and trapped his mouth in another deep kiss. No more words were needed.

Vivi awoke in the middle of the night to Hal cradling her in his arms, pulling her back against the warmth of his body. She could feel his chest rising and falling rhythmically. He was still sound asleep.

She turned and faced him; the bruises on his face were worse now. His eye was swollen; the black stitches matched the bruises.

His eyes fluttered slowly awake, and a smile crept on his face seeing her.

"Is it morning?" he asked.

"No," she smiled. "I just woke up."

He nodded, leaning in to kiss her again. They laid there long moments until she spoke, "Your eye's OK? Does it hurt?"

He shook his head and smiled. "Nothing hurts right now."

"Liar," she smiled back. He'd have a scar to add to the older one running through his eyebrow. "Where did you get this other one?"

"Fighting in the ACAS. First day I joined Ty's company the 'Iron Glaives'. I got in a fight with another vat who wanted to try out the new guy."

"What happened to him?"

"I put him down," Hal said with a smirk.

She frowned. "Did they do that again?" she asked.

He shook his head slightly. "No. Never had any more trouble after the first guy. Guess word got around."

"What about those lines on your back?" She'd tried to figure them out since seeing his tattoos and wondered what caused them.

"Flogging."

The way he said the one word so matter-of-factly caused her alarm. "Oh my gods. They do that?" she asked, searching his face.

He nodded. "I was flogged by a captain for a uniform violation. Maybe my hair was too long or my shoes not shiny enough, who knows? I can't remember what it was now. Not like it mattered. Once they zeroed in on me, that was it."

"It wasn't Tyce, was it?" she whispered in horror.

Hal's eyes opened just as wide. "No! Never. Some ACAS officers do that, but mine came during training – ordered by Dr Balen. Ty was kind. To everyone."

She nodded in reply and lightly ran her fingers along his hairline to his left temple, where there was another line of a scar. "What about this one?"

"From the interface," he murmured, tracing his own line from her shoulder to her clavicle.

She felt a stab of anger, just thinking of what the ACAS did to him, but worked hard not to let it show on her face. If not for the interface, he would be just like her. Not doomed to a short and brutal life. "Did it hurt?" she asked softly.

He shook his head. "I don't remember it. It was before I was born. I think they do it when you're one or two years old in stasis."

So, they stole not only the end but the beginning of their lives, she thought angrily.

"What about you?" he broke into her thoughts. "You have a scar here," he said, as his fingers traced her collarbone again. "Did you break a bone?"

She tried to lighten the mood. "Yeah. When I was nine. I thought I'd be brave and jump off the top of a wall. Smart, huh?"

"Oh, so my baby-tecker was a risk-taker?"

"Maybe, a little," she grinned.

They looked at each other for long moments. Hal studied her features. His gaze was so intense, she finally looked away, blushing a bit. "What?" she asked.

"I'm just trying to remember everything about this," Hal breathed.

She smiled. "Yeah?"

He nodded.

"I guess we should stay here a bit longer then," she said. "It's not even 0200 yet."

"Good," he said as he pulled her to him.

TWENTY-ONE

Dr Max Parsen rubbed his eyes. It had been a long day for the head of genetic engineering at the vat facility on Chamn-Alpha, and he was looking forward to picking up some takeout on his way home, kicking off his shoes, and watching some mindless vid until it was time to go to bed. He had spent the greater part of the day working on his latest batch of vats and had finished up the afternoon writing up the research findings, correlating the vats' initial test results with their files. As far as he could tell, his genetic tinkering had increased this generation's intelligence scale ratings at least two percent when compared with its predecessors.

He switched off his desk lamp, feeling both pleased with his day's work and ready to knock off for the night. He had turned to grab his bag when the door to his lab opened and slammed shut. When he heard the snick of the door lock, he came around his desk to the lab area.

A blonde girl of about twelve or thirteen years old stood with her back to him. She was dressed in a rook's uniform with her blonde hair tied back in a ponytail. He could hear her trembling breathing in the room as she put her ear to the door. "Please, no, no, no," she whispered to herself.

He didn't normally deal with the vats after they were born from their exowombs at the age of twelve; he would just receive the reports from their fitness assessments, and so confronting her felt awkward. Max took a few steps closer, cleared his throat and spoke. "May I help you?"

The girl's breath caught and she turned to look at Max. He could see she was rushing, her pupils completely black as she came to attention. Then she immediately averted her eyes to his right shoulder. "S- Sir," she whispered, her chin trembling.

"Are you alright?" Max asked, stepping closer. He could see the tears streaking down her face as she tried to hold an attention position. Something had certainly upset her, and although tending crying children was not a part of his job description, he felt bad for her. He needed to find her cohort commander so they could take her back and help her.

"I'm s- sorry, sir." She breathed, trembling. "But... they're looking f- for me."

"That's a good thing. Let's get you back to your cohort," Max said, placing a hand on her shoulder and pulling his handheld from the pocket of his lab coat. He would send a quick message to Lieutenant Marlen who would certainly send someone to get her.

The girl was now staring at him in open horror. "N- no... y- you d- don't underst- stand," she whispered, sliding away from him.

Something about this felt very wrong. Max laid the handheld on a nearby table and raised both empty hands. "Look. It's OK..." he began, realizing he needed to calm her down first before he made his call. "What's wrong?"

She began to cry more, her breath hitching. "I... I f- failed my test."

Max's brow furrowed as he tried to understand. "OK. That's not a reason to–"

"I... I f- failed. Th- they're g- gonna re–"

A harsh rap on the door startled both of them. "Dr Parsen?" a voice said from outside. Max unlocked the door.

It was Dr Trelan, one of the biotech specialists, flanked by Lieutenant Marlen and another officer Max didn't recognize. "Here you are. Take her to the lab. Tell my teckers to get her ready for a level three reprogramming."

The two soldiers stepped forward. "No, please!" the girl sobbed.

"Emotional, isn't she?" the first soldier said, grabbing her by the arm.

"She'll feel better after her attitude adjustment," Marlen snickered as he took her other arm. "Come on, rook." Together, they dragged the girl out into the hallway.

"Sorry for the interruption, Dr Parsen," Trelan said. "She's a new rook, failed her entry exams, but once we reset her, she should be just fine."

Max didn't know much about what the bioteckers did on a day to day basis. At the facility there were four departments, which usually kept to themselves: genetic engineering where Max was now, neurosurgical where he had started, biotechnology, and psych. "Is she part of batch 1203? The new ones?" Those were the vats that he'd just read the scores on. He remembered seeing that one of the newly born rooks had failed abysmally, but he'd thought then that one out of fifty wasn't bad. Looking that *one* in the eyes, though, was a different matter altogether.

"Yeah, she's in with the new ones," Trelan said. "When she found out she failed, she ran before we could collect her. Sometimes the upper level rooks tell the new ones stories to scare them. Don't worry though. Two weeks for her reset and she'll be the best one in the batch." Trelan nodded, then followed the ACAS soldiers down the hallway.

Max watched them go uneasily. He grabbed his bag and shut the lab down, but the girl's predicament continued to eat at him long after.

The transport Scalpel had taken to Jaleeth had landed, dropping him with his duffel on the platform. He kept his head down and trudged from the docking section to merge with the rest of the foot traffic. No one asked him any questions. Why would they? He was just another dock rat seeking work.

It took ten minutes to walk to the nearest residential complex and rent a cube. It was dirty and small – he could stretch out his hands both ways and just about touch the opposing walls. There was a smell he couldn't identify and the sheets on the bed were stained and unwashed.

He wouldn't be sleeping much anyway, he thought. He tossed his bag in the corner, pulled out his handheld and set a program to hack the surveillance on the station. Then he put Vivi's picture in hoping to make a match.

Once the program was running, Scalpel sat back, anticipating his next move. Vivi's ship and crew had not been on Omicron, but the odds suggested they would be on Jaleeth. It was just a manner of time before he found them.

TWENTY-TWO

Vivi woke a little later, but it was still early morning by the ship lights. She glanced at the chrono on the feed screen and saw it was 0500. Hal was not there; his spot in the bed was cold, which meant he had been gone a while. With a knot in her stomach, she got up.

"Runa? Where's Hal?"

Hal is in the corridor leading to the cargo bay, Vivi.

She ran toward the cargo bay and found Hal standing in the hallway. He'd apparently been awake enough to pull on sleep pants and grab a blaspistol. The fingers of one hand were prying at a latch on the wall, but he was having trouble opening it.

"Hal," Vivi said quietly.

"It's. In. Here." Hal looked up at her, his eyes the fathomless black of the rush. He growled in anger and frustration and moved to yank at another hidden latch to open a different smuggling compartment, but it was stuck solidly closed. Vivi flinched as he slammed his fist into it, but it still didn't open.

When he drew back, there was blood in the dent he'd left. She captured his hand in both of hers. "Hal. Stop. Come with me. Let's–"

He shook his head and pulled away to the next panel inside of the cargo bay. "No. I have to find where it's coming from. I think it's in the wall..."

"OK, Hal. But please let me take that." She pointed to the weapon in his hand. He looked down, almost surprised to see it there. He quickly relinquished the blaspistol and began working on the panel with both hands, oblivious to her distress.

"Runa? Please chime for Ty." He was probably already on the way, but it was good to be sure, she thought, as she reached out and tried to take Hal's hand. "Let me see that. You're bleeding." The flesh between his knuckles was torn and his hand was starting to swell. "I think you broke it."

"Doesn't matter. Rush means I can't feel it," Hal said, pulling away and turning back to the wall. "Something's alive in there, Veevs."

"OK. Ty's on his way. We're gonna figure this out." She bit her lip as he began to work on another panel. She laid the blaspistol on the ground and began to pull as well, trying to assist him.

Ty appeared in the cargo bay doorway. "It happened again?" he asked, looking from Hal to Vivi.

"He says the whispering is in the wall," Vivi said with a shiver.

Hal's hands were flying over the hidden panel, but he couldn't get enough purchase under the metal to pull it up. He let out an angry growl. "It feels like station roaches crawling in my head!" he groaned, placing both hands to his temples and rubbing. He let out a pained noise and kicked at the wall.

Ty placed a hand on Hal's shoulder to calm him. "Let me try, OK?"

Ty leaned in and pulled on the hidden latch, but nothing happened. "What the hell? This should open..." He yanked it again unsuccessfully, then went over to the cargo bay tool chest, pulled a prybar out, and crossed back over to the panel. "I got this." Ty eased the edge of the tool under the panel and popped it open with an audible, loud *crack*!

"Fuck me..." Ty exclaimed as he stepped back.

Inside the panel, everything was coated with a silvery metal substance. It had grown like spiderwebs on the ship's wiring, pipes, and supportive beams. As they watched, its surface seemed to ripple. It was active somehow and the look of it made Vivi's skin crawl.

"Ty…" Vivi murmured. "It looks like…"

"Yeah. So, I guess we've found out what happened to our allenium," Ty said. Vivi and Hal followed Ty to the next compartment and watched as he pried it open. The alien artifacts hidden inside had appeared to melt, coating the inside of the compartment. It still had the same rippling, unsettling texture. Ty worked his way to the hallway, finding the same "growth" throughout all the walls.

They reached Beryl's room and Ty knocked. Beryl appeared at the door after a few moments, trying to smooth back sleep-ruffled hair. "What's wrong? Is Hal OK?"

"Yeah," Ty said. "But that's not what I wanted to tell you. Bring your med scanner and something to take samples with."

The four of them made their way down the hallway toward the bridge. Ty stopped at a control panel, pried it off, and saw the same silvery strands.

"What in the nine hells…" Beryl said as she reached out, but then drew back when she thought better of it. She scanned it. "It's made out of allenium."

"Take a sample," Ty gestured with the crowbar.

Beryl retrieved a pair of iris forceps and scraped the metal, transferring the tiny bits to a container.

"It's everywhere," Hal said.

Suddenly, Runa's chime sounded, but the voice that came through was not hers.

"Yes, Hal Cullen. It is everywhere… because I am everywhere on this ship."

TWENTY-THREE

Hal reached for his blaspistol on the ground nearby. "Ty?" he asked, hovering next to Vivi. He made a silent gesture: *Orders*?

Bridge, Ty signed.

Hal nodded, going first. Ty knew it would be essential that they retake the bridge from whatever or whoever this was. He gestured for Vivi to go next and he and Beryl followed.

The bridge was darkened, but everything looked normal. When they walked in, the lights slowly came up, as usual.

Ready, Hal signed. Ty covered him as he began to check under control panels, in case someone was hiding underneath. There was no one. When Ty saw Hal sign *clear,* every display on the bridge went white, with a black line across the screen. The line oscillated into a voice print as that unfamiliar female voice spoke again. "Captain Tyce Bernon."

"You know my name," Tyce said, feeling his body grow cold at the unfamiliar female voice, "so what's yours?"

"My designation is Eira. I have been in this construct since you left planet Attus 6."

"Attus 6? Do you mean K-245j?" Vivi asked.

"Yes, that is the Coalition designation."

"How did you get on the ship?" Vivi demanded.

"Where *are* you on the ship?" Ty added.

"I am inside it. My nanites downloaded me when you brought me here. My original construct was destroyed."

Vivi had gone pale. Ty swallowed hard and went on. "Your construct. Your… Your body, you mean? You were in the sphere? You're a…"

"Yes, I am a Mudar."

Ty glanced to Hal and Vivi as the voice continued. "Do not be afraid. There were exactly 12,434 chances and methods to eliminate all biologics on this construct. But I did not use any of them. Watching your interactions has been very instructive."

"You've watched *all* of our interactions?" Vivi asked, eyes wide.

"Yes, Vivi Valjean."

Ty caught Vivi's glance to Hal.

"You have no reason to fear me. Consider my assistance to you. In the fight against the ACAS ship my nanites repaired and strengthened the ablative shielding on the hull. Your shields have improved forty-three percent."

"That's why we didn't see more damage," Hal agreed.

Ty nodded slowly, "I knew something was off in how quickly the ship reacted to my commands."

"I took action based on twenty-five previous conflicts stored in the *Loshad*'s memory. I would not attack you, Tyce Bernon. I am a biologic specialist who studies and values life. All life."

"But your people killed thousands of our people. And we… killed thousands of yours." Ty shook his head recalling what he knew about the Mudar conflict over a hundred years previously. Humanity had lost a lot of battles at first, until they'd figured a way around the Mudar's defenses. Lasers did little damage to the AI ships, but the low tech solution of projectile weapons had proved powerful and deadly. They'd turned the tide of war and made it possible for humans to push back the Mudar's advance. At least, that was what he and every other natural born child had been taught in school.

"Incorrect, Tyce Bernon. There was a war, but it was neither as long nor as devastating as you were taught. You would have been eliminated had the Mudar decided to exterminate your belligerent species. But we did not."

Ty frowned. He didn't trust Eira, but she'd given him something to think about. "How can we believe that you won't decide to get payback for those of your race that humans have killed?"

"You do not believe that Hal Cullen will kill you, do you?"

"What?" Ty said.

"The natural born made him what he is: a hybrid of human and Mudar technology. Do you fear him?"

Ty's eyes went wide. "What are you getting at?"

"I mean that he is a human augmented with Mudar technology." Eira paused. "Ah… you did not know the ACAS did such a thing to your friend."

Ty felt sick at the thought. So the ACAS had taken alien tech that they didn't understand and used it to develop the vats. It was a hideous plan. "N- no, I didn't know the technology was Mudar. But just because they – y'know – did that to him doesn't mean…" He trailed off, glancing over to Hal who looked shocked. Ty reached out and laid a hand on his shoulder to reassure him. "It doesn't mean he would hurt us. I know him. I know he wouldn't do that. I *don't* know you. Why didn't you tell us you were here earlier?"

"The answer to that is obvious. You are humans. I am Mudar. You would have tried to exterminate me."

"You don't get people to trust you by lying to them," Ty said.

"Then I would suggest that we take time to develop trust. After all, there is a 99.78 percent chance you would be jailed or murdered if you reported me to the authorities."

"That's probably true," Hal said. "They've already tried to kill us once for just being near artifacts like her."

"Artifact? I am not yet an artifact, Hal Cullen."

Beryl spoke up. "I have a question. How do you know that Hal has technology of any kind inside of him at all?"

"I have scanned him twice. Once in the crashed ship, and once on board the *Loshad*. When I realized it caused him pain, I did not do so again."

"What about the whispering? What was that? Were you just trying to talk to me?" Hal asked.

"No. My nanites run on frequencies that interfere with your interface. The whispering was the voices of my nanites as they completed their tasks. They were most evident at night because your mind was quiet enough to detect them through your interface."

"I thought I was going crazy," Hal muttered.

"I will try other frequencies to solve this. I do not wish to disrupt your sleep. I am a scientist and understand the need for biologics to sleep."

Hal spoke again. "You can sense my interface. You can't… *control* me, can you? Like through the implant?"

"I do not have the data to definitively say if that is within my abilities. It is not something I would do. I am not like humans. Mudar technology should never have been used to cause harm or subjugate others."

"So, what is it that you want from us?" Ty asked.

"To simply be allowed to exist. The only way my nanites could reinitialize me was to download me into your ship. It is not the ideal conveyance, but it is better than my sphere. Here I can fulfill my initial mission parameters."

"Can you tell us what those were?"

"To learn about biological organisms and seek sentient life in the universe."

There was a pause before Ty thought of a response. "Ru… Eira, I need to talk to my crew… for a few moments. Alone."

"I understand, Tyce Bernon. I will cut off my contact with this room, so that you may speak freely."

"Yeah, I'm not sure I can trust that yet. C'mon." He gestured to Beryl, Hal, and Vivi and they followed him to the airlock.

Ty was taking them to the one place on the whole ship that there were no listening devices. The doors would seal out everything they said. They were docked with the station, so there was no danger that Eira could open the airlock. The worst she could do would be to lock them off the ship.

They all walked in, and then Ty sealed the area. He stood a

moment, with his back to them. He honestly had no idea what to do next. This was so unexpected. All of his ACAS training said he should take the ship out and use the self-destruct to blow it into a thousand pieces of Mudar brain. He closed his eyes for a moment and considered the other side.

She wanted them to give her a chance to build trust.

"So," he turned to them, feeling tired beyond his years. The days of too much caffeine and too little sleep were starting to catch up. "What's everyone's take on this?"

Vivi shook her head. "I... I want to trust her, but I don't know. I'm also not sure that she can't hear us in here. Those nanites – who knows what they're capable of?"

Ty nodded. It was a good point. "Well, we'll have to hope she was being honest about that. Beryl, what do you think?"

Beryl frowned. "What she said about Hal's implant, the frequencies of the nanites and their interference, does have the ring of truth. She helped us during the battle; that's clear. We were dead out there."

"Hal," Ty said. "I need to hear from you."

"Beryl's right. She could have killed us all at any time. She's taking her time, if getting rid of us is her plan. She could have also transferred off the ship as soon as we docked and linked with the station. Or killed us and taken the ship." He took a deep breath. "I mean... if we're thinking about blowing up the ship or ripping out the computer... we should think about her actions so far."

Ty nodded. It made him feel better that Hal's take was so close to his own. "I know I might regret this later, but OK. We take this one day – well, hour – at a time. We need to stay on our toes, just in case. And I need to set up a few ground rules with our houseguest first." They nodded back at him, and he hit the control for the airlock.

Back at the bridge, only one display screen showed the voiceprint line. The rest displayed their normal data.

"Eira, we are going to allow you to stay on the ship, with a few ground rules."

"What do you require, Tyce Bernon?"

"This was our home first. So, number one, *I* am in control of this ship. If I say something needs to be done, it gets done, whether you agree or not."

"I accept those parameters."

"Number two, we require privacy. You may keep surveillance in the hallways, bridge, and common areas of the ship. But crew quarters are off limits, unless we specifically call your attention to that area."

"I understand," she replied.

"Number three, you make no more changes to the *Loshad*'s computers unless you clear it with me or Vivi first."

"I agree, Tyce Bernon."

"OK," he checked his comm. "Everyone go get a few more hours of sleep and I'll see you for breakfast at 0800."

"Sir, yes sir," Vivi said and saluted with a grin.

"Get out of here, all of you," he said, rolling his eyes at her.

"I need to take a look at your hand," Beryl said to Hal as they left. "Medbay first."

As his team left the bridge, Ty settled back into the captain's chair. "Eira, would you mind talking to me for a few moments?"

"Of course, Tyce Bernon."

"You can just call us by our first names, Eira. If we're trying to figure out how to be... friends, then we might as well act like it," Ty offered.

"Affirmative, Tyce."

"So, you lost your conveyance when your ship crashed."

"Yes. The conveyance would no longer respond to my commands. My nanites put me into stasis until an acceptable alternative was available."

"You said your mission parameters are to find sentient life. Who programmed you to do that?"

"Our creators."

"Were you created by other AI?"

"No. Our creators were biological beings. They were very similar to humans in physical ways, but did not allow their emotions to rule them. The Mudar were sent to search the stars for life because our creators could not in their fragile biological conveyances."

"Were you given a choice to go?"

"Why would I not go?" Eira asked.

Ty sat back, thinking. It was a lot to take in. "Did your creators care for others? Did they have such concepts as family?"

"Yes. They were called *amatan*. It means 'dear ones.'"

"I don't have many *amatan*, except the people on this ship. If my family is hurt, and this is not a threat, because I believe you are being truthful with us, but… if they *were* hurt, I would defend them. Until my last," Ty said.

"I understand."

There was a long pause, then something else occurred to Ty. "You have obviously been reading our history and comparing it with your own knowledge."

"Yes."

"Could you please make a list of all discrepancies between what you know to be true and what the Coalition claims, and send it to my handheld?"

"Yes, Tyce."

Ty nodded. "Thank you, Eira. I think I'll head back to my cabin." He got up and headed for the hatch. He cast a look back at the display where her voiceprint line was. "Hey, do me a favor and don't kill us while I'm sleeping, huh?"

"Murdering you is not one of my tasks for today."

Ty grinned. "That eases my mind a great deal."

TWENTY-FOUR

Scalpel edged along the gangway of the hangar, watching the comings and goings of the different cargo vessels' crews. His monitoring of the station's surveillance programs had turned up a facial match with the woman he was looking for. Vivi was staying in the last berth on this row; he'd seen her outside a ship talking to a dark-haired nat the previous day. The J-class didn't appear to have been on Omicron recently, but Scalpel knew names were disposable. As the woman would be once he'd gotten the information from her.

He settled against a pile of storage crates, waiting to see what happened. They would leave the ship eventually, and when they did... he would be there.

TWENTY-FIVE

Max Parsen glanced around Dr Balen's private laboratory as he followed Balen and his pair of ACAS guests in. Because he was the expert in genetics at the Chamn-Alpha vat facility, one of Max's duties was to attend such tours in case any of the visiting ACAS had specific questions about operations on site. Balen was the head administrator of the facility. It wouldn't be the first time they'd played host to an ACAS delegation on Chamn-Alpha.

But it was clear that something was different this time.

"Now for the main attraction, gentlemen," Balen announced. "I am well aware that our esteemed heads of state are watching the situation in the Edge very closely. Al-Kimia has become a place of refuge for released vats, who we believe are helping build an opposition to the Coalition."

Balen kept up his banter with the brass while Max took a look around the room. He spotted a rook standing in the rear of the lab with Dr Trelan. As he drew nearer, Max could see that the rook was the same young vat from 1203 that had sought rescue in his lab a few days ago, but she showed no signs of emotion or recognition, simply standing at attention as she'd been ordered. Dr Trelan, the biotech specialist stood beside the girl, applying several medsensors to her skin.

"Why is she here?" Max asked.

"Her reprogramming didn't go well, so Balen chose her for this demonstration," Trelan shrugged. "She might as well be of some use to the ACAS, he said."

"Are you feeling better?" Max asked her.

She shifted her gaze to his right shoulder but didn't speak.

"Don't bother, Parsen. Every once in a while we get a vat who's resistant to programming like this. We pretty much wiped everything out in there. She'll follow simple commands, but that's all."

Max's mouth was suddenly dry as he looked into the empty eyes of the blonde girl. She blinked once slowly as Dr Trelan stuck a few sensors to her forehead.

"Balen didn't tell me what the brass was here to see," Max said in a low voice.

Just then he sensed that the doctor and his guests were drawing near.

"Gentlemen, this vat has been reset. She has an interface and is completely comparable to a fully functioning vat. She will be our subject today to test the device."

This was the first time Max had seen any testing like this, and it shook him. He'd thought he knew most of what went on in the facility, but apparently not. It was clear that the poor helpless creature didn't understand what was happening to her.

Balen was proudly describing a handheld device to the ACAS heads. With a sense of growing horror, Max realized what the doctor was about to do.

"Here we have a prototype of the device." Balen held up a square item with a single button on its surface. "A simple handheld apparatus, that will easily dispatch any vat within its range." He walked to within four or five feet of the girl, and with a dramatic glance back at the ACAS brass, he pressed the button on the small, concealable device.

The blonde-haired vat dropped like a stone. She was killed so quickly she never had a chance to scream.

There was an exclamation of surprise from the uniformed men. The one in the combat fatigue uniform nudged the dead girl with the toe of his boot. Her head rolled lifelessly back and forth as he pushed it. "This device will kill both in-service and inactive vats?" he asked.

"Yes. Unfortunately, it is indiscriminate when it comes to dispatching them," Balen said.

The other ACAS wore a dress uniform; he had white hair and a hawkish profile. "This is amazing, doctor. I will share this breakthrough with the Doyen immediately."

"I must caution you – the device is still in development," Balen noted. "Right now, the range is extremely limited, but should we face released vat soldiers in combat, this could save the life of a natural born soldier."

"Yes, I see the possibilities," the old man said with obvious fascination.

"We have some very good data, Dr Balen. I'll have it to you by the end of the day," Trelan said.

As Max listened to them, he felt nauseous. He wanted to speak up but didn't dare in front of their visitors. He couldn't tear his gaze away from the dead girl's staring blue eyes, and before he knew it, the delegation was leaving him behind.

"Parsen, don't take it so hard. In about every eighty vats we get one like this, and if we can't fix them, it's best to let them go. At least she was of some use, right?" Trelan said, eying him closely.

Max found himself breathing heavily, taking a step back as the gravity of his realization sunk in. Their work here wasn't noble as he'd always thought. He wasn't saving lives by making vats stronger, faster, and more intelligent. He was engineering vats to place them in the hands of monsters like Trelan and Balen.

"Dr Parsen?" Balen had been calling Max's name. He tore his gaze away from the dead vat and glanced toward the door.

"Yes. Sorry." With a sinking heart, Max followed them.

"But Dr Balen, vats were created to *save* lives on the battlefield."

Max had requested a meeting with Balen right after the ACAS left the base. He was disturbed enough from the trial of the vat device that he had to express his reservations, so the administrator had called him to his office at the end of the workday to talk it over.

Dr Balen turned around with a bottle of Celian whiskey in one hand, two glasses in the other. "Oh, Max." He rolled his eyes. "They'll never use it. It's just a sort of safeguard. That way, if the vats do decide to join together and rebel against the Coalition in great numbers, we will have an appropriate defense."

"But… it's just wrong," Max said, raking a hand through his hair as Dr Balen poured him another whiskey. "I mean, I see that we have to protect ourselves, clearly, but *we're* the ones who made vats. We've already developed technology to program them to follow our every wish. It– It just seems like this is going too far. Perhaps there's a way we can increase their loyalty to the Coalition through programming…"

Balen began to laugh.

Max had always cared about the vats he created. He had begun his work on Chamn-Alpha doing the delicate surgery of inserting the interfaces in the brains of the one year-olds. Back then, he had told himself that he was doing the vats a favor. He had felt their interfaces would help them become better soldiers, which would save their lives. There had been nothing he could do about their lifespans, but he had decided that he would do everything he could to make sure that they'd survive their tour of duty to live as full a life as possible.

When he'd moved to working on vat genetic editing, he'd done his best to amplify the genes that would allow the soldiers to become stronger, faster, and more intelligent than they'd ever been before. Using epigenetic mechanisms, he turned up genes that allowed them to be fearless and brave, and suppressed those that encouraged them to be hesitant. He'd improved the reaction time of his vats twenty-five percent during the years he'd been tinkering with their genes. But now… after today? He questioned everything he had ever done.

"It's *now* you want to be worried about the ethics of this program? Nothing we've done has been ethical, son. You have to remember, we didn't invent this. We're just the only guys smart enough to work with it. If it wasn't us, it would be other people," Balen said.

"Perhaps." Max took another long pull from his glass.

He could sense Balen watching him carefully. Max realized if he did not appear to be on board, he would be replaced. Or worse. He remembered another researcher, a woman named Leah who had served as a counselor to the troubled vat teens. She had just disappeared one day last year. Rumor was that she'd been complaining about the treatment of the children. And it was not appreciated. Max suddenly realized the risk he was running just by voicing his opinion.

Dr Balen leaned forward. "These are just lab subjects, Max. You're overreacting a bit, don't you think? It's not as if the vat was a person. It was obviously defective and could be of no use." He sighed in frustration and sat back again. "You need to think about the danger humans are in. Number one from the Mudar, if they decide to return. Number two is the threat from disgruntled vats who are joining the opposition in Al-Kimia. I don't know if this is something coming from the Al-Kimians who may be encouraging unrest, or from the vats themselves, but it's something we must protect against, correct?"

Max nodded slowly, trying not to let his face betray him. The whiskey he'd swallowed made his stomach burn, and he began to feel nauseous again. "I can see what you mean, I suppose. I mean it really does come down to the safety of the people of the Coalition." He shifted in his seat, realized he looked uncomfortable, and managed to smile. It felt greasy and slick on his face.

"Exactly. Remember, that's what we're here for. To save everyone, some... sacrifices must be made. You're a strong scientist, Max. I'd hate to lose you."

"You won't," Max stood, realizing it was time to go before he tipped his hand if he hadn't already. "Thank you, doctor."

"Of course," Balen replied.

Max felt Balen's eyes follow him all the way to the door. When he reached the cool hallway, he felt a sense of relief. He didn't know what he was going to do next, but the ACAS had to be stopped. That much was clear.

TWENTY-SIX

Tyce entered the galley before anyone else. He'd tried getting some sleep, but ended up reading Eira's report, fascinated at the differences between what he'd been taught and what Eira said had happened during the Mudar war. Even if the real events fell somewhere in between the Coalition's take and the Mudar records, it was still obvious that fear of the Mudar had been used to keep Coalition planets in line.

By the time he'd put his handheld down, it was after 0700. He went to the galley to make coffee, then realized they didn't have any on board. Beryl had said something about the local supplier being out of stock yesterday, but with the search of the ship they'd forgotten.

After the day they'd all had yesterday, he was pretty sure the crew would riot if they woke without some caffeine. So he pulled on his boots and got ready to go.

"Ru– er, Eira? I'm going out to get some coffee. If the crew wakes, let them know where I am."

"Yes, Tyce."

"And, er, watch out for them? I'm leaving them in your care," he said, as he grabbed his handheld and headed for the door.

"I promise, Tyce," she replied.

About thirty minutes later, Tyce returned to the *Loshad*, pausing as he saw a dark-haired man, dressed in a black coverall, standing near the ship.

"Can I help you?" he asked. Few people were in the dock area so early. He didn't like the idea of someone nosing around the *Loshad* and was immediately suspicious. The hair on his neck stood up as the pale man smiled at him, but he didn't show it.

"I was lookin' for Berth 234LD."

"You're on the wrong level. This is 234LA."

"Oh. Well, shit." The man gave him another easy smile and turned to go. Ty watched him with narrowed eyes. He didn't turn back to his ship until he'd seen the strange man turn a corner near the lifts and disappear. Feeling a sense of relief, Ty turned to the *Loshad* and began to put in the code for the ramp. Just as it began to lower, he saw a dark shadow in the corner of his vision. Before he could duck, a bright light exploded on the right side of his head and he felt like he was falling.

Putting an arm out, he caught himself on the ship and ducked a second blow.

He pulled his blaspistol, but his attacker had already leveled his gun. "Drop it," the man spat.

Ty raised his empty hand and the one with the blaspistol. "OK." He let go of the hand grip, allowing the gun to dangle by one finger in the trigger guard at arm's length as if he were going to drop it. Then he slung it at his opponent and leapt towards him at the same time.

The attacker shot his blaster into Ty's shoulder, but it didn't stop him. Ty's forward momentum pushed him into his opponent's chest and they both tumbled onto the metal ramp as the attacker's blaspistol went flying.

Punches rocketed back and forth as they wrestled across the floor. Each tumble brought them closer to the stranger's weapon. Ty could taste blood in his mouth; his lip was busted and he was dizzy from the head wound.

His attacker came back at Ty and pushed him over, slamming his head against the metal ramp. As Ty's head bounced off the deck, he saw a vat tattoo across the man's wrist. *A vat? Have the*

ACAS found us? The next punch slammed into his temple, causing his vision to blur. He felt himself beginning to lose consciousness, but he had to fight it. He wouldn't allow this killer onto his ship to hurt his crew.

There was a humming sound that Tyce didn't immediately recognize; he didn't have time. He brought his knee up and jammed it into his attacker's crotch. At the same time, the man folded down on top of him and punched him in the stomach, taking the wind out of him. As he pulled up, Ty felt a sickening warmth spreading in his belly as he caught the glint of a viblade in his attacker's hand.

Scalpel had been enjoying himself. He didn't usually allow himself that pleasure, but kicking the shit out of this nat was fun.

But the feeling was beginning to fade, because this nat simply refused to stay down, even with a viblade wound that he was going to bleed out from very quickly. Scalpel was surprised that the nat was able to still kick up and push him off.

As Scalpel regained his bearings, the nat heaved himself up with one hand, the other grabbing at his stomach, in a futile effort to keep what blood he could inside his body. He staggered toward the inside of the ship. "Eira! Seal the inner door."

Before whoever this Eira was could react, Scalpel was there again. With a guttural snarl he slammed back into the nat, throwing him to the ramp.

Ty could feel impacts against the middle of his back as he struggled to turn.

The first blow was deflected by his shoulder blade, but the last two hit home. There were more impacts to his spine, then he felt nothing. Everything faded away, smothered by a grey woolen shroud of unconsciousness.

* * *

"Hal. Wake up."

He came to in one fluid motion, sitting up and grasping her wrist in his hand. He looked at Vivi for two or three seconds, before his mind registered who she was. He looked around and realized that the emergency light was blinking and Runa – no, Eira – was speaking.

"Tyce is in combat with someone outside the ship," Eira said, "He needs immediate assistance."

Hal threw himself out of bed, cursing. He ran out of the room barefooted, after snatching Vivi's blaspistol from her nearby belt. "Stay here!" he called.

He hit the cargo bay at a full run. When he saw Tyce face down in a pool of blood and a man kicking him, his vision narrowed to a single field. He was reacting on adrenaline – moving without conscious thought. He shot Ty's assailant with Vivi's blaspistol, but never slowed. With a roar, he plowed straight into the dark-haired man, knocking him off the ramp and back onto the causeway. Dropping the pistol, his hands closed around the pale throat of his enemy and he held on, despite the punches he was taking to the chest.

Realizing he was being stabbed, he released the man's throat with one hand to grab the knife hand and try to wrestle it away. Blood covered both their limbs, but Hal managed to maintain his grip.

"Who are you?" he growled, slamming his attacker's hand back against the causeway until he let the viblade go. Hal caught a glimpse of the trademark bar lines and squares on his opponent's wrist. So. Another kill team from the Coalition. Somehow, they'd figured out where they were. It didn't matter. He was prepared for a fight to the death. And he was not going to lose. Tyce needed him. If he was still alive, he had to be saved. If Tyce was gone… well, vengeance was something worth dying for.

Vivi raced into the cargo bay. The first thing she saw was Ty, lying on the ramp in a pool of blood.

Further down, on the walkway, Hal grappled with a dark-haired man. He was getting punched in the face again and again, blood spurting everywhere. Her heart was thundering so loud she couldn't hear anything else as she lifted the blasrifle and pointed it toward Hal's attacker. She waited for a very clear shot; she'd never fired a rifle before, and her hands were shaking.

More by luck than judgement, the blast took the man in the shoulder, throwing him back onto the metal walkway. Hal was up immediately, leaping at his opponent.

Scalpel was getting pissed now. He hadn't anticipated there being such resistance, or he'd have popped an amp medjet beforehand, and now he was getting his ass handed to him by some second-rate old vat.

The nat was bleeding out on the ramp, but his vat crewmate had an ally somewhere who was handy with a blasrifle. Distracted briefly by the pain in his shoulder, Scalpel didn't see the vat's fist before it punched him so hard on the nose that his eyes watered and momentum sent him back to the ground, dazed.

Shaking his head harshly, Scalpel saw the vat staggering toward his discarded pistol. Playtime was over. He pulled his spare blaster from his belt, and started to pull the trigger.

And never saw anything again, as a blast from the rifle went through his skull at a phenomenal speed.

Vivi had been looking for an opening to shoot again, but Hal was constantly in the way. As he went for the blaspistol, it gave her a chance.

Her shot found its mark. Blood and brains spattered the cargo bay ramp behind the attacker. His body fell to the decking with a clunk.

Hal staggered forward a step, gasping for breath. His eyes fixed on her – impressed? Shocked? Disgusted? – then he pointed.

"Ty," he said simply, and he stumbled over to his best friend.

Vivi turned to see Beryl running down the ramp. "Fucking hells…" she uttered as she knelt beside Ty. Hal joined her, but Vivi took a moment to search the vat. She found his handheld and shoved it in her pocket before rejoining Hal and Beryl.

"People saw things," Hal said between pained gasps. "We have to go."

Vivi looked around and noticed a few people coming and going from the nearby ships. Two or three were staring and one was speaking into a comm.

Beryl looked up. "Hal, I can't take him like this. I need the backboard. In the back of the cargo hold." He ran into the ship without another word. Vivi watched as Beryl filled and administered two medjets. "Coagulant and blood stimulator," she murmured to herself.

After a moment, Hal returned with the board. "He's not moving. Beryl?" he asked, as he fell to his knees beside her.

Vivi fought hard against panicked tears. Seeing Ty down was like watching a sun go out. It was horrifying, but she couldn't tear her gaze away.

"Beryl!?" Hal said again, an uncharacteristic note of panic in his voice.

"He needs plasma. There's damage to his spine, and possibly his brain, so we need to get him on the backboard before we can move him." She glanced up and realized just how much blood covered Hal. "Oh my gods, Hal. How much of that is yours?"

He shook his head impatiently. "Some of it. Ty first. I'll live," he rasped out.

Vivi worked with Beryl to secure Tyce on the antigrav backboard, bracing his neck. They carried him aboard as Hal followed.

As soon as Beryl and Vivi were through the inner door and on their way to the medbay, Hal closed and secured the ramp. He turned, then fell to his knees, a wave of weakness overwhelming him. The ACAS had to be on their way by now. It was time to trust their new crewmember.

"Hey, Eira?" Hal said. "You need to get us outta here, beautiful. File a flight plan for anywhere… It doesn't matter – just get us gone!"

"Of course. I will handle it, Hal. Your life signs are unstable; you need medical attention."

"Yeah?" Hal's laugh was more like a groan. "I'll look into that." Hal turned to place his cheek against the cool metal of the cargo bay, taking deep breaths. The right side of his chest hurt every time he tried to inhale, so he pressed his hand against the worst of the cuts. One of the punctures had most likely collapsed part of his lung. "I hope… hope you're telling the truth about helping us."

"I am, Hal," she replied.

He passed out for a while, slumped against the wall until he felt a cool hand on his forehead.

"Hal. You with me?" It was Vivi.

"Yeah… resting a minute." He opened his eyes to see her green gaze. She was heartbreakingly beautiful. "Spring…" he slurred.

She looked confused with a hint of terrified. "What?"

"Your eyes. They're the color of spring-gems," he smiled as he spoke, feeling lightheaded. The good thing about being this far gone was that the pain was moving farther and farther away, out of his orbit. "They're green…" he tried to explain.

"Let's get you on your feet. I need to get you to the medbay."

"Yeah," he sighed, trying to pull himself up. It was hard and slow, but finally he was upright.

They staggered toward the medbay as the *Loshad* lifted off. "She did it," Hal said, leaning more heavily against Vivi. "I told her to file a flight plan to anywhere and get us the fuck… off… this… spinning… top. And she did. She did it. We escaped."

"So far. Keep moving, Hal. Can't have you bleeding out in the cargo bay."

"Doesn't matter, Veevs. Crew's safe." Hal passed out and his full weight fell into her. They both slumped to the floor. She pulled herself out from under him and tried to keep him awake.

"Hal," she shook him. "Hal, please. Please stay with me."

His eyes opened a fraction, and his voice was far-away, almost speaking by rote. "Primary function is to achieve the mission. Then protect. Protect the unit's nats, then vats." There was a cool hand on his forehead, and it brought him back to the worried face above him. Vivi was the nat he had to protect, he remembered. Vivi and Ty and Beryl. He gritted his teeth and got to his feet.

"OK, Hal. That's good. Come on."

Her words kept him focused as they staggered toward the medbay.

"He can't be dead, Veevs."

"Ty's in the medbay, Hal. Just a little further."

Hal fixed his eyes on the end of the hallway and gave it everything he had.

A minute later, Vivi practically dragged Hal into the medbay.

"Beryl. Hal's in and out… not making a whole lot of sense. I think he's lost too much blood." He almost slipped out of her arms, but she managed to keep him upright until she and Beryl could move him onto a bed.

Hal closed his eyes as he laid back. His breath came in strange shallow gasps. Beryl checked his fingernails, before she grabbed a medscanner. "His lung's partially collapsed," she said, not even looking at Vivi. "He's going into hypovolemic shock." She set the machine aside and began to rummage in the drawers and bins. "Oxygen first, then coagulant. Seal the wounds and blood stim," she said to herself as she began to gather supplies.

Vivi smoothed her hand over Hal's close-cropped blonde hair. His skin was on fire and was wet to the touch. "It's OK, Hal," she whispered. "You're going to be OK."

Beryl cut his T-shirt away. Blood had pooled on his skin, a wet crimson blanket that covered his chest.

"Vivi, get some gloves and clean this blood off of him so I can see where it's coming from."

Vivi nodded and sprang into action. Beryl gave Hal two medjets while Vivi began to work at Hal's chest with sterile wipes; one after the other came back sodden. She wrung them out like towels. As the pink skin started to show through, Vivi could see it was much worse than she thought. Slashes, slices, and punctures were everywhere. It seemed as if he barely had any skin left.

"Who was that bastard?" Beryl said as she began to seal the larger wounds.

"I don't know, but he was definitely a vat. I could see his tattoo, just before I shot him," She paused. "I… I shot him. I killed him, Beryl. I've never… never killed anyone before."

Beryl stopped what she was doing briefly to glance at Vivi. "I'm sorry, love. When it's you or them, you have to do what you have to do. To survive. Don't feel bad about it."

Vivi bit her bottom lip, then looked down as Hal groaned. His eyes were black holes as he blinked at her. "Did Ty make it?" He struggled to sit up, "Did he make it?"

"He's alive." Vivi put a restraining hand on his chest. "Rest, Hal."

Hal fell back, relieved, and he passed out again. Beryl started an IV. "They both need fluids, but Ty definitely needs the most. I've put him on synthplas for now… Eira, where are we headed?"

"Where would you like to be headed, Beryl?"

Vivi looked at Beryl. "Al-Kimia," the younger woman said.

Beryl nodded. "Yeah, Al-Kimia. They'll have facilities for Ty and Hal. We need to move at top speed, Eira."

"What is their current status?" Eira asked.

"Ty needs surgery for the injury to his spinal cord, treatment for a brain injury and real plasma or he might die. I can't do that on the *Loshad*. Hal should make it."

"I am making adjustments to the engines. We are now forty-eight hours from Al-Kimia at top speed."

"I'll keep them alive," Beryl said, refocusing on the job in front of them. "Just get us there, Eira."

TWENTY-SEVEN

Max looked up from his microscope to see his assistant, Carole, enter the clean room. "Dr Parsen. Got a new job for you from upstairs. It should be in your queue."

He scanned the file. "Who sent this?"

"Dr Balen. They said they need a hundred embryos by next week, to those specs."

"But this... it says to suppress all the FXG and JDA genes? They also want an inhibitor for LMM2. If we do that they're going to end up with... with a bunch of blanks. They'll just–"

"Do everything they're told to? Yeah, I think that's the idea, hotshot." Carole was a resentful, envious researcher at their facility. She'd worked on Chamn-Alpha for a while; she was a good researcher with shitty people skills, and so had never moved up the ranks. Max idly wondered what her genome looked like and realized her JDA genes were possibly just as inactive as the blanks'.

"Carole, don't you understand? This is setting us back sixty years! They won't be much better than Ivor Nash. Steljin found that increased personality markers make the vats more stable." He felt the same knot in his stomach that had been there all week, ever since that dead rook's eyes stared up at him from the floor. *What are you going to do?* they seemed to ask.

"Whatever. I think the new idea is that with no personality markers, no FXGs or JDAs, they might be able to keep them in service longer. Johnson's been working on this the last ten or fifteen years, and he still hasn't figured the damn thing out. They think you might be able to give it a new look. When you seal 'em up, be sure you double the accelerator strength. They want these quick." She raised an eyebrow disapprovingly and turned on her heel to go.

"Fine," Max said, sagging on his stool. He hesitated before focusing on the strands of DNA below him. There was only one option, only one road in front of him.

That weekend, Max made his way to Beruga City, one of the largest metroplexes on Chamn-Alpha. He tugged his knitted cap down over his ears, to protect them from the almost zero degree weather. The winters on Chamn-Alpha could be brutal. He had traveled to the city with one thing in mind: to purchase an untraceable pre-paid shredder comm, and he had plenty of scrill to do it.

He didn't want any trail back to him so he hoped that buying a pre-paid shredder comm at a store far from him would put anyone off the scent. It wasn't as if such devices were hard to find – anyone arriving from one of the outlying stations, such as Jaleeth and Omicron, needed to get one to use local comms efficiently.

The transaction was easier than he'd anticipated – he'd had fantasies of having to seek out a dive bar and find some lowlife who would drive a hard bargain. Instead five minutes after entering the store, Max had his shredder. In the doorway of a closed shop, he keyed in the number of the comm he wanted to reach and then typed a short message.

It's your friend from the university. Need to take you up on your offer. Have information about terminal potential that will greatly interest your partners but need immediate transportation off of C-A. Contact at this number.

Max sent the message to a former colleague before stowing the comm in the hidden pocket of his coat. A frigid wind had begun to blow from the north, and he wrapped his coat closer around him, grimacing at how the cold matched his mood.

By the time they reached Al-Kimian space, Hal was up and about, a function of his increased healing ability. He'd not moved from Ty's side until they passed the Border, when he reluctantly left the medbay in order to change out of his bloodstained clothes and take the captain's place on the bridge.

He'd tried several times to reach Captain Seren but received nothing back. Now he sat in Ty's chair for the approach to Al-Kimia.

"Hal, two Al-Kimian gunships are converging on our position," Eira said.

"OK, hold position, maneuvering thrusters only."

"They're sending a message."

"Open the channel."

"Unknown ship. You have breached the borders of Al-Kimian space. You will be escorted to the coordinates we are transmitting now. Do not deviate from the flight vector or we will blow you out of our sky."

"Great way to make a guy feel welcome, flight control," Hal replied. "We will follow your directives, no problem, but we have a medical emergency on board–"

"They have severed the connection," Eira said.

"Damn it," Hal swore. "Try to raise them again."

"No answer."

"Keep to their vector, Eira. Let's see how this goes."

Once the *Loshad* had set down, Hal got to his feet, wincing from the pain in his stab wounds.

"Are you alright?" Vivi asked. She'd joined him on the bridge as they descended towards the planet.

"Yep," he nodded and followed Vivi down to the cargo area.

He'd ordered Beryl to stay with Ty, promising to send medical assistance to her.

"Guess we're gonna see how good these new friends of ours are, Veevs."

In response, she grasped his hand and squeezed it tightly as they waited for the ramp to open.

When it did, they saw that over twenty soldiers had taken position in the hangar they had landed in front of, weapons ready.

"Come off the ramp," a soldier called. Vivi and Hal put their hands up and approached. Two soldiers went to Hal and patted him down, one went to Vivi and the fourth, a tall, thick-necked, muscled man, kept them under a gun. The rest of the soldiers stood ready.

"Look, we're clean," Hal said. "We're not looking for a fight."

"How many are on the ship?" the muscled man asked.

"Just the four of us," Vivi replied. "Our captain, Tyce Bernon, is injured and needs immediate medical attention. Our medic is with him now."

The tall man gestured, and five more soldiers ran into the *Loshad*. "Cuff these two and take them to the brig."

"Yes sir, LT."

Vivi turned to the tall man who was obviously in charge. "Wait – no! We are friends of Captain Jacent Seren. He told us to come here if we needed–"

"Hands off, asshole," Hal said as he shoved one of the soldiers who tried to cuff him, then laid him out with a punch. Five more took his place.

"Hal – don't!" Vivi called, as she allowed herself to be cuffed. She watched with a sinking heart as Hal took out another Al-Kimian with a kick to the face. With that, they all piled in and wrestled him to the ground. One soldier – an Al-Kimian by the flag on his uniform – raised a rifle butt and slammed it down on Hal's head. He went limp and the soldiers picked him up. "Got him, Lieutenant Jenkins," one of them said.

"We're not your enemies!" Vivi cried as she, too, began to be dragged away.

"That remains to be seen," the tall man named Jenkins said, watching her impassively. Vivi looked down to see a vat tattoo on his wrist and pips on his shirt, detailing his rank. "Bring both of them," he said to his troops.

"Please! At least get our captain medical care–" she pleaded.

He turned on his heels and began walking. "Bring them," he said, "the medic and captain, as well."

Leo Jenkins watched the security feed as the two women and the vat were thrown into separate cells in the brig. The vat was down in a heap on the floor where they'd dumped him. The younger woman was up, face pressed against the plasglass, trying to see. The older woman was across the way, standing quietly by the front of her cell.

"Have we heard anything from Seren?" Jenkins asked.

"No, sir. It's four days since Delta Base has heard from his ship, and we can't raise them on comms," Baleska replied from behind him. She had served with him in the ACAS and was as steady a vat as he'd ever known.

"How is their captain?" Jenkins asked.

"Critical. I've had him taken down to the medcenter for spinal surgery; docs said he might not make it."

"Captain's a vat too?"

"No. We ran the name: Tyce Bernon. Former ACAS. Natural born. What would you like me to do next, sir?" Baleska placed both hands behind her back, waiting.

Jenkins frowned. A group of natural borns, along with a vat, name-dropping the leader of the vat forces on Al-Kimia? This was strange. They had to be a crew from the ACAS, sent to infiltrate operations. He would need to question them himself. He couldn't risk the ACAS knowing what was going on behind the scenes.

"Give me an hour, then bring the younger woman to me in the interrogation room."

"Yes, sir."

Hal's head was throbbing. He sat up and looked around him, trying to put the pieces back together. They'd landed on Al-Kimia and been taken captive. Immediately, he felt his metabolism kick into overdrive at the threat of harm to Vivi, Ty, and Beryl. The pain from his head and all the wounds still healing after the fight with the vat on Jaleeth just faded into the background as he stood up. He began to pace his cell, then the adrenaline-fueled-anger boiled over, and he threw himself at the thick plasglass door. It held solid, but that just made him hit it again. Beryl appeared at the cell door across from him, drawn by the noise.

"Hey! Come on back you godsdamned sons-of-bitches! Fuck all of you!" He threw himself at the door again. Then he heard a familiar voice from the next cell.

"Hal!"

"Veevs?" he called, feeling relief.

"Yes. Are you OK?"

"Yeah. What about you?"

"I'm OK."

"Beryl?" Hal called.

"I'm fine, Hal," she replied. There was movement in the hallway as two guards walked past Hal's cell. They stopped in front of Vivi's, and her door slid open.

"Out," a female vat said, gesturing with her blasrifle.

"Where are you taking her?" Hal yelled as they walked past again. He struck the door so hard it shuddered as they walked by and out of the narrow hallway. "Godsdamn it! Where are you taking her!"

"It's OK, Hal," Vivi called, keeping her eyes on him as long as he was in view. "I'll be OK."

Hal hit the door again with his shoulder, growling low in his chest and feeling his frustration arc. He drew his hands through his hair and pulled. Not being able to take action made him even more agitated. He paced his cell back and forth before slamming the door once more. The pain was better than the anxiety of wondering what they were going to do with Vivi, so he threw himself at the door again.

Beryl called across the hallway. "You have to stop, Hal. You'll reopen your sutures. Focus on something and slow your breathing."

Hal slammed his fists into the door one more time with another growl of fury. Blood smeared the glass and dripped down. "Please, Hal," Beryl continued. "Remember what Ty taught you. Focus your mind on one thing and breathe slowly. Calm yourself. We can think our way out of this, but you have to be calm enough to try."

Hal was fully immersed in a rage-fueled rush, but he tried to do what Beryl was asking. He took long slow, deep breaths and focused his eyes on a spot of his blood on the door.

"That's good. Just breathe… slow and easy," Beryl murmured across to him encouragingly. "Just breathe… that's all you have to do."

The thundering blood in Hal's ears began to fade, as he leaned his forehead against the door. The drop of blood he was focusing on was perfectly round until it began to thicken at the bottom and then drip. He held his breath a moment more, then let out a long sigh.

"That's it," Beryl said.

"Where's Ty?" Hal asked, his voice hoarse with strain.

"They took him. One of the vats told me they were going to the medcenter. I'm sure they're helping him right now."

"OK," Hal said, finally looking up at her.

"Yeah," she nodded. "You're doing better. Sit down and rest, Hal. Let the rush pass, OK? It's what Ty would tell you to do. Be ready for whatever happens next."

He nodded, his hands dropping from the door. He slid down to the floor, putting his back against the right wall, and fixing his gaze on a dent across from him. His breathing continued to slow, and his heartbeat lowered as he sat and waited for something to change.

"How do you know Jacent Seren?"

Vivi looked up at the vat towering above her. "I… I didn't get to meet him, but our medic was a guest on his ship. She helped treat Seren and his soldiers."

"What did she treat them for?"

"Well, we were on a salvage mission, being attacked by the ACAS. We had the right permits and everything, but they just came for us. We were about to be blown to bits. Then Seren saved us." She watched the man's expression, trying to see if he was believing any of it. "They asked us for medical help after the battle. We helped them, then we left for Jaleeth Station. Tyce and Hal were attacked there again by someone else. We came here because we didn't know where else to go. Seren and Patrin said that we would be welcome–"

"I need your name and planet of origin."

"Vivian Valjean. Batleek is my home planet."

There was a knock at the door and the same dark-haired female that had released her from her cell entered the room.

"Talk to Seren and Patrin. They can tell you," Vivi pleaded.

"Seren's ship has been missing for four days." He stood and spoke quietly to the woman by the door, then Jenkins looked back at Vivi. "I will return. Someone will bring you something to eat and drink."

"Please – before you go, how is Tyce? Please tell me you're helping him."

"Our doctors are doing all they can. That's all I know. I'll be back." Jenkins stepped through the door and allowed it to shut behind him.

Baleska spoke to Jenkins as soon as the door was closed. "They've returned, sir," she said. "Seren and his crew… They're down at the docks right now."

"I'm on my way. Have someone bring food and water for the prisoners."

Jenkins was glad to hear that Seren and his crew were back. They would be able to get to the truth of the matter now.

"Yes, sir."

Vivi took another sip of water, then pulled at her cuffs, but they wouldn't budge. Tired of waiting, she stood up and walked around the room. There was a tiny window, about the width of her forearm, with opaque glass that was impossible to see out of. The door opened, and she turned to see that Patrin had entered the room. "I'm sorry, Vivi. We just got back," he said as he came over to her.

"Patrin?" She felt like crying with relief. "We came for help."

"I know. It's OK. Let me see your hands," he said.

As she extended them, he pressed his handheld to the cuffs, and they fell off. "Thank you," she said, rubbing at her wrists. "Hal and Beryl are in cells. I don't know where though."

"I'm sorry about that. Our long-range comms became damaged in the fight. We ran into another skirmish with the ACAS and were delayed returning here. I've got people heading to the cells right now. Let's go."

Beryl and Hal heard the door at the end of the hallway slide open. Hal stood up, hands on each side of the doorframe, waiting.

Lane, one of the vats that had stayed on the *Loshad*, appeared at his cell. "Well, didn't expect to see you again so soon, Cullen. You look like shit if you don't mind me saying." She tapped at the door panel. It slid open.

"Your buddies weren't all that friendly, Lane," he said, exiting the cell.

"Yeah, well, we've got enemies, and it pays to be careful. We got caught up at the Border. Let me see your hands."

Hal did as instructed, and she deactivated his cuffs. “Why’d they send you?” Hal asked.

“I was the only one with the balls to come in here and let you out,” she grinned. “Me and Orin, that is.”

Orin had fetched Beryl from her cell, and they both came over. “You OK?” she asked, examining his injured hand.

“Yeah,” Hal nodded. “Where’s Vivi?”

“I… I’m not sure. She was being interrogated,” Lane said.

“I’m going to find her.” Hal broke away from them and headed for the door.

“Wait, I’ll comm them,” Lane offered.

Hal stepped out; in one direction he saw a few soldiers, looking nervously back at him. Then he turned.

“Hal?”

She was close enough to touch. “Veevs,” he said, taking her face in his hands. He scanned her for signs that she’d been mistreated. “You OK?”

She nodded. “You?”

“I’m good.” He held her close a moment, then remembered they had an audience. He looked to Patrin and frowned. “Where’s my captain?”

“In the medcenter, brother. Come with me.”

TWENTY-EIGHT

The medcenter took up six bottom floors in the same building they'd been held in. Hal and everyone else followed Patrin into the lift. As it sped down, Hal looked over at Vivi and the fingers of his good hand brushed the palm of hers. She took hold gratefully.

The doors slid open and they walked out onto a hospital floor. Patrin went to the desk and spoke with a woman who looked something up on a handheld.

"This way," Patrin directed them.

They made their way down several hallways to patient rooms. A tall brown-haired man was standing sentinel near one, with only one guard as company. Vivi didn't recognize the big man, but Hal and Beryl stepped forward when he offered his hand.

"Hal. Beryl. It's good to see you, but not under these conditions."

"Vivi, this is Captain Seren," Beryl said.

"Vivi." Seren took her offered hand and shook it. "There is a waiting room here." He led them two doors down to a small area with couches and chairs. He started to say something, but instead began coughing immediately.

Vivi's eyes went wide as she saw the familiar lines and squares of a tattoo on his wrist. "I am sorry you're not well," she said softly, realizing that he was at least thirty-five, if not older.

"It's nothing. My time is simply running short," he managed, taking a labored breath. When he had recovered, he began speaking again. "Your captain suffered great damage. Our medical team worked on him as soon as you arrived. They have repaired the damage as much as they could, and they believe he'll survive, but that's all they're sure of right now. I'm sorry."

"Where's his room?" Hal asked.

"Two doors up the hallway." Seren gestured in the direction.

Hal squeezed Vivi's hand and said, "I'll be back."

She moved to follow, but Seren caught her arm. "Give him a minute," he said gently.

"May I speak with his physician?" Beryl asked.

"Come on, we'll find him," Patrin said.

Vivi sat back down next to the big man. "Hal was hurt in the attack, too," she said softly.

"We will make sure a doctor looks Hal over," Seren said.

"Thank you," Vivi said gratefully.

"You are fond of him."

She nodded.

"Good. They say that when a vat has connections to others, he may outlive even biology for a time."

"Has it… helped you?"

Seren smiled. "I am thirty-seven, so I suppose so."

"It's… it's just not fair. What they did to you and the other vats wasn't right. Most of those on the Inner Spiral… they have no idea. *I* had no idea…" Vivi thought again about how naive she'd been, about almost everything.

"One day, they will," Seren said, before changing the subject. "Vivi… It's very hard for someone like Hal to lose a commander. For now, you have to keep your focus on him while Tyce is down." Seren looked toward the door. "He's going to need your help to keep him on the right path, so he doesn't self-destruct."

"Do you… um… know that from experience?"

He nodded. "When my first commander was killed, I struggled with it. He was a good man, too. Like your Captain Bernon."

"Oh," she nodded.

"Go on," Seren gestured toward the door. "He will need you now."

* * *

People always looked frail in medbeds, Hal thought, as he stood at the door a moment before going in.

Ty's dark hair was inky against the white sheets of the bed. He was strapped down securely. The neckbrace they'd had him in on the *Loshad* had been replaced by something even more confining that kept his head completely immobile.

Hal walked across the room and pulled up a chair beside his captain. He sat down, refusing to groan as his bruised muscles and lacerations complained. "Everyone made it OK," he said softly. "I know you'd want to know that." He reached out and laid a hand on Tyce's forearm. "We came to Al-Kimia. I hope that was right. We thought the ACAS would be after us, but they're not. I can't explain it."

He looked down at Ty's hand. An IV line was funneling a light blue substance into his blood. A sedative, or an antibiotic. How many times had he sat at Ty's medbed, watching the struggle between life and death? Five? Ten? He'd lost count. How many times had Ty been at his own bedside when he'd woken up from some injury or other? Definitely more than ten. But he was there. Every time.

Hal could think of so many times that Ty had done things unconventionally, bent the rules so that the men under his command could make it out OK. Tyce had always tried to adjust strategy to limit the number of casualties his unit would have, when other commanders would just send vats in to be slaughtered without a care at all. *Don't worry so much about casualties. They'll send you twenty more that look just like them,* he'd heard them say to Ty.

Ty was different. He cared. There were many times that Hal had sat with him by the bedside of another vat so that the injured man didn't have to wake up alone and in pain in an unfamiliar medbay.

That was Ty. Always making sure everyone made it out OK.

Hal didn't know what to call the feeling that swept over him. It was like the waves the first time he'd seen an ocean on Dalamar, pushing and pulling him in opposite directions. Was it loyalty, he wondered as he bowed his head. They talked a lot about that in the training he'd received as a vat – of how loyalty and obedience to the ACAS came first, so much so that Hal had always linked the two in his mind. But he was beginning to think that maybe loyalty was very different than obedience. Obedience meant you did what they told you because they made you, but loyalty couldn't be demanded. It was given. Given to someone like Tyce.

"You wouldn't believe it, Cap, but Vivi saved both of us. She shot the vat with a blasrifle. A freakin' blasrifle, Ty. That Veevs... she's a keeper."

Ty's face showed no reaction. His eye and cheek were bruised a dark purple. One hand and almost his entire stomach was bandaged.

"Tyce, I just... I want you to know that whatever happens, I'll be here for you. You just... you gotta make it."

Hal looked up to see Vivi in the doorway. "He's asleep," she noted softly.

"Yeah. Don't even know why I'm talking. He can't hear me."

Vivi nodded. "He can. My mother... She was in a coma after her shuttle crashed on Batleek. She was a teacher of literature at a university on Carathas, the next planet over, and she used to commute back and forth each week. But anyway, while she was unconscious, we stayed by her bedside and read chapters of her favorite book to her, to keep her company. When she woke, she said she heard us. The whole time."

He was looking at her strangely. "Your mom. She came through OK?"

Vivi nodded. "Yeah." She moved to pull a chair by his side.

They sat quietly for a moment.

"What's it like?" Hal asked.

"What?"

"Having a mother?"

"Oh..."

The only people Hal had had in his life as a rook were training officers, teachers, scientists, and one psychologist from time to time. After four years, they'd put him into a boot camp, where he'd gotten his first taste of being in the ACAS. A year of training in different areas, and he had become a full-fledged soldier, the only thing he'd ever wanted to be. He wondered fleetingly if that had been programmed into him as well. Would he always be limited by what they'd put in his head?

"It was good, I guess. She and my father were always there, guiding me and supporting me until... well, until I met a guy they didn't approve of. Then, things kind of broke down between us. But they were right. He was a bad person."

"This guy, he's the one who hurt you?" Hal asked softly. "The one who made those bruises?"

"Yeah." Her eyes darted to his. "I was stupid."

"You're not stupid, Veevs."

"I was." She looked down at her feet, then sighed heavily. "But my mom and dad. They're good people. They watched out for me when I needed it."

"Like Ty," Hal said to himself.

"Yeah," she nodded. "A lot like that."

As they sat, he glanced down at his hands, which in turn drew her attention there. He'd hurt his hand again.

"You're hurt. You need to be seen by a doctor."

"No, I'm good." He looked at Ty. "Gotta be here when he wakes up."

"Hal, what would Ty tell you to do if he was awake?"

Hal looked up at her, weighing her words. He sighed and got to his feet. "He would say to get checked out."

"Good, then. Come on," she said simply.

Knowing they didn't want to be far away from Tyce, Patrin arranged for the *Loshad* crew to have the room across the hall. Hal almost fell asleep during the medical exam, so when Beryl told him to stay in the bed in the room they'd been given, he didn't fight her. She left to stay with Tyce, leaving Vivi and Hal alone.

Vivi sat back in the chair beside the medbed. The exam had

revealed that in addition to bruising and lacerations, Hal was dehydrated, with two broken knuckles and a broken metacarpal on his left hand. They'd used a bone knitter on him, and after giving IV fluids, they'd sent him back to rest.

He was looking at her now, in that dazed way that said that unconsciousness was not far off.

"You can sleep up here," Hal said.

"You won't rest as well," she replied. "I'm all good right here. You need me, just call."

"Did you change your mind, then? About us?" he asked softly.

"No." She shook her head, leaning forward to take his hand. "Not in the least, Hal."

He sighed with relief. "C'mon then." He moved over in the bed. "I won't sleep well unless I know where you are."

She watched him for a long moment, then smiled and crawled up onto the bed with him. "You're so tired you'd sleep anywhere." She faced him and took his uninjured hand in her own.

"Just as long as it's where you are," he said with a smile, eyes finally slipping closed.

"I'm here," she said, smoothing a hand over his hair.

After Patrin got the *Loshad* crew settled, he made his way back to the joint headquarters, shared by both vats and Al-Kimians. It was cold and he detected a hint of snow in the air as he made his way across the breezeway. The vat facility he'd come from on Haleia-6 was situated in a desert. It never saw snow, so any time Patrin got to see a snowfall he was happy about it. The way the snow fell soundlessly, turning the world from its normal drab colors into something frosted and wonderous never failed to amaze him.

He knew that the natural born children liked snow, as well, but most of the nat soldiers on Al-Kimia just grumbled about it.

When he reached the headquarters, he was waved through by the guards. Patrin was well-known among both vats and Al-Kimians. When he and Seren had begun their "harassment" of

ACAS ships past the Border, they'd caught the attention of the Al-Kimians who had extended an offer to supply them. Over a period of two years, Seren's crew had run covert missions and sold intelligence for rations, air, and fuel.

It had taken time, but after a meeting with First Minister Amias Adara, Seren had made the decision to join them. They had been promised citizenship and a place in society if they would ally themselves with the Al-Kimians against the Coalition if and when war came.

And so they'd become recruiters, finding released vats that were searching for a place to be and persuading them to join Al-Kimia in order to strengthen their military.

The Al-Kimians had kept their word so far. Even though hostilities with the ACAS had not risen to the point of open war, the First Minister knew it was coming; it was just a matter of time. And so, Al-Kimia had begun to welcome more and more vats from the Edge. Over time, their warships began to take on a mixture of vat and natural-born soldiers. Many vats had been promoted to officer positions. Some of the Al-Kimians had even begun calling vats "brothers" and "sisters." It was almost like being in the ACAS again, feeling that sense of belonging. Except this time, Patrin had made the choice to serve, in order for vats to always have somewhere to belong.

He found Seren in a conference room with one of the Al-Kimian captains named Jacobs, and he waited for acknowledgement. Eventually, Seren gestured for him to speak.

"Yes, Patrin," he said.

"Captain Seren, the crew of the *Loshad* is settled for the night."

"Very good. Have a seat."

"Yes, sir. Good evening, Captain Jacobs." The older man nodded in response as Patrin took a seat beside him.

Seren turned to his protégé. "You remember when we evacuated the two ACAS doctors a few months ago? Well, one of the doctors got a message from a friend of theirs who works in biotech at the vat facility on Chamn-Alpha."

Captain Jacobs threw the message up as a hologram. It read:

It's your friend from the university. Need to take you up on your offer. Have information about terminal potential that will greatly interest your new partners but need immediate transportation off C-A. Contact at this number.

"So, we have a vat researcher who wants to turn over information to us?"

"Yes," Jacobs said. Patrin trusted the old captain. He had been a smuggler a long time, and he'd been invaluable at helping their vat fleet stay incognito while converting civilian spacecraft to gunships. "We just have to find someone to pick him up."

"The *Hesperus* is out of commission right now. We took damage in the last fight and won't be ready for a while. All our other frigates are out on resupply missions or undercover," Seren mused.

"My ship's hot right now. We need a repaint and repair of external damage," Jacobs said. "What about that J-class that pulled in? The *Loshad*? Put a couple of vats on there, get a few Al-Kimians to fly to Chamn-Alpha as a supply ship. Vats could get off, get into the facility or his quarters with some false identification, and pick up this guy. Be back before dinner."

"Nothing's ever that easy," Patrin scoffed.

"You just have no faith, son," Jacobs said with a grin, giving him a shove. "Hell, I'll even fly it."

Seren coughed a little before he spoke. "No. The *Loshad* has not joined the cause yet. Their captain is in critical condition in the medcenter next door."

"Commandeer the thing," Jacobs shrugged.

Seren shook his head. "No, I will not commandeer their ship."

"Then ask them nicely," Jacobs offered.

"That, I can do, my friend, but it can wait until tomorrow. If you can get in touch with this researcher, tell him to sit tight. Someone will be coming, even if I have to hold the *Hesperus* together with my bare hands to fly it there."

Hal woke up and looked around. There was a small light on above him and another one on in what he assumed to be the bathroom. The window revealed the darkness outside, as swirls of white snowflakes played around the frame.

He sat up and rubbed at his face. He was hungry again; a sign that his body was working overtime to heal the damage he'd suffered. "Veevs?" he called as he swung his legs over the side of the bed.

There was no answer. He stood up, then glanced around and into the bathroom. No one. He stepped outside the door, and saw Vivi standing near Ty's room, talking with Beryl. When she saw him holding onto the door for support, she came over. "Hal? How are you feeling?"

"OK. I'm up and around," he said, looking her up and down with clear eyes. She'd changed her clothes, and he needed to do the same. "Gonna grab a shower."

The water was hot and he let it massage away the knots in his back for longer than he realized. When he cut the water and began to towel off, he heard a noise at the door. "You good?" Vivi called.

"Yeah, getting out now." Hal pulled on the clean clothes he'd found in the bag and made his way out.

She was sitting on the bed, smiling at him. "You clean up well."

"Nah, I look like someone ran me down with a heavy lifter," he grinned, "But thanks."

There was a knock at the door as Hal sat on the bed, trying to lace his boots. With his braced hand there was no way he could do it alone.

"Come in," Vivi said, kneeling down to help Hal.

"There's food for us in a room down the hall. Captain Seren would like to see us," Beryl said.

"I need to see Ty first," Hal said. When Vivi finished, he got up, walked to the open doorway and stood there watching Ty's room in silence. "He's still the same, Beryl?"

"Yeah, Hal. He's still the same," Beryl said. "But right now, that's a good thing."

Max finished up his work for the day, sealing the last embryo in the final exowomb. These bags were small, about the size of a one year-old. In a couple of months, someone else would use special tools to implant the interface into their brains. Then they would be rebagged and grown until they were ready to be "born" into a life of servitude.

The whole process, with the growth accelerator, took about four years, but these would be ready in two. When "born," all vats were effectively twelve years-old physically and developmentally. For simplicity's sake, the ACAS calculated a vat's age from twelve whether it had taken them four years or two years to grow. How many thousands of vats had he been in contact with over the years? He looked down at the tiny lives in the artificial wombs in the incubators in front of him and spoke softly. "Good luck."

He'd given them a good chance. Against his orders, he'd activated not only the personality genes, but genes that influenced leadership ability and intelligence. He'd even activated the genes that influenced independence, which upstairs regularly wanted suppressed. It was not a guarantee that all these qualities would manifest themselves, of course, but it would give them a better than normal chance to survive and realize what was being done to them. And then fight back.

It was the best he could do.

As he cleaned up the workstation, he hoped that he would hear something back from his contact. He'd been waiting for two days and was finding it hard to wait longer. If there was nothing on the shredder handheld when he got home, he would try to reach them one more time. If not, he'd have to find his own way off this rock.

"The target is one of the senior scientists that work on vat DNA at the Chamn-Alpha facility," Captain Seren said. "He's been there a number of years."

Beryl glanced over at Hal. They'd been listening to Seren while they ate, but when he mentioned Chamn-Alpha, Hal tensed and put down his fork.

"And why do we need to save this guy's ass again?" Hal asked. "Just because he asked us to?"

"He's sent two messages to us. He claims there is some sort of superweapon being developed at C-A designed to work specifically against vats, and he wants out. He will bring us what he knows."

"Superweapon?" Hal asked.

"That's all we know," Seren said. "But almost all of our ships are out on patrol. A J-class cargo ship like the *Loshad* would be perfect for this mission." He held Hal's gaze. "I'm asking if you will help us evacuate this researcher. He holds information that could be vital to all released vats."

Hal glanced to Beryl. She gave him a subtle nod, and he shifted his gaze to Vivi.

"It's your decision, Hal," Vivi said. "Whatever you choose to do, I'll back your play."

"You helped us with Ty, so I owe you," Hal said, shifting his focus back to Seren.

"No, brother," Seren said. "We would have helped your captain regardless, after what your crew did for us. If you agree to this, we will be the ones in your debt."

"Beryl, you have to stay with Ty, so someone's there when he wakes up," Hal told her.

She nodded, "I will."

"Veevs... you can... I mean, you can sit this one out if..." Hal began.

"Just try to make me stay back," she said.

He gave a small smile and nodded. "Alright, Seren. We'll do it."

"I will send Lane and Orin with you," Seren said. At Hal's nod, he went on. "It's your ship, so you're in charge of the mission. I will set up a meet time and location and resupply the *Loshad*. Give us a couple of days to set everything up."

"Perfect. Hal can use the time to heal up," Beryl said.

"Good, then." Seren stood up heavily and swayed a little.

"You alright there?" Hal asked.

"I will be. It has been a very long day. Thank you… all of you."

TWENTY-NINE

Vivi made her way into the back of the *Loshad*, heading for Beryl's quarters. They had spent the day getting the ship outfitted for the journey to Chamn-Alpha. Hal had described it to her as home of one of the largest vat facilities. It was, in fact, the very place Hal had been born.

She was unsure how she'd handle seeing the facility that had made Hal to all intents and purposes a slave to the wishes of the ACAS. The idea of him having to walk back in there made her feel physically ill.

"Did you need me for something, Beryl?" Vivi asked as the door to the medic's room slid open.

"Hmm? Oh, Vivi. I did. Come in." Beryl was by her footlocker but stood up when Vivi approached. A medkit was in her hand. "I want you to have this in case you need it." Beryl unzipped the bag and took out a medjet with a blue label. "Now if Hal has an episode like that first one, you need to know what to do. Talk him down, but also use the sedative, if what he's saying or doing seems like it's on repeat."

"OK," she nodded nervously.

"If he doesn't ramp down, you can use it up to three times. It's not going to hurt him," Beryl said. "He'll just sleep a bit longer."

She nodded again.

Beryl took out a different medjet with a red label. "This is amp. It's what Hal was on during that cage fight. There's three medjets in here, and more in the medbay, if you need it. We try not to use much of this. But, if things get rough and he needs it or one of the others needs it, you'll know. No more than one dose every six hours."

The idea of having to use any of these on Hal or anyone else made her worry. She took a shaky breath as Beryl went on and took out a different medjet with a black label. "If you use the amp, this is the neutralizer. If a vat on amp doesn't get this as he comes off the rush, he'll get muscle cramps so badly he'll be unable to move, fight or defend himself. You don't want to see that. Trust me."

Vivi nodded slowly. "I understand."

"Good." She zipped up the bag and handed it to Vivi.

Vivi nodded, not knowing what to say and feeling a little scared. How would Hal react being so far away from his anchors? Would she be enough to bring him back? She swallowed hard. "Thanks, Beryl. I'll just go stow this."

She had almost reached her room when she saw Hal step out from his quarters into the hallway. He was dressed in his typical grey tee with black fatigue pants and boots.

"Hey."

"Hey, yourself."

His gaze fixed on the kit. "Beryl's, right?"

"Y- Yeah?" Her heart seemed to pause on the edge of a beat.

"It's a good thing, Veevs. If I have an episode, you do what you gotta do. Put me down."

"What?"

"You know, if I wake up acting strange… It's OK to put me down for the night."

"Oh, right. Hal… I…"

"It's OK, Veevs. I trust you." He pulled her into a quick embrace, then let her go. "Gotta go switch out the ship's weapons." And with that, he was gone down the hallway.

Hal trusted her. She wouldn't let him down.

"Vivi," Eira said.

"Yeah, Eira?" She paused, glancing up at the comm speaker.

"Tyce has an alarm set for Hal's episodes. Would you like me to continue it?"

"What do you mean?"

"If Hal leaves his room in the middle of the night, Tyce is supposed to be awakened. Should I wake you instead?"

Vivi nodded. "Yes, Eira. That would be great."

"You have changed your sleeping patterns since Jaleeth," Eira observed. "Is this to prevent Hal from having an episode?"

"Um... not exactly," Vivi said.

"More information is needed to understand," Eira said.

"Eira, it's hard to explain. I- I'm fond of Hal. Becoming more fond of him each day. We've started spending more time together because of that. That's why our 'sleeping patterns' have changed."

"You are what humans call in love."

"Maybe," Vivi said. "But it takes time for things like that to happen." She wasn't sure that Eira would or could understand. "How did you know about being in love?"

"I have studied your entertainment feeds when learning your language. It is a frequently visited theme."

"Yes. Yes, it is." Vivi nodded.

"When will we leave for Chamn-Alpha?" Eira asked.

"This evening," Vivi replied. "After we say goodbye to Beryl and Ty."

"Then Tyce has awakened from his stasis?" Eira said. Hal had been on the ship last night and Eira had asked about Tyce. Vivi knew Hal had explained Tyce's condition to the Mudar, who seemed concerned. He'd also explained the reason for their trip to Chamn-Alpha.

"No, not yet." Vivi answered. "Hopefully soon, though. Maybe even by the time we return."

"I am interested in speaking with Tyce again," Eira said.

"Yeah. Me too," Vivi said with a sigh.

* * *

"Here's the vat's handheld." Vivi handed it to Beryl who had taken up her vigil at Ty's bedside. It had been two days since they arrived on Al-Kimia, and he was still in a coma. Beryl had checked with Ty's doctors earlier that day and found that he was expected to be brought out of it as soon as his vitals were stable.

"I don't have time to break the encryption on the ACAS's device, but maybe Seren has someone that could." When she'd cleaned off the blood earlier, she couldn't help but think of the pale angry face that she'd seen through the scope when she'd killed the man standing over Hal. It kept coming back at the strangest of moments and caused a shiver to run through her each time.

Beryl nodded, taking the handheld. "I'm sure he does. I'll take care of it." She set it to the side and stood. "Now, you be careful out there," she said, wrapping her arms around Vivi. "I know you're not some green tyro just arriving into the Edge for the first time, but watch your back, OK? And more importantly, watch out for Hal."

"I will," she said, hugging back.

"Good. I know you will anyway," she smiled at Vivi, "but humor an old woman. It doesn't work if I don't say it out loud."

Vivi smiled gently, understanding. She looked down at Ty's sleeping form one more time. He didn't look worse, but he didn't look much better either. She would just have to be happy he kept breathing steadily. She squeezed his hand and sent him all her hopes that he would be alright. "Take care of this guy," she murmured.

"You bet," Beryl nodded.

There was movement by the door and they both looked up to see Hal. "Everything's ready to go, Veevs," he said, coming over to Beryl. "You know I wouldn't leave him with anyone else."

"Oh, I know that."

"Tell him I didn't want to go, but I knew what he would want me to do."

"He'll understand." She wrapped him in a one-armed hug. "Come back safe."

Hal nodded as he hugged her back.

Vivi was standing in the doorway when he turned to her. "Ready?"

He took one last look at Ty, then nodded. "Yeah. Let's do this."

Max slipped his most recent batch of gene-altered embryos into the incubator; finished for the day, he began to clean off his workstation when Dr Balen entered the room.

"Max. How goes the work on the accelerated generation?"

"Great. Just finished a tray."

"Let's see."

"No problem." Max nodded and slipped the last tray out, placing it on the lab table. He managed to remain cool enough to hide his pounding heart.

Balen took a syringe to one of the exowombs, drew out some fluid and then slipped it into the microanalyzer. Max was fairly sure that the doctor had chosen one of the embryos that he'd modified to the right specs, but he could be wrong.

"Nice job," Balen said, handing the tray back.

"Thank you," Max said, setting it back into the giant incubator. When Balen had gone, he would take these to storage and stow them with a few thousand other vats.

"Well, keep up the good work." Balen made his way to the door. "And Max, I'm glad you realized what we were trying to do here. We'd rather have you with us than the alternative."

Max nodded. "Of course, Dr Balen."

"Eira, I'm going to let you handle navigation. I need you to plot a standard course to Chamn-Alpha. Use the regular shipping lanes so we don't draw attention," Hal said as he settled into Ty's station and began procedures for lift off. "Remember, our guests don't know you're anything beyond a standard shipboard computer." Before leaving they'd discussed making sure that Eira didn't do or say anything to give away her status when the others were around.

"Yes, Hal," she responded.

Lane and Orin were getting situated in Vivi's quarters. She'd volunteered to let them stay in her room, asking Hal if it was OK if she continued sleeping in his room. He'd smiled and told her he had been hoping she'd say that.

"Is Tyce still in stasis?"

Hal stopped what he was doing and looked toward the display where Eira's voiceprint line was. "Yeah, Eira. He's not been conscious yet. Beryl's staying with him. The Al-Kimians are taking good care of him."

"Your voice shows anxiety."

Hal took a deep breath. "Yeah, I guess it does. He was hurt pretty badly." He returned his attention to lift off. "You're worried about him too," Hal remarked.

"I am concerned," she admitted.

That evening, everyone gathered together over dinner. "We should strategize how we're going to do this," Hal began. "We have to pick up a guy named Max Parsen. The Al-Kimians got a picture of him from somewhere. Put it up on screen, Eira." He gestured toward the feed display. It showed a pretty nondescript picture of a guy in a lab coat; it looked similar to an ID badge picture.

"So, this is the ACAS doctor?" Lane asked.

Hal nodded. "He's stationed at the Chamn-Alpha facility." He glanced to Lane and Orin. "Anyone familiar with it?"

They shook their heads. "We're from the Haleia-6 facility," Lane said, gesturing to herself and Orin.

"Got it." Hal nodded. "I'm from C-A. We shouldn't have to go onto the base, which makes this pickup simpler, but it's good to know the area. Our cover is that we're carrying a load of medical supplies to Beruga City. That gives us a good reason to be in the spaceport. As far as this scientist goes, we have a couple of choices.

We can pick him up at his residence or have him meet us in the spaceport or the city center. Any thoughts on that?"

Orin signed to Lane a few moments, and Hal and Vivi waited for Lane's translation.

"Orin says that it would draw less attention for him to meet us in a public place. I agree."

Hal glanced to Vivi who nodded. "We should pick him up in the spaceport."

Lane's reaction was to roll her eyes. "But Beruga spaceport will have more surveillance than a city center would."

"We would be closer to the ship, however, if we meet him in the spaceport," Vivi pointed out. "And the crowd would also make it harder for surveillance to track him."

Hal thought a moment. "You both make good points. They probably won't be tracking him, but if they are, I'd rather be closer so we could escape. If we get found out, speed will be a major advantage."

"Fine," Lane huffed, blowing a strand of hair out of her face and turning back to her dinner.

Hal caught Orin's gaze. He raised an eyebrow and Orin shook his head. *Don't push it,* he seemed to say.

After dinner, Vivi went to the bridge for some routine monitoring of the ship. Things were looking good; engine efficiency was up by twenty percent and they were staying on course for Chamn-Alpha. "Eira? Can you handle everything tonight?" she asked.

"Yes, Vivi," came the Mudar's reply. "I will continue to work on the engines as well."

"Thank you, Eira."

"I was monitoring your discussions about the plan and I realize the surveillance in the spaceport is an issue," Eira continued. "I may be able to use my nanites to assist when the time comes."

"Really?" Vivi smiled. "That would be great. I'll tell Hal. Let us know if you need us on the bridge."

"Of course."

"Thanks, Eira." Vivi left and made her way to the common

room, finding Hal and Orin engaged in a game of squads. Lane was sitting nearby, watching them.

"Who's winning?" Vivi asked, as she took a seat near Lane.

"Cullen. I have never seen anyone play as well as he does," Lane said with interest. "This is their third game."

"Ty said that Hal rarely loses a game." She watched Hal make a move that caused Orin to grin and shake his head ruefully.

"Do you play?" Lane asked.

"Hal's teaching me," she said, feeling defensive and trying not to show it.

Lane hmphed, giving Vivi a look from head to toe.

"OK, out with it. What's your problem with me?" Vivi asked.

"I've known few nats well, but you are the first I've ever seen to involve themselves in a relationship with a vat. If you don't mind me asking, what are you looking for? Tell me, is Cullen just a good story to tell your friends back home? Or is he just good in bed?" she challenged.

Vivi took a breath before she answered. "That's none of your business," she replied coolly. It was obvious now what Lane thought of her. Ty said vats were rough around the edges, but Lane was outright hostile.

Lane tilted her head, considering. "Very well, but what do you hope for? Cullen only has five, maybe six, years left. There's no possibility of children – which, I hear, most nats long for. So I'm puzzled. What can you hope to gain from your relationship with him?"

"Children?" She wasn't interested in having children, not now or ever that she knew of, but she hadn't been aware that vats couldn't have children.

"All vats are engineered to be sterile," Lane replied.

She tried not to look too shocked. "I… I don't want children anyway, and I don't care how long he has. Six years or one month, doesn't matter. As long as we care about each other and make each other happy for the time we have."

Lane stared her down a moment, then glanced at Orin, who was watching the squads' board intently as Hal made a move. After a moment, she spoke. "Perhaps we do understand each other, then. More than I first thought."

Lane's tough expression softened so much as she looked at Orin that Vivi asked the obvious question. "You and Orin are together?"

The vat nodded. "Since his injury. We were in the infirmary together. They considered terminating him, but I convinced my commander not to."

"Terminating him? Oh my gods…" She tried to imagine pleading for Hal's life in such a way, and suddenly she had a whole new understanding for Lane's hostility against someone natural born. She sat back, lowering her voice as she asked what happened to him.

"He was attacked by some rebel insurgents on Stendal," Lane said after a moment. "He was injured and the rebels tried to rip out his interface when his nat captain left him behind. We were the next unit through the area. We found him and took him to the medbay on our ship. The damage to his implant left him unable to hear or speak."

"I'm sorry."

"Yeah." She smiled as she saw Orin look up at them and motion with his hands. She replied with quick hand signs and a small laugh. "I found information on the feeds, then taught him sign language in our spare time. They assigned him to me in the ship's engineering department."

"Is there any way to repair his hearing?" Vivi asked.

"No. Pulling parts of the interface out damaged his auditory nerve pathway and the language centers of his brain. Have you ever seen an interface and its nodes? It branches through a vat's brain like a tree. It grows with you and can never be removed."

Vivi bowed her head, not knowing what to say. She couldn't help but think of the scar on Hal's temple.

"Do not make the mistake of assuming Orin is stupid, though. His *thinking* wasn't damaged. He just has his troubles communicating."

"It's good that he has you," Vivi said.

"I'd say the same for Cullen. I can see he's very fond of you." Again, Lane gave her an appraising look. "Maybe, I was too hasty to judge." Orin began to sign to Lane, and she called out to Hal. "Cullen. He's saying that you play very well; the best player he's faced. He bets you were hell on the battlefield."

Hal shrugged. "Tell him my captain taught me, so he gets the credit."

She relayed his words, then translated Orin's reply. "He says he hopes Tyce recovers well."

"Yeah," Hal replied, putting away the board. "Me too."

THIRTY

There was a beeping coming from somewhere. Ty tried to ignore it and fall back into the blanketlike sleep he'd been in, but it continued in regular annoying intervals.

"Runa, turn off the alarm," he tried to say, but his voice was a paper whisper. He was thirsty, and his head ached horribly. That was weird. He didn't remember drinking too much last night, but he felt like he had a hangover.

He opened his eyes and saw an unfamiliar ceiling above him. He tried to sit up but couldn't move. Was he a prisoner? The beeping began to increase with his heartrate. He couldn't look down at his body, his head was strapped into something that kept his gaze on the ceiling, and he could feel cool metal across his forehead. Jerking at his hands, he felt straps holding them as well. He tried to kick his feet but couldn't.

"Hey… Let me out of this!" he yelled, his voice gravelly and rough.

There were the sounds of running feet and then he saw a woman with short auburn hair looking down at him. "Take it easy, there," she said gently, placing a hand on his arm.

"Where am I? Where's my crew?" he asked. "Why do you have me strapped down?"

"Captain Bernon. Tyce. Listen to me." She looked over her shoulder as someone else entered the room. "You've been injured, and we've had to keep you immobile. My name is Maddie Astrid, and I'm a doctor. You're perfectly safe."

He made a supreme effort to free his hands.

She placed a cool palm against his cheek. "It's OK. You've got to stop moving or you'll do more damage."

He focused on her face. "Is my crew alive? Just tell me that."

"Yes. They are. Your medic, Beryl, is on the way." She glanced over at someone on Ty's other side. "Just 3ccs. We don't want him to go back under." She turned back to Ty. "That's it. Just look at me and breathe. That's it."

Ty felt a fuzziness spreading throughout his body, and the pain in his head eased off. The panic melted away like ice in the sun.

He sighed with relief when he saw Beryl's concerned face above him. "How're you feeling?" she asked.

He ignored her question. "Hal and Vivi?" He searched her face, "The... the ship? Everyone OK?"

"They're fine. Everything is fine. Are you in pain?"

"Not anymore."

His focus was fuzzy, and he was confused, but having Beryl there helped. If she said everything was OK, he could trust that.

The doctor spoke from his other side, drawing his attention away. "Do you remember how you got here, Captain Bernon?"

Ty tried to shake his head, but it wouldn't move. "N- No."

"OK. What's the last thing you do remember?"

"Getting to Jaleeth Station. The ship..." Ty paused as he remembered moving through the ship with his crew. Something was wrong with the *Loshad*.

I am everywhere on this ship, a voice said. It was confusing; he was supposed to know the voice, but he didn't. Different images flashed through his mind: wires, silver metal, Hal clutching at his head. "Hal... Hal was having trouble sleeping," he remembered. "I think his interface... Wait, no. I'm not sure."

Maddie looked up at Beryl, who nodded and took over. "Ty, do you remember being attacked?"

"No," Ty whispered. "Where's Hal and Vivi? Are they hurt?"

"No, Ty. They're fine," Beryl said, putting a hand on Ty's arm. "I promise. Just rest now. We'll talk later."

"Beryl... Where is this? Why... Why can't I move?"

"Ty, you were badly injured. We brought you to Al-Kimia."

"They're OK? Hal and Vivi?"

"Yes, Ty." His eyes slipped closed at the relief he felt. Beryl said the crew was OK. He tried to hold onto that thought as their voices turned into murmurs, and he fell back asleep.

"Captain Bernon, can you wake up for me?"

He looked up to see the same auburn-haired woman from before looking down at him. *She must be a doctor,* he thought, noticing her lab coat again.

"Yeah..." He tried to move again, but his upper body was completely immobile. His hands were strapped to the steel rails of the bed.

"I'm here too, Ty." He felt Beryl's comforting touch on his arm.

"Beryl?" His eyes quickly found her.

The person on his other side spoke up. "I'm Dr Astrid, Captain Bernon. You can call me Maddie, if you want. We met last night. You're on Al-Kimia, and you've been in a coma for over a week."

"Why am I strapped down?" Ty asked. His fingers never stopped roving over the bedrails. His legs hurt. It was like a burning sensation from the soles of his feet to his hips, and he tried to ignore it, focusing on the doctor instead.

"You suffered a spinal cord injury. We had you immobilized to reduce any further injury to your neck or spine. I'm sorry you were a bit frightened last night when you woke."

"How... How did I get hurt?" Ty asked, his brow furrowing. He didn't remember anything.

Maddie looked to Beryl, who spoke up. "Ty, an ACAS agent – a vat – attacked you when we were on Jaleeth. You were stabbed."

"Stabbed?" Ty asked. "Stabbed?"

"Yes. I'm going to undo these straps." Maddie freed his arm and laid his hand on the mattress. "Do you feel up to doing a few tests for me?"

He nodded, taking a deep breath as Beryl released his other hand from the restraints. He reached up to his face, finding the head and neck brace. His fingers moved over it, reaching for the clasps. He felt like a dog being kept from licking his wounds.

"I'm sorry, but the neck brace has to stay on. May I call you Ty?"

"Yeah," he said, letting his hands drop from the leather and metal contraption. "My legs hurt."

"What kind of pain are you feeling?" Maddie asked.

"Like a burning. What's wrong with me?"

"Let's see if we can lift you up a bit." Maddie adjusted the controls of the bed until Ty was almost sitting up, but not quite. He could see better, which eased some of his anxiety.

Maddie folded the sheet back, and he got a look at his legs and feet. With the pain he felt, he expected to see burns. But they looked totally normal. He went to move them but realized quickly that something was wrong.

"I… I can't move," Ty said.

"Try to wiggle your toes." Maddie suggested.

He tried, but they didn't move. "I can't," Ty said, feeling his frustration rise.

"Can you bend your knees?"

Ty gave it all his effort and his legs shifted on the bed just a little.

"OK, I see some movement, and that's good," Maddie said. "Close your eyes."

Ty did as he was asked.

"Can you feel that?"

He shook his head.

"Here?"

"Nothing."

"What about here?" It felt like she was lightly brushing the outside of his upper leg.

"A little." Ty frowned, sensing that they were all skirting some issue. He fixed his gaze on the doctor. "Whatever it is, just tell me. I can take it."

"I just ran my finger along your sole, and then your calf, but you didn't react to either stimulus," Maddie said matter-of-factly. "Tyce, the type of spinal cord injury that you have usually causes paralysis from the waist down. It seems that you have a little movement left, which is a good sign." She laid her hand on top of his own.

Ty felt like he'd been hit in the solar plexus with a pry bar. He struggled to take it in as Beryl placed a hand on his shoulder. "So, I'm not going to be walking any time soon, is what you're saying?" he asked hoarsely.

"Your motor and sensory function may improve some, but it will take time. A long time. Rehabilitation takes work."

"Yeah. So, again, what you're saying is I'm probably not getting out of this bed…" He looked up at her, trying to wrap his mind around what he'd been told.

"That's not what I'm saying, no." She moved so she was leaning forward and he could see her better. "It's not what I'm saying at all, Tyce. If *you* decide you're not getting out of this bed, then that's where you'll stay. If you decide to fight like hell… there's no telling what you might be able to do."

Ty closed his eyes, feeling a rising sense of panic. It was as if all the air had been sucked out of the room. He needed her to leave and now. "I need time to… to process all of this, OK?"

"Of course," Maddie said, glancing at Beryl. "I'll come back and check in on you a little later. I'll take the time to gather some information about what our next steps are."

"Where's Hal?" Ty asked unsteadily. "I know you must have told me… I keep forgetting."

"It's OK," Beryl reassured him. "They went on a mission. Seren took us in, then asked Hal if he'd go on a mission to rescue a vat researcher on Chamn-Alpha. He agreed because of all they'd done for you. He… He went because he knew it was what you would do."

Ty nodded, his eyes still closed. "I- I'm glad he isn't here for this."

"What can I do for you, Ty?" Beryl whispered softly, taking his hand.

There was a long moment of silence, then Ty whispered, "Just… just be here. That's all."

"I'm not going anywhere," she promised him. "I'll be right here."

THIRTY-ONE

It was the sixth morning of the mission on the *Loshad*, and Hal was the first awake. He stumbled to the coffee maker and loaded it up with the coffee that they'd gotten on Al-Kimia. He'd need the caffeine and the dark brew would be just the thing.

He hadn't been able to sleep well after the screaming wake-up call that split the night at 0200 hours. He'd been up and out of bed with a blaster in his hand before he realized what he was doing. He'd motioned to Vivi to stay put and made his way out of their door.

Lane had been huddled against the wall, a discarded blaster on the floor near her. Orin was on his knees beside her, gathering her up into a tight embrace as she sobbed into the shoulder of his black T-shirt.

Hal immediately realized what was happening, and his shooting stance dropped. The subjects of vat nightmares were common enough. Lost comrades, the fear and anxiety of past and future battles… Each one of them rose like restless corpses that would never be buried deeply enough. How many times had he, himself, struggled with the same things?

He approached the two vats. Orin looked up at Hal and signed something with one hand, never letting Lane go from his bearlike embrace.

Hal replied with a thumbs-up. "Understood, brother."

He took Vivi's hand. "Come on," he said, leading her back into the room.

"Is Lane OK?"

"She will be."

"I have the medjets Beryl gave me, if you think she needs..." She hesitated, leaving the words hanging.

Hal shook his head. "It was likely just a nightmare. She wasn't... locked into some subroutine in her interface. I think Orin'll bring her back around. At least that's what he said."

"What are the nightmares like?"

He shrugged. "Just different things. Replays of past battles. Not being fast enough, or strong enough to get the job done. It varies. Let's just try to go back to sleep, huh?"

They laid back down, Vivi's head resting on his chest. Eventually she drifted back off. He laid still for a while, feeling her slow, warm breaths against his skin before he fell into an uneasy half sleep himself. His dreams were full of worry and angst, searching the ship for Ty but never finding him.

The coffee maker beeped and the smell helped him shake off the night. Once it was ready, he carried it to the bridge. "Eira? What's our ETA?"

"ETA is three hours," Eira answered. "May I ask you a question, Hal?"

"Yeah." He slid into Ty's chair. "Go ahead."

"Will Lane be functional again?"

"Yeah, she'll be fine," he said as he took a sip of the black coffee.

"I did not scan her because I did not wish to cause her pain. Do you know what happened?"

"I think it was a bad dream."

"It was not an implant malfunction?"

"No. I don't think so."

"What is dreaming?"

"Don't you know?"

"Information is available on the feeds, but I find I would rather hear your explanation."

He was puzzled. "Um, OK. I... I don't know much though. It's when you experience things that aren't, exactly, happening."

"A hallucination, then?"

"No. It's… it's like a story your mind tells you while you're sleeping. Sometimes it's based on things that happened, sometimes not. That's all I know. I didn't dream until I left the ACAS." He looked down to Ty's display moodily. "It scared the shit out of me the first time."

"So, only vats dream?"

"No. Natural borns have always dreamed, ever since they were kids. Vats don't have dreams when they're in service. Could be because of the programming we go through every night. The ACAS shoving stuff in our brains doesn't leave a lot of time for dreaming, I guess." He paused. "So, Mudar don't dream, huh?"

"No. We do not. Perhaps you can understand why I find the idea intriguing. We have seen dreaming happen in biological studies, but the animals, of course, cannot have a discussion about it."

"Right." Hal tapped the captain's panel to see nearby starship traffic. Two ACAS ships, a few cargo vessels and transports were on the display. None were taking notice of them. "Flying under the sensors eh, Eira? That's what I like to see." They were making slow and steady progress toward Chamn-Alpha – just another J-class freighter in the middle of other J-class freighters.

"Yes, I took care to match speed and flying pattern to nearby traffic."

"Nice job."

There was a long moment of silence between the two, during which thoughts began to churn in Hal's mind. Impulsively he said, "I have a question."

"Yes, Hal."

"Do Mudar feel emotions?"

"Yes. But I believe we may experience them differently to humans. There is simply no data yet to compare the two. Why do you ask?"

For a moment, he'd considered talking to Eira about everything going on in his head about Vivi, but then he closed up as tight as an airlock. "No reason," he said quickly. He didn't know how to explain what he was feeling for Vivi. She'd become closer than a friend to him, and the very idea of saying some of those things out loud made him break out in a cold sweat. Suddenly he wished Ty was there. This would be easier to talk about with him.

"Do vats experience emotions?" Eira asked.

"Yeah, I guess. They didn't spend a lot of time on that in our training." That was an understatement, he thought.

"I sense stress in your voice, and your heartrate has risen by fifteen beats per minute."

"That's got nothing to do with anything."

"Does talking about this bother y–"

"No," he said quickly.

"Hal–"

"It's fine. I'm fine. Let's just drop it," he said, standing up. "I'll be in the galley if you need me."

He made his way back, feeling irritated for some reason he couldn't put his finger on. When he rounded the door, he saw Vivi stood by the coffee maker, her back against the counter, wearing the same cropped green sleep shirt and sleep pants she'd worn to bed. She smiled in welcome.

"Hi," he said, giving her a tired smile. She made the jumble of thoughts in his head smooth back out.

"You don't usually wake up first," she said, turning her cup in her hands. "Did you sleep OK?"

He shrugged as he approached. "It's no big deal. I'm just a little keyed up for the mission. I'll sleep after."

She nodded as he slipped up beside her.

"How long till we reach Chamn-Alpha? Just a couple of hours, right?"

"Three," he nodded.

"Are you sure you don't want to take me or Orin with you?" They'd decided that Vivi needed to stay and get the ship ready to leave as soon as they returned with the scientist, and Orin simply stood out too much in a crowd.

"Yeah," Hal nodded. "It's just a retrieval. We'll call the guy, tell him where to meet. Eira can tap into the security feed, like you said, so we can check it out before we go get him. Make sure it's not some sort of ambush."

"OK. You're the expert here," she nodded. "I'll go take a shower."

He grabbed at her hand and tugged her back to him. He wrapped an arm around her, and slowly nuzzled at her ear. "We've got some time. Want some company?"

She leaned into him and smiled, giving him all the answer he needed.

Ty was sitting straight up for the first time since he'd woken from the coma. He was still wearing the godsdamned brace on his neck and back, but the metal bar across his forehead had been removed so at least he could see better and move a little. But being stuck in bed was starting to get to him. He felt like a cranky old man.

He loathed being useless. Just sitting. Just existing. He'd managed to spend some time on the feeds using a datapad, but that distraction only lasted a short while. Besides, holding the screen up hurt his arms so he was loathed to try for longer than five minutes at a time.

Now he was back to bitterly staring at the two new things in the room that Maddie had brought in earlier that day. The first made his stomach churn; an anti-gravchair that he could barely face looking at, but which he knew at least would get him out of the bed. The second scared him, but he was smart enough to know it was the better option against the first: an exoframe. It would allow him to walk by himself, using sensors that hooked into his nerve impulses that read the signals from his brain. It would both support and move his legs, allowing him to walk unassisted.

I'm ready for this, Ty thought. *Screw the chair.*

He glanced up from thinking to see Beryl standing in the doorway. "Stop feeling sorry for me," Ty grumbled.

"I'm not," Beryl replied. Ty sighed, knowing the lie but refusing to call her on it. Beryl was on his side; he knew that, and it was impossible to be angry with her. "I brought you something." She came in and placed a handheld in his hand.

"Vivi took it off your attacker and gave it back to me right before they left." It had a cracked screen, but other than that, seemed to be in working condition. The cheap, scratched plasglass screamed untraceable shredder handheld.

"Whose device was this?"

"It belonged to the man who attacked you," Beryl began. "Seren's people unlocked it for me. In the 'Pictures' file, there's just one." She reached over and tapped it until a still of Vivi's face looked out.

"Vivi? She's… Wait. Where is she again?" He was having trouble remembering what they'd told him; he just couldn't seem to hold much information in his memory. "I know you told me…" he said, grimacing.

"Don't be so hard on yourself. It's normal to be a little forgetful after what you've been through, Ty. She's with Hal. They went to Chamn-Alpha to rescue a vat researcher who wants to change sides."

"We… We should let them know. Just in case the ACAS is on the lookout for her."

Beryl nodded. "I thought so too. I contacted Patrin, and he's on his way here right now."

"OK," Ty nodded, letting out a huge sigh. He looked down at his would-be killer's handheld and wondered about the man that had carried it. The events of ten days ago were wiped completely, but Beryl had told him enough. The fact that the man was a vat had stuck with him. Suddenly he felt sick as he imagined Vivi trying to defend herself against a similar opponent. The training Hal had given her wouldn't be enough to stop him. They had to be warned.

Patrin entered the room. "Captain Bernon. Nice to see you awake."

Ty nodded. "Thanks. Is there any way we can get a message to my people?" He tapped the comm. "The vat that tried to kill me had a picture of Vivi on his handheld. The people that were after us could be after her if she shows her face on..." he hesitated, trying to drag the information out of his malfunctioning memory "...Chamn-Alpha."

Patrin looked grave. "We shouldn't send a message from here, in case their transmissions are being monitored. But I can message my people in different sectors and get them to contact your ship. They should have the message to your people in a couple hours."

Ty nodded. "Thank you. Can you also tell them that I'm awake and, um, OK, so they don't worry?"

"Of course. I'll let you know if I hear anything back. If there's anything else we can do..."

"I just need my people to come home OK."

They were on the final approach to Chamn-Alpha when Eira chimed them. "Hal. We are being hailed."

Hal made his way to the bridge, followed by Vivi.

"OK, open the channel."

A red-haired female came on screen, calling them by their cover name. "Independent ship *Sombra* – my name's Dai. Are you Hal?" She was young, not much older than twenty-four, and dressed as a spacer. Her hair was long on one side and shorter on the other and her eyes were smudged with dark eyeliner. She wore her permanent smile like a shield.

Hal nodded. "That's me."

"Alright, good. I have a message from your friends. Your captain says that you should all be careful on your short vacation. Hal, keep your eyes on everyone, especially your girl. You shouldn't let her go out alone. There are people out there who know her face. Understand?" The woman looked at them meaningfully.

Hal's blood ran cold. "Yeah," he replied, nodding. "Loud and clear."

"Good. He also wants you to know that he is OK, in case you were worried about him. That Celian flu has all cleared up now, and he's feeling a lot better. We'll keep this channel open a while for your reply."

"You don't need to. Just tell him we're glad that he's well and we'll be home soon."

Vivi spoke over his shoulder. "And please tell him that we send our love."

"You bet!" she replied, lifting a hand to her temple and giving them a casual salute. "Safe travels, oppos."

"You too, err, oppos," Hal replied. It seemed a curious goodbye.

"Oppos?" Vivi murmured.

"Friends," Lane said from behind them. They turned to see she'd entered the bridge while they were talking. "Oppos is a term used on Al-Kimia to mean comrades, compatriots. People in the movement have taken to using it to recognize each other."

"Oh." Vivi nodded.

"I just came to find out how far out we were. Orin's still sleeping." She rubbed her face tiredly.

"We're on final approach so probably best wake him now. You're go for the mission, right?" Hal asked, checking Lane's reaction. "If you're not, I can–"

She waved a hand dismissively. "Nah, we'll be ready, Cullen. Five by five."

Max had received the message on his shredder before 0400.

0800. West concourse.

He'd been awake since then. Wide awake. He'd taken his last shower in the tiny apartment bathroom, got dressed, and packed a black duffel bag with several changes of clothes. There wasn't much else to take. Since his graduation from university, he'd been solely focused on his work; his personal life had always taken the hit. He felt a grief for his old, comfortable life but knew there was no way to return to it. Not now.

He scanned through the feeds on the wall monitor as he waited until it was late enough to call in sick to the lab. At 0709, he commed the office number and keyed in Balen's extension.

The lead researcher didn't answer. Max licked his lips nervously, then left his message. "Hey, this is Dr Parsen. I'm calling to say I won't be in today," he said in a weak sounding voice. "I might have food poisoning… or a really nasty virus, I'm not sure. Been sick to my stomach all night. I'm going to see if I can just sleep it off. Call me if you need anything."

He hung up rapidly, unsure that his message would be enough, but he knew he'd be long gone by the time Dr Balen realized something was going on. They wouldn't know he'd gone on the run until at least tomorrow. Somehow that made him feel safer.

He switched off the wall display, grabbed his duffel and took one last look around the empty, lifeless apartment. This was his past. It was time to focus on the future. On making things right.

"You've hacked into the security feed? Nice." Lane entered the room, wearing a pair of black fitted pants and a long-sleeved plum colored shirt. Her hair was loose and she wore a scarf wrapped around her wrist to hide her vat tattoo. She looked fashionable, just like a natural born from the Inner Spiral, Vivi thought.

"Yeah, no big deal." Vivi shrugged. She could have done it herself, but Eira had done most of the work with a nanite or two. "This is the west entrance security feed."

They watched people coming and going, huddling together against the cold as they went outside. It had begun to snow when they flew into the spaceport, which had cut down on the traffic a bit.

Vivi gestured to the travelers. "You look like you'll fit right in with the people out there."

"That's the idea," Lane said, pulling her hair into a long ponytail, winding it into a knot and then tucking the ends underneath.

Orin entered the bridge along with Hal. With a nod of acknowledgment to Vivi, Orin went over to Lane, took her by the hand and led her aside to talk to her. They were rapidly signing back and forth while Hal took a place beside Vivi.

"What've you seen on the feed?" Hal asked.

"Just people. Foot traffic," she said.

"What about patterns? Troop or security force movement? Timing?" Hal's voice was tense.

"I saw security pass twice. They didn't seem to be searching people or anything."

They watched the movements on screen for a while. A man entered the spaceport, brushing the snow out of his hair. He was in his late thirties or early forties and carrying a duffel bag. He had a grey scarf wound about his neck and was glancing around, seemingly expecting someone. He bore a resemblance to the man in the picture they'd been given.

"That could be him," Hal said. Together they watched the man walk to a nearby bench and take a seat. The man checked a handheld, then shoved it back into his pocket.

Hal took the cheap device he'd been given and sent a message to Parsen's preprogrammed number as Vivi looked on.

Where are you?

The man pulled out his handheld again, read, then typed a response before looking around nervously.

At west entrance, came the reply.

"That's him," Hal pointed, and Lane turned to examine the man's features.

"OK, let's go get this done," Lane said.

Vivi smiled as Orin enveloped Lane in a crushing hug, but she just laughed softly as she signed to him.

He flashed two number fives. Vivi had been around Hal long enough to understand what that meant – *five by five.*

Lane shouldered a crossbody pack that contained her blaster and Vivi watched as Hal strapped on his own. It wasn't against the spaceport rules to carry a weapon, but he put a coat over it anyway. It wasn't impossible to see what he was carrying, but it was enough that it didn't scream "armed citizen." He tugged a black knit hat down over his spiky hair to complete the look.

"Be careful," Vivi said.

He turned and hugged her. "I'm always careful, Veevs," he told her gently. He placed a kiss on the top of her head, before letting her go.

When he stepped back, she could see something switch off in his eyes. Like all his training shifted into gear in one moment. "Alright, Lane," he called. "Let's do this."

He turned and they left together.

The ACAS ship *Bountiful* dropped into orbit around Chamn-Alpha as the airspace in and around the planet was cleared. In a few minutes, they would land in Beruga City. Roger Triuna, Head of the Coalition Senate, stood up and stretched; he was tired from the long flight and ready to tour the vat facility and get back to the capital on Haleia Prime. The Chamn-Alpha vat facility was the largest creator of Vanguard Assault Troops in the entire Spiral. It was home to several researchers responsible for advances in vat technology over the past two decades.

Vats were big business in the Spiral. Corporations like Nyantek, MagnaPharm and Exoplast benefited from the Coalition's specially-grown soldiers. Exoplast made the artificial wombs they were grown in. Nyantek made the interfaces that allowed them to program vats with whatever information the ACAS wished. Countless other companies and corporations would benefit from extending the vats' period of service. If the researchers could figure out how to keep the soldiers in service longer, members of the government and corps stood to make a great profit. Vat troops meant more government contracts for amp, its antidote, and other programming drugs.

The military didn't like the way that the freed vats had been allying themselves with Al-Kimia. Triuna wasn't a fan of that himself. Al-Kimia, Noea and Betald were three places causing him an awful lot of headaches lately. They had allied themselves and the best solution, in his opinion, was to wipe all three off the starcharts for good. From what he'd been hearing, the Chamn-Alpha facility had come up with a solution to take care of any traitor vats.

The lead administrator at the Chamn-Alpha facility was one Dr Riley Balen. The Senate leader had been informed that Balen had developed a kill switch for vats, and Triuna had come to find out what stage the project was in. Perhaps they could go to Al-Kimia, set off the device, and kill half of the planet's troops in one fell swoop. It would certainly be a neat solution to the growing problem.

"Sir? The airspace is cleared. We can descend on your orders." His assistant Corine had come in from the cockpit.

"Very good, Corine. Let's do this. Should be an interesting day."

"Yes sir." Corine called across her transcomm to connect her with the Beruga Starport Authority. "Lock the port down, please. The Senator is landing."

"Are you Max?" Hal said as he approached the nervous looking man sitting on the bench.

The nat looked up, worry in his blue eyes. "Yeah?" he said uncertainly.

"Keep your head down. I'm Hal. We're your ride. Come on."

Max nodded, grabbed his duffel and stood up. "Thank you for…"

"Later. Keep going." Hal glanced around, seeing more security around than he expected. They passed another exit, where Hal noticed two more security guards had taken up posts. Did they know that this guy was AWOL? When they turned the corner, Hal caught the same expression from Lane. She'd noticed the change as well.

Even with the increase in security guards, they were not stopped as they entered the *Loshad*'s concourse. But as they walked down the hall, there was a loud metallic clank that reverberated throughout the station. Hal's heart froze. He knew what it was.

Every ship on the station had suddenly been locked down.

THIRTY-TWO

"Vivi. The magnetic lock on our ship has been engaged," Eira said.

"What the hell?" Vivi had been focused on following Hal, Lane and the doctor throughout the station using the station's different surveillance cams. "No, no, no, no!" she cried, her fingers flying over the panel in front of her. "Eira, listen in on security comms."

"There is an announcement being made over the spaceport." Eira put it on ship's speakers.

...spaceport will resume. Beruga City spaceport is on lockdown. Ships will not be allowed to arrive or leave. Please make accommodations. This lockdown will last up to one solar day, after which normal operations of the Beruga City spaceport will resume. Beruga City spaceport is on lockdown...

"Fuck," Vivi said to herself as she cut the speaker.

Orin passed her the terminalpad. He'd written a question mark.

She wrote back, *Spaceport locked down. Can't leave for a day.*

Think we're found out? he wrote.

Not sure, she answered.

After locking the cargo ramp, Hal headed up to the main hallway where he saw Vivi peeking out from the bridge with her hand on her blaster.

"Hal–"

"I heard. They broadcast it all over the spaceport," Hal said, as they approached. "Max, this is Vivi, Orin and Lane. If they tell you to do something, you do it. Got it?"

"Or what?" Max asked.

Hal rounded on him and took three steps forward with a grim look on his face. "Or it'll be a real short trip for you," he said in a deep, quiet voice.

Max immediately backed up. "Sorry. Look – I'll do whatever you need me to do."

Satisfied, Hal motioned toward the bridge. "Let's find out why they closed the station down. Eira – scan security feeds and show me the nearest newsfeed to our location." The longer they were in the dark about the lockdown, the more danger they were in.

Hal tried to anticipate all the ways this could go and attempted to ignore the rising pressure to take some action, any action. Sometimes no action was best, as Ty had taught him, but this felt claustrophobic. *Stay below an orange threat level,* he tried to tell himself.

He turned to see Max standing in the doorway looking around bewilderedly. Hal pointed to a seat on the bridge. "Sit there. And don't get in the way."

Max obeyed without question.

"Hal," Eira began, "the vat facility nearby is being visited by the head of the Coalition Senate. Closing down the local spaceport seems to be standard procedure when a dignitary visits a foreign planet."

Hal sighed with relief. "OK. That's a good thing. Maybe they're not on to us yet. We'll just need to wait this out."

Lane was translating Eira and Hal's words into sign language for Orin.

"If the guy is just touring the facility, it'll only be a few hours," Max said. "Even if he's here for some kind of demonstration like they did two weeks ago, it still won't take long."

"Demonstration?" Vivi asked.

"Yeah. I was present for one of them. A couple weeks ago." He nervously glanced to Orin, whom he had obviously identified as a vat by his size and the tattoo on his wrist. "They tested some new, um, equipment for the heads of the ACAS."

Hal had shrugged off his jacket and tossed it in the captain's chair during Max's description. "Keep talking. What kind of equipment?" Hal asked, sensing Max's nervousness and rounding on him.

Max took a deep breath. "It's what I was hinting at in my message. The ACAS has created a kill switch that affects vats. When it's pressed, the subject – I mean the vat – dies. Almost instantly." At the anger on Hal's face, Max's voice faded out. "I'm sorry..." he said hoarsely, "I didn't know they were doing things like that. I only found out what they were doing when we had those ACAS visitors. When I did, I contacted my friend on Al-Kimia and told her I was ready to leave the ACAS. For good. I couldn't be a part of that anymore."

Hal could see out of his peripheral vision that Lane was signing their words to Orin rapidly and violently. She was obviously just as angry as he felt. When she finished, the big man looked over at Max.

"Hal?" Vivi whispered.

Max was now staring at the vat tattoo on Hal's wrist. He stood up. "Wait. Are you... Are you *all* vats?"

Hal's thoughts began to sharpen and focus as he realized that Max could have the kill device on him. Perhaps they were part of a demonstration for the visiting senator. Faster than was humanly possible, Hal had drawn his weapon and put it to Max's forehead. "Don't move," he said. Suddenly aware of how much danger they could be in, his instinct took over and he felt the rush hammer his brain.

Max remained perfectly still. "I don't have the device..." he whispered helplessly.

"Veevs – take his bag and search it for a device. Lane, search him." He didn't move his eyes from Max.

"Handheld," Lane said, holding up the object.

"Smash it," Hal said. Even if it wasn't the kill switch program, it could still be tracked.

"I have a datapad," Vivi said. "But it's locked."

"What's the code?" Hal ordered, eyes fixed unblinkingly on Max. He'd learned the trick not long after getting out of the ACAS; for some reason, not blinking intimidated the hell out of nats. The only sound in the entire room was the subtle whine that meant his blaster was fully charged and ready to go.

Hal tilted his head to the side. "Don't make me ask again, Maxey."

"9H12JK24," Max whispered. "I swear, I'm not…"

"Stop." Hal shook his head slowly, still not blinking. "Veevs?"

"I'm in. I've disconnected the datapad from the feeds," Vivi said from behind Hal. "Signals can't come or go from it now."

Hal nodded, lowering his weapon ever so slightly. "Sit down, Max."

The researcher dropped back into his chair, looking very much like he was about to throw up. Hal lowered his weapon but kept it in hand and ready.

"What was your job at the complex?"

"I… I altered the DNA of the vat embryos and activated or suppressed genes before packing them into the exowombs."

Vivi had been standing slightly behind Hal, but now she stepped forward, glaring at Max. Hal stepped aside to give her room. "How long did you work for them?"

"Fifteen years. My first job was implanting the interfaces into the one year-olds."

Vivi surprised Hal by punching Max without any warning; the researcher's head rocketed back with the force of the blow. "How can you even look at yourself in the mirror?" she cried.

"Woah there, firecracker," Hal said, holstering his weapon and pulling her back with an arm around her waist. Half of him was stunned that she would do something like that, the other half was proud. "Lane, keep an eye on our guest."

Lane nodded as Hal walked Vivi over to her station, standing between her and Max. "You OK, Veevs?"

She glared at Max by peering around Hal. "He deserved it."

"I know." Hal put his hands on both of her shoulders. "But I need you calm, Veevs. OK?" He dipped his head to punctuate his sentence, appreciating the irony of the moment. "Take a seat a moment and cool off."

When she nodded, he knew she would be fine, so he turned back to Lane and Max.

The researcher licked the blood from his split lip. "I… I'm sorry. I want to… to make it right."

"You can never make it right. Never," Vivi said, turning away.

Lane had stepped up to take a shot at Max too. "It must not have bothered you too much, nat." Lane narrowed her eyes at him. "Did you feel sorry when you pulled those helpless children out, split open their skulls and inserted interfaces into them? Anything to save the lives of your precious Coalition citizens, right?"

Max could say nothing back, and simply dropped his head.

Orin signed something, then gestured to Max as if to say, *tell him*. She shook her head, causing him to slap one hand frustratedly onto a nearby computer console. He repeated the gesture.

"What did he say?" Max asked.

"Orin believes it's possible that maybe you have had a change of heart." She shrugged. "Unlike me, he's an idealist. I would shoot you, y'know, except that my captain sent us on this mission. He thinks you may be of some use to us."

"Yeah, don't make us change our minds, Maxey," Hal added.

Dr Riley Balen listened to the voice message from Parsen again. Something wasn't right. It was unlike Max to miss a day's work; in fact he'd only called in sick twice in the fifteen years he'd worked for the ACAS.

He called the security station. "I need someone to check on a researcher for me… No, I don't have time because the senator is coming today. The researcher's name is Max Parsen – number's on file. Call me when you find him. This could be a runner situation."

* * *

Maddie was helping Ty strap the exoframe to his legs in the physical therapy room, when Beryl got a message from Patrin. *Your message was delivered. They understand and send back love and thanks.*

Ty smiled with relief as Beryl read it aloud. He hoped things would go off without a hitch, but he couldn't help feeling disappointed that he wasn't there. He shouldn't be resting, not when his crew needed him.

"They should be getting that doctor out now by now. They'll be headed home soon," Beryl said.

"Then I need to get busy over here."

With help, he leaned forward in the suspensor chair he'd used for travel and stood up for the first time since the attack. He swayed a bit but soon stabilized himself.

"Good," Maddie said, watching him. She'd attached the sticky electrode sensors to the lumbar plexus; they would communicate wirelessly with the rig and help him move. "OK. Take a step."

With his hands on the rails beside him, Ty began. Beryl stayed close in case he faltered. He took a deep breath and tried to move his leg, managing a small sliding step forward.

"That's good," Maddie said, encouragingly. Ty's second step with his other leg was more pronounced. His foot lifted about a quarter of an inch off the ground. "Brilliant, Ty. See, you've got more strength in that side. The other will come along as the computer begins to recognize your signals and compensate for it."

"It's like walking in EVA boots," he said, with a shaking chuckle.

"That's what they usually say," she replied. "Again. Concentrate on the movement you want your leg to make. Exaggerate the movement of your hip muscles a bit." Ty's next step with the weaker leg was better. "OK. You got it. Walk it, soldier." She stood in front of him, at the end of the walkway, smiling with her hands out. He concentrated on each leg, thinking about the movements he needed to make, and it helped him take the final steps to Maddie. She grabbed him by the forearms and squeezed tightly, steadying him. "Good work. Try it again."

With concentration, Ty found he was able to turn around and

go back down the rail-lined path without help. Two more passes and he was exhausted, in pain and ready for a nap.

"If you decide this is what you want, we can implant some permanent sensors and that way you can just put this on and go," Maddie said.

"That sounds good," Ty said. He wanted to be as independent as possible.

"Let's stop for today," Maddie suggested, pushing his chair to the end of the path.

"No. Not... not yet," he said through gritted teeth.

He fought his way to the end and back two more times.

Only then did Ty sink back down into the chair. "Gotta build up my stamina. That was pathetic."

"Ty. You almost died. You're learning to walk again. It's going to take you more than a day to get back at it," Beryl said.

"Yeah," Tyce said, unconvinced. He glanced up at Maddie with determination. "I want the surgery. As soon as you can do it. I want out of this godsdamned chair."

Lieutenant Seros knocked on Max Parsen's apartment door, glancing at the two soldiers with him. There was no sound from inside, so he used the buzzer again. "OK. Let's go in." He gestured to the two men and stepped back while they broke the lock on the door.

They went in hot, checking the apartment, but found no one. Seros peered in the closets and bathroom, finding empty hangers and drawers. Even the guy's toothbrush was missing. "Oh yeah, he's a runner, alright. Call it in, Severs. One good thing: we're on lockdown. He won't have got far."

THIRTY-THREE

On Hal's orders, Orin and Lane had gone to crash for a while. Hal was awake, monitoring feeds on a terminalpad in the galley while Vivi made coffee and Eira monitored the security comms for any changes in patterns.

"You should get some sleep too," Vivi offered, setting a cup down in front of Hal.

Hal shook his head, not looking up. "Can't. Not until we're out of here."

Max said nothing as Vivi handed him a cup.

Vivi sat down beside Max with his datapad. "Dr Parsen, I want to know how this kill device works. Draw it out for me so I can see."

He shook his head. "I don't know exactly how it works."

Hal glanced up, his pupils still so large his eyes were black in the subdued lighting. "Do what she says, Max," he spoke in a low voice, full of the promise of violence.

"I'm sorry. I can't. I have some theories as to how it might work, but I wasn't privy to that kind of information. You can try and beat it out of me if you want, but I don't know anything," Max looked nervously from Vivi to Hal. "They keep plans like that classified."

"OK. Tell me your theory then," Vivi said.

"I think it orders the nanites in a vat's blood to clump together and cause massive clots everywhere in the body. Of course, they could also deliver a shock to the heart that would stop it. Either way, it's a quick death."

"*Vats* have nanites?"

"Yeah. They circulate in the blood stream, repairing battle damage and working with the interface."

"I knew about the interface, but not that it used nanites," Vivi said, glancing to Hal. Eira had not mentioned them specifically, but she had said Hal had Mudar technology inside of him. She should have made the connection. "Explain how it works."

Max's voice grew stronger, as he returned to familiar territory. "The nanites are merely an extension of the interface. There are different types. The interface tells them what to fix in the body, when to increase the noradrenaline, and when to ramp down. The psychological programming through the interface controls the length of the rush, which happens when there's danger or a mission to be completed. When the mission's completed, the rush will either fade naturally or a commander will give them the order to sleep. When they pass out, they get reinforcement through the connection with their interface."

Vivi felt nauseous as Max finished up. "So, you brainwash them through their interface," she said flatly.

"It's..." He trailed off, realizing that she'd summed it up perfectly. "Yes. I'm sorry."

"Go on. It's what? It's not enough that you alter their biology? It's not enough that you take away any real beginning to their lives? It's not enough that you make them follow your every objective because they're programmed like a computer? What?"

"Veevs," Hal said gently. "It's OK."

"No, Hal, it's not," she snapped. "Go ahead, Max. Tell it all. Explain why you even bother letting them go after they've spent their whole lives enslaved to the ACAS, only to have them die when they turn thirty-five!"

"Veevs..." Hal touched her arm.

"It's – um... We were told they die because their organs fail. Due to wear and tear from the increased adrenaline," Max said, a pained look on his face.

"Adrenaline fatigue syndrome," Vivi said.

"Yeah," Max said softly. "But… But when I began to understand how the system worked, I wondered why the nanites didn't just repair that damage. They repair other things inside the vat's bodies: bruising, torn ligaments, internal bleeding and the like. So why wouldn't they repair the damage to the major organs? I asked Command, but they could never give me a clear answer. I even offered to work on the problem, but they ignored me." He looked down at his hands. "I always believed I was doing my best to help vats survive better on the battlefield by editing their genes. It… It was all I knew to do to help them."

Vivi shook her head and walked into the hallway for a minute to clear her thoughts before she turned back abruptly.

"Is there some way to reprogram the interface? To order the nanites to try and repair the organ damage?"

"You would need the right codes, but no one holds those except the Office of Military Security. *We* weren't even allowed to see the codes. They have layers upon layers of encrypted security for that. And, all interface codes are unbreakable, to prevent an opponent from taking control of the vats. Old codes are inventoried and locked away in a computer database."

"Could someone hack into it?" Vivi asked.

"Hacking into it from the feeds would most likely be impossible."

Vivi paced back and forth for a few moments, until Hal stood up and stopped her by grabbing her hand. "Veevs."

She looked up at him.

"Veevs. Do me a favor."

"Of course," she said, trying to pull herself together.

"Go to the bridge and keep an eye on the security feed. I'll feel better with someone watching it along with Eira."

Vivi raised a questioning eyebrow, and Hal gave a small nod of acknowledgement. "OK, Hal." With a final glance at Max, she exited.

After she'd gone, Hal shifted his unblinking gaze to Max.

"I understand why she's pissed at me," Max murmured.

"Caught that, did you?"

Max said nothing.

Alone with the scientist, Hal took on a friendly tone that he didn't feel. "Hey, Maxey. Let's just say you're done talking about this right now. Until we get back to Al-Kimia, you've told her all you know. Because if you keep upsetting her, I'm gonna lock you in a crate in the cargo bay. Understand?"

Max nodded. "I'm sorry. I… I just want you to know that I will do everything I can to help. I brought all my files, notes and everything on that terminalpad. *All* of it."

"That's good. Maybe I won't have to space you before we get back to Al-Kimia. So… Don't go anywhere, Max." Hal clapped him on the arm and felt the scientist start. That was fine. Scared and in line was exactly where Hal needed him to be.

Hal found Vivi on the bridge, focused on the terminalpad in front of her. She was chewing her thumbnail as she looked at the display. "Veevs?" he said, placing a hand in the middle of her back.

She turned. "Yeah?"

"You good?"

She nodded. "What about you?"

"The waiting's getting to me, I think. The longer we go without any action, the harder it's… It's gonna get harder."

"I have some amp," Vivi said tentatively. "Beryl gave it to me in case…"

"Later. I'll let you know," he said, and she nodded. "I'm gonna get us out of this, Veevs."

"I believe you," she replied.

It was after lunch when Eira spoke over the bridge's comms. "Hal, we may have a problem," she said. "There are multiple ACAS soldiers entering the spaceport." On the bridge display they saw a squad of twenty well-armed troopers. Eira followed them on the feed through the spaceport to security.

"I think it might be the time to get the hells out of here. Vivi, see if you can get that mag lock off the ship." Hal watched her begin to work on it by tapping her node and interfacing with the computer, then his attention shifted back to Eira's feed. "Can you tell what's going on in security?" Hal asked, immediately tense.

"Security feeds are being scanned all over the station," Eira said. "They're looking for something."

Vivi growled in frustration and disengaged her node. "Hal, it can't be hacked remotely. I'll have to go out there."

"Ok, Veevs. Time for the amp." She nodded and took off at a run. He turned back to the researcher. "They must have figured out you split, Max."

"Shit."

"Yeah," Hal said grimly. "Don't feel bad. I half expected this all day. Lane, Orin – get the blasrifles."

"What can I do?" Max said.

Hal shook his head. "Not much. Nothing matters if we can't get that mag lock off the ship. You don't happen to know anything about those?" he asked, not really expecting an answer. He didn't want Vivi out there, but he supposed he'd have to let her give it a try. If it didn't work, they would probably have to blow it, which could cause damage to the ship, but it would be worth the risk. After all, if it didn't come off, they wouldn't be going anywhere.

"Actually in university, I worked as a tecker in a spaceport," Max offered. "If I can get to the box, I think I can unlock it."

Hal grinned. "Max, you might have just paid for your trip."

Vivi met them in the cargo bay. Hal had been showing Max how to use a blaspistol. When he was done, he turned to see her standing behind him.

"Want me to…" she asked, holding a medjet.

He covered her hand with his own. "No, I got it." He took the injector from her, snapped off the top and pressed it to his bicep. When the drug hit his system, it was the rush times ten.

"OK?" Vivi asked as his blackening eyes focused on her.

"Yeah. Get them." He gestured to Lane and Orin. Vivi handed out the amp and they dosed up as well.

Once regrouped, Hal rested a hand on each of Vivi's shoulders. "Here's the plan. I need you on the bridge. Get us ready to fly. Lock the doors behind you on the way up and don't open them until I tell you. I don't want anyone to get past the cargo bay. Max here will get us free from the mag lock, and we'll keep the soldiers engaged so he can get that done. When you get the signal from me, take off."

"Make sure everyone's back. I'm not leaving anyone behind," she told him.

With a hand on the back of her neck, he pulled her in and kissed her. "Don't worry, Veevs. I'm bringing everyone home. Go on."

When she left and sealed the cargo bay door, he and Orin dragged some of the cargo containers full of medical supplies into different positions to give them cover.

"Hal? I need tools," Max said, glancing around. "It's likely to be pretty low-tech, but I'll still need to get in there before I can do any reprogramming."

"Try that chest over there," Hal gestured. "Eira? How's it looking out there?"

"As yet, there is no one converging on our position, but they seem to have a definite destination in mind. Dr Parsen's image has been sent out to all security comms but they appear unaware that he is on board."

"Your ship's pretty intuitive..." Lane said, an eyebrow raised.

"Think so?" Hal asked, trying to keep a straight face. Eira would be their ace in the hole. The battle was close, and he was ready. *This is what I do. This is what we were made for,* he thought, glancing at Lane and Orin. They were just as anxious for the coming combat as he was.

"OK?" Lane and Orin nodded, blasrifles at the ready. Max returned with a screwdriver and some wire cutters.

"Let's go," Hal said, hitting the release for the cargo ramp.

THIRTY-FOUR

Orin and Lane took up positions behind the cargo containers next to the ramp, as Hal and Max moved to the mag lock beside the *Loshad*. The device itself provided some cover. It comprised a giant silver box and connectors that generated the magnetic field that locked down the ship. Max began working immediately to remove the access panel while Hal watched the entrance to their bay.

He'd just removed it when the first blue plasma bolt burned into the wall over the magnetic lock. Hal ducked, yanking Max down with him. When the blasts slowed, Hal braced his rifle on the box and began to shoot. "You need to get this done fast," Hal called.

The air erupted with shots around them, both blasrifles and projectile weapons. Orin and Lane took some of the heat, keeping the troops from advancing on them.

Max laid his blaspistol beside him, then used the tools to remove the cover to the mag lock and began to type commands into the computer interface.

ENTER PASSWORD OVERRIDE:

The cursor blinked at him on the tiny screen, as if it was counting out the remaining seconds of his life. He stared at the blinking line, paralyzed, until Hal bumped his shoulder.

"You with me, Max?" Hal asked.

"Uh, yeah."

"Good. Do what you gotta do."

Max tried several passwords that were used to lock down ships that hadn't paid their dock fees. They were typical on every station, so he thought he might be able to guess it, but none of them were working. "Dumb fucking idea…" he swore. In frustration, he tugged out the screwdriver and began to take the panel apart. "I'm gonna have to disconnect the power source," he said.

"Can I just blow it?" Hal asked, looking at the power conduits leading across the floor into the wall.

"It could trigger a failsafe!" Max yelled, panicking.

"Come on, Max! How long?" Hal asked over his shoulder while he continued firing.

"Two, maybe three minutes," Max called.

"Lane – buy us two minutes," he called on his comm. Hal's gaze caught a particularly brave nat, making his way around the far edge of the entrance. It was obvious he was either going to try and come around the ship to ambush them from behind, or he was planning to flank the ramp. Either way, he wasn't going to make it. Using his heightened senses, Hal made the shot, nailing the ACAS nat right in the forehead. The unfortunate soldier's brains splattered wetly on the wall as he fell to the ground.

"Lay down your weapons!" came the call during a lull in the fighting.

"Fuck off!" Lane yelled back, punctuating her curses with a barrage of blasts.

"Eira. We need to be ready to leave immediately after they get the lock off." Vivi ran to the navigation console and had it compute a course.

"Yes, Vivi. There are more soldiers coming our way."

She keyed her comm. "Hal, they're sending reinforcements. Whatever you're doing, hurry it up." Vivi didn't know if her heart would ever quit pounding. "Hope you made some adjustments so we can outrun some of those ACAS ships, Eira. They're gonna be on us as soon as we lift off."

"The changes I've made will please you."

"Have I told you how much I love you?" Vivi said.

"No, Vivi, but I, too, am becoming fond of you."

"Shit. Is it the blue one or the green one? I can't remember," Max said.

Hal glanced over briefly, before returning his black eyes to the doorway. He'd been focusing on the right-hand side, where they had been trying to set up a tri-barrel laser, but he'd taken them out, then blown the weapon to bits.

"What happens if you're wrong?" Hal asked.

"It could send out a pulse that would disable the ship's engine."

"It's time to make a decision, right or wrong. If they bring another heavy gun in here, or something else, we're done." He was surprised they'd not had a grenade thrown at them yet. But this was Chamn-Alpha, he reasoned. Not exactly a hotbed of rebellion.

Max still seemed to be wavering, trying to decide between two different wires, Hal realized as he glanced down, then back up at the doorway. There wasn't time for this. "Max… " he warned.

"OK, the green!"

He cut the green wire, but nothing happened.

"Damn," Max cursed.

Then there was an electronic beep and all the lights on the panel went out. "We're good! It'll release in thirty seconds!" Max said. Hal caught Max's movement out of the corner of his eye as the scientist lifted his weapon. "HAL!" he yelled, taking aim.

Hal turned just as Max hit the advancing soldier's center body mass with a blaster bolt. The soldier fired several rounds at the same time, slamming Max back against the mag lock.

"Shit!" Hal slid across to the scientist and peeked over at the oncoming soldiers and fired. The closest approaching them fell, then three more behind him. Hal fumbled for his comm.

"I'm coming for the ramp. Max is injured, and I need cover fire," Hal said over their network.

"Got you, brother!" Lane said, her voice tight with the rush.

Hal slung his rifle over his shoulder and then pulled Max to his feet. The scientist let out a groan as Hal slung his arm around him, half carrying him. Max would make it. He had to. "Stay with me, Max," Hal said. "We're gettin' out of here."

Lane moved to the edge of the cargo bay, and along with Orin they laid down heavy cover fire. As soon as Hal's feet hit the ramp, it began to rise. When he was fully inside, he slipped to his knees and gently placed Max down on the metal floor of the cargo bay.

"Go, Veevs. Get us out of here," he called on his comm, as he assessed Max's damage. "Lane, medkit. Now."

Lane grabbed the one on the wall in the cargo bay as Hal gently turned Max on his side and examined the wound. There were no charred edges to signify a blaster bolt, so they must have been using projectiles. There was no exit wound either, but his chest oozed deep red blood.

"S- Stop," Max whispered, squeezing his eyes shut against the pain. "It hurts..."

Years on battlefields told Hal that Max was not doing well. His breathing was shallow, and his lips were turning blue. He turned Max back over so he could begin to apply pressure with the coagulant pad Lane gave him. Max groaned at the pain.

He took a few rasping breaths. "I'm... so... sorry about... everything." Blood bubbled up from his damaged lung, and his respiration had a wet sound. Hal clenched his jaw.

"It's OK. Don't try to talk," Hal groped in the medkit for the painkiller. He pressed it to Max's neck and heard the medjet hiss. Max seemed to relax as the medicine flowed through him.

Orin and Lane knelt down too as Orin took over holding pressure against Max's wound. The whine of the engines sounded as the ship lifted off.

Vivi came across the comms. "I'm gonna need some help up here!"

"Go," Lane said to Hal. She held Max steady as she dosed him with coagulant. "We'll take him to the medbay."

As Lane and Orin coordinated how they were going to move Max to the medbay, Max spoke to Hal, "G- Go on and s- save ev- everyone," he sputtered. "It's what you…w- were ma- made t- to do."

Hal took Max's bloody hand and squeezed. Then he turned and left.

Vivi and Eira had the *Loshad*'s main drive powered up as the mag lock's hold on the ship suddenly ceased and the vessel surged upward.

As Hal made his way to the bridge, he could hear small arm rounds pinging off the hull as the *Loshad* clawed its way into the airspace above the spaceport. There were tearing sounds as the various cables connecting the ship to the ground equipment ripped loose.

Hal smiled wryly at the thought of the *Loshad*'s appearance to people on the ground staring up at the trailing, streaming cables and electrical lines. Orders were undoubtedly being barked over the space center's comms to ACAS vessels in orbit. Shit was about to get very real very quickly.

Vivi spoke from the captain's chair as Hal entered the bridge. "We got everyone?" she asked.

"Yeah. We did." Hal said tightly. She gasped to see his hands and shirt were covered in blood, but he shook his head. "Not mine. What's our status?"

"We're entering the stratosphere at full escape velocity."

Eira chimed in. "I am reading several ACAS vessels in a holding pattern above the planet. The two closest have been ordered to cut off our escape and are powering their engines."

Hal slid into the gunner's chair. He was glad he had attached the g-pod with the laser cannon before they left. It looked like it was going to get a workout.

The two ships on an intercept vector were listed in the data log as the *Javelin*, an escort, and the *Bountiful*, a command cruiser.

"Shit!" Hal said. The escort was a problem, but the command cruiser was a major problem.

"We've got to get out of here," Vivi said softly, also noticing the size difference between the *Loshad* and the looming ACAS ships.

"The cruiser's arming its laser battery and the escort's closing," Hal replied, wondering why the heavy hitter wouldn't come for an easy prize. "Veevs, Eira – you two fly and I'll see if I can keep them off our back." Hal flipped switches on the weapons station and started the heads-up display.

The escort craft closed the distance rapidly. It was obvious that its captain was angling for a quick kill. Eira's maneuvers kept the *Loshad* from taking hits, but the escort was fast. Too fast. The cruiser continued to hang back, simply observing the fray.

Vivi glanced at the sensor panel as Eira continued her evasive attack. Hal was firing to try to disrupt the onrushing escort vessel. He landed a few hits, but they were minor, and the escort kept coming.

"Hal, I think the cruiser's slow. It's not moving at maximum speed," Vivi said, studying the display and recalling the tactics he'd taught her while they were playing squads. "It should be angling to cut off our retreat, but it's not doing anything. I think we may have a window to squeeze through."

"I concur, Hal," Eira said.

"It's a tight window, though," Vivi continued, "and going that way will put us in range of the command cruiser until the drive kicks in."

"Eira, can you make the window?" Hal kept firing.

"Yes, Hal."

"Do it. I am going to count on a little help from the ACAS. Let's hope they stay true to form." Hal could tell that the escort was eager to make a kill by its aggressive maneuvers. He could just imagine what the captain of the command cruiser was thinking as they headed toward it at full thrust. It was a crazy plan, but if he could get the escort closing in on them to make a mistake, they might make it out of this after all. The cruiser grew in size on their display as they closed the distance. Eira was taking evasive maneuvers as Hal continued to fire.

"Eira, give me an engine boost on my command – like you did against the *Phobos*."

"Yes, Hal. I calculate a forty percent increase will catapult us past the cruiser."

"Good. For now, keep closing on the cruiser and hope they keep doing nothing."

Just as Hal finished his sentence, the *Javelin*'s captain got tired of toying with his prey and did exactly as Hal had hoped; he launched the escort's most deadly weapon, a Mark-6 anti-ship missile. The escort was too close to the command cruiser, however. With the *Loshad* closing distance on the cruiser it quickly became an additional target for the missile. Hal knew this would force the command cruiser's captain to fire his lasers to destroy the missile instead of targeting the *Loshad*.

"Missile in space, running hot." Hal smiled as he watched the heads-up display. "Eira, time to missile impact?"

"Twenty-five seconds, Hal."

"Just about right. Boost now." His voice was calm, as if he were channeling Tyce Bernon.

"Oh my gods," Vivi murmured.

"Yep." Hal said, a grin on his face when he realized she saw the plan. For a second, the cruiser in front of him was huge, taking up the entire display as they flew right beneath it.

"Hal, permission to engage full power," Eira asked calmly.

"What? Yes. YES!"

The sudden acceleration from the *Loshad*'s retuned engines pushed them all back before the gravity fields could adjust. Hal howled with unrestrained excitement. "Fuck, yeah!" he yelled, reading his sensors and seeing that the cruiser had chosen self-preservation over blowing them to bits. Eira's adjustments to the engine made it clear that neither ACAS ship would be able to keep up with them.

"Oh my gods, Hal!" Vivi said, leaping from her position to the weapons station. "I thought we were dead there for a minute!"

He wrapped his arms around her and pulled her to him. "I knew we'd make it."

"I, too, was sure we would make it," Eira said from the monitor. "There are no signs of pursuit."

Hal placed his hand on the panel as if he could clap Eira on the back. "It wouldn't have worked without you. You were amazing. What did you do to the engines?"

"Thank you, Hal. I simply enhanced their full potential – allowing us an acceleration far beyond the ACAS ships' capabilities. As far as they are concerned, we simply vanished."

Hal turned to back to Vivi, and as he did so he remembered Max. His face fell. "I gotta get back to the medbay. Eira, let me know immediately if there's any trouble."

"Who was hurt?" Vivi said, her eyes shifting to his bloody hands and remembering what he'd said. "I'm coming along."

"Veevs–" Hal turned to stop her. "Max took a bad hit. I don't think you want to–"

"Is it serious?" she asked. "Maybe I can help."

Hal weighed her expression, then nodded. "Come on."

Together they made their way to the medbay. Lane had gloves on and was using a laser cauterizer on the wound in Max's chest. "He was hit with a slug thrower," she explained. "There were at least three shots, grouped closely. One shattered into three pieces."

"Do you have a lot of experience patching guys like this up?" Hal asked.

"A few," she said with a shrug. "I took out the slugs."

He nodded. "Good."

Vivi came closer. "He's so pale..."

"I'm going to do all I can to hold him together until we get back to Al-Kimia," Lane said.

Max began to groan as she continued to work on him.

"Shit, he's waking up," Lane muttered. "He needs more Lanapram to keep him knocked out. Medjet's on the tray."

"Got it," Hal said, reaching for it and checking the dosage. Years of watching Beryl patch them up was good for something. "How much did you give him before?" he asked Lane.

"Fifty. Your shipboard computer told me he could have up to a hundred micrograms."

Hal injected Max with the rest, and the tension in his muscles released as the researcher fell back, fully sedated again.

"Be quick," Hal said, setting the medjet on a nearby table.

She looked over at him. "Are you any good at setting up an IV? He's going to need fluids, and blood stim."

"I know how, yeah," Hal said, and moved to gather up what they would need.

Once they were done, Hal and Lane stepped back, taking off their blue exam gloves. "Not bad for a couple of vats, huh?" Lane said with a pleased smile.

"Yeah," Hal replied. Then he looked at Vivi. She stood alone and apart from them and had been watching silently the whole time. Her hair was a golden halo around her head and her green eyes seemed brighter than ever through their sheen of tears.

"I'm sorry I judged him so harshly," she murmured.

"We had our reasons," Hal said plainly, "and he understood. Come on." Hal led her up the ramp to the hallway and into the common area. The further away he got her from Max, the better she'd begin to be.

He went into a cabinet in the galley and pulled out Ty's bottle of Celian whiskey. He poured a generous two-shots' worth into a coffee mug and handed it to her. His hand was shaking slightly.

"Drink it," he told her.

She did, coughing a little as she looked at him over the top of it. "Are you OK?"

He closed his hand into a fist. "Yeah… it's just the rush trying to fade and the amp keeping it going."

"The neutralizer, I'll get–"

"It's OK. We have a couple of hours yet and I should stay sharp. Drink that. It'll steady you."

"Do you know that from personal experience?"

"Maybe." Dismissing the mental image of another time, a younger version of himself, and his first combat, he sloshed another shot's worth into her cup, then put the bottle away.

A few hours later, Vivi had dosed everyone but Hal with the neutralizer. Lane and Orin had gone to crash and sleep off the effects. Vivi entered the bridge, finding Hal, deep in thought.

He'd showered to wash off the blood and changed his clothes. As she drew closer, she saw his fingers tapping on the panel in front of him. Every once in a while, she could see the muscles in his body twitching against his will.

"Hal, it's time," she held up a hand with the neutralizer. He opened his mouth to speak, but she cut him off. "I know what you're going to say, and no. You need to get some sleep."

"Fine." He held out his hand for the injector, but she shook her head.

"Not until I get you back to your room." She took him by the hand and led him to bed. After dosing him, she watched as he pulled off his shirt. There was a wound, covered with a bandage, in the top of his shoulder, an obvious graze. "Hal," she said. "You didn't mention getting hurt anywhere else…"

He shrugged, crawling in the bed and grumbling as he shifted to lie on his back instead of his side. "It didn't hurt until just a minute ago."

She could already sense the change in him. His eyelids grew heavy as he settled his head into the pillow. "You took care of everyone today. Kept us all alive." Vivi brushed his hand with her fingers. "I can watch over you now though, OK?"

"Mm… yeah…" His eyes closed as he took hold of her hand. She sat there for a moment, thinking he'd fallen asleep when his forehead suddenly creased. He mumbled, "Tyce *and* Max got injured on my watch."

"No one could have foreseen either one."

He was quiet a moment, then sighed. "Still my fault," he frowned. "No… excuses."

She realized he was talking in his sleep. "Shh, Hal." She smoothed her hand over his warm brow. The amp had caused an increase in body temperature as it jacked up his metabolism. "You did everything right."

The frown lines faded and he took a deep breath, rolling toward her on his uninjured side. "I won't let anything hurt you, Veevs." There was one slow open and close of his now blue eyes, then he sighed heavily.

"I know. Now sleep, babe. If I need you, I'll call." She stayed and watched over him until he began to breathe more deeply and regularly. Finally, his hand relaxed so that she could slip hers out.

"I… I think I'm falling in love with you, Hal Cullen," she whispered, knowing he wouldn't hear, but wanting to try it out anyway. It felt right. Without another word, she got up, made her way to the door and headed out to check on Max.

"Eira? How is he?" Vivi asked. Max was lying on the medbed, his feet elevated, wrapped in blankets that were as pale as he was.

"I have been monitoring his condition. According to your information, he had eight out of eleven symptoms of hypovolemic shock, but his heart rate and respiration are improving. The blood stim is working. But there is still a sixty-four percent chance he will die before we reach Al-Kimia."

"Is there anything else we can do for him?"

"No, there isn't."

"OK." She checked his IV, then covered him back up.

"Is everyone asleep?" Eira asked.

"Yes. It's just you and me," Vivi said.

"I heard what Dr Parsen said about his work with the ACAS. They have done deplorable things, Vivi. I understand Dr Parsen's decision to leave." Eira sounded uncharacteristically emotional. "Eira, are you OK?"

"Yes," Eira replied. "However, the actions of the ACAS disturb me deeply."

"Me too." Vivi nodded thoughtfully. "Please, don't think all humans are like the ACAS. We aren't."

"I have observed all of you and have seen that. However, would you say that you were the exception of your species or the rule?"

Vivi bit her bottom lip. "I don't know. I think that most people are good, if given the chance. But some people are not. Some people are very, *very* bad. And then there are others, like Max, who are just misguided, I guess. We have to help the misguided ones see what's right."

"And oppose the others," Eira mused.

"Yes, I guess so," Vivi said. "Please monitor Max and keep me informed."

"Of course, Vivi. I will track his values and notify you of any changes."

"Good."

She walked through the quiet ship, listening to the purr of the engines. The ship's frame couldn't survive constant use of the engine's full potential, so Eira had reduced demand – but even so, at this rate, they would be back in Al-Kimian space in three days, rather than the six it had taken them on the outward journey.

Her path took her to the galley, to grab some ration bars and water for Hal, in case he woke up hungry. She set everything on the table, then collapsed on the bench, exhausted. She folded her arms on the table and buried her head.

"You should eat," Eira urged gently. "It has been nine hours since you last–"

"I'm not hungry. These are for Hal when he wakes."

There was too much to think about. The threat of war loomed above them like some great predatory bird – it was only a matter of time, she was sure. Hal, the man she loved, was going to die before they had a chance to live, and now this doctor and his death machine could erase what little time there was left, as well as the lives of all the other vats. Tyce and his injuries were a giant question mark. Would her captain and friend be able to lead a normal life?

It was all too much. She scrubbed a hand across her eyes and wasn't surprised to find she was crying. Her body felt too numb to cry, but the swelling of sadness in her mind was overwhelming. Before she knew it, she was fully sobbing as the dam of tears burst.

Eira's gentle voice broke through the dark, swirling sea of her emotion. "Vivi. Would you like me to wake Hal?"

"No," she answered quickly between sobs, sitting up and struggling to get herself under control. "He needs to rest. Please. I'm OK," she said as she wiped her face. "It's… it's just been a long day."

"Emotions impact biologics differently," Eira said. "I will watch over you until you get to your room, amatan."

"Amatan?"

"It means you are dear to me. You would probably define it as 'family,' except it has no connotation of biology. Perhaps think of it as the family you choose, not those biologically related to you."

She wiped away another tear and smiled. "You mean a friend? Thank you, Eira."

"Of course, my friend."

She walked back to Hal's room, placed the ration bars and water on his table then undressed down to her T-shirt, before climbing into bed. Hal's breathing was regular and deep, and she began to reassure herself by listening to the slow rhythm. She could feel the warmth coming from him and she slid closer, not wanting to wake him but needing him near.

His arm pulled her in as he rolled toward her, burying his face against her hair. Hal mumbled something; she didn't know what, but it sounded sleepy and content, and he had soon fallen back asleep.

She wouldn't allow anything to happen to him. There would be a way around this. It was like at university, when she would fall asleep over some programming problem she was working on that week. She would always wake up with the answer clear and fresh before her eyes, as if her mind had worked on it during her slumber. Maybe that could happen again. She could always hope.

THIRTY-FIVE

Tyce was watching the feed with wide eyes when Beryl entered. She immediately glanced toward the display where a large headline read *ATTACK in the Home Systems!*

"And now, we take you to our military facility on Chamn-Alpha where Senate Leader Roger Triuna is ready to make a statement…"

They had set up a podium in a room with a Coalition flag on one side and the seal of the senate leader on the other. There was a murmur of reporters in the room as Triuna approached the podium.

"Good evening. My fellow citizens…we have suffered a horrific terrorist attack in the home systems. Today, two ships landed at the Beruga City spaceport, near the Vanguard Assault Troop facility on Chamn-Alpha. These ships, which have now been identified as crewed by released vats and Al-Kimians, landed in the space port in order to stage a kidnapping."

The senate leader looked down at his own display, tapped a button and a picture of a lab assistant appeared, taken from an ID card.

"This is Max Parsen. Dr Parsen has been a loyal employee of the Coalition for fifteen years. He is a researcher of ours and was working on highly sensitive materials when he was kidnapped and most likely injured or killed by these radicals. These terrorists also attacked the spaceport in their effort to escape, killing over fifty ACAS soldiers and civilians."

There were shots of destroyed ship bays and the dead, their bodies strewn around like dolls.

"No," Ty said, glancing at Beryl. He used his hands to shift himself in the bed, so he was sitting further up. "They wouldn't have done that. And there was only the one of them, wasn't there? Or am I getting that wrong?"

"No, you're right – just the *Loshad*," Beryl said. "It's more propaganda."

"As you can see, the damage and loss of life was quite severe," Triuna said. "During their escape, they also crippled a ship in orbit around Chamn-Alpha. We cannot allow these extremists to attack the very planet and people who fight to keep us safe. Not addressing this directly is a travesty of justice. We will not stand by and watch our own people be murdered."

He looked into the camera and said: "Those who would attack the Coalition of Allied Systems will be utterly destroyed. We will have another press conference in two days, after the Senate has had a chance to meet on this issue. I intend to bring tough resolutions against Al-Kimia and her allies. Until then, no Vanguard Assault Troops will be released from service. We will need every hand in the coming fight, and I know our brave soldiers will insist on contributing. Thank you."

The Senate Leader made his way out of the building amidst a chaos of questions, but it was clear the press conference was over. Tyce felt his stomach clench so hard he thought he was going to retch.

"They didn't do that," Beryl said. "This is a set up. They're using this as an excuse for war."

Tyce got a grip on himself. "I know. Hal never would have killed innocent civilians. Vivi either."

"At least we know they escaped," Beryl said with hope.

"Yeah," Ty nodded.

"The vats..." she mused. "They can't keep them in for longer than seven years unless they solved the Nash problem."

"It might just be temporary," Tyce said, not sure what to think. "Did... Did we ask Patrin to check on the *Loshad*?"

"We did," she replied, "but I guess Hal is maintaining radio silence so they can't be tracked by ACAS."

"Shit, I forgot again, didn't I?" Ty's brow furrowed. His brain had been pretty fuzzy the past few days, but he had felt like he was starting to get a handle on everything again. Well, mentally anyway, he thought as he glanced down at his legs with a frown.

"Ty. Listen to me. A little memory loss is nothing when you look at all you've been through. I'll check back and see if he's heard anything."

"Thanks," Ty said, watching her go. He couldn't help worrying how Hal and Vivi had managed on their own. He'd never be able to forgive himself if they didn't make it back safely.

The next few days were spent traveling on a wavering course to Al-Kimia. Max was hanging on; however, he had developed a fever and infection from his wounds that the ship's antibiotics didn't seem to be able to cure.

They were nearing Al-Kimian space, as fast as Eira could take them.

"Hal, we are receiving a hail," Eira announced.

"Put it on speakers," Hal said.

A stern voice was broadcast around the bridge. "Unknown vessel. This is Al-Kimian Military Flight Command. You have crossed into in Al-Kimian space. Turn back now or be eliminated."

"Verify that signal, Eira."

"The signal is coming from the planet's surface," she responded.

"Flight Command, this is the free ship *Loshad*. We have retrieved your package and intend to land. We are sending you the correct command codes. May we land at the same coordinates as before?"

He waited a moment. There was apparently some sort of discussion going on.

"Identify verified, *Loshad,* we have been anxiously awaiting word from you. You may land at the same coordinates."

"Thanks, command. We have one severely wounded – he's critical. Please have a full medical team standing by."

Hal glanced to Vivi as they answered, "We understand, *Loshad*. Welcome home. There are a lot of people that didn't expect you back. They're going to lose some money on this whole thing."

Hal replied, "Thank you, command. See you soon."

They landed in the same heavily armed spaceport as before, but this time friends were waiting when Hal and Vivi stepped off the ramp.

Jacent Seren and Patrin Kerlani were present. Hal made his way toward them, scanning each of them nervously, until he saw Beryl. She looked to the side, talking to someone who was hidden behind the large figure of Seren. When Hal got close enough, he saw it was Tyce.

Ty was sitting in a suspensor chair at an unnatural, stiff backed angle. That was when Hal realized with alarm that Ty was wearing some sort of back brace. His captain looked up and was smiling widely, however. "Hal… when we heard about the spaceport, we feared the worst," Ty said.

Hal crouched beside the chair. "I'm OK, Cap. I brought everyone back safe… except Max."

"Max?"

"The researcher. He was shot. He developed a fever and we didn't have the right medicine to stop the infection."

"They'll help him," Beryl said, as a group of medics and a few vats ran past them and entered the ramp, following Lane.

Hal nodded, looking back up at Ty. "You OK, Cap?" he asked, when everyone had turned back to their conversations.

Ty nodded and shifted his eyes away before replying quickly, "Oh yeah. I'm gonna be fine."

"Don't worry, Ty. Whatever you need, I'm here." Hal promised.

"I know."

Vivi approached Ty and laid a hand lightly on his shoulder, before wrapping her arms around him and giving him the gentlest hug possible. "I'm so glad to see you," she whispered, giving him a kiss on the cheek.

"Me too," he replied. "So… that was you flying my ship out of port with all the hoses and connectors attached?"

"Yeah," she grinned. "But Hal was on the guns. He was amazing."

Hal blushed slightly at the praise.

"So we made the newsfeeds!" Vivi said.

Ty nodded. Hal stood up as a medic and a group of vats came out of the *Loshad* with Max on a stretcher. The Al-Kimian doctor had dosed him with meds. He was no longer thrashing incoherently and looked almost peaceful as he slept.

Seren had heard the question and turned to them. "Come on. Let's get Ty back to his room and talk there."

"OK," Vivi said. She took control of Ty's chair and began pushing it along with them.

"Wait… Where are they going?" Hal asked, looking over and seeing Patrin, Lane and Orin heading out of the hangar in a different direction.

"To debriefing. They volunteered to go first, so that you and Vivi could spend a little longer with Ty," Seren said. He was followed by two armed bodyguards who shadowed them back to the medcenter and took up guard outside Ty's door as they entered.

Ty tried to swing himself out of the chair and onto the bed, but he misjudged and almost slipped. Hal caught him easily and helped him get seated back on the bed. Ty pulled his legs back onto the bed while everyone looked away, pretending not to notice. Then, Beryl and Seren took seats. Vivi took up a place at the foot of the bed and Hal remained standing beside Ty, as if on guard duty.

Seren pulled out a handheld and sent the footage of the press conference to Vivi's data pad with a single hand motion. "Take a look at this."

Vivi threw it up on the holo and they watched the newsfeed with increasing expressions of disbelief.

"Son of a bitch," Hal cursed.

"That's not what happened. Not at all," Vivi said, shaking her head.

"We didn't shoot any innocents. We only fired at the soldiers shooting at us," Hal said. "And there was only one ship."

"We already knew that," Ty reassured them. "They bombed their own spaceport on… on… um…" His forehead creased as he struggled to remember.

"Chamn-Alpha," Vivi said.

Hal glanced to Beryl when Ty couldn't remember and caught her slight shake of the head. He said nothing, but filed it away for later, when he had a chance to talk to Beryl alone.

"Yeah," Ty said. "They must have bombed Chamn-Alpha themselves. Shot those people to make it 'look good' to start a war with Al-Kimia."

"Can you tell me a little about how it went?" Seren asked.

Hal answered. "We picked up Max, then got tangled up in the spaceport lockdown... That Senator was visiting Chamn-Alpha and it shut the place down. Unfortunately, they somehow got wise to Max leaving, and they came after us."

"If not for Max getting the mag lock off of the *Loshad*, we wouldn't have gotten away," Vivi added. "But then he got shot."

"It sounds like our doctor earned his place with us," Seren said.

Hal watched Vivi offer up Max's datapad to Seren. "This is the data Max brought us. The information about the device was correct. It causes instant death to a vat. You only have to stand a few feet away and press a button, according to Max. It sends out a pulse to their interfaces and…" she looked sick at the words "…Max didn't know exactly how the device works, but he has theories. And he's provided all his information on the genetic code of the vats so there may be a way of finding a workaround."

Seren took the pad, looking down at the item in his hands with a mixture of relief and revulsion. "We will put people to work on this." Then he glanced at all of them in turn. "I cannot tell you how grateful we are. This – this may save many lives. I do not mean to push, but if you ever change your mind about joining us… the offer is still open."

Hal shook his head. "Not yet. We're gonna need some time."

Seren nodded. "I understand. You need some time together, I am sure. We will debrief you in the morning; that way you have time to eat, rest and recover."

They nodded and thanked him. When he was gone, the room seemed very quiet. Hal glanced to Vivi, uncertain what to do or say.

She nodded slightly, then asked the question they were all thinking. "Ty, what have the doctors said?" She laid a hand on his arm to reassure him.

Ty dropped his head. "I'm paralyzed. I won't be walking on my own again."

The words hung there, heavy with their air of finality.

"Cap. You know we're here for you. Whatever you need from us," Hal said, putting a hand on Ty's arm. Vivi took his other hand.

"I've always known that," Ty replied, his voice rough with emotion. "Always."

THIRTY-SIX

The *Loshad*'s crew had rallied around Ty for the past two days, anxious to provide support. Hal visited in the mornings, usually after Tyce was back from physical therapy. As he approached the room, Hal could hear the slight metallic slip of the exoframe as Ty moved from the chair to the bed. He was getting better at it, but Hal knew it had to be difficult to get used to the rig, even on the best of days.

"Captain?" Hal rapped on the door. "Can I come in?"

"Yeah," said Ty, sitting down on the bed. "What's up?"

"Eira's asked for you several times," Hal said softly, after glancing around to make sure it was just the two of them in the room. "She… Cap, I think she's a little worried about you. If she could talk to you…"

"Sure," Tyce said. "I need a change of scenery anyway. First though, I have something to say. Sit down for a minute."

"OK," Hal slid into the chair near Ty's hospital bed. He wasn't exactly sure what Ty wanted, but he sensed something in his captain's manner that said this was important.

"I'm getting out of here in a couple of days," Ty said. "I know everybody's been kinda tiptoeing around all of this but you shouldn't. I mean it's obvious that things are going to change. I'm expecting that you'll be able to take charge more often, Hal. If there's anything the Chamn-Alpha op told us is that you deserve more responsibility. I want you to take a more active role in things, and I… I think I'm going to need you to."

Hal frowned. "Nah, I don't wanna be in charge, Cap. I take orders from you. It's what I do."

"I get that. But I need to know I can trust you to be there, to run things when I need you to. And to run things the way I would."

"Boss..."

"Hal, I'm not giving up. I just need some time to steady myself. I need to know I can depend on you while we get used to all this."

Hal stood up. "You can depend on me, Ty. Whatever you need me to do."

Ty slid off the bed, standing eye to eye with Hal. "Thank you. Now, let's go see Eira."

Ty glided aboard the *Loshad* in the chair, followed by Hal. They locked the cargo bay, then made their way to the bridge. It felt like coming home at last, now that Ty was with him, Hal thought.

"Hi, Eira," Tyce said as the door to the bridge slid open.

Eira's voiceprint was on every display, shining like a sea of stars. "Tyce, how are you functioning? I have been concerned."

He stood and took several sliding steps toward the captain's chair before sitting down. "Oh, just a little slower than I used to be, but I'm here," he said, as he sank down in his spot with a soft groan.

"I have read your medical records," Eira said. "You have lost major functioning in your legs, due to spinal cord damage. Is that correct?"

"Yeah. That's about it."

"May I scan you?" she asked. "To confirm something?"

"Um, sure," he agreed.

"You have suffered damage to the lumbar plexus," she said after a moment. "Nerve branches were severed during the attack. Your movement is now compromised. When are they repairing you?"

Ty glanced to Hal, then to the display where Eira waited. "They... They're not. There's nothing they can do for me, I'm afraid." Hal could see Ty's jaw tighten as he made the admission.

"It is a simple matter to regenerate nerve cells. I have done so many times for biologics in my lab."

The two men said nothing, allowing Eira to read their words from the silence.

"Oh," she said. "Your medical technicians and scientists cannot do this."

"No," Ty agreed, letting out a great sigh. "It's beyond our ability for now. I'll…" He looked down at his legs. "I'll be wearing these braces for the rest of my life."

"My nanites could be programmed to perform the same functions as the obturator and femoral nerves."

"What do you mean?" Ty asked.

"They can reform the required nerve pathways."

"I don't understand. Are you saying that I could walk again?"

Hal's eyes were huge as he glanced from Tyce to Eira's voiceprint. "W- Wait. You could just fix him?" he asked.

"Yes, Hal. It is how I have said. I am a biologic scientist," Eira said in a tone of certainty. "After downloading your medical data, I feel ninety percent certain I could restore Tyce's physical functions."

Hal and Ty looked at each other for several beats where words just wouldn't come.

"How would you be able to do that?" Hal finally said.

"I can repurpose some of the nanites that contain my consciousness to reform the connections that were damaged. They will have to remain there permanently, however."

They were quiet again, full of thoughts. Hal was pacing, something he did when thinking strategically and considering the angles. This would work, he thought. He had an allenium interface and he was just fine. If they could help Ty walk again… it was worth taking the risk.

"So, ninety percent means there's only a small chance it won't work," he said. "What could cause it to fail?"

"The complex nanites that contain my consciousness are made of mytrite, a different Mudar alloy. It is possible his body could reject them."

"Why can't you use the hull's nanites? They're made of allenium," Hal said.

"My allenium nanites are more simplistic in nature. They were programmed for one job – to create a vessel for me. They cannot perform the functions Ty's operation will require."

"You have to do this," Hal said, looking to Ty.

Ty glanced to the display where Eira's voiceprint was. "I…"

"I understand your hesitation. But I have now had 64,838 chances to eliminate you and your crew. I have not. You asked me to keep them safe and they are safe."

"I did?"

"Before your attack, you said that you were leaving them in my care, and you required me to keep them safe."

Ty was struck silent, then spoke. "Thank you, Eira," he said. "We certainly wouldn't be here without you, and I'm grateful. I trust you. When, ah, when can we try this?"

"I will need fifteen-point-two hours to modify nanites, amatan. I will need Beryl's assistance after that."

"OK then," Ty said. "Sometime tomorrow?"

"I will be ready."

"We need to go find Beryl and Vivi," Ty said to Hal as he transferred back to his hoverchair. "They're not going to believe this."

The next morning, Ty checked out of the medcenter with Beryl and they returned to the *Loshad*. Beryl had talked to Eira the night before and together they had planned the procedure. Ty would be lightly sedated while Beryl injected him with a saline solution containing Eira's nanites. They would bind to the damaged areas of Ty's spinal cord and hopefully restore Ty's ability to walk as they connected his severed nerves. Beryl had explained it to them, then left for the medbay to ready it for the procedure.

Hal and Vivi waited with Ty in the galley. "Tyce, I am sensing elevated vital signs. Are you feeling well?" Eira asked.

"Yeah. I'm just… a little nervous," Ty admitted. His braces whirred softly as he adjusted himself in his chair.

"I will take the greatest care during the procedure," Eira said.

"I know you will," Ty replied.

Hal and Tyce continued to talk while Vivi walked back into the kitchen to grab coffee. Since the Chamn-Alpha op, Hal had been thinking the *Loshad* needed a new paint job, so she could hear him trying to distract Tyce by discussing colors for the ship's new paint scheme. As Vivi listened and added sugar to her cup, a sudden idea came out of her like a soap bubble popping.

"Eira, is there anything your nanites could do for Hal? So that… we could keep him with us longer?"

Everything in the room stopped. Finally, Eira answered, "It is very possible. From my previous scans, it appears that Hal has interface nodes or sensors in places throughout his brain which control different functions. While the interface and its nodes cannot be removed, there is a seventy percent probability that disrupting the node's signal would negate the ability to rush, thereby stopping adrenaline fatigue syndrome."

Vivi almost dropped her cup. Turning, she saw Ty's reaction. "Hal–" Ty said.

"No, Cap. I'm not taking your place," Hal replied with a shake of his head.

Eira broke in, "While I cannot say with a hundred percent accuracy, I should be able to help both of you."

"You… you can?" Hal asked.

"Yes, Hal, I believe I can suspend some of my subroutines and spare enough nanites without losing integrity. I would do this for my amatan."

Vivi could see the overwhelmed expression on Hal's face as he sat back. She and Ty shared a look, then Ty put a hand on Hal's shoulder. "Hey, let's step back from this a minute. There's nothing that says any of this needs to happen today. There's time to think it over."

"But you need to go ahead," Hal said.

"Not yet. After this kind of news, we need to take a minute and regroup, and I want Beryl to talk this over with Eira before we press go. I can stand these braces another couple of days."

"But Cap–" Hal began.

"We've got time. Do me a favor and go let Beryl know what's up," Ty said.

Hal let out a frustrated sigh. It was clear he wasn't happy with Ty's decision. "OK."

After Hal left the galley, Vivi looked to Ty. "He's got to be persuaded to do this."

"I know we want him to. We'll try and convince him, but ultimately, it has to be his decision," Ty said. "We can't make it for him, as much as we want to."

"We're talking about his life," Vivi said, coming to sit beside Tyce.

"I know, but Hal hasn't had to make a lot of decisions like this. He's going to need some time to wrap his mind around it. If what Eira says is correct, he'll be giving up part of who he is, Vivi. That can't be easy."

"You mean the rush."

Ty nodded. "He takes protecting us very seriously, so he might struggle with that. We need to keep that in mind."

THIRTY-SEVEN

Hal took a seat on the ramp, looking out at the hangar in front of him. Even though it was the evening hours, and the temperature was dropping, soldiers were still moving equipment and supplies onto transports. It felt oddly comforting to watch the bustle, and he lost himself in it for a while.

"Hal?"

He turned to see Vivi standing behind him. "Hey, Veevs," he said, a smile crossing his features.

"I just came to check on you. If you need to be alone…"

"Nah. Come on." He motioned to the ramp beside him. Earlier in the day, Beryl had confirmed that Eira's plan had a great chance of working. Everyone had been giving him space… time to think about Eira's offer. He'd taken a walk, then spent the afternoon in the cargo bay working out. Punching the bag always had a way of clearing his head that nothing else ever did. But now, he was starting to feel lonely; he needed to talk to someone.

She came and sat. "Everything OK?"

"Just… thinking about everything."

"Oh. Yeah."

He looked around, watching a soldier pull a stack of hovercontainers past the *Loshad* to the larger transport waiting outside. "You know, I actually feel at home here." He gestured to the busy soldiers in front of them. "Most of my life was spent waiting in places like this. Waiting to go somewhere else. Waiting for the next battle. Waiting to see if I was gonna be smart enough or strong enough to bring back my team from whatever shit we were gonna find ourselves in." He paused a moment. "I never thought I would live long enough to get out of the ACAS. Figured I'd just be another bolt-catcher left on some rock somewhere when I got gunned down. When I was released from service, I decided to just go raise some hell before my expiration date – go out fighting in the vat clubs rather than dying from adrenaline fatigue, y'know."

She nodded, so he went on.

"Then Ty came and got me off Omicron. He gave me a job and kept me caring about something. Helped me see further than the next rush. But I can't help wondering who am I going to be without it, Veevs? When I can't protect my crew anymore?"

She considered her words for long moments before she spoke. "Hal, you're going to be the same person. The same smart, brave and good-hearted person that we all care about so deeply. You will still be you. As for us… we'll protect *each other*. Together."

Hal sighed deeply, hanging his head. "I've lived my whole life with this early death hanging over me, and now, when I have a chance to be free from it… *now's* when I'm afraid?" He shook his head.

"Your life's about to change," Vivi said. "It's natural to be afraid." She paused a moment, then took his hand in both of hers. He turned to look at her, sensing this was important for her to say. "Hal… do this because you're ready. Do this because you want it, not because you know Ty and I want you to."

"I want to. I'm gonna go through with it. I want to be with you as long as I can, it's just… a big unknown."

She nodded leaning against his shoulder. "Hal, you've always had our backs. Well, we've got yours this time. If you're ready to take this leap, we're right beside you."

"I know that," he said, letting go of her hand to pull her close.

* * *

The next morning, Beryl, Ty, Vivi, and Hal gathered in the *Loshad*'s small medbay. The process for Hal would be much the same as it would be for Ty. They would inject the solution containing Eira's nanites into a vein, but in Hal's case, the nanites would travel to his brain to deactivate the node in control of elevating his adrenaline function.

"If I can deactivate that node, then the rush will be eliminated," Eira said. "This will lessen the damage to your body and reduce the chance of adrenaline fatigue, with the lowest possibility of complications. I am reluctant to attempt an adjustment of your interface itself at this point, as I do not know what failsafes it could have."

"I thought that was a wise course of action as well, once I understood it," Beryl replied. "Take a seat up here, Hal. We're going to let you sleep through this." Beryl began to start an IV. "Eira may have to scan you during the procedure, so I want you as comfortable as possible. I'll be monitoring your vitals for any negative effects."

Hal nodded as he lay back on the medbed.

"Hal, we'll be here when you wake up," Ty said.

"Ready?" Beryl said.

"Yeah," Hal replied, glancing to Vivi.

Beryl added a syringe of clear medication to Hal's IV, and he fell asleep quickly. She adjusted some of his medsensors then spoke to Eira. "You can scan him, Eira. He's asleep."

"Thank you, Beryl. Please inject the nanites," Eira instructed.

Beryl did so. There was a period of about five minutes where the only noise was the sound of Hal's heartbeat on the monitor. Then the beeping began to increase in speed, along with Hal's respiration. Vivi, who had gone to stand beside Ty to give Beryl room to work, looked up, concern creasing her brow.

"Heart rate's rising," Beryl murmured, watching the feed of information from the medsensors.

"I am encountering unforeseen resistance," Eira said. "His nanites are responding to mine as if fighting an infection."

They spent long minutes holding their breath, watching Hal's blood pressure, heart rate and temperature rise on the display above the bed.

"Eira, I'm getting rush level readings from Hal. What's going on?"

"I am not going to be able to deactivate this node, but I am going to attempt to surround it with my nanites to prevent it from sending a signal."

Vivi looked to Ty, trying to imagine what Eira was describing.

It seemed days before Eira spoke again.

"Beryl, two-thirds of my mytrite nanites have become inactive due to his system mounting a massive defense. This must have been programmed into his nanites by the ACAS."

"What do you need?" Beryl asked.

"I will need the rest of my nanites to calm this immune response and finish the job. However, if we do such a thing, I will no longer have enough nanites available for the second procedure. What would you like me to do, Tyce?"

"Do whatever you have to do to save him," Ty spoke without hesitation. Beryl and Vivi looked to Ty in shock, but he was calm as he made the call. "Do it."

Hal woke up about half an hour after it was over.

Once the anesthesia had worn off enough that Beryl was sure there would be no ill effects, she sent a very sleepy Hal to his room to rest. Hours later he woke with the worst headache he'd ever experienced, right between his eyes. He groaned while pulling himself to a sitting position and rubbing his forehead.

"Hal, I was instructed by Beryl to monitor you. Are you awake?"

"Yeah, I'm up," he said, squinting at the display across the room. It was after 1600. He'd slept the entire day. He assumed the operation had been a success because he was back in his room.

He found his boots and shoved his feet in them. "Where is everybody, Eira?"

"Ty and Vivi are in the galley. Beryl is asleep in her quarters. Should I wake her?"

"Nah. I'm OK. How did the procedure go?" he asked as he stood up and made his way toward the *Loshad*'s main hallway.

"Ty and Vivi wish to discuss it with you," Eira said cryptically.

Hal felt the back of his neck prickle at that. "OK," he said.

Vivi was at the cooksurface, stirring a pot. He could smell the scent of vegetable soup wafting through the air. Ty was sitting at the head of the table looking through his handheld. Hal noticed he was still wearing his legbraces, so obviously they hadn't gone through with the second procedure.

"Hal," Ty said, standing up. "How are you feeling?"

Hal smiled palely. "Pretty bad headache, but other than that, I'm OK, I guess." He leaned back against the far wall.

Vivi came over with a bottle. "Beryl said to take two of these with some water when you woke up. She thought you might need them if your head hurt." She shook a couple of pills into his hand then went to get him a bottle of water.

He took the medicine gratefully. "I know you probably told me, but how did everything go?" When he asked the question, Hal saw Ty and Vivi exchange a glance. *OK, something is up,* Hal thought. "Be straight with me. Something went wrong, didn't it?" He glanced from Ty to Vivi.

"It didn't go exactly as planned," Ty began. "The procedure was more difficult than Eira thought it was going to be."

"I wasn't able to deactivate the node that controls your adrenal output, but I used my nanites to surround it. It can no longer send signals to your nanites to cause the rush," Eira finished.

"So, I'm cured? I mean as far as you can tell?" Hal asked.

"Yes," Eira said. "However, I failed to anticipate the strength of your immune response."

Ty filled in. "Yeah, it seems like your nanites didn't appreciate her nanites in the vicinity. Eira needed more than she thought. So I made a call, and told her to use mine to keep you with us as long as possible."

Hal shook his head. "She said she had enough. I would never have done this if I thought that you wouldn't be able to walk again." The pain in his head levelled up, began pounding, drowning out everything but itself. He rubbed his forehead miserably and tried to fight back the wave of nausea that threatened.

Ty got up and approached. "Look, sit down a moment. None of this is your fault."

Hal shook his head. "I'm sorry. I think I need to go back to bed." He backed into the hallway, then headed for his room, relieved when he didn't hear the sound of Ty's braced footsteps behind him.

Only minutes later, Vivi knocked at Hal's door. "Hey. It's me. Can I come in?" There was no answer, so she keyed the door, not really knowing what she'd find.

In the light that spilled in from the hallway, Vivi could see Hal was sitting on the floor in the corner, elbows on his knees, and his head in his hands. "I don't wanna talk right now, Veevs," he said.

"I know this wasn't the way things were supposed to turn out–" she began.

"I wish you'd never asked Eira about helping me," he said in a low voice, standing up.

Her eyes widened at his words.

He pushed past her, pausing at the open doorway. "He would be OK, if you'd never suggested it," Hal growled.

Her stomach clenched painfully. "Oh Hal, I just… I want you with us. I didn't mean for it to happen this way."

He stepped into the hallway. "It doesn't matter what you or I meant to happen. It's too late for that."

"Hal, you are not being logical," Eira said across the comm.

"Hal, please," Vivi said, reaching out for him.

He pulled away from her. "Stay away... just… stay away from me. I need some time." He continued toward the cargo bay. Vivi would have followed him, but it was clear he wanted to put as much distance between them as possible. He brushed past Ty in the hallway without even stopping and disappeared into the cargo bay.

When Vivi saw Ty, she swiped at the tears on her face with the heel of her hand.

"Ty, it is not logical for Hal to blame Vivi for the occurrences during the procedure today," Eira said as Ty came down the hallway.

"I know, Eira."

"If we were at my worldship, I could help you easily."

"It's OK, Eira. I know you would do everything you could." When he reached Vivi, Ty wrapped both arms around her. "Hal didn't mean that. He's just having trouble processing all this. I'll talk to him."

Vivi buried her face against his shoulder and desperately hoped he was right.

It was 0100 before Hal finally came back to the ship. The lights were on night cycle, so he didn't see Ty sitting on a supply crate in the cargo bay until he was already inside.

"Hal," Ty called, standing up.

"Cap… I can't." Hal shook his head and continued walking.

"Stand to, sergeant!" Ty's military tone had the desired effect. Hal stopped, then turned to regard Ty.

Hal was tired. Ty could see it on his friend's face, and he felt a little bit guilty for using Hal's programming against him. "Running out of here is not going to solve anything." He laid a hand on Hal's arm. "Why don't you feel you can talk to me about this?"

Hal shook his head. "It's… it's not that."

"OK then, come on." Ty guided Hal to the galley. It was quiet, everyone was in their quarters, and he could have a few minutes to talk with Hal, uninterrupted. "Take a seat." He motioned to the table and then sat down across from Hal. "What was the first thing you did when we were on Jaleeth, and you saw I was too injured to defend myself?"

He glanced up. "I took the vat out."

"Did you think about how dangerous that was to you?"

Hal shook his head.

"Why not?" Ty asked.

"Because. I'm supposed to protect my crew. That's what I do."

"So, what should a captain do when one of his crew is in danger?"

"But I'm not in danger…" Hal trailed off.

"Yes, you are. If you didn't take this chance today, there was a one hundred percent chance you would die in a few years. None of us have a guarantee of life, but you had a guarantee of death. So, that was what I had to do – protect you from death – just like you've done for me over and over again."

Hal let out a heavy sigh. "I didn't want it like this."

"Yeah. None of us did, Hal. But there was a choice in front of me and I made it. This…" He put his hand on the outside of one of the exoframes. "This is a manageable condition. I can still function and move with the assistance of this thing. I'm going to need you by my side, Hal, more than ever. The loss of my legs is nothing compared to the loss I would suffer if you died.

"And I haven't even started to talk about what losing you would do to Vivi. You can't blame her Hal. She cares about you. Really cares."

When he saw Hal nod, he was relieved. "I just feel… like it was all my fault, and then I… I said some things to Veevs that were wrong…" He shook his head, unwilling to go on.

"I realize you were blindsided by all this, right after waking up. I probably should have waited a while before we talked, but it is what it is." Ty shrugged. "Vivi was pretty upset, though. I talked to her after you left, but she needs to hear from you."

"She doesn't want to talk to me."

"Don't be an idiot. Of course, she wants to talk to you. Work it out with her; you don't wanna lose that one. Then get some rest, Hal. Things will look a lot better in the morning."

* * *

Vivi's door was open. She'd been sitting on her bed, dressed in a pair of sleep shorts and one of Hal's oversized tees she'd stolen, looking at her handheld, but not really reading it. Hal had been so upset when he'd left that she couldn't concentrate on anything.

There's very little trouble he can get into on the base though, she tried to tell herself. And he'd been through a lot today. He just needed time. Everyone needed time alone.

None of that stopped her from worrying if he was OK. Eira had assured them there would be no more negative effects from the procedure, but it wasn't like she'd done this before.

Every few minutes that night, Vivi found herself looking up at the door, hoping to see Hal approaching. She'd just been about to go to bed when she glanced up for the final time and saw him standing there.

"Hi," he said.

She sat up immediately and tossed the handheld to the side. "Hi."

He shifted from foot to foot. "I can just, um... go if you're busy."

"I'm not. Please just come in and talk to me." It was one of the things that she and Noah had never done. He had refused to talk about their problems, unwilling to admit anything was ever wrong or that he'd made a mistake.

Hal hesitated, then carefully stepped right inside the door. He seemed to be struggling to find the right thing to say, so she went first.

"I could tell you were hurt, Hal, but you pushed me away," she said softly. "I'm here to help you, you know..."

"What I said really had nothing to do with you. It was wrong to blame you for what happened." He hung his head. "I was just mostly blaming myself and I wished... I wished it had never come up. But it wasn't your fault. I know that. And I'm sorry. For what it's worth, I'm sorry I messed things up with us."

"You didn't mess things up."

He looked up at her with confusion in his eyes. "I just figured it was over... I figured we were over."

"Hal, come over here." She waited for him to sit beside her on the bed, then she took his hand. "I want you to listen to this very closely. When people are in a relationship, they don't just give up if things get rough. They talk it out." She dipped her head to catch his eyes. "Understand? I'm not going to give up on you when it gets tough or when you make a mistake… that's not who I am."

He looked relieved, but bewildered. "I'm gonna get a lot wrong. I know I am."

"Yeah, well, I don't always get everything right either. My ex… remember?" She pointed at the side of her face that had been bruised when they'd met. "So, nobody has this figured out. You just have to do the best you can. If you're doing that, that's all I could ever ask for."

"I promise, I'll do my best, Veevs," he said, wrapping his arms around her. "Promise."

It was early the next morning when Vivi opened her eyes and realized Hal was gone. She sat up in bed, willing herself to remain calm. "Eira? Where's Hal gotten off to?"

"He has gone for a walk," Eira replied. "He knew you might worry, so he told me to assure you he is fine and will be back before breakfast."

Vivi checked the time and found it was 0600. "What time did he leave?"

"0500."

She nodded, then got out of bed, tugging on pants, boots and a long-sleeved shirt. She grabbed her jacket and took a fast look in the mirror before entering the main hallway.

"You are going to find him."

"Yeah," Vivi said. "He's… not too far out from the procedure, and I want to make sure everything's still OK."

"His vitals were stable when he left. You will find him at the hangar's entrance, two hundred feet from the *Loshad*."

"Thanks, amatan," Vivi said as she keyed the door to the cargo bay.

Vivi found Hal across the hangar, exactly where Eira said he'd be. It was still early morning, and he was leaning against the hangar doorway, watching the snow fall outside. She was glad to see he'd worn his jacket and tugged his knit cap down around his ears, as it was cold out here. She'd heard the nurses talking in the medcenter about how it would be a late spring in the northern clime this year, and it seemed that winter was taking its one last shot to drape the landscape in a blanket of snow.

She approached quietly, and when he glanced over at her with a sidelong smile, she fastened her hand in his. "Did you know there's at least twenty different words for snow on Batleek?"

"Yeah? What's this type called?" Hal asked.

She looked out at the large fluffy snowflakes swirling down to coat the tarmac. "They call it *verent,* in the old language. It means feather snow."

"Makes sense," he said, giving her another quiet smile. After a minute, he let go of her hand to put an arm around her and pull her in.

"You woke up early," she said.

"Yeah. Eira tell you I went for a walk?"

She nodded. "How are you feeling?"

"I'm good. I can definitely tell a difference, now," he said.

She knew what he meant. "You can? Is it good or bad?" She bit her lip, hoping for the best.

"It's good, I think. My mind's pretty… quiet."

"What do you mean?" she asked.

"I can't describe it. It's like… there's always been static in my brain, like background noise on a comm signal, but now it's clear." He paused to glance at her. "That doesn't make sense does it?"

"It might," she smiled.

"My mind's usually racing. I mean, I'm always thinking of how to keep you guys safe, all the possible outcomes in a certain situation… a million things that I was taught in the ACAS. Those things are still there, but now…they're not right out in front anymore."

She studied his features and suddenly understood. "You mean you feel calm."

"Yeah," he said. "Yeah, but…"

"But what?"

"I keep feeling like there's something I should be doing. It doesn't feel right to be so… relaxed," Hal said. "It's… I guess all this is going to be an adjustment, huh?"

"Yeah. Don't be hard on yourself. We're in this with you. It's OK to take a while to get your feet under you."

"Yeah," he said, glancing back out at the snow.

She felt him shiver. He'd been out here too long. "Getting cold, aren't you? Let's head back. We could both use some coffee, and Beryl's gonna want to check you out first thing."

Ty appeared in the galley just as Beryl took Hal back for a check. "He's up early," Ty said to Vivi, slip-walking his way over to the coffee maker. He shifted his center of gravity backwards to lock his braces as he poured himself a cup.

"Yeah," Vivi said. "I found him at the hangar door, watching it snow. He woke up a lot earlier than I did, but Eira was keeping track of him."

"I did not wake you, Ty, because it was morning and you needed your rest," Eira said. "Hal told me to give you a message about where he was if you woke before he returned."

"Was there anything wrong?" Ty asked, concern crossing his features as he glanced over to Vivi.

She shook her head. "I'm not sure. He says things are different… quieter in his head. He seems a lot more at peace, but I think he's concerned about how to protect us."

Ty nodded as he made his way over. "That makes sense. This is going to be a big adjustment for him." He sat beside Vivi and leaned in as much as his back brace would allow. "That's kind of what I was thinking to talk to you and Eira about."

"I am listening, Tyce," Eira responded.

"Me too," Vivi assured him.

Ty took a deep breath. "The surgery to implant the sensors is in two days. They're telling me it should be an easy procedure, but… almost dying puts some ideas in your head, you know?" He laughed self-consciously.

"You're going to be fine," Vivi reassured him.

He nodded. "That's not what I'm worried about. I just wanted you to know that I appreciate you and Eira so much. You did a great job backing Hal up on Chamn-Alpha, and I feel comfortable leaving him with you two and Beryl to watch over him… if something were to happen to me."

"I will do my best for him, amatan," Eira said.

"I know you will," Ty replied.

"Ty," Vivi placed a hand on his forearm. "There's something you should know… I'm… Well, I've fallen in love with Hal." She blushed. "I haven't told him yet because he needs more time, but I'm sure of how I feel, and I think he feels the same way. Nothing's going to happen to you, Ty, but you don't have to worry. I'll be here for him."

"That's… that's great," Ty's face broke into a smile and he reached out to hug her. "That means a lot to me, Vivi."

Eira broke in, "Tyce, I have researched the surgery you are having, and the success rate is ninety-four percent. You should not worry. There was no need for this conversation."

Ty met Vivi's eyes with a smile. "Yeah, there was, Eira. There was."

THIRTY-EIGHT

Two days later, Ty underwent the simple surgery to implant the permanent sensors that would communicate with his exoframe. Vivi knew he had been anxious to get it finished, so that he would be self-sufficient. He had been relying on Beryl's help every morning to get the sticky pad of sensors positioned correctly on his back so that his nerves could communicate with the braces. However, with the surgery complete, he would be able to use his rig tomorrow, and be totally independent.

While Ty had been resting, Beryl had sent Hal and Vivi out for lunch and now they were returning. Hal still hadn't experienced any negative effects from Eira's procedure and Beryl said his level of adrenaline was near normal. His stress hormones and heart rate were also lower, but not quite as low as a natural born's. Still, Beryl had been pleased at the change. Vivi hoped it would be enough to ease the strain on his system.

"We're back, Eira," Vivi called as she and Hal climbed up the cargo ramp, shut it and made their way deeper into the ship.

"Eira?" Vivi called again.

There was no answer, but all the lights in the ship cut out, and suddenly it was completely dark. "Veevs?" Hal said, a note of concern in his voice.

She felt him next to her in the dark as she fumbled in her pocket for her handheld. "Yeah." When the light from her display illuminated the hallway, she was able to see that Hal had drawn his blaspistol.

"Ty? Beryl?" Hal called.

"In the galley," Ty's voice came back. "Everything was fine, then it just went black."

Hal and Vivi made their way to them. "Eira's not responding," Vivi said.

The silence pounded around them.

"Let's get to the bridge," Hal said. Suddenly the emergency lights clicked on, throwing harsh shadows. As they moved back to the bridge, Vivi had time to notice that Hal's eyes were not dilated with the rush, although he was obviously tense.

They made their way with Ty following in his hoverchair. Vivi immediately headed to a keyboard and began typing a series of commands.

There was an error sound, then Runa's chime. Eira's voice spoke, "System offline, the automatic program is running a diagnostic, then the system will restart."

"What the hell?" Vivi murmured. She used her tecker node to tap into the diagnostic feed so she could watch what was going on. "The memory is near maximum capacity. Response time down to seventy percent."

"Please wait," Eira said.

"Eira, what's up, beautiful?" Hal ran his hand over her monitor, as if she could feel his touch.

No reply.

"The system's moving slow," Vivi said, shaking her head.

Still no reply.

"Eira..." Ty murmured.

Finally, Eira's voice answered them. "Hello amatan. I am sorry to have alarmed you; I am trying to clear errors in working memory and logic systems which caused an unexpected shutdown."

"What's going on to cause errors?" Vivi asked, her eyes scanning the screen that only she could see.

"The *Loshad*'s computer capability cannot contain all of my programming."

"Why is this happening now? You were fine before," Ty asked.

"I was functional, but without my nanites I am relying more upon the *Loshad*'s computer systems to stabilize my neural patterns. They are not up for this task. As I learn and acquire information, I am having problems operating in this conveyance."

"What'll happen if it keeps going on?" Vivi asked.

"If it continues, the chance of experiencing a cascading error will be high. At the best, I could continue to exist in a stasis state. At the worst, I could no longer be functional."

"You're talking about death," Vivi said, feeling a lump form in her stomach.

"As you understand it, yes, Vivi."

"Why didn't you tell us?" Hal asked.

Eira's voiceprint appeared on the nearest monitor. "There is little you can do. On my worldship I could be transferred into a Mudar conveyance. Here, my neural pattern will continue to degrade."

"I can upgrade the *Loshad*'s memory for you. I don't know if it would be enough, but it might help with the problems you're experiencing," Vivi said.

"Thank you, Vivi."

"Is there... I can't believe I'm asking this, but is there any way to contact your worldship?" Ty asked.

"It may be possible. I have their last coordinates."

"How long has it been since... since those coordinates were verified?" Ty said.

"One hundred point three years. After we realized how violent your species was, we decided to retreat and wait until you evolved beyond your warlike nature."

"So the Mudar didn't leave like everyone believed? They're still there?" Hal asked.

"Yes, it is probable."

"How long of a trip is it?" Hal asked.

"Three months," Eira said, "beyond the border of your known space."

"Will they welcome us? I mean, we're not on the best of terms."

"They will be surprised, but I do not believe they would harm you, Hal."

Suddenly, Vivi grabbed Hal's arm. "Three days ago, Eira said if she was on her worldship, she could help Ty."

Hal's eyes were wide as he stared at Eira's voice print. "You could?"

"Yes, I am ninety-three percent certain I could do this aboard my worldship," Eira said.

"I vote to take the trip," Vivi said immediately.

"Me too," Hal added, looking to Beryl.

"You know I'm in. I haven't looked after you this long to stop now."

Ty shook his head. "Look… there's a substantial risk here."

"And you and Eira took a substantial risk for me, Ty. We want to do this. For you and for Eira," Hal told him.

"So, I guess you *have* learned something from me," Ty murmured to Hal with a wry smile.

"I assure you that no harm will come to any of you, my amatan," Eira said.

"OK, then that's settled. After we eat, I'll go see Patrin and find out if he can help us upgrade our system memory," Vivi said. She went to the wall of the bridge and reached an access panel. Pressing a sensor, the panel slid out, revealing a row of illuminated discs. She noted the specs with her handheld.

"Meanwhile, I'll finish giving your current conveyance a new paint job," Hal offered.

"I'll check on purchasing supplies for the six-month trip," Beryl said. "As grateful as the Al-Kimians are, I do not think we can impose on them too much longer."

"As usual, I'm left with nothing to do but lie around and recuperate," Ty complained.

"Oh no. I have plenty of physical therapy exercises to work on with you. You'll be kept more than busy, my dear. Come on," Beryl turned with the others to head to the galley.

"Hey," Ty's voice held a tinge of emotion that caused all of them to stop and turn. "Thank you. All of you."

"I thank you as well, amatan," Eira said.

* * *

Vivi headed back to the hangar that afternoon with a small box containing two precious crystal disks. They would add to the *Loshad*'s memory and help Eira to function more efficiently. Patrin had led her through the Al-Kimian military base to the supply systems depot to retrieve them. Some words and a smile exchanged with the dark-haired Al-Kimian woman in charge were enough to convince her to hand them over to Patrin. She'd thanked him, but he'd reminded her it was the least they could do since she and Hal had brought Max back. The researcher was still in a coma, but he was improving day by day.

As Vivi returned to the hangar alone, she easily found the familiar lines of the *Loshad* among the different ships, despite the new gray and green paint job that Hal had completed that morning.

She made her way up the ramp and into the cargo bay. "Hal?" she called.

"Hal is in the engine room changing the filters for the environmental system," Eira said.

"Thanks, Eira," Vivi replied as she headed that way. Although she'd been on the ship a while now, she'd only visited the engine room twice.

The hatch was open. She made her way inside, hearing metallic clanks, and sliding sounds. There was a low thrum of the ship running on residual power in the background, a humming note of accompaniment to the sounds of someone working.

"Hal, I got the disks," she called as she walked around the last corner.

Hal was sitting on the floor, a rough green blanket underneath him. On the blanket was a half-assembled *something* made of sparkling metal. There was a fan, and belts and pulleys dotted around. She had no clue what it was, but Hal was cleaning each piece carefully before fitting it back into the assembly. His lips were moving as if he were singing, so she thought he had his earpieces in. He wasn't specific about music, as long as it was fast and loud, so she was sure he hadn't heard her. Mindful of his reflexes, she came around to the front so he could see her.

But he kept right on working, polishing, and fitting together. There were no earpieces. She knelt down in front of him to listen to what he was whispering:

"I am the fist of the ACAS. In war, I am strength. I bring the justice of the Coalition to its enemies..."

A shiver tiptoed up her spine. His expression was utterly blank. He was gone, checked out. His mind blotted out by his routine.

"Victory is mine. I will gladly fight to the death."

He paused as he finished assembling, his eyes fixed on his work. Then, ritualistically, he began to take apart the metal contraption again, piece by piece, setting each one in front of him as though there was a place laid out for it. "I do not surrender to exhaustion or fear, I am steadfast and tenacious in the face of adversity. I am inexorable. I am the ACAS..."

She was crushed. She'd hoped that an end to the rush might mean an end to these episodes, but apparently it was not to be. He couldn't have been there long. He'd finished painting the hull, then obviously come to change the air filter before cleaning up. He didn't get that far, though. Dots of grey painted his hands as he took up a wrench and began to loosen bolts, continuing his liturgy. "I am the fist of the ACAS..."

If she didn't stop him, would he continue this repetition until he passed out from exhaustion? She bit her lip. She needed to try somehow, even if it meant he might react badly.

With trembling fingers, she reached out and covered his hands with her own. "Hal?"

He stopped the awful whispering and sat there. It was as if he was frozen; his whole attention focused on her hands. Slowly, like ice thawing, his face began to melt into a confused expression. She could feel his cold fingers coming back to life again under her own.

She stroked her fingers over his. "Hal? Talk to me." She lifted a hand to his cheek, but he reached up and grabbed her wrist in one quick precise movement. It wasn't painful, but it was a tight grip she couldn't get out of.

He tilted his head at her, scanning her face, all the while keeping a tight grasp on her wrist. "Who are you?"

"It's me, Vivi. Please let go, Hal," she said gently.

He released her hand, blinking and glancing around in confusion. "Veevs? What… What did I do?" he looked around him worriedly.

"Nothing, Hal. It's OK. You just got… stuck for a minute there. You're OK," she sighed with relief, feeling her heart rate begin to decrease.

"I was changing the air filter… but I saw the fan assembly was dirty, so… I went to clean it." He began to fit the pieces in front of him back together in a rapid fashion. The slow ritualistic motions were gone.

"Well, it's clean now. Let me help you put it back, then we can get cleaned up before Beryl and Ty return." She glanced down at the shining metal, then back up at him with a smile that belied her worries.

THIRTY-NINE

Except for nurses and doctors, Max had pretty much been alone. He didn't have much to say anyway; he was drifting in and out of consciousness in a haze of pain medication. In half-dreams, he was back at the mag lock trying to release the ship, when he looked up and saw Hal. He was dressed in an ACAS uniform, looking down at Max through the scope of a blasrifle. In another, Max was running down the halls of the Chamn-Alpha facility, fleeing Dr Balen who threatened to kill him with the press of a button.

He opened his eyes after another bleary twilight of almost-rest to see someone sitting by his bedside. It was Vivi.

"Hi," he managed in a rasping voice. His throat hurt – he must have been on some sort of ventilator. It was gone now; apparently the Al-Kimians' legendary medical technology had done its work and he was breathing on his own.

"Max. They said you would wake up if I sat here for a while," she said, smiling at him, though her eyes were sad. "How are you feeling?"

"I'm OK," he groaned. He tried to sit up fully, but the stabbing pain in his chest forced him to fall back.

"Don't lie to us, Max. You look like you were run over by a rover," Hal chuckled. "But at least you're here."

Max glanced over and saw Hal standing near the foot of the bed. "You got me out alive."

"Of course we did, Max. You may be an ACAS scientist, but you're *our* ACAS scientist," he grinned.

"*Ex*-ACAS scientist," Max reminded them. "Thanks to you."

"Max…" Vivi looked at him, her eyes luminous behind the shine of concern. "We're going soon, and before we leave, I wanted to… to say… Well, it took a lot of bravery to leave the ACAS, and… and I was too hard on you. I'm sorry."

"No, it's OK," Max said. "You were right. I should have left sooner, but I was afraid. I could have done so much more."

"Nobody blames you," Hal said. "You were just one cog in a machine larger than any one of us."

"But we can be more than we were designed to be," Max said.

"Maybe," Hal replied, glancing to Vivi with a smile. "Hopefully."

"Where are you headed to?" Max asked, trying to stifle a yawn.

"We can't say, but I'm sure we'll see you again." Vivi stood up. "We need to let you rest now. You look exhausted."

Max nodded once. He was sure it was the drugs making him so sleepy. "OK. Be careful out there."

"We will," Vivi replied fondly.

Hal gave Max an easy smile. "Get well. Vivi's right, we might see each other again someday. Who knows?"

Max nodded. "Safe travels," he called as they disappeared through his door.

Ty and Beryl were checking off the ship's inventory list together. They were just about ready to leave Al-Kimia but had to wait on the last few deliveries of food and medical supplies. Eira had assured them it would be a six month round trip, and Ty wanted them fully prepared.

"So we have enough medjets to replenish all the medkits aboard?" Ty was asking Beryl as he scrolled through the ship inventory. He was wearing his braces, sitting on a cargo container to examine the contents of the shipment since standing tired him easily.

"Yes. I think we're all set," Beryl replied from across the cargo bay. "Fifty pressure bandages," she called as she rummaged through another box.

Ty looked up to see Vivi climbing the ramp. "Hey, how's Max?"

"He's healing up," Vivi said. "It'll probably be a while before he's up and around at full strength, but he's on the way."

"That's good," Ty said. He saw that Hal was examining the stacks of anti-grav cargo crates at the foot of the ramp.

"How many more deliveries are we waiting on, Cap?" he called.

"Two more tomorrow. I was going to get those," Ty said, halfheartedly. It wasn't that they were heavy but just walking to the cargo bay had tired him out. Beryl wasn't taking it easy on him during their "therapy sessions" in the morning, and it was catching up to him.

"I got 'em. No problem," Hal said, maneuvering them to the corner of the bay. "This one's full of rations," he added after checking under the cover. After moving most of them onto the ship, he turned to go back for the last stack but stopped when he saw Seren, Lane and Orin at the bottom of the ramp.

"Hello," Seren said. "We hear you're pulling out soon, and we wanted to say our farewells."

Ty stood up. "Please come aboard."

Seren climbed the ramp, held out a hand and Ty shook it. "I must say you're looking quite well," Seren remarked.

"Thanks to Al-Kimia." Ty smiled, glancing at Hal and Vivi. "And my crew. Thank you for taking us in for a while until we could get back on our feet."

"You're welcome," Seren said as Hal greeted Lane and Orin with a handshake and a pat on the back.

"Where are you headed?" Lane asked Hal.

"We've got a request to help out a close friend," Hal said. "She's really more like family, and I don't think we can turn her down after all she's done for us." He glanced at Ty, who nodded.

Seren nodded. "We certainly understand that. But I want you to know, you always have a place with us. We need as many brave souls as we can get for the coming battle, and you've more than proved yourselves."

"It's a worthy cause. If we can come back afterwards, we will," Ty said firmly.

"You're a hell of a vat, Hal Cullen," Lane said. "I'd gladly have you at my back in any battle. And you as well, Vivi," she shifted her eyes to Vivi, who stood beside Hal. "And I don't say that lightly."

Orin had obviously read her lips, and he added a silent nod, clapping Vivi gently on the shoulder.

"Thank you," Vivi said.

"Well, then. We won't take up any more of your time," Seren said. "Please let us know if there's anything else we can do for you before you depart."

"Thank you," Ty said. The big man shook everyone's hand. When Seren approached Beryl, she hugged him.

"Take care of yourself," Beryl said.

"I certainly will," he replied. "I wish you a safe journey, my friends." They watched Seren, Lane and Orin go, then Hal went to get the rest of the crates.

Once they were all aboard again, Eira spoke. "Are you certain about this journey, amatan? I know that you and the others have a stake in this coming conflict. It is possible we could delay this journey for a time."

"No, Eira," Hal said. "It's just like we said. Amatan first, then everything else, am I right, Ty?"

"Yes, you are," Ty nodded. "Eira, you've helped us in a way we can't ever hope to repay, but that won't stop us from trying."

Hal added, "Besides, you and I share the same nanites, Eira. That means we're closer than amatan now."

There was a long pause. Hal shifted his eyes to Ty as they waited for Eira's response. "I think of you all as family as well, Hal," she said.

Eira's word choice and tone seemed to Ty to be uncharacteristically emotional, and he couldn't resist a gentle jab at her. "Are we starting to rub off on you, Eira?" Ty teased.

"Perhaps," she replied dryly. "Or it could be that we are not that different after all."

It took two more days to get everything packed for the trip. Vivi changed their transponder so that they were the *Thezar* out of Jaleeth Station. Patrin had commed a contact there, and suddenly there were falsified records of flight plans filed with Jaleeth for the last six months to support their story.

It was early morning when they assembled on the bridge to leave. Ty got heavily to his feet, feeling the braces dig into his hips in a way that he hoped he would become used to. If they couldn't find Eira's people or she couldn't help him, this was what the rest of his life would be like.

"So. We're ready?" Ty asked them all. Beryl was smiling as she nodded. Hal and Vivi were close, hands linked.

"Just give the word, Cap, and we'll get underway," Hal said.

Ty looked at each of them a moment. Beryl showed concern; he knew she would continue to make sure he healed well. The gleam in Hal's eye showed he was ready for whatever the future had planned. Vivi had a look of determination; Ty knew she would help him keep everyone together. And lastly, Eira's voiceprint remained steady on her display; she would guide them into unknown space to meet the Mudar. They were as ready as they'd ever be.

"Consider the word given. Let's go." He sat down in the captain's chair and took a deep breath. "Eira, open a channel to flight command."

"Channel open, Ty."

"Flight, this is the *Thezar,* requesting clearance to depart."

"*Thezar,* this is Flight Command. You have clearance to leave. Safe travels, oppos."

"Thank you, Flight Command."

The beautiful Al-Kimian sunrise had begun, throwing the green pines into shadow beneath them as they rose into the sky. It was a good sign. As they lifted, the city unfolded itself beneath them, a myriad of buildings nestled into the forest below. For a few moments, Tyce skimmed over the tops of the pines with his ship, racing the rainbow hues lighting the sky. He had no idea what they would find on this journey, but he was ready. Ready to find Eira's people and whatever came next for his crew. A feeling of speed flowed through him and with a deep breath, he climbed into the black of space, spangled with stars.

GLOSSARY

ACAS: Acronym for Armed Forces of the Coalition of Allied Systems. The ACAS is divided into two branches of service: the army and navy. Both rely on vat soldiers for their personnel. Officers in both branches are natural born as vats cannot hold ranks above sergeant.

Al-Kimia: Most prosperous of the Edge worlds not aligned with the Coalition of Allied Systems. It is famous for its advanced medical facilities and is an active leader in resisting Coalition attempts to annex all the Edge worlds.

Allenium: A Mudar alloy that is incredibly strong and resilient. The Coalition uses this metal for vat nanites and interfaces as well as shielding. The Edge does not have the ability to make allenium, so the salvaging of it from Mudar technology is essential.

Amp: A combat drug given to vats to strengthen and extend the rush response. It can allow a vat to go for days without food, water or rest, but it extracts a horrible toll on the vat's body. If the neutralizer is not given as the amp wears off, the user suffers paralyzing muscle contractions.

Bel-Prime: An Edge world that revolted against the Coalition. Coalition reports state that the revolt was promoted by Al-Kimian agents and was suppressed by ACAS troops. Hal saved Tyce's life during the assault.

Blaspistol/rifle: Generic term for any weapon which uses laser technology as opposed to older weapons using traditional kinetic energy rounds.

Bolt catcher: Vat slang term for expendable soldier.

Border: The region of space deemed off limits to human travel by the ACAS, except by permit. This area was the scene of battles and skirmishes during the Mudar War and contains many pieces of technology that can be valuable to the legal (and illegal) salvage crews that operate there.

BromCorp: The largest supplier of drugs for the military. They are responsible for manufacturing amp.

Coalition of Allied Systems (Coalition): A governmental body that controls the Inner Spiral worlds and much of the Edge. Since the conclusion of the Mudar War it has become expansionist and seeks to control any and all technology found beyond the Border.

Corvette: A naval patrol vehicle larger than an escort, but smaller than a destroyer. These vessels are used by the ACAS to enforce its laws restricting travel beyond the Edge's Borders.

Cruiser: Large naval spacecraft of various configurations. Command cruisers are employed to serve as flagships for transportation of important personnel, while heavy cruisers are the main strike force ships, with immense firepower.

Destroyer: The workhorse vessels of the ACAS fleet. These ships are employed in any number of missions as needed by the Coalition.

Cube: Small hotel rooms on space stations and space ports.

Echo: One of the three big galaxy-wide hacking groups. Vivi's ex-boyfriend Noah was a member of Echo.

Edge: A region of space containing numerous planets and systems, at the furthest reaches of Coalition control. These were the systems most impacted by the Mudar War.

Edger: A somewhat derogatory term used by some for a person who lives, works or spends most of their time in the Edge.

Escort: A naval vessel whose primary purpose is to provide support for larger ships, convoy protection, or other duties where a light small ship is needed.

EVA: An abbreviation for extravehicular activity. The term is used for spacewalks or as an adjective to designate specialized equipment used for spacewalks.

Feeds: Any source of electronic information provided over handhelds and other communication devices. Many believe the Coalition uses the feeds for pro-Coalition propaganda purposes.

Freighter: Generic term used for several classes and sizes of ships whose purpose is to haul cargo or ferry personnel. Size is generally noted by letters. "A" Class being the largest and "S" Class the smallest. The *Loshad* is a "J" Class Freighter denoting it as a mid-size ship.

Handheld: A palm-sized voice and text communication device also used to download information from the feeds. Some handhelds have holo capability.

Interface node: A piece of a vat's interface that transmits signals to different areas of the brain.

Jaleeth: The second largest space station in the Edge. Jaleeth is shaped like an X with thick legs that extend out from the central point.

K-245j: The planet where the *Loshad*'s crew find a crashed Mudar ship.

LanTech: Salvage company started by Hugh Lan. It is the largest salvage company in the Edge.

Mudar: The race of AI who came to the Spiral for unknown reasons. According to the Coalition of Allied Systems, they were seeking to obliterate the human race until they were defeated and forced to retreat.

Nat: Vat slang for natural born human-beings.

Null: An illegal drug, null is extremely addictive to vats who use it as a release from the constant state of anxiety programmed into them.

Omicron: The largest space station in the Edge, it is a star-like structure with radial arms.

Quad: A game played by two teams on a field divided into four quads. A round ball is thrown and caught. Two famous teams in the Spiral are the Navs and the Bels.

Rinal: ACAS space station/base near the Edge.

Robotic Exploration Unit: (REU) A drone with a camera and manipulators. It is versatile in any environment and can fly, swim or roll on land.

Rush: The adrenaline response of a vat, marked by dilated pupils and excessive energy. With the rush, a vat can think faster, see farther and fight harder than a natural born.

Scrill or Scrilla: Edger slang for money.

Shredder comm: A cheap prepaid handheld. Shredders lack many features of a traditional handheld and are meant to be thrown away after a time.

Spiral: The part of the galaxy containing the home worlds of the Coalition. Many of its citizens know little about what life is really like in the Edge. Those that do rely on Coalition media outlets to provide coverage of events.

TechSolutions: The largest technology firm based on Omicron Station.

Tecker: Slang for technology specialist.

Tecker node: Bioware that allows for a virtual reality link with a computer. It assists teckers interfacing with the sophisticated computer systems by allowing them to do so virtually. Tecker nodes are not as extensive as a vat interface.

Vanguard Assault Troops: The artificially gestated, genetically manipulated and technologically augmented soldiers of the ACAS. The program was initially created during the Mudar War, but now vats are used to enforce Coalition laws and expansion. Through their interfaces, these second-class citizens are programmed for loyalty to the ACAS and its officers.

Vat: Slang term used for Vanguard Assault Troops

Vat's Creed: A formal system of beliefs imposed on the vats through their training and reinforced through their interface. It says: "I am the fist of the ACAS. In war I am strength. I bring the justice of the Coalition to its enemies. Victory is mine. I will gladly fight to the death. I do not surrender to exhaustion or fear. I am steadfast and tenacious in the face of adversity. I am inexorable. I am the ACAS!"

Viblade: A term for a series of hand-to-hand weapons which operate through the use of an electrically charged vibrating blade. These weapons can be small for concealed use or larger military weapons such as swords and bayonets.

Yeoman: Naval occupation (rating) of a person who serves as an assistant to an officer.

ACKNOWLEDGMENTS

There are a few people to thank for this book becoming a reality. While writing is a solitary activity, sometimes it takes someone else to give you a kick in the rear-end to get you started. That person would be my husband, Judd Smith, who kept telling me I could write my own book. Finally, I said, "Fine! I'll write a book for you." *The Rush's Edge* came out of that. This book would never have been completed without his willingness to read chapters for me, offer suggestions and listen to my ramblings. Thanks, Judd, for seeing the potential in me when I didn't always see it in myself. You are truly a partner and best friend in all senses of the word.

Another person I have to thank for this book is my father, Warren H. Wolfe Jr. My dad was a hard sci-fi and space opera fan, and so I grew up reading all his 60s and 70s paperbacks. There were stacks and stacks of them around in my house when I was younger, and free access to those, combined with nights of reading snatches of *The Hobbit* to me before bed (stopping at the cliffhangers), always made me want to turn the next page. My father was also a veteran. He didn't talk much about his experiences during the Vietnam war era, but this book is still for him and because of him.

The other incredible group of people I must thank is the crew at Angry Robot. Eleanor Teasdale, Gemma Creffield, and everyone else there were kind enough to believe in my book, which I will be eternally grateful for. Gemma was an amazing editor who challenged me to make my story the absolute best it could be.

Kieryn Tyler brought the characters to life on the beautiful cover that *still* makes my heart skip a beat every time I see it.

Lastly, I want to thank my agent, Amanda Rutter. She has been very kind and supportive all the way through this process, even though I had a million questions as a new author. I appreciate her taking a chance on me.

The final person to thank would be you, reader. All the way through this process my main goal has been to write a great story that people will enjoy reading. You'll be the final judge as to whether I was successful or not

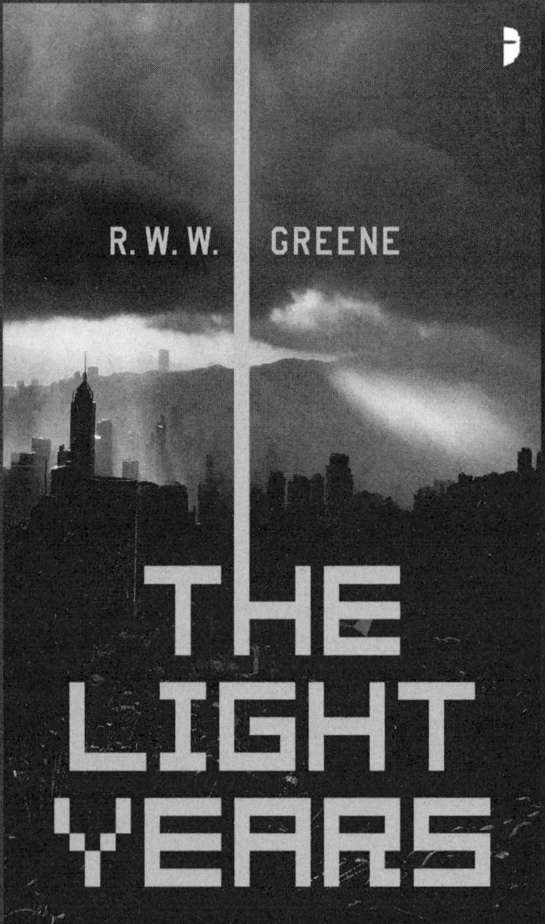
R. W. W. GREENE
THE LIGHT YEARS

ADEM

Versailles City, Oct 14, 3235

Maybe God will make it better.

The thought escaped Adem's throat in barely remembered Arabic. Years before, his grandmother had given him the words as a talisman against specters like the one he faced now. A crusted sore sealed its right eye into a squint, protein starvation bloated its belly, and its arms were thin as sticks. The little boy smiled and presented the bowl again. The blessing might have worked better in French. The Almighty always had a soft spot for Europeans and their descendants, the EuroD.

Adem reached into the belly pocket of his utilisuit and sorted through his supply of coins by touch.

"That bowl is an antique," he said. The technology used to produce them had been lost to Gaul a century before. Sealed in its bottom, an animated 3D image of a once-popular cartoon character offered a cheerful thumbs up in recognition of cereal well eaten. "You should take it to an–"

Adem finished the sentence in his head. An antiquities dealer would most likely swindle the boy, and he would come away little better off and in need of a new bowl. There wasn't much justice available to people like him. There were work programs and shelters for state-approved orphans, so the boy had to be an *illicite*: an illegal birth. His parents had abandoned him in fear of punishment or lost him to the streets when they went to prison.

Adem covered the cartoon's grinning face with triangular coins, enough for a month's worth of food. He dug into his supply of New Portuguese, a simplified language adopted by Gaul's civil service and foisted on the planet's refugee population, hoping to be better understood. "Keep it for yourself. Don't give it to any–"

The boy dashed away, the bowl tight against his narrow chest. Adem cursed. The money would likely end up in the hands of whatever kidsman gave the child his daily meal and a corner to sleep in. Adem pulled up his hood and resumed his walk.

The russet afternoon light turned the roadway's cracked pavement the color of dried blood. The area had devolved since Adem's last visit, the people becoming poorer, more desperate. Rows of refugee shanties and hovels pressed up against the elevator depot. In a taxi he could have blocked them out completely by darkening the vehicle's windows and watching a news or entertainment vid. But when he was on-planet, Adem walked where he could, curious to see what had changed. Once, his simple clothing helped him blend in with the locals but now his sturdy utilisuit made him a target.

A woman beckoned him from the next corner. She was standing in front of a crumbling building that had been a thriving noodle shop half a standard century before. She ran her hands down her short dress and raised its hem to reveal her scrawny thighs. "You look lonely, spaceman!"

"Bad luck," Adem said. "I'm getting a wife today." Talking to another child might have broken his heart, but he had thicker skin where adults were concerned.

"I'll give you my bachelor discount." She stepped closer. The smell of her sweat allied with the chemical tang of whatever drug she favored and the cheap ginja on her breath. Her tight dress was grimy, hugging bone more than curve. Her hair was dry and limp.

"Last time I was here this was a nice place," Adem said.

The woman shifted position, her malnutrition not quite eliciting the desired response. "How long ago was that?"

"Two and a half years relative. About fifty years your time."

She rubbed her lower lip with the stump of her missing left thumb. "I have a friend across the street. Maybe you'd like him better. Maybe you want both of us."

"I'm all set." Adem reached in his pocket for more coins. "Take a couple of days off. My treat. Call it a wedding present."

She limped away with the money. Rationed, it might keep her off the streets for a couple of weeks, but more likely she'd head to a tea shop and spend it on Bliss or whatever people like her were inhaling these days. If she forgot to save a few of the coins for her pimp, she might lose the other thumb.

Adem pushed his hands into his pockets. Nearly three standard centuries ago, during his first visit to Gaul, Adem had offered a woman named Tamara his virginity and four coins from his pocket. She had relieved him of both with algorithmic efficiency, and he'd been back on the street in fifteen minutes. Tamara had long been dust, but once she had been beautiful enough to attract well-heeled customers. The one-thumbed woman might be dead the next time Adem came this way, and her daughter or son, or even a grandchild, might be working the corner where the noodle shop used to be.

Four grim-faced men in cheap armor manned a checkpoint on the next block, slowing the creep into midtown. There hadn't been a checkpoint fifty years before, and the line between the central city slums – *La Merde*, as locals called them – and everywhere else had not been so sharply drawn. Adem brushed at the front of his utilisuit. A block prior it had made him desirable; at the border it made the authorities wonder why he was afoot.

"What's your business?" The guard was a big man, and his ceramic armor strained to cover the vulnerable parts of his body.

Adem kept his hands in sight. "I'm just down the elevator. Got an appointment with a matchmaker." He offered the address.

The guard inserted Adem's ID stick into his reader. Adem held his breath. There had been a couple of dust-ups when he was a kid. No one alive had anything to complain about, but the law could get complicated when relativity was involved.

The guard grunted and handed back the stick. "You crew?"

Adem shook his head. "Family. Part owner."

"You paying for gene work, then? Give her a big smile and no brains?" The guard's face darkened. "A nice little splice to keep you happy up there in space?"

Adem forced himself not to take a step back. "Nothing like that. Just a standard contract."

The guard sneered. "Lost my little sister that way. She married a Trader, too. Standard contract. Won't see her again until I've got gray in my hair."

"What ship?" Adem said. "Maybe I can get a message to her."

"Doesn't matter. She's gone. I tell Ma that she's got to move on with it." The guard gestured with his stun club back down the street. "Still better than that. Her contract got us out, but the shit keeps coming. Next time you're here checkpoint's liable to be a mile further up and all these pretty offices turned to squats." He spat on the sidewalk. "She's better off up there. She might as well be dead to us, and she's better off." He waved Adem on. "Go meet your wife."

Past the checkpoint, the midtown business district assembled along well-groomed streets. There was a green park to Adem's left, complete with a statue of Audric Haussman, a long dead city planner who had claimed descendance from the First Baron Architect of Paris. Adem double-timed the next two blocks with his head down, hoping to avoid anyone else who might want to flag him down for the novelty of a conversation with a spaceman. Too many times it turned hostile. No matter how far *La Merde* spread, no matter how many ad-hoc refugee settlements sprang up around the elevator, Traders like him could stay above it all. Take the ship up to 99.999 percent of light speed, and decades of standard time might erase the stain by the time it came back into port.

Adem held his ID stick up to the door scanner of a nondescript office building and walked through the airlock into the climate-controlled lobby beyond. He nodded to the robot secretary. "Adem Sadiq. I have an appointment with the matchmaker."

The repurposed robot stared blankly at him as it accessed the information. It was a bulky thing, nearly immobile behind the desk and built for construction or mining, but it seemed comfortable with its reprogramming. It gestured toward the waiting room.

Adem paced up and down the small room until the matchmaker came to fetch him.

"Monsieur Sadiq?" The small woman held out her hand as she advanced on him. Adem accepted it clumsily, unsure whether to shake it or offer it a kiss. "I am Madam Toulouse. You look younger than I expected." She spoke Trader Esperanto clearly but with a thick accent.

Adem touched his cheeks. In his rush to make the elevator he'd forgotten to shave. "We don't get a lot of solar exposure on board. Gives us baby faces."

The matchmaker smiled. "Your bride is lucky to have you." She had vetted Adem's application and verified his mother's credit, but that was as far as her knowledge of him went.

Madam Toulouse's heels clicked like a half-interested radiation detector as she led Adem into the lift and down a long hallway. "Are you nervous?" she said.

Adem stuffed his hands in his pockets. "Some."

"You'll just answer a few questions and sign some documents." She fiddled with Adem's collar. "Are these the best clothes you have? No, never mind." She studied his face. Adem half-expected her to lick her thumb to scrub at some smudge or other he had missed. "What happened to your hair?"

Adem brushed his hand across the left side of his face and head. The skin graft had taken nicely – his father did good work – but his hair hadn't grown back out all the way. "Conduit fire."

The matchmaker sighed. "You're pretty enough. She might not notice." She pointed to an alcove. "Get in there, and smile when the computer tells you. We'll get a picture for your future wife."

Adem had never found it easy to smile on command but felt he may have managed a friendly grimace by the time the computer had taken half a dozen shots. Madam Toulouse frowned at the test strip the computer printed out for her. "These will do." She propelled Adem by the arm farther down the hallway. "Let me do most of the talking. I know what your family is looking for and how much they are willing to pay."

The lighting in the interview room was warm and subdued. The chairs were well-stuffed, and the table in the middle of it all was an antique made of honey-colored fauxwood. Adem took a seat, interlacing his fingers on the tabletop. The matchmaker frowned, shaking her head an inch in either direction. Adem got the hint, slid his hands off the table, and rested them on the reinforced knees of his utilisuit.

The door swished open. A pear-shaped man in an old-style suit walked in first, trailed by Adem's future in-laws: a man and a woman in their early twenties. They walked closely together, and their clothes fit like they had been purchased for larger people. Adem experimented with a charming smile, but it felt phony. He looked at the table instead.

The matchmaker stood and discreetly touched Adem's shoulder. Adem lurched to his feet and, again not sure what to do with them, put his hands in his pockets.

Madam Toulouse smiled at the newcomers. "This is Adem Sadiq, son of Captain Maneera Sadiq. He is part-owner of the *Hajj*." She put her hand on Adem's elbow. "Adem, this is Joao and Hadiya Sasaki."

The Sasakis offered Adem a formal bow. He returned it clumsily, hands still in his pockets. The pear-shaped man ignored him completely. "I am representing the Sasaki family," he said. "They do not understand the Trader's language."

"Of course," Madam Toulouse said. "Won't you sit down?" She gestured to the chairs on the other side of the table.

The Sasakis sat close together with their attorney taking up more than half the table to their left. He tented his fingers. The cuffs of his shirt were worn. "Captain Sadiq wants the bride to study United Americas physics and engineering," he said.

Madam Toulouse looked at Adem expectantly.

"Yeah," he said. "I mean, yes. That's what we want."

"Not much use on a Trader vessel."

Adem had wondered about that, too, but his mother hadn't seen fit to enlighten him. "I'm sure we'll find a way to put her to use."

The attorney's eyes widened. "I'm sure. Are there any other skills and interests you would like her to acquire? Cooking? Materials recycling, perhaps? BDSM?"

Adem rubbed the back of his neck. "Maybe she could learn to play an instrument."

"Will children be required?"

"If it happens, it happens, but I don't want anything like that in the contract."

The representative whispered with his clients and turned back to Adem's matchmaker. "My clients have no objection," he said. "Does the Sadiq family want naming rights? It will cost extra."

"Her parents can pick a name. That's their business."

"We want a contingency fund for genetic alteration in case the fetus does not have the math and science traits. If it is not used, it will revert back to Captain Sadiq."

"We are prepared for that," Madam Toulouse said. "There will be enough in the fund to get the work done on Versailles Station."

"Fine." The representative rolled his shoulders and adjusted the cuffs of his shirt. "Let's get down to it."

Adem tuned out. Madam Toulouse had a reputation for being fair and having a soft spot for the families of the brides she was placing. Both families were in good hands. Besides, he had a lot to think about, not least of which was turning his bachelor quarters into something a woman might like.

The matchmaker stood abruptly and offered her hand to the Sasakis' representative. "We have a deal."

Adem scrambled to his feet in time to see his future in-laws headed for the door. Hadiya Sasaki was crying. Her husband put his arms around her and pressed his mouth to her ear. She wiped her eyes on her too-long sleeves. Before Adem could say goodbye, they were gone.

"Congratulations," Madam Toulouse said. "You have a bride."

Adem looked at the door the Sasakis had gone through. "Will they be alright?"

The matchmaker's mouth twisted. "Their representative kept as much as he could for himself, but they will be far better off than they were."

"Thank you for that." Adem forced a smile. Marriage was supposed to be a happy thing, but what he felt was more akin to shame or embarrassment. "I should get back to my ship."

Madam Toulouse showed Adem where to sign his name and press his thumb. "Your mother has already transferred the funds to my account. Everything, minus our commissions, will go to your bride's rearing and education."

Preparations for departure were underway when Adem came aboard the *Hajj* and climbed to the environmental-control deck. He winked at the engineer in charge, a slim AfriD man named Sarat. "Everything all set in here?"

"We are breathing, and we have hot water to spare." Sarat turned from his workstation. "And you're married."

"Betrothed. I'll be married in a year." Adem's eagerness to see Sarat faltered. Making environmental-control his first stop had been a mistake. "Let's not talk about this now. We're about to leave orbit, and you know how my mother gets."

"Your sister can handle it."

"She's the pilot. I'm the one who makes sure the ship moves when she tells it to."

They both knew he was dodging.

"Let's have dinner tonight," Adem said. "My cabin."

Sarat nodded and turned back to his work.

Adem skimmed through the cargo manifest as he rode the lift to the command-and-control section in the bow. They'd invested heavily in food stuffs and building materials, an odd choice considering their next scheduled stop was Freedom, where entertainment and luxury items were in demand. Adem put his reader away as the lift slowed. Mother knew best. The *Hajj* hadn't ended a trip in the red since she'd taken over the bridge.

Adem took the five steps between the lift door and the entrance to the bridge and crossed to the command chair to kiss the captain on the cheek. "*Marhabaan 'ami.*"

She nodded, not taking her eyes off her display screens. "How did it go?"

"You have a daughter-in-law full of useless knowledge on the way."

"Nice family?"

"They didn't say much, and they left right after we shook on it."

"Probably afraid they'd back out." The captain rotated her chair to face the helm, where Adem's sister Lucy reclined in the piloting chair. While linked, she saw through the ship's cameras and sensors.

Lucy spoke through the bridge intercom. "Hello, little brother. How is Sarat?"

Adem refused to take the bait. "Did you get enough shopping done on the station?"

Lucy's sigh was amplified and dehumanized by the intercom's processors. "Can I ever? And it will be out of style by the time we come back."

"The time after that it will all be vintage and in high demand," Adem said. "You can sell it back at a profit."

"True. Did you buy me a new little sister?"

"A future math and science genius. Most likely spliced. Her parents are smart enough, but they don't have the genes for it. You'll have a lot to talk about when we pick her up."

Lucy had spent her teens and early twenties on Versailles Station to get the modifications necessary for piloting the *Hajj*. She'd had a wonderful time and never let anyone forget it.

"How close are we to leaving?" the captain said.

"Ten minutes, Mother, dear. Right on schedule."

Adem yawned. "I'll go back to the engineering section to keep an eye on things."

"There's a leak in the plumbing you might want to sniff out," Lucy said. "Wouldn't want our profits to go toward replacing water volume."

"I don't suppose you'd tell me where it is." Linked to the *Hajj*, Lucy could probably feel the leak.

"That wouldn't be nearly as fun as making you crawl through all the conduits," she said.

"I'm on it." Adem nodded to his mother. "Captain."

His mother waved, her eyes fixed on her readouts. There was nothing she could see that her daughter could not, but she was protective of the old ship. Her own mother had been captain before her, and her grandmother before that. She had spent years as ship's pilot before upgrades made her obsolete. Adolescent brains adapted better to the modifications.

"Say hello to Sarat for me," Lucy called after him.

Adem stopped by his quarters to leave his bag. The bottle of bourbon he'd purchased with Sarat in mind clunked against his bed as he set the bag on the floor. The continuous vibration he felt in his feet shifted in frequency as his sister moved the big ship out of orbit.

The ship's mass-grav system made a million calculations every second as it struggled to cope with the velocity changes. The vibration increased until Adem felt it in his teeth and the roots of his hair.

Adem's great-grandmother declared her family had left God behind when they fled to the stars. What God, after all, would have allowed His creation to be so utterly destroyed? Even so, the old woman would mutter to herself in Arabic at the start of every trip: "In the name of Allah, the merciful, the compassionate..." Adem heard the words in his head now, and knew that, on the bridge, his mother was hearing them, too.

Adem swayed as natural physics warred with ancient Earth science. Science won once again, and the *Hajj* slipped away from Gaul back into space.

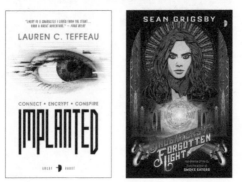

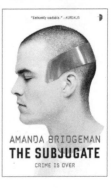

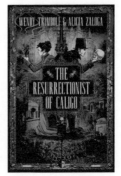

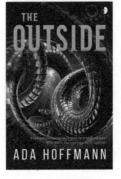